PRAISE FOR TESSA

—◦∾◦—

THE HIDDEN PRINCE

"A fascinating and engrossing read, with a brave protagonist living in a world where the threats are all too real. . . . The ancient world of the Persian Empire comes to life . . . [with] beautifully written characters, who come across as being genuine, human, and easy to relate to. . . . All in all, this is a deeply moving read."

HISTORICAL NOVEL SOCIETY

"Tessa Afshar combines adventure and romance in a fast-paced novel that kept me turning pages. I loved the way she brought so many historical figures to life. I highly recommend *The Hidden Prince*!"

FRANCINE RIVERS, *New York Times* bestselling author of *Redeeming Love* and *The Lady's Mine*

—◦∾◦—

JEWEL OF THE NILE

"Afshar's excellent latest follows a young mixed-race woman in the first century CE as she embarks on a quest to find a father she thought long dead. . . . Exquisite plotting and outstanding historical details set this apart. Afshar's fans will be overjoyed with this tale of love lost and found."

PUBLISHERS WEEKLY, starred review

"Tessa Afshar's novels are well worth waiting for and *Jewel of the Nile* is certainly no exception! What a lovely book and what a beautiful message."

CHRISTIAN NOVEL REVIEW

—◦∾◦—

DAUGHTER OF ROME

"With meticulous research and a vividly detailed narrative style, *Daughter of Rome* . . . is both an emotive biblical love story and an inherently fascinating journey through the world of first-century Rome and the city of Corinth."

MIDWEST BOOK REVIEW

"This is a lovely slow-burning, faith-filled exploration about overcoming trials and accepting past mistakes."

HISTORICAL NOVELS REVIEW

"Afshar brings in a thoughtful consideration of whether or not there are behaviors that cannot ever be forgiven, and her intricate biblical setting will engross readers. This is [her] strongest, most complex Scripture-based story yet."

PUBLISHERS WEEKLY

"Tessa Afshar inhabits the world of early Christians with refreshing clarity. From life under the threat of persecution to domestic details and her characters' innermost thoughts, she makes early Christianity spark."

FOREWORD REVIEWS

"Tessa Afshar has the rare gift of seamlessly blending impeccable historical research and theological depth with lyrical prose and engaging characters."

SHARON GARLOUGH BROWN, author of the Sensible Shoes series

"Tessa Afshar's ability to transport readers into the culture and characters of the biblical novels is extraordinary. . . . *Daughter of Rome* is a feast for your imagination as well as balm for your soul."

ROBIN JONES GUNN, bestselling author of *Becoming Us*

—— ⌘ ——

THIEF OF CORINTH

"Afshar again shows her amazing talent for packing action and intrigue into the biblical setting for modern readers."

PUBLISHERS WEEKLY, starred review

"Lyrical . . . [with] superb momentum, exhilarating scenes, and moving themes of love and determination. . . . Afshar brings to life the gripping tale of one woman's struggle to choose between rebellion and love."

BOOKLIST

"Afshar's well-drawn characters and lushly detailed setting vividly bring to life the ancient world of the Bible. A solid choice for fans of Francine Rivers and Bodie and Brock Thoene."

LIBRARY JOURNAL

---—⟶—---

BREAD OF ANGELS

"Afshar continues to demonstrate an exquisite ability to bring the women of the Bible to life, this time shining a light on Lydia, the seller of purple, and skillfully balancing fact with imagination."

ROMANTIC TIMES

"Afshar has created an unforgettable story of dedication, betrayal, and redemption that culminates in a rich testament to God's mercies and miracles."

PUBLISHERS WEEKLY

"With sublime writing and solid research, [Afshar] captures the distinctive experience of living at a time when Christianity was in its fledgling stages."

LIBRARY JOURNAL

"Readers who enjoy Francine Rivers's Lineage of Grace series will love this stand-alone book."

CHRISTIAN MARKET

"With its resourceful, resilient heroine and vibrant narrative, *Bread of Angels* offers an engrossing new look at a mysterious woman of faith."

FOREWORD magazine

---—⟶—---

LAND OF SILENCE

"Readers will be moved by Elianna's faith, and Afshar's elegant evocation of biblical life will keep them spellbound. An excellent choice for fans of Francine Rivers's historical fiction and those who read for character."

LIBRARY JOURNAL

"In perhaps her best novel to date, Afshar . . . grants a familiar [biblical] character not only a name, but also a poignant history to which many modern readers can relate. The wit, the romance, and the humanity make Elianna's journey uplifting as well as soul touching."

ROMANTIC TIMES, Top Pick review

"Fans of biblical fiction will enjoy an absorbing and well-researched chariot ride."

PUBLISHERS WEEKLY

"Heartache and healing blend beautifully in this gem among Christian fiction."

CBA RETAILERS + RESOURCES

"An impressively crafted, inherently appealing, consistently engaging, and compelling read from first page to last, *Land of Silence* is enthusiastically recommended for community library historical fiction collections."

MIDWEST BOOK REVIEWS

"This captivating story of love, loss, faith, and hope gives a realistic glimpse of what life might have been like in ancient Palestine."

WORLD MAGAZINE

THE
PEASANT
KING

TESSA
AFSHAR

Tyndale House Publishers
Carol Stream, Illinois

Visit Tyndale online at tyndale.com.

Visit Tessa Afshar's website at tessaafshar.com.

Tyndale and Tyndale's quill logo are registered trademarks of Tyndale House Ministries.

The Peasant King

Cover designed by Jennifer Phelps

Edited by Kathryn S. Olson

Published in association with the literary agency of Books & Such Literary Management, 52 Mission Circle, Suite 122, PMB 170, Santa Rosa, CA 95409.

For information about special discounts for bulk purchases, please contact Tyndale House Publishers at csresponse@tyndale.com, or call 1-855-277-9400.

Library of Congress Cataloging-in-Publication Data

A catalog record for this book is available from the Library of Congress.

ISBN 978-1-4964-5826-1 (HC)

ISBN 978-1-4964-5827-8 (SC)

Printed in the United States of America

29 28 27 26 25 24 23
7   6   5   4   3   2   1

For my dearest Leila:

Kind, deep, caring, clever, beautiful.

You won my heart the first moment I saw you.

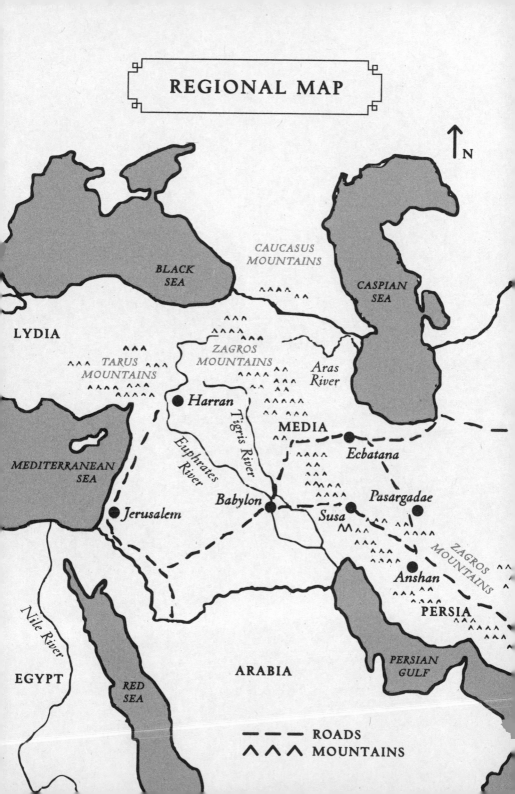

ONE

*So David triumphed over the Philistine with only
a sling and a stone, for he had no sword.*
1 Samuel 17:50, NLT

The Eighth Year of King Cyrus's Reign in Persia

War came slinking into Jemmah's world, stealthy and sudden, advancing without regard for the comfort or convenience of those in its path. Having lived through two years of it, and three years of civil skirmishes before that, Jemmah had thought herself inured to its interruptions. Yet when the clatter of horse's hooves startled her out of a sound sleep, she sat up abruptly in bed, pulse thrumming like a tambourine with too many cymbals. Bleary-eyed, she drew her knees to her chest and tried to calm her racing heart.

When she heard a low whinny and the answering whisper of a man's calming voice out in the yard, she scrambled to gaze through the lattice window above her bed. The stocky, broad-shouldered rider dismounted, hand lingering on the neck of his lathered horse, his face hidden in the shadows.

Jemmah's father emerged into the yard, calling a low greeting to their unexpected visitor. His tone sounded friendly. Jemmah exhaled. A guest, then, and not an intruder.

The lamp Father carried shed its weak light on the rider. Jemmah recognized the haggard profile as he turned to extract a scroll from its leather cylinder. One of Cyrus's couriers.

He had made several stops at their new home in recent months. But this was the first time he had arrived in the middle of the night. Jemmah could hear the murmur of her father's voice as he accompanied the stallion and his master into the stables, where both would be treated to food and a good rest before doubtless leaving on another errand for the Persian king.

Hurriedly, Jemmah pulled her tunic over her head and grabbed an old shawl from the top of a stool, impatient to hear the latest news. Cyrus must be hard-pressed if he was sending midnight messages.

Two years earlier, the young Persian king had refused to pay the compulsory annual tribute to the Medes. That simple act of defiance was tantamount to a declaration of war. A war Cyrus welcomed if it meant freedom from having to surrender the best of his land and resources to Media.

Jemmah's mother said Cyrus was like David fighting against Goliath, except the young Persian king had fewer stones for his sling. As the daughter of Judean parents in a Persian court, Jemmah understood the reference only too well.

Her mother smiled with relish when she made the comparison, as though facing a giant represented some glorious adventure. Jemmah fought a slight shiver whenever she thought of the odds in that story. Facing the Goliath of Media meant that, for months, Cyrus had lived barely one step ahead of disaster.

And the Median king, Astyages, was only just turning his full attention toward Cyrus and his modest territory.

Splashing her face with tepid water from a bowl, Jemmah bent to grab a towel from the foot of the bed. Round yellow eyes stared at her unblinkingly.

Jemmah gasped, taking a hasty step backward.

Slowly she let out her breath. She had forgotten that she had brought the owl into her room before retiring for the night. Zarina had found the injured bird in one of her wild rambles through the cliffs of Pasargadae the day before and brought him home for Jemmah to tend.

"You startled me," she said to her wide-eyed guest. The owl bobbled his head from side to side.

It had taken Jemmah hours to coax a bit of meat down the owl's throat. She had wrapped the shivering bird in the folds of a soft blanket, tucked him snugly inside a basket, and left him by her bedside before crawling between her own sheets to fall instantly asleep.

Pale-bellied and speckle-backed, the owl's torso now emerged from his cocoon, turning to follow Jemmah's every move.

"I suppose you would like to join me," she said, stroking the silky feathers. "Come then, Master Curious." She lifted the basket with gentle hands, careful not to jostle the bird's injured wing.

In the rectangular chamber that served as a dining room on one side and a comfortable reception area on the other, Jemmah found her parents, already dressed for a day that had started closer to midnight than dawn. At the dining room table, her mother's ink-stained hands were making quick work of a missive.

"What's happening?" Jemmah said by way of greeting.

Her mother ignored the question. "Did you have to use my best blanket for your owl, dear?" She laid aside her bronze stylus long enough to give Jemmah the look. It had been quite effective when Jemmah had been nine. At twenty, it was more adorable than fearsome.

She grinned. "It's not my owl. Zarina found it."

Her mother, who had seen an endless procession of needy, broken creatures—not to mention people—come and go through their doors since Jemmah had learned to walk, was not fooled. Sighing, she returned her attention to her letter. It did not escape Jemmah's notice that her mother had deliberately ignored her question.

Jemmah's brother, Johanan, was leaning against the wall, his arms crossed, his brows lowered in a knot. They were twins and, having shared a womb for nine months, had somehow learned to read one another like a scroll. Without a word passing between them, Jemmah now sensed the ball of apprehension that her normally coolheaded brother was trying to hide.

She followed his gaze to a spot on the scarlet carpet and felt her eyes widen. Next to her mother's feet sat an open travel chest. She had not had time to pack properly. But at the bottom lay her mother's sky-blue shawl, neatly folded. Her mother had a firm attachment to that shawl, which had been the first present their father had given her. Jemmah often teased that she protected that thin piece of cloth as though it were a newborn babe.

In a world of arranged unions and practical marriages, her parents had made a love match, and their devotion to one another had only grown with time. Her mother would certainly not pack that treasured love token for just any trip. She would never risk losing it. If the shawl was going, it meant either her mother believed she would be gone a long while—which, considering the size of her diminutive chest, seemed unlikely—or she felt anxious and needed extra reassurance.

"Who are you going to visit, Mother?"

Her mother sighed and laid down her stylus a second time, looking like a warrior who had dropped his sword as a mark of surrender. "I have received a letter from the king."

"And here I thought we had gathered for midnight refreshments," Johanan said dryly.

Jemmah picked up the abandoned stylus and twirled it absently. "I saw the messenger in the yard. The king has summoned you?"

Mother recaptured the stylus and tapped its pointed tail on the table in the quick succession of a drumbeat, making the owl look at her with alarm. "I beg your pardon," she murmured to the bird and laid down the writing implement. She turned to Jemmah. "The king bids me to Anshan. I must meet with . . . an old friend."

Early in the course of his uprising, Cyrus had moved some of the residents of the Persian capital, Anshan, about two days' ride northeast, and settled them in what had been little more than a village. Once the ancestral home of Cyrus's clan, the Achaemenids, Pasargadae made up for its lack of grandeur by the unique advantage of being ringed by mountains. Their sharp peaks and crests provided a steely wall of protection more defensible than any bulwark in the capital. An important advantage lest Astyages should descend upon them with the full force of his army.

Cyrus had entrusted Jemmah's father, Jared, with the task of looking after the civilian population as they settled in Pasargadae. He had grand plans for the place. "I will make these plains my new capital," he had promised, green eyes hard with purpose. "Once I have dealt with Astyages, Persia will need a better fortress than Anshan."

Jemmah's father had set about his new tasks with his usual efficiency, rationing stores of food, digging wells, building homes, and gaining detailed knowledge of the topography so that in case of battle, the women and children could be carried into the safety of the mountains. Over the past two years, they had built the rudiments of the city that would one day serve as Cyrus's new capital. They had constructed houses and even dug the preliminary foundations of the king's palace.

Until now, the king had kept Jemmah's mother safely tucked away in Pasargadae, using her immense talents as a scribe to establish a network of lightning-fast communication centers across the far-flung hills and mountains of Persia. Here in Pasargadae, her mother trained scribes before sending them off to new posts, enlarging an already-impressive information hub the likes of which even Babylon did not possess.

Jemmah chewed her lip. Though Anshan lay only two days' ride to the east, travel in these war-torn times was never safe. While Astyages kept the bulk of his army to the north, small Median search parties had been seen roving through Persian territory. A trip to Anshan was more dangerous than it sounded. The thought of her mother riding through those passes sent a chill down her spine.

"Will you also be going, Father?"

Her father adjusted the leather patch that covered his left eye. He had lost the eye in an accident in his youth. He never spoke of the incident, nor had Jemmah ever known him to complain of the loss or of the occasional headaches it caused. "Cyrus will not allow it."

Father did not look happy about the king's decision. But they all knew Cyrus needed him here in Pasargadae. Jemmah felt torn between relief and alarm. "Who will go with you, Mother?"

She rubbed her eyes. "Cyrus has promised two of his personal guards. They should arrive before dawn."

Jemmah exhaled. Cyrus's men, though few, included some of the best soldiers in the world. The most talented were assigned to the king's imperial guard and formed the backbone of Persia's standing army. An elite group, Cyrus had named them the Immortals, because as part of their training, they learned to step into the empty spot an injured or dead man left behind during combat, giving the impression they were indestructable.

That the king had spared two of his finest warriors to ensure Keren's safety was a mark of his regard for her. As well as a sign of the danger inherent to this mission. The king could hardly afford to spare two of his best fighters while facing a much larger force a few days' march from Anshan.

"Why does Cyrus not dispatch one of his generals on this mysterious errand?"

Her mother sighed. "Because this is something only I can do."

Having served as Cyrus's chief scribe since he had been a lad of eleven, and as his teacher before that, Jemmah's mother had received her share of delicate assignments. But none had entailed travel during an escalating war.

Jemmah chewed her lip. Whatever the risks, her mother would face them willingly because she believed in the utter necessity of Cyrus's undertaking. She would go where she was sent and do her best to accomplish her task.

Jemmah could either make her mother's going easy or make it hard. She could act as a brace or become a barrier. If she obeyed the needling voice of anxiety, she would only prove an obstacle, blocking the way with questions and objections. She sighed. Worry was a self-serving taskmaster. And while Jemmah could not keep its sharp fangs from sinking into her own soul, she could at least keep its venom from spilling into those she loved.

She wrapped her arms around her mother. "You keep those Immortals in line. We'll muddle along in your absence while you are saving the kingdom."

For a moment, her mother's eyes glistened. She gave Jemmah an approving nod. "You always know how to bolster my heart."

Zarina padded into the room, her face splitting into a feline yawn. "Why does your heart need bolstering?" She gazed into the half-packed chest. "What's all this? Going somewhere, Keren?"

Although she had lived with them as a daughter of the house for eight years and been repeatedly invited to call Keren and Jared *Mother* and *Father*, she had never accepted the invitation. Perhaps her memories of her father remained too vivid. She had been seven when Jemmah had found her in the baggage train of vanquished Saka warriors, half-dead from starvation and thirst. Her father had died fighting the Persians, not realizing that his little girl had sneaked to hide amongst the baggage before he had set out for battle.

The sick child of a conquered enemy would, in the normal course of things, have been left to die. But Jemmah had nursed the little girl back to health with her parents' help and come to love her as a sister. "Mother is going to Anshan," she explained.

Zarina's exotic eyes with their slight tilt at the edges, which she had inherited from her mother, lit up. "Can I come?" she cried.

"No!" Keren and Jared said in unison.

She threw herself sideways on a chair. "I am never allowed any fun. I bet there will be a sword fight."

"I hope not," Jemmah's mother said, sounding appalled. She had a peculiar sensitivity about swords, though she knew how to wield them well enough.

"But if there was, I could fight for you. I could keep you safe."

She probably could, at that, Jemmah thought. Zarina was almost as good as Father with the bow and terrifyingly accomplished with a sword.

Come to think of it, Jemmah's whole family had exceptional gifts. She was the only ordinary person amongst them. Sometimes it gave her a headache.

Her father mussed Zarina's silky black hair. "How about you keep *me* safe? I hear Astyages is planning to bring his army south."

Jemmah's belly tightened into a knot. Her father had spoken lightly. But the information in that quip was accurate enough. Whether they stayed or went, danger shadowed them.

TWO

The LORD your God will make you abundantly
prosperous in all the work of your hand.
Deuteronomy 30:9

ASHER

Ornate double doors swung open to reveal a long chamber with gilded columns and a high, domed ceiling clad in silver tiles. The guards on either side of Asher tightened their hold on his arms, forcing him to stand still at the entrance, awaiting permission to proceed.

"Mind my tunic, boys," he said, curling his lip. "Try not to wrinkle it."

The guards ignored him. At the far end of the rectangular room, a man occupied a bejeweled throne. Rings flashed as he signaled with an impatient hand for them to approach.

Astyages.

He had ruled the Medes for almost thirty-five years, and he had not been young when he had ascended the throne all those years ago. The sallow, sagging skin of his cheeks and neck contrasted with the black ringleted wig that sat slightly askew on his pate.

A few steps before reaching the dais, the guards shoved Asher down roughly until his knees hit the marble tiles with bruising force. He flinched. "No need for such rude treatment."

"I hear you are getting too big for your trousers, pup," the king drawled.

"My trousers fit me perfectly, I assure you, my lord. I am very particular about my tailoring." Asher made an exaggerated adjustment to the soft wool that enveloped his legs in a tight-fitting line. Every bit of him was covered in the latest fashion favored by young Median lords. It was an annoying but neces-sary part of his disguise. The iron chains hanging from his wrists jangled discordantly with the movement.

"Don't be clever with me." Astyages leaned forward. "I am speaking of the new chariot you have designed. My spies tell me it can mow down a row of infantrymen in full armor."

Asher's pulse skipped a beat. How had the king known about the chariot? Where had he gained that piece of information which Asher had kept so carefully concealed?

He forced his eyes to widen in mock innocence. "A chariot, my lord? Your spies must surely be slipping. What have I to do with chariots?" He shrugged. "If it is something new you want, may I recommend these boots?" He lifted his foot to show off the blue leather. With their elevated heels, they had become the latest rage amongst the wealthy young men of Media. "Not the pinnacle of comfort, I admit. But they do add to one's height. An advantage in our family line, wouldn't you agree?"

The king's face turned magenta. "Don't presume to take advantage of our connection."

"Do we have a connection?" Asher's smile flashed with genuine amusement. "I hadn't realized."

"A tenuous one."

"I cannot express my gratitude for that small comfort," Asher murmured, leaving the king to form his own conclusions as to whether his comfort lay in the connection or in its tenuous nature.

Astyages might be his father, but there had never been a meaningful relationship between them. Although for years Asher's mother had written the king to remind him of his responsibility to his son, Astyages had never acknowledged the boy. Even when the leader of their tribe had approached the king personally to ask him to publicly accept the child, the king had ignored the request. Until a few years ago, Asher had met Astyages only once, an occasion which had not left him with warm memories.

The king's interest in Asher had only sparked when the son he had never formally recognized started to produce some of the best weaponry in the region. The king had summoned Asher to court then and interviewed him attentively. Astyages had applied a mix of heavy-handed demands with a few spurious compliments, expecting his abandoned son to melt at the first sign of his royal father's attention.

Asher had other ideas. Filling Astyages's stockpiles with his superior weaponry hardly fit into his plans. He had had to come up with a scheme that would repel the king's interest quickly.

"Much too hot and greasy for the likes of me," he had told Astyages when the king demanded to know what he had done with his arsenal. "Sold the whole lot off to an Ionian with garlic breath. He's better suited to coarse labor."

A new Asher had been born the day he had hidden away his workshops. A primped, pampered Asher who had burst upon the world with a delectable sense of style and a fastidious refusal to get his hands dirty with anything resembling hard work. So convincing had been his fashion-crazed disguise that the king and his spies had swallowed the illusion whole and, with no little disgust, had washed their hands of him.

Astyages, who hardly knew the son he had sired on a lowly slave, had believed the lie of Asher's distaste for drudgery and promptly lost all interest in him. For years, the dandified disguise Asher had adopted kept the king and his hounds at bay. They had never connected the source of the fine armaments produced in the area back to the long-haired, fastidious illegitimate son of the king. Which was just what Asher had intended.

Until his arrest today.

Astyages ground his teeth. "I want the plans for that chariot. And I want the stockpile of swords you promised Nabonidus." A tiny muscle jumped in the corner of the king's eye as he spat the Babylonian ruler's name.

Asher's face went still. The extent of the king's knowledge sent a chill through him.

"I have never made the king of Babylon any promises." That was true, though amid a heated war over disputed territories, Asher needed no formal agreements with Babylon to know they would welcome stores of high-quality weaponry. Astyages had been correct in assuming that he had a cache of swords earmarked for Nabonidus. In fact, he had a stockpile of well-made bows, arrows, spears, and daggers accumulating in several secret hideaways, ready to be delivered to Astyages's most powerful foe.

"You play with words." The king snapped to his feet. With an agility that belied his age, he raced down the steps of the dais and came to tower threateningly over Asher. "I am about to lose my patience with you. Be mindful, pup, or you will find those chains have become your permanent companions. Where have you hidden the swords?"

Asher exhaled. The king's guards had captured Asher before he had been able to transfer his small fortune in arms to northern Mesopotamia, where the Babylonian king could access them. Which made his arrest a significant inconvenience.

He rubbed the bruise he could feel forming on his wrist, causing his chains to jangle noisily again. It was time for honeyed words. For bootlicking and reassurances. Anything to unlock these chains. But twenty-seven years of resentment rose in objection to the very idea.

Carelessly he shook the iron bonds at his wrist. "I've had prettier bracelets."

It was a mistake to show that he did not fear the king. Astyages relished the terror of men, mistaking it for power. By displaying his disdain, Asher had only made the king more determined to subdue him.

Astyages growled like a wolf with toothache. At a signal from him, a guard kneed Asher in the gut, followed by a sharp elbow into his ribs. Asher bent over in agony. The blows continued until his vision blurred.

As the king's men dragged him out of the ornate chamber, Asher watched his blood drip onto the polished stones, staining them in a trail of scarlet. He grimaced.

That could have gone better.

* * *

Astyages's prison proved as filthy as his throne room had been pristine. Asher grunted when the guards flung him onto the dirt floor and barred the wooden door in his face. He wiped his split lip using the corner of his sleeve and crawled until he could sit with his back against the damp stone wall.

He tried to inhale through his nose and found it blocked with blood. With careful fingers, he prodded the swelling flesh. Sighing, he ripped a narrow band of fabric from the inside edge of his tunic and, rolling it, inserted the wool gently into one nostril and repeated the procedure with the other. In an hour or two, when the pain subsided a little, he might try to snap the dislocated bones back into place. He closed his eyes and laid his head against the wall, battling a wave of dizziness.

A single thought nagged at the edges of his mind, keeping him from the sleep his body needed. How had Astyages gotten hold of his information?

The king was sly. He would give him that. He was slippery. Perhaps his agents had discovered one of Asher's workshops without Asher noticing. Astyages might have even uncovered the cache of swords Asher had hidden away, and finally come to realize that he had lied about selling his armory.

But the new chariot was not even in production yet. Although Asher had created one wheel to determine its viability, he had no finished prototype sitting all shiny and inviting in a field somewhere. Except for his drawings and a few key pieces, the chariot remained a dream in his head.

Which could only mean that Asher had a mole in his trusted network.

He hated that thought. He had handpicked every single man who had served him over the years with careful consideration. These men were his friends. His trusted companions. Who amongst them would have broken that trust?

More importantly, how was he going to get himself out of this hole so that he could discover the answer to that question?

CHAPTER

THREE

Though he fall, he shall not be cast headlong,
for the LORD upholds his hand.
Psalm 37:24

Jemmah arched her back. After hours of copying complicated text on a wet clay tablet, she had developed a crook in her neck. She took a moment to examine the clay, noting its drying edges. If she could not finish the full text before the tablet dried, she would have to throw it away and start fresh.

She gave vent to a long sigh. Johanan glanced up and grinned. "Maybe you should ask the owl to help."

Jemmah pretended to consider the suggestion. "Do you want to lend a . . . talon?" she asked the bird.

The owl wobbled his neck from side to side.

Jemmah laughed. "He is too bright to be roped in."

Round yellow eyes turned their full focus—and charm—on Jemmah.

"You are a beauty!" she exclaimed and caressed the soft

feathers, enchanted. Ignoring his dazzled admirer, he returned his attention to the dead barn mouse sitting before him. With a delicate poke from his sharp beak, the owl grabbed a fat piece and swallowed it whole.

"He seems to be on the mend." Johanan wiped the nib of his stylus on a wet rag. "When Zarina brought him home, I thought nothing would save him. You seem to have pulled him off the edge of death."

Jemmah shrugged. "I did little enough. He managed most of the work himself." She studied the half-finished tablet before her. "Unlike you, I have no truly useful skills."

She pushed her stylus into the wet clay, forming a diagonal groove, repeating the motion in a precise parallel line. With her mother gone, the scribes were shorthanded, and Jemmah had offered to help. Her skills were adequate for simple letters. But these complicated Elamite documents pressed her to the edges of her ability.

Her brother could have finished this copy in half the time. He already had skill and experience enough to slip into their mother's shoes as head scribe. But one of Cyrus's first acts as king had been to launch the development of a written language for the Persians. Though cousin to the Median language, the Persian dialect had never been recorded in writing. Instead, Persians used the ponderous Elamite script for their written documents and legal records.

Cyrus knew that an independent kingdom needed the faculty of the recorded word—one not borrowed from previous conquerors. If Persia wanted to become a power in its own right, it needed tools that stretched beyond bows and arrows. Words could have more power than swords.

Having studied under Keren's tutelage from a young age,

Cyrus had a surprisingly good grasp of linguistics. His early training had come to his aid as he set into motion the development of the new script. If battles and the concerns of court had not consumed so much of his time, he would have probably completed the entire process himself.

As it was, the constant interruptions of war and politics had convinced him to seek help. Johanan had been the perfect partner for Cyrus's bold venture. The two of them had created the initial concepts. Now Johanan found himself neck-deep in finalizing the text and grammar that would give the Persians their own written language.

Jemmah pressed the sharp tip of her reed stylus into the wet clay, determined to complete the copy before the tablet dried beyond use. Two lines short of the end, Zarina strode into the room, silky braid flying behind her as she threw herself into a chair next to Jemmah.

"I found a fat rabbit for that greedy bird of yours."

"He is not my bird. You found him." Jemmah's brows knotted in concentration as she drew double horizontal lines.

Zarina plucked a pistachio from a silver bowl and cracked the shell. "You *kept* him."

"Only until he is well enough to hunt on his own."

Zarina cracked another pistachio and played with the half shells without eating the green nut. "No letter from Keren?"

"I asked Father earlier," Johanan said without lifting his head from his work. "Nothing yet."

Zarina snapped to her feet. "It's been five days since she left! We should have heard from her." She paced restlessly. "I told her to let me go with her. If there was trouble, I could have helped."

Jemmah cast a regretful glance at her letter. Only one line left, and if she did not stop, she might finish before the clay set. Gently she set down her stylus. Reaching out, she snagged Zarina's wrist and pulled until she flopped into her lap like a toddler.

The world saw a fortress when they looked at Zarina. It wasn't merely the muscle-bound shoulders, the hard, powerful legs, the iron abdomen. Everything about her seemed to radiate an unapproachable strength.

But underneath the layers of stone-hard armor she wrapped around her heart lay a vulnerable core. Few suspected the existence of this sweet, fragile center, least of all Zarina, who had bought the fiction of her own toughness as fully as the world had.

Jemmah knew better.

She could read those hidden delicate emotions with the same fluid ease that Johanan could understand the cuneiform symbols of his new written language. Jemmah knew the path to that fragile place. Knew how to calm its fears and comfort the tears that never made their way to the gray eyes. She wrapped her arms around the girl—her sister every bit as much as if they had shared a womb—and poured into that embrace all the love and safety Zarina did not realize she needed.

"Five days. Only one day late, assuming she arrived in Anshan with no delays and had time to send a letter immediately. All the reliable messengers are doing Cyrus's bidding these days. She was probably left with an old, limping man and an ancient, blind donkey. They are shuffling over the passes as we speak."

Zarina grinned. "You're not worried?"

Jemmah was not about to lie. "Of course I am worried. I was worried before she left. But I think our anxiety is premature. Ask me again in two days if we have heard nothing yet."

Zarina gave a curt nod. Jemmah felt the coiled tension drain out of her as her body slumped with relief. As if becoming abruptly aware that she had been lounging on Jemmah's lap, babyish and clingy, she jumped to her feet, back ramrod straight. Jemmah hid a smile before returning to her clay tablet. Ruined, as she had suspected.

Father walked in, blowing into his cupped hands. It had been an unusually cold and wet autumn, which meant the end of the campaign season was, thankfully, only weeks away.

"All my beautiful children in one place." He sank heavily into the chair before the hearth.

Jemmah noticed his wet hair and fetched a towel for him. "Still raining?"

"Enough to turn everything to mud." He kissed the crown of her head before rubbing his drenched hair with the towel.

She saw his fingers tremble and gave him a sharp look. "You seem flushed."

"A little chill, only." He leaned against the back of his chair. "Don't forget your training, my girl."

About to sit down, Jemmah snapped to her feet again. "Fire and lightning!" Cyrus's favorite expression came to her lips with casual ease. The king had only been twelve when the twins were born. They had all grown up together. To Jemmah, Cyrus felt more like a glamorous uncle than a distant king. "Irda will skin me. How late am I?"

Johanan grinned. "No more than usual."

"I will work on that Elamite tablet when I return!" she cried, grabbing her cloak on the way out.

The armory, a rectangular wooden structure with few embellishments, had been erected earlier that year on the grounds of what would one day become the heart of the palace. As well as housing a rather sad collection of old weaponry, they used the place for training, especially in bad weather.

Jemmah shrugged off her damp cloak and, grabbing a wooden practice sword, found Irda taking three women through basic drills. In her rough leather trousers and tightly bound hair, Irdabama might fool the casual observer into thinking she was a man. Nothing could be further from the truth. With her curls loose down her back, and wearing a feminine tunic, Irda could take a man's breath away.

Persian women grew up accustomed to harsh terrain, unfriendly weather, and poor crops. In this dearth of comforts, they became tough and enduring. Jemmah had watched women rise from childbirth, wrap their newborns to their chests, and join their husbands in the field during harvest. A few, like Irda, were expert hunters who wielded bows and arrows with the same ease as they carried a babe in their arms.

Now that most of Persia's able-bodied men were serving in Cyrus's army, the women of Pasargadae had risen to do the jobs usually given to their husbands and sons. They helped construct houses and hunted for meat. They cooked bread and minded children while sharpening axes and digging trenches.

And they learned to wield weapons lest there should be a surprise attack on Pasargadae. Irda was their primary trainer. An experienced swordswoman and ardent patriot, she would have joined her husband on the battlefield if Cyrus had not set her the task of training the women.

Jemmah could hold her own with a bow or sword, though she would never have the speed or power of Zarina nor the technique of Irda. Like everything else she tried, her talent proved ordinary. Irda had shrugged her shoulders when Jemmah had said as much. "Even a mediocre archer can be useful in a melee," she had said matter-of-factly.

Now Jemmah watched with admiration as the trainer led the

women, each movement executed with precise control. When she finished with her pupils, she dismissed them with a few last instructions. Without taking a beat to wipe the glistening sweat on her brow, she waved Jemmah over.

"Do you want a moment to rest?" Jemmah asked.

Irda quirked a brow. "Are you trying to delay sparring with me?"

"Absolutely."

"Good. A touch of caution will help you live longer." Again, she gestured Jemmah forward and converged on her before either had inhaled.

They danced and hacked and lunged and parried for long minutes. Jemmah was holding her own, mostly because after training a dozen pupils in a row, Irda was growing a little winded.

Abruptly Jemmah realized Irda had been driving her backward with purposeful, strategic steps, intending to trap her in the tight space where two walls met. Impossible to maneuver in that narrow space. It would be the end of the match if Irda's strategy succeeded. Jemmah tried to wriggle to the right and found Irda's sword blocking her path. She swiveled left and found the sword swinging with incredible speed in that direction.

Jemmah took two enormous steps backward, thinking to squirm her way out at the last moment. But Irda followed step for step and slammed her into the corner, the wooden hilt of her weapon pressing against Jemmah's abdomen. Jemmah looked up, a small, instinctive movement of her neck, and froze.

Above her, a timber overhang cast its shadow over them. She found herself wedged between two walls, with Irda pressing in. Surrounded in every direction.

The world closed in.

Jemmah felt a terrifying fog encroach, cutting off her breath. Her vision darkened. She could feel her legs give way, and sagged, held up merely by the edge of Irda's sword.

From a distance, she heard Irda's savage exclamation. The weight against her lifted, and gentle arms gathered her away from the oppressive walls. She felt the drip of chilled water against her lips. Her eyes flew open. She was lying on the dirt floor of the armory, Irda crouching next to her.

"I am all right," she said, her voice unsteady. Finding a thread of strength, she pushed herself to a sitting position.

"Forgive me." Irda pulled away to give her more room. "I forgot your . . . condition." She gestured toward the wall.

The pity in Irda's eyes skewered her. Jemmah forced a smile to her trembling lips. "Good thing for you I have a condition. I was about to crush you." She had learned to dispel that hated pity with humor.

Irda threw her head back and laughed, the tension easing from her hunched shoulders. "I can see you visited some strange dreamworld when your eyes rolled up in your head, girl. Now return to the real world where I can beat you one-handed."

Feeling still sluggish, Jemmah came to her feet. Carefully, she avoided looking at the dark corner, which had, with cold indifference, sucked her into the vortex of her old ghosts. It had been months since she had suffered an attack. Long enough to pretend that the fanged monsters in her mind no longer existed. Long enough to convince herself that she had outgrown her . . . condition, as Irda so quaintly called it.

The problem with ghosts that hid in your mind was that they could crawl out anytime they wanted.

FOUR

Because of the LORD's great love we are not consumed,
for his compassions never fail.
Lamentations 3:22, NIV

Jemmah took the long way back, walking in a wide arc so that she could calm the mad beating in her chest before she arrived home. If Johanan took one look at her now, glimpsed the wide, wild terror in her eyes, he would know the monsters had returned.

That was the extent of his knowledge. Even her twin could not cross those borders. No one went into that place but her because she had been the only one who had crawled out of it alive.

She picked up her pace, clambering over the rocky ground until her breath came out in gasps and her muscles burned. With every step, the memories grew dimmer, until they lost their immediacy, fading again as they crawled back into hiding.

In the distance, the sun glinted off the stones of the new

canal, which they had finished building the previous year. The canal carried water from the Pulvar River and fed the dry plains that ran alongside it, transforming a parched wilderness into farmland and gardens. Cyrus had spared two engineers for the work, and its completion had meant that Pasargadae had harvested its first rich crop early that fall. No one in Pasargadae was going hungry this year, and they had even sent grain to Cyrus's always-hungry army.

The fields lay fallow now, bleak and muddy from the rain. Come spring, they would be plowed and planted with wheat and barley and, where space allowed, a few small vegetable patches.

A month ago, her father had started the construction of another canal, where a handful of women and girls were now hard at work laying stones. An old man standing in their midst seemed to be busier giving orders than actually lending a hand.

Even after two years, it still struck her with a pang to see women alone where once young men would have labored, the sound of their cheerful laughter bouncing from the hills. Some of these women had already lost husbands, sons, brothers, and nephews to the point of a Median spear or the sharp edge of a Saka sword. Their men were never coming back. Still, they poured their hearts into this land, the new capital that Cyrus dreamed of for his free Persia.

As she drew closer, Jemmah waved, and the women straightened from their work to call out a greeting.

"How is your little one, Barsine?" she asked, coming to stand by the diminutive young woman whose arms were covered in mud all the way to the elbows. "Is she over her fever?"

Barsine's grin flashed shyly. "She is, mistress. Thank you for the physic you brought her. It soothed her throat right away. Now if only you could make a remedy for all her words."

"Her words?"

"She chatters more than a broody hen. From the moment her eyes open at sunrise until she lays her head down, she talks and talks, though I barely understand her lisping, baby words."

"Takes after your man, that one," one woman pointed out.

Barsine gave a rueful nod. "True enough. He has probably killed more Mede soldiers with his tall tales than with his arrows." She sighed. "I miss those stories more than you'd believe."

"He will return soon. Less than a month, I reckon, before we have our men back." Jemmah waved at the heavy pile of stones stacked nearby. "Then we'll put them to work."

"Truth preserve you, mistress," one of the older women said. "After so many months gone, there is better work for them at home. Persia needs more sons."

Everyone laughed before returning to their backbreaking task, lining the trench with heavy stones quarried from the mountains. Jemmah did not offer to help. She had tried to join them once, rolling up her sleeves and stepping into the dirt, only to be welcomed by scandalized expressions. After an hour, she had realized she had made a nuisance of herself and, with an apologetic smile, left them to it.

The Persians had strict social conventions. As a rule, the peasant classes did not mix with the aristocracy or those associated with the ruling classes. Since Jemmah and her family were close to the king and regular visitors at the palace, the peasants considered them as good as nobility. The common folk expected them to stick to their side of the palace wall, undertaking their own duties, leaving the manual labor to the ones who knew how to do it right.

Like an undigested lump of stale bread, it sat ill in Jemmah's belly, this separation. Every stone these women laid, every trench they dug, every seed they planted would one day benefit her. She gave what she could in return. Her simple remedies in times of illness, her tightly woven wool blankets for the frosty days of winter, meat for their barren tables, letters for their men at the battlefront. But it never seemed enough.

After taking her leave of the women, Jemmah wended her way to the family orchard, the plot of land Cyrus had gifted to her parents the previous year, which they had planted with hundreds of fig, pomegranate, and almond trees. A small grapevine spread over the sunny, gentle curves of the hillside.

It would be years before they would harvest any fruit. Right now, the plantings looked like an orchard of bones. In the spring, they would turn green with new leaves. But they were too young to bear fruit. Maybe that was what she loved about this place. The far-off promise that one day something good would come, though it seemed so unlikely now.

She found her favorite squat boulder and leaned against its edge where the stone had been worn smooth by countless storms. The damp seeped through the thick folds of her cloak and sank into her wool tunic, making her shiver. A nagging unease nipped at the edges of her mind.

She felt as though she was running barely ahead of a gale, and it would break in upon her at any moment. The incident in the armory had fingered the disquiet. Deepened it. Whatever premonition was dogging her steps, it gave rise to a baffling dread she could not shake.

When she had been very young and some agitation took hold of her, her father would lift her onto his lap and whisper something from the Scriptures into her ear—some divine assurance that seemed enough. *"His compassions never fail,"* or *"The Lord your God is with you wherever you go."* Sometimes, he would tease her and make her laugh by asking whether she believed the Lord was like the gods of Canaan, and quoting Elijah, say: *"Perhaps he is daydreaming, or is relieving himself. Or maybe he is away on a trip, or is asleep and needs to be wakened! Perhaps that is what you think?"* .

She would giggle and say, "Abba! Of course he is not!" Then she would shake her finger at him chidingly and her troubles would slide off her shoulders.

She felt again that odd shiver of dread. And even the memory of childhood comforts could not silence this murmuring anxiety as she made her way home.

Her steps were heavy as she walked inside. "Father went to bed," Johanan informed her, frowning over some detail in his clay tablet.

Jemmah halted midstep. "So early?"

"I think he has a chill," Johanan said. "He stayed in the rain too long, inspecting the course for the new canal."

Jemmah recalled the tired way her father had sat by the hearth earlier and the hectic color that had stained his cheeks. A good sleep would do him good.

But when he did not show up for breakfast after sleeping through dinner, Jemmah knocked quietly at his door. "Father?"

"I'm all right, my girl." His voice sounded raspy.

She cracked the door open. "May I bring you some warm bread and honey?"

"Not hungry."

Jemmah slipped inside. "Is it one of your headaches?"

"No, my love."

As her eyes grew accustomed to the darkness of the room,

she saw that his hair was damp with sweat. She stepped close enough to the bed to touch his forehead. "You are feverish!"

"I'll live."

"No doubt, especially once I fetch the physician." Jemmah's tone brooked no opposition. Her father sighed and, turning over, pulled the blanket over his head.

During the campaign season, Persia's civilian population suffered from a dearth of capable healers. Most of the best physicians were traveling with the army or serving the aristocracy that had remained in the fine villas of Anshan. The only physician serving the needs of the people of Pasargadae was an old man whose creaky bones could no longer keep up with the demands of a marching army. That frail body did nothing to detract from his sharp mind, however. What little Jemmah knew of herbs and healing, she had learned from Pharnaspes. She ran to fetch the old man and found him in the middle of his breakfast, though he came without a grumble.

It took him long moments to complete his careful examination of the patient. "Third case today already, and another dozen over the past week. Fever seems to be going around."

Jemmah forced calm into her voice. "Is it dangerous?"

The old man shrugged one bony shoulder. "I don't believe so. Not to a man as healthy as your father, in any case. But you must rest." He pointed a bony finger at his patient, who lay in bed, arms crossed over his chest, staring at them with a narrowed eye. "Plenty of sleep, and no more running about in the rain for you." Pharnaspes left a bag of herbs before returning to his meal.

"He says you must remain in bed." Jemmah straightened her father's tangled blanket.

"I heard." His lips twisted into a grumpy line.

She handed him the cup of herbs she had steeped in hot water. "Until the fever is broken."

He sniffed at the cup and made a horrified face.

"You are to drink that twice a day."

"Twice a day? Twice in a lifetime would be too many times."

CHAPTER FIVE

He is not afraid of bad news;
his heart is firm, trusting in the LORD.
Psalm 112:7

— CYRUS —

Cyrus gazed into the horizon, careful to keep his expression blank. Eight years of rule had taught him to keep his feelings to himself.

"Any sign of them?" Harpagus asked as he clambered up the hill to join him.

"Not yet."

They were both silent for a beat, leaving their concerns in an unspoken heap between them. "They will come," Cyrus said. Keren had never let him down.

"You will manage, even if they cannot join us. You always do." Harpagus gave a knowing nod of his regal head. He had the carriage of a Median nobleman, with mild manners that seemed better fit for court life than on a battlefield. In fact, as Cyrus knew firsthand, he was a capable and ruthless general.

"I will manage better with a thousand fresh fighting men by my side."

Over the past two years, Cyrus had won many battles and skirmishes against Astyages, starting with the one he had waged against the man standing by his side. Harpagus.

It had been the greatest shock of Astyages's long rule to watch his famed general defect to Cyrus at the beginning of that assault, taking with him most of the infantry and cavalrymen under his command. The few soldiers Harpagus had left behind took flight, refusing to engage in a clash against the commander they loved and respected.

It had been the easiest battle of this long war. The one he had not fought.

Now, close to the end of this second campaign season, Cyrus's army was bone weary. To weaken Astyages's superior forces, Cyrus had had to be relentless, pressing hard, even when his troops were desperate for rest. His men were all heart now, with little strength left. Short on weapons, short on food, short on supplies, they faced the last battles of the year, before the encroaching winter forced Astyages's men back into their holes in Media. But these concluding battles of the year could be the last his brave men would fight if he could not support them with something more than sheer determination and clever strategies.

In the distance, he saw a quick flash, followed by another and another. Metal from weapons. Narrowing his eyes against the pale sun, he stared hard into the horizon. If these were Media's soldiers that had somehow given his spies the slip,

Cyrus's troops would face grim odds. He had not expected a frontal assault, and certainly not so soon.

Slowly the rigid line of his back relaxed. He had to swallow before he could speak. "They have come! Gaubaruva's men have arrived."

"Just in time!" Harpagus cried, slapping Cyrus on the back.

Cyrus studied the long column of men and horses, followed finally by a baggage train of plodding mules and camels. Expertly he assessed armor and supply carts as they wended their way toward them. A thousand fighting men.

"I knew she could do it," Cyrus said with grim satisfaction. "Gaubaruva can deny me. But he couldn't say no to Keren."

Harpagus shook his head. "I don't understand. How did that woman manage it? Not that I underestimate her abilities. I know better than most what she is capable of. Still, this—" he nodded toward the ranks of soldiers snaking their way toward them—"this is another matter. Gaubaruva is a cautious man. He has sat on the sidelines of this rebellion for two years, finding excuse after excuse not to join in."

"He owed Keren a debt."

"He owed his king a debt!" Harpagus said, his voice raspy. His notions of loyalty were quaintly old-fashioned for a defector.

Of course, had it not been for Astyages's barbaric brutality— murdering Harpagus's fourteen-year-old son in recompense for sparing the life of Cyrus as a babe—Harpagus would still be serving him. Cyrus owed this man his life twice over.

He grinned good-naturedly. "Gaubaruva has done his part. Over the past two years, he has fed our men with his fat cattle and put much-needed weapons in their hands."

"But he has never given us what we needed most. Soldiers."

Cyrus shrugged. "As you said, he is a cautious man. And this war—" he spread his hand in a gesture that took in the ragtag appearance of his army, along with the tired visages of soldiers pressed too long without reprieve—"is much too perilous."

"What power does Keren hold over him?"

"She saved his life once. More importantly, she saved his reputation."

"That, I can believe."

Cyrus glanced at the man who had once paid the ultimate price for protecting him. He kept few secrets from Harpagus. "Eight years ago, when all the tribal leaders had gathered at Anshan for my coronation, Keren discovered a plot against Gaubaruva and warned him of it."

"Chieftain rivalry?"

"Mother-in-law trouble."

Harpagus loosed a bark of laughter. "I thought *my* wife's mother had a sour disposition."

"You laugh. But Gaubaruva had a serious problem on his hands."

"I suppose it is awkward to put your children's grandmother to death."

"Worse. This tiny woman had plotted to assassinate a nomadic chief and had come very close to succeeding. A cattle lord cannot afford to show himself vulnerable to the machinations of his aged mother-in-law. It makes him look weak."

"Ah. Though the plot had been foiled, its very existence would open the door to a dozen more assassination attempts by every power-hungry rival."

"Precisely." Cyrus nodded approvingly, pleased with Harpagus's grasp of Persian politics. "Keren saved Gaubaruva's life by catching the plot. But she ensured his continuing rule by covering up the whole matter."

"That's why you sent her instead of one of your generals. She has the old man by the hair of his chin."

"Not that she would ever stoop to pulling. But I hoped the sight of her would be enough to move him to action."

Harpagus watched as the column of men climbed the rocky hill, closing the distance between them. "However she managed it, we now have the means to withstand Astyages until the end of this campaign season." He caressed the hilt of his bejeweled sword. "He will come himself next spring. Mark my words. He was hoping his generals and hired soldiers would defeat you once and for all before winter. Once he is robbed of that ambition, he will have no choice but to deal with you personally. He cannot afford to allow this war to drag on."

Cyrus thought of the old man who had tried to kill him as a babe. His own grandfather, the king. He had only failed thanks to Harpagus. He flashed a smile that was at once confident and ferocious. "Grandsons can be as problematic as mothers-in-law."

"He knows if he cannot put you in your place, the head of every vassal nation will soon rise against him."

"Let him try. I look forward to it."

Cyrus strode back into the camp and, with an easy efficiency that flowed partly from his nature and partly from long experience, made necessary arrangements so that by the time Gaubaruva's forces arrived, they found themselves welcomed into a camp well prepared for the addition of so many newcomers.

It took only an hour for the new officers to be apprised of the current situation. Cyrus poked at the map his cartographers had prepared, detailing with precision the area surrounding them. He pointed out the location of the Median army.

"We will leave camp before first light tomorrow. Astyages's men think they have the upper hand because of their superior numbers. They plan to attack us when it is convenient to them, imagining we are cowering up here, licking our wounds from our last encounter. We will have surprise on our side when we show up at their door."

"You want us to leave *before* first light?" one of Gaubaruva's officers asked. "We'll be blind in these hills. Astyages's soldiers won't have to kill us. We'll break our own necks trying to get to them."

"Not at all. My troops know every handsbreadth of these hills. Dark or light. We know our way and will look after your men."

By the time Cyrus had seen to every detail of his plan and read through the latest reports from his spies, the sun had set. Wearily he stepped into his plain tent, collapsing on his folding chair with a sigh. His servant unstrapped the leather thongs of his boots and placed his swollen feet into a basin of cool water.

Cyrus exhaled and, closing his eyes, slid down the hard chair.

"My lord!"

Cyrus's eyes snapped open. He recognized the dusty messenger standing at attention as one of the Immortals he had sent to accompany Keren. Cyrus frowned. "Aryasb! What are you . . . ?" His words died as he noticed the dried blood on the man's temple.

He sat up so fast, the bowl of water at his feet overturned. "Where is she?"

"After she met with Lord Gaubaruva, the mistress began the journey home immediately rather than spend another night at Anshan."

Cyrus felt a trickle of icy dread. "Where is she, man? Out with it!"

"A party of Medes attacked us. Eight men on horseback. They took her, lord."

"But she lives?" Cyrus came to his feet.

"Last I saw, she was slung over a Median horse, being carried north. I tried to follow, but . . ." He pointed to his head. "Too much blood loss. Fell off my horse. By the time I came to, they were long gone."

"They took her? As hostage?"

The Immortal nodded.

"Fire and lightning!" Cyrus brought his fist down on the scarred surface of his travel desk.

Aryasb dropped his head. "They must have been hiding around Lord Gaubaruva's pasturelands when Lady Keren came to see him. Likely they were hoping to pilfer a sheep for their dinner. Instead, they saw her walk into Gaubaruva's tent and recognized her."

"How? She wasn't garbed in rich clothing, if I know Keren."

"No, lord. But these men were no regular soldiers. They knew their way around our hill tracks too well."

"Spies?"

Aryasb nodded. "Lady Keren is known as your chief scribe and your particular friend. Men like that would recognize her, even plainly clothed as she was. Astyages would be generous with his silver for such a rich prize."

Cyrus squeezed the bridge of his nose. "Where is your partner?"

"Dead, lord. Though he took two of those devils with him. I dealt with three myself, and the lady left a fourth incapacitated. I lugged him here on the back of my horse hoping to get some useful information out of him."

Cyrus nodded. "That leaves two guards to deal with if only we can catch up with them."

"I tried to track them. But they had already gone underground.

No trail. They are good, lord. If we can intercept them before they reach Ecbatana, we might save her. Otherwise . . ." The Immortal shook his head. "Once she is in the king's clutches, he will want to squeeze her for whatever information he can."

Cyrus went still. "If my grandfather harms a hair on her head," he spat out, "he will pay dear." His mind whirled furiously as he weighed various plans. None seemed perfect. He scraped a tired hand over his short beard. "I have few men to spare. What we lack in brute force, we must make up for with cunning." He pointed at Aryasb's head. "Seek the physician. I will have need of you soon enough."

Taking his seat again, he asked for ink and a fresh scroll. He was a king and a warrior. But all he could do for his dear friend now was to write like an assistant scribe.

CHAPTER

SIX

Rise up, set out on your journey and go.
Deuteronomy 2:24

Cyrus's letter arrived as the sun was setting, turning the mountains into the vivid orange at the heart of a fire. Jemmah flew to the courtyard and came to an uncertain halt before the two mud-splattered Immortals who had already dismounted from their stallions.

She recognized the pale man who stood playing with the bridle of his horse. Cyrus had sent him to fetch her mother. At the time, he didn't have a great bruise that extended from his temple to the corner of his swollen eye, accompanied by an angry gash the length of a man's finger, barely closed with fat sutures. "Aryasb!" She remembered his name. "Where is my mother?"

A muscle jumped in the man's cheek. "I bring a letter from the king, mistress. Is your father at home?"

"I am here," Father said, stepping into the courtyard, his hand already outstretched. His skin looked pasty and damp. Two spots of high color on his cheeks bore witness to the fever that yet burned in his blood. His fingers trembled as he grabbed the papyrus roll Aryasb was offering. Forgetting to offer hospitality to Cyrus's messengers, he turned on his heel and withdrew into the house.

Jemmah stood frozen, her breath emerging in one long gasp.

A horse whinnied. She turned and saw the stallion drop his neck in a weary gesture. Years of training in the Persian court gave her a backbone when the rest of her dissolved into a gelatinous mass. She called for the stable boy and caught the eye of their Judean cook, who was making fresh bread in the outdoor oven, silently signaling her to look after the Immortals, before rushing indoors.

Her family had gathered in the reception room. Father stood bent over the unfurled scroll, his lips stretched thin and white.

"She's dead?" Jemmah's question emerged like a puff of air, barely audible.

"No!" Father's head snapped up. "No, Jemmah. But she's been kidnapped."

"Kidnapped?"

He nodded. "Astyages's henchmen attacked them. His spies recognized Keren and took her captive on her way here."

"She lives?" Jemmah felt her legs give and sank abruptly onto the soft Persian carpet with its thousand-thousand knots.

"She lives. And we are going after her." For a moment he did not resemble the mild-mannered man who administered a city but rather the warrior he had once been. The one who had fought alongside Immortals and defeated Cyrus's foes in more than one skirmish. The fierce expression could not quite undo the weakness of the fever, however, and with a lurch, he sank into the chair near the hearth.

Jemmah crossed her arms over her chest, trying to hold herself together. "Who will go?"

"Cyrus could only spare two Immortals. Aryasb and Megabyzus are good men. Aryasb fought hard to save your mother and will fight even harder to get her back."

Johanan stepped forward. "I would like to join you, Father."

Father's eyes softened. "Cyrus wants you to remain and assume your mother's duties." He gave Johanan an apologetic look. "And mine, while I am gone."

Johanan frowned. "I would prefer to go with you."

"I know, Son."

Johanan gave a sharp nod, a perfect combination of frustration and duty. "I will look after the scribes and Pasargadae in your absence."

Father stood on legs not quite steady and pressed Johanan's shoulder. "You make me proud. My thanks."

"I am coming," Zarina said, grabbing her favorite bow. "I should have gone the first time."

Father frowned. "Zarina—"

"She is right," Jemmah interrupted. Father gave her a surprised look. He would have expected Zarina's insistence to join this expedition. But not Jemmah's. She squared her jaw. She doubted her father should go on this mission at all. The fever had weakened him too much. He could barely stand, let alone ride long distances.

"You are not strong, Father. Not with that fever. And besides, you will likely need more than the skills of a warrior on this mission. You may find yourself in need of a fast messenger. Or if the trail leads in two different directions, you will need enough riders to cover both. Numbers matter. And three are simply too few."

"Don't forget me," said a voice from the door.

Jemmah jumped to her feet. "Irda!"

Irda stepped into the chamber. "I saw the Immortals riding toward your house. Aryasb is a friend of my husband. He explained what has taken place." She pressed a hand to her heart and bowed her head. "I will accompany you, Lord Jared. It would be my honor to serve."

Before Jemmah's father could respond, Irda held up a hand. "I know what you wish to say. But the women will survive without me for a few weeks. I have two assistants who can take over the training. And we have drilled our escape routes so often, should there be an attack before the passes close, they could find their way to our hiding places even in the dark."

Father was silent for a moment. Then he offered Irda a courtly bow so deep she might have been a queen. "I thank you, Irdabama, and accept your aid."

Jemmah sprinted to her tutor, subjecting her to an exuberant embrace. "You are a champion."

Irda offered more than an unerring sword arm and a straight arrow. She represented the comfort of friendship—the surety of a wall during a gale.

"Watch my trousers," Irda said in her usual dry tone. "You are wrinkling them."

Chuckling, Jemmah stepped away. Her father was fond of leather trousers too. But that leather had been fashioned by expert hands, tamed into a supple softness that sat against the skin like a slab of creamy butter. Irda's trousers were made of rough, homemade leather so thick they would stand up on their own even without a pair of legs to occupy them. Not even Jemmah's friendliest embrace could put a wrinkle into them.

Irda turned to look at Zarina with raised brows, as if to say, *Do you also want a turn at an embrace now?*

Zarina put her hands up as if to respond, *Not in this lifetime. But thank you all the same.*

Jemmah faced her father. "You still need Zarina. And me."

Father grimaced. "It is true our numbers are against us. I don't seem to have much choice in the matter." Tiredly, he drew a hand over his face. "Your mother and I have done our best to prepare you for such a time. And although everything in me rises to shield you from all harm, I know you to be capable of this challenge. Come if you wish it. I welcome your help."

The rigid line of Jemmah's back loosened. She had worried he would refuse her suggestion out of a surfeit of concern for their safety. Her argument, elaborate and insistent, sat at the ready on the tip of her tongue. She sheathed her words, relieved she had no use for them.

For a moment, everyone lapsed into silence. Within hours, they would have to set out on a perilous journey whose end could shatter their hearts and their bodies. Jemmah's mother was the warmth of their home, the center that pulled everything together. She could not imagine life without her.

Father sent for Aryasb and Megabyzus. They arrived armed with a detailed map, which they spread on the dining table, quickly explaining what they knew. "Here is where we were ambushed," Aryasb said, pointing to a narrow pass.

"Do we have any possibility of catching up with them before they reach Ecbatana?" Father asked.

This was the key question, Jemmah knew. On the highway, in good weather, travelers on horseback could ride to Media's capital in two weeks. Ten days, if they rode horses bred for endurance on mountain trails. This gave them a narrow window to catch up with her mother's captors.

Aryasb placed his index finger on a spot about two days' ride from Ecbatana. "This is the last stop where Astyages's men usually hole up to change horses and rest before heading for the capital. It offers us the best place for an ambush."

Jemmah studied the map with a frown. "Eight days' ride from here? They have quite a head start on us. How can we catch up?"

"We leave tonight," her father said. "And hold on to the main highway as long as we are on Persian land. That will buy us time. Astyages's men must travel by rough trails while they remain this side of the border, or risk being spotted. That will slow them down."

Aryasb nodded. "Our horses' night vision will allow them to navigate in the dark, especially while we are on the highway. Astyages's spies don't have that luxury. The back routes they use for the moment are too treacherous for night travel. They must stop after sunset until they enter Median territory and switch to the highway."

"The horses won't last if we push them that hard," Zarina said.

Johanan pointed his stylus at three different spots on their route. "You can get fresh horses here, here, and here. These are the secret outposts where Cyrus has stashed his scribes. They always have fresh horses on hand in case a messenger has to dispatch urgent news."

Aryasb nodded. "The king has given us the authority to requisition whatever we need on the way."

"What about when we cross into Median land?" Jemmah

asked. Half their journey would take place inside Media's borders.

Father gave her an approving nod. "Then we switch to goat tracks and fields."

"Astyages will have men guarding every road that leads to the capital," Aryasb admitted. "Even the paths known only to shepherds are likely patrolled."

"Though not nearly so well as the highway," Jemmah's father pointed out. "For now, the Median king is more interested in the movements of an army than in small bands of riders."

"True," Aryasb said. "We are unlikely to encounter any large troops."

"Only small ones," Zarina quipped. "With sharp, pointy swords and plenty of arrows in their quivers." She rubbed her hands together. "Excellent. Let them see what we do to oafs who take our kin."

At the mention of *kin*, Father gave Zarina a warm glance. "My bloodthirsty girl." He pulled gently on her braid and bent over the map, studying the minute details which had probably taken years to complete.

He reached for Johanan's stylus, and dipping it into the ink bottle, he carefully drew a black line through the map, starting in Anshan and ending in Ecbatana.

"Lord Jared!" Aryasb yelped, appalled at the defacement of his valuable map.

"In warfare, Aryasb, strategy is more important than tools. Cyrus has at least two more copies of this map. He can always make more."

Jemmah studied the bold line, puzzled. "But, Father, this is not the route you described. The opposite, in fact."

"Precisely."

Irda traced the newly drawn black line with a tapered finger. "If the map should fall into enemy hands, they will not know where to find us. That's why you spoil the cartographer's excellent work?"

Father nodded grimly. "Now we will all memorize the real route."

Jemmah frowned, wondering why everyone had to learn the route when they could simply follow her father and the two Immortals Cyrus had sent them. Then it sank in. If the men were lost, the rest could still go on and attempt to free her mother. An icy hand ran down her back, making her shiver.

Quietly she followed her father into his chamber. "How are you?"

"I will live."

She pressed a hand to his brow and felt herself wilt. "You are burning! Your fever is worse. How can you even consider going?"

He turned on her, eyes fierce. "I will not leave her in Astyages's hands."

"Of course not. Which is why we are going in pursuit. But, Father, you must be reasonable. You cannot join us. Not like this."

He ground his teeth. "I am coming."

She said nothing, gauging the desperate defiance that rode him. At times words were not equal to the intentions of someone's heart. She saw this was such a moment and judged it wise to keep her own counsel. God would have to do what reason could not. Either by the time they left, her father would start improving, or he would hit a wall of fever-induced weakness in a few hours. That would convince him better than any argument she could pose. She pursed her lips. She only hoped that the realization would not arrive at the wrong moment.

* * *

They packed light, though their cloaks and boots were heavy in anticipation of the frigid cold they would encounter as they traveled further north. Jemmah's father had two extra horses loaded with food, water, and supplies, and they were on their way within the hour.

Having been introduced to horses as a toddler, this was not the first time Jemmah had ridden in the dark. She allowed her stallion, which had much better night vision than a human, to pick his way to the gate.

Johanan's voice followed her as they loped out of the yard. "What am I supposed to do with your owl?"

"Set him free as soon as he can fend for himself," she said over her shoulder. "Until then, feed him. He likes the little mice in the barn. And don't forget to talk to him, or he'll grow lonely."

The sound of her brother's groan followed her all the way to the road. Jemmah laughed tiredly. The entire world seemed to have gone mad. She was riding in the pitch of night, an old sword strapped to her side, chasing after Median spies, while her brother looked after an injured owl and her father clung to his stallion, trying to hide the weakness of fever. She blamed it on Astyages. All of it. The years of war. The endless loss and grief and separation. And now her mother's abduction.

Her mother would disagree. "It's not Astyages who controls our world, Jemmah," she liked to say. "He has his role to play, and he plays it a little too well. But were it not for Astyages's greed and cruelty, perhaps Cyrus would be content to rule in Persia. Content to be the king of a small kingdom. Now his reach must extend beyond these narrow borders, all the way to his own grandfather's throne. To free his people, Cyrus must conquer Media. And when he conquers Media . . ."

"He will have the power to set the captives free," Jemmah whispered, just as if her mother were here and she and Johanan were finishing her sentences.

Her mother's faith, like her father's, had been shaped in a furnace of trials. Somewhere over the years, they had learned to rely on God's provision beyond what could be reasonably expected from hard work or mental and physical acumen. They had come to believe in God's intervention in their lives, come to expect the miraculous when the ordinary simply proved insufficient.

Jemmah had yet to learn that kind of faith.

Her father pulled alongside her. "What did you say about the captives?"

"She was speaking to Keren," Zarina explained.

"It was more that Keren was speaking to me."

CHAPTER

SEVEN

*Today you are drawing near for battle against your enemies: let not
your heart faint. Do not fear or panic or be in dread of them.*
Deuteronomy 20:3

They traveled most of the night, stopping only to allow the
horses short respites and to stretch their own sore muscles. Her
father managed to cling to his stallion, though Jemmah's brow
puckered with worry when she saw him weave atop his mount
a few times.

She navigated the dark ride with ease, her black stallion
answering the light pressure on the reins and the guidance of
her knees smoothly, which left her mind free to generate too
many painful questions. The kind of questions that had claws.
Like what would Astyages do to her mother if he got his hands
on her? And what were his men doing to her right now? Had
she been injured? Was she in pain?

An hour before dawn, they arrived at the first of Cyrus's
hideaways. A plain mud dwelling, at first glance it looked like

a small farmhouse. But a thick oak door rather than frayed curtains at the entrance and a spacious stable with a new roof hinted at something more. Two scribes and a soldier manned this outpost. In spite of the early hour, all three welcomed the group with swords drawn. Whoever had been on guard duty must have spotted them even in the darkness. They sheathed their swords as soon as Father presented Cyrus's sealed letter.

The guard told them that two days earlier, he had discovered tracks in an obscure trail half an hour west of the outpost. "Two horses, lord," the young guard explained. "And one heavier, like it carried extra weight. Could be the party you are seeking."

"Show me where," Jemmah's father rasped. But when he turned to follow the guard, he stumbled and fell to his knees.

Jemmah rushed to his side. Gently she helped him rise. "Go to your bed," she chided. "Rest with the others. I will go with the guard. If there is anything to be found, I will report it to you. I promise."

Reluctantly he jerked his chin down in mute assent and retreated into the house. While her companions wrapped up in felted wool blankets and stretched out on rush mats to snatch an hour of sleep, Jemmah went off with the young guard to examine the tracks by torchlight.

The way had become cumbersome with mud, slowing their pace, and they traveled for close to an hour before the young guard pulled on his reins and came to a stop. "This is where I saw the tracks."

A close examination of the ground revealed nothing but a sodden mess. The rain had washed away the tracks, leaving no fresh clues for Jemmah to examine. She heaved herself back on the stallion and calmed him with a reassuring hand as he pranced a few steps. He was as weary as she.

"Poor boy," she said, plodding him on. "Lots of hay for you, soon. And a good long rest, too." She would miss him when she exchanged him for a fresh mount later that morning. The stallion was her own horse, familiar to her every shift and signal. She patted his muscular neck. "I will come and fetch you home. Don't you worry, boy."

To the east, the sun broke over the horizon, lighting up the morning with fingerlike rays. In the pale light, Jemmah caught sight of a skinny magpie pecking at something shiny dangling from the sparse bushes that grew at the edge of the track. The magpie's black-and-white body twisted one way, then another, as it tried to shake the object loose from the grasp of twigs. Something about this sight tugged at Jemmah. Without volition, she pulled lightly on the reins, signaling her mount to halt. For a moment she watched the little bird struggle in the bushes, beak pecking and plucking at its sparkling prize. Narrowing her eyes, Jemmah dismounted in a swift, smooth arc, startling the magpie into flight. Her knees were unsteady as she knelt to retrieve the shimmering object.

A bracelet.

Her heart picked up its tempo as she stared at the golden circlet in her hand. She recognized the petal pattern etched into its smooth surface. It belonged to her mother, one of the simple pieces of jewelry she often wore. Tied to a corner was a wisp of blue fabric. She had torn a thin strip from her beloved scarf to show that she had left the bracelet on purpose. To let them know she was well. And to guide them to her.

Her heart was lighter as they rode back to the outpost. She ran inside, clutching her prize, and sank down beside her father's bedroll.

"Jemmah!" He opened bleary eyes and rose on an elbow. "Were the tracks helpful?"

"Washed out in the rain. Found something better than horse tracks, though." She opened her hand.

Father sat up. For a long moment, he stared into her palm. Gingerly he reached for the bracelet. Without a word, he bent his head and kissed the gold circlet, its ragged ribbon of blue clinging to his damp cheeks. Tucking the bracelet inside his quilted vest, he patted Jemmah on the arm. "Well done, my girl."

"A magpie found it first. If not for his inquisitive eyes, I would have missed it."

"Now we know with certainty that they came this way two days ago. And that she was safe when she left us this token."

"If she could bring herself to tear that scarf, it means she has given up all hope of escaping by herself."

"It also means she knows I am coming for her." Her father's smile burned slow. But his body could not keep up with his determination. No sooner had he climbed his brown stallion than he toppled in a heap on the cold, wet ground.

Zarina reached him first, hefting his torso against her, trying to warm his shivering body by draping her cloak over him.

"I'm a fool," he slurred. "Help me back on. I'll keep my seat this time."

Jemmah knelt on one knee before him. "You know you can't."

His eye narrowed, flashing fire. Jemmah swallowed. Gently she took his hand. "You would only hinder us."

He ground his teeth until his jaw bulged out in a square knot of frustration. "She is waiting for me."

"She would never want you riding in this condition."

Jemmah dropped her head. "I could not bear to lose both of you. You understand?"

"You will not lose her," he rasped.

"I will not lose either of you." She squeezed his hand.

He pressed his fingers to his temple. "Curse this fever."

She grinned at him. "Perhaps you think the Lord is like the Canaanite gods? *Perhaps he is daydreaming, or is relieving himself. Or maybe he is away on a trip, or is asleep and needs to be wakened!* Perhaps that is what you think?"

A reluctant grin pulled on her father's lips. "Using my own words to foil me. Worse. Using God's Word. There must be a law against that somewhere."

"I meant no disrespect."

He tapped her gently on the cheek. "I know, my girl."

"God is here and well aware of your fever. For a reason he alone understands, he does not want you on this part of the journey with us. Your job now is to rest. Heal. Be here for us when we return."

He took a steadying breath. "Send me a message when you can. And tell her . . . tell her my heart goes with her, though my body cannot."

Jemmah wrapped her arms around him and held on for a long time, trying to draw from him the strength she would need to go forward. Trying not to feel like a lost child without his presence to guide her. Trying to believe herself equal to the task that she now faced.

* * *

They encountered no further obstacles as they made their way to the second outpost and, after changing horses once again, managed to maintain a brisk pace on the open highway. By then, lack of sleep and the demands of a brutal ride were making Jemmah ache all the way to her bones. She ignored her body's mewling needs and pressed herself to the limits of her endurance.

They arrived at the third outpost after sunset. Jemmah slithered from the back of her horse and sat hard on the rocky ground, trying to call forth enough strength to rise and make her way to the door.

They were surprised to be greeted by one of Cyrus's regular messengers. "The king sent me."

"How goes the war?" Aryasb demanded.

The messenger's face split into a quick grin. One of his two front teeth was missing, giving his mien a fierce cast. "Mistress Keren managed to convince Lord Gaubaruva to part with a thousand armed men. They arrived just in time. Astyages's army retreated after our initial surprise attack. We hold the higher ground now. Reckon we'll live to see another campaign season."

He withdrew a small papyrus roll from a fold inside his padded coat. "I did not expect you to arrive so early. You must have made good time."

"We have been riding flat out. At my best estimate, we remain about a day's ride behind them."

The messenger craned his neck to look behind them. "Where is Lord Jared?"

"Fever," Jemmah explained. "We had to leave him at the first outpost."

Aryasb handed the reins of his mount to Irda. "Is that the letter the king sent?"

The messenger handed his tightly wrapped scroll to Aryasb, who frowned at the message before passing it to Jemmah.

Cyrus certainly did not believe in wasting words, she thought. The letter merely read, *Should the need arise, seek Prexaspes. He will render whatever assistance you require. You know where to find him.* If that message had fallen into enemy hands, they would have been hard-pressed to unravel its meaning. Then again, without her father to decipher it, so would she.

"Is that all?" she asked the messenger.

"Yes. The king said Lord Jared would know what he meant."

"Who is Prexaspes?" Zarina asked.

Aryasb shook his head. "Do you know, Megabyzus?"

"Never heard of him."

Jemmah frowned. "That name. It sounds familiar." She blinked. "Surely it can't be."

Fourteen years earlier, when Jemmah and her brother had turned six, their family had moved to Ecbatana and lived there for two whole years. Having celebrated his eighteenth birthday, Prince Cyrus had accepted Astyages's invitation to settle in Ecbatana, not as a hostage of Persia, which would have been common practice for a tribute-paying nation, but as a guest of his grandfather.

At first, Cyrus's father, King Cambyses of Persia, had vehemently objected to Cyrus's decision to live in Ecbatana, not trusting Astyages with his son's welfare. Queen Mandana, Astyages's own daughter, had been even more vociferous in her opposition than her husband the king. Her father had already tried to kill her son more than once, after all. Astyages had for years tried to convince his estranged daughter and her royal husband that his love and admiration for his only grandson had long since erased any enmity he might have felt for the boy. Neither had believed him.

But Cyrus had pointed out that the Median king was busy

fighting a long, bloody war with the Lydians to the north and would surely be too preoccupied to foment any murderous schemes against him. Most importantly, Cyrus had convinced them that the best way to defeat an enemy was to know him better, to make friends of his enemies and friends alike. As always, Cyrus's near-supernatural charm and patient persistence had opened the way, winning for him the permission to move to Media.

He had brought a small household with him, amongst them Jemmah's parents and a coterie of trusted personal guards. For two years, Cyrus had served his grandfather as a courtier, learning as only a man of his sharp intellect could the intricacies of ruling a large and complex court. He had served as a warrior prince, forging new treaties as much with the blade of his winsome charisma as the threat of his sharp sword. He had followed the Median king's orders for two years and proven himself worthy in wit and war. In the process, he had gained a large circle of admirers and quietly won friends in high places as well as low.

Jemmah still retained some vivid memories of the two years she had lived in Ecbatana, though her childish recollections did not always prove helpful. But the name Prexaspes stood out from that time.

"What?" Irda asked. "What can't be?"

"That name. Prexaspes. I seem to recall such a man in Ecbatana from years ago."

"Who is he?" Zarina asked.

Jemmah pulled on her ear. "As I recall, he is in the . . . removal business."

"Removal of what?" Irda asked.

"Waste."

"As in garbage?"

Jemmah's mother had once escaped arrest by hiding in a basket of week-old rubbish. She would have understood the usefulness of a man in such a trade and appreciated the symmetry of a rescue plan that included him. Jemmah wrinkled her nose. "No. The other kind. He removes excrement."

Aryasb slapped his forehead with the palm of his hand. "I remember now. One of the king's agents in Ecbatana is a waste remover."

"Ecbatana?" Zarina crossed her arms. "I thought we were going to intercept Keren before she reached the capital."

"Every good plan should provide a contingency for unforeseen events." Jemmah's face lost expression. "In case it fails."

Irda nodded with approval. "That man is our contingency?"

"So it seems."

A wall of shocked silence followed Jemmah's pronouncement. Jemmah supposed that most of them would have preferred a warrior or someone high in the ranks of courtiers, or at least a man of influence.

"We'll make our original plan work," Jemmah said. "No one is going to Ecbatana." Or to Cyrus's waste-removing agent, she thought fervently.

* * *

Before leaving the third outpost, once again they switched their exhausted mounts with fresh horses from Cyrus's stables. Jemmah's new mare had a broad back and an odd lilting gait that proved hard on her backside after several hours. The mare made up for her discomfort with gratifying agility once they entered Median territory and began traveling on narrow trails that were little better than goat tracks—and often worse.

From the hour they crossed the border into Media, the weather turned against them. Deluge after deluge made the tracks dangerous, if not downright impassable. Astyages's men would have to contend with the same elements. But they were traveling on a level highway now that they had entered friendly territory, which meant they were making faster progress.

In spite of their grueling pace earlier on the Persian roads, Jemmah was aware that they still had not gained enough ground to arrive at the Median post by the eighth day. Their only option now was to risk traveling on the Median highway for short spurts, an unavoidable necessity that forced the companions into strained, unbroken silence for long hours at a time.

The morning of their seventh day, they crossed a barren field, and after ensuring there was no sign of Median soldiers, they made their way onto the highway. Icy rain dripped on Jemmah's head and snaked its way down her neck and under her tunic. She shivered. She had not been dry for two days, though it felt more like a century. She threw a look behind her, searching for riders. The downpour made for poor visibility.

Without warning, Zarina slowed her mare and then stopped altogether, her head tilted to the side as though listening for something beyond the endless patter of raindrops. Jemmah reined in her horse, signaling the others to do the same. Zarina was known for her legendary hearing.

"Get off the road!" Irda cried. "Now!"

Only then did Jemmah hear the faint reverberation of pounding hooves. Many hooves. A large party. She pressed her heels into the sides of her mare, driving her into the field. The horses slipped their way through the mud, finding little cover. Behind them, Jemmah picked up the sound of hooves closing in. They had been spotted.

Until they reached the rocky foothills and made their way to one of the trails, they would remain dangerously exposed. Jemmah swallowed hard as she heard the swoosh of an arrow flying too close to her cheek. She flattened her body against the horse's back and focused on the outcropping of rock ahead. Behind her, Jemmah heard a cry, then a great crash. She slowed down to look back.

"Keep going!" Irda cried and flicked the mare with her whip.

Jemmah's mare shot forward, pushing into the protection of the craggy boulders, followed closely by Zarina and Irda. Clunky on flat terrain, her horse became sure-footed as soon as they reached the entrance to the rocky trail.

Once behind the wall of rock, she slowed her mount to a halt and bent to peer through a narrow opening. Megabyzus's horse lay on her side, an arrow protruding from her neck. Under her muscular flank, Megabyzus lay trapped, trying desperately to free himself. In a moment, Aryasb had dismounted and rushed to the aid of his companion.

"Dismount!" Irda hissed. "To your bows."

Jemmah understood Irda's command instantly. The men's open position left them utterly vulnerable to the arrows of the approaching Medes. Years of training took over Jemmah's fingers. Throwing herself flat on the ground, she nocked her arrow and aimed through a narrow slit in the tight rock formation.

Rain blinded her, and she blinked the fat droplets out of her lashes. She had never shot at a human being before. She aimed for an arm and loosed her bow. The man dropped the arrow he had been pointing at Aryasb and screamed as his arm bloomed with blood.

There was no time to think. To feel. She nocked another arrow and aimed for a wrist and missed. She aimed for a thigh and hit the horse instead. Good enough to break the man's advance and throw off his aim. Arrow after arrow, she nocked, aimed, loosed, until her arm shivered. Swallowing, she tasted salt and realized her face was not wet merely from raindrops.

Next to her, Zarina and Irda proved their prowess in archery, never slowing down until Aryasb had managed to half carry a hobbling Megabyzus into the shelter of the rocks.

Aryasb assessed their surroundings with an experienced eye. "Zarina, climb that rock and cover our flank lest they find a way around and attack us from behind." He dropped next to Irda and pulled out his bow in the same motion. "Count?"

"Ten at the outset. Three are down. Four injured, though some are still in the fight. That leaves three. How is Megabyzus?"

"His leg is bad. Jemmah, will you see to him?"

In answer, Jemmah crawled toward the wounded Immortal. In truth, she felt more at home tending the injured than she did causing the injury. Coming to her knees beside Megabyzus, she looked at the leg for a moment without touching it. The Immortal's face was gray with pain.

"I have to tear the trousers to have a better look. It will probably hurt."

Megabyzus nodded. Time slowed as Jemmah focused on her patient. Arrows whistled overhead. Every once in a while, one of her companions would cry a warning. She ignored the intense battle that surrounded them and set her entire focus on the wounded Immortal. In the absence of a trained physician, Jemmah knew she was the best chance Megabyzus had. The horse had pinned him against a rock, which had cut into the flesh of his thigh a jagged line so deep she could see the bone, and a thin, faint line near the top where it had fractured at the hip.

She fetched wine from the packhorse and was about to clean the wound when Megabyzus held out a trembling hand. "Me first," he gasped.

Silently Jemmah handed him the skin. When he had drunk several long swigs, she gently removed the wine from his grasp and began to clean the mangled flesh.

"Do you know what you are doing?" His words slurred at the edges, whether from pain or the effects of the drink, she was not certain.

"Your chances would be better if you were a bird or a dog."

Megabyzus sputtered and held out his hand for another mouthful of wine. She gave the skin over without demur and was glad for it when he barely made a sound as she began plying a needle to the deep cut. She had finished sewing the laceration and was looking for an effective means of immobilizing the thigh when Zarina cried out.

Jemmah's head snapped up.

Zarina had thrown aside her bow and was trying to defend herself against two Median soldiers wielding swords. She whirled to one side to evade a downward thrust only to be met with the sword of the second man. Barely she managed to parry it, swinging her body around to avoid another attack from the first.

Jemmah gasped. They had her ringed between them now, one behind and one to the front. In another moment, Zarina would have no way to defend herself against both. Jemmah reached for the short dagger still sheathed at Megabyzus's side. In one smooth motion, she pulled it loose and rose to her feet, her hands and eyes already taking aim before she could form a thought. The dagger flew, end over end, and found its target in the man's back. Soundlessly he dropped to his knees.

With a short feint left and parry right, Zarina disabled her remaining opponent and turned in time to see the Median soldier fall behind her. She whirled and caught Jemmah's wide eyes.

"You might reconsider your occupation," Megabyzus said through dry lips. "That was a credible throw."

Jemmah stuffed a trembling hand painfully against her lips in an effort to suppress the sobs that threatened to choke her. She was fairly certain she had killed the man. The thought made her want to retch.

In a moment, Zarina landed at her side. "You saved my life," she whispered fiercely against her cheek. "Hold on to that, my sister."

She did not wait to see her nod as she disappeared to help Irda. Jemmah wiped at the salty tracks on her cheeks and tried to still the chattering of her teeth.

Megabyzus patted her hand lightly. "No need for tears. Your stiches aren't that bad. I've seen worse."

She gave herself a mental shake. She had done what she had to do. Now was not the time to drown in emotion. Now was not the time to think of the life she had taken. She managed to shove the horror and shock of that moment deep beneath the surface of her mind and pressed the dead soldier where it could keep company with another ghost.

Dredging up a weak smile for Megabyzus, she said, "We need strong splints to keep that thigh immobile. Any ideas?"

Megabyzus shifted, trying to find a more comfortable position. "How about the haft of my spear? You can cut it into half lengthwise."

"That could work." She crawled to where the Immortal's pack had dropped when his companion had dragged him behind the protection of the rocks, and grabbed the short spear from its loops. She gave it an approving nod after examining the thickness of the wood.

"This will do, if I manage to cut it right."

"Will I be able to ride?"

"Not even if I rig you up with twelve splints."

CHAPTER

EIGHT

Because the LORD your God walks in the midst of your camp,
to deliver you and to give up your enemies before you . . .
Deuteronomy 23:14

"Considering we were outnumbered two to one, we came out of that better than I expected," Irda said, glancing in the direction of the surviving Median men. Most of them had suffered a collection of various injuries. After trussing them up like geese, they had hidden the prisoners inside the bowels of a narrow cave. "We only sustained one injury," she said, sounding pleased.

Jemmah massaged the back of her aching neck. "We had the advantage of cover. If they had managed to reach us on the open road, we would not have fared so well. As to our one injury, it is enough to place us in an awkward position. Megabyzus cannot ride." She gestured at the prone body of the Immortal, snoring softly under the folds of a blanket. Jemmah had put a few drops of the milky juice of the poppy in his wine, before making a poultice of honey, frankincense, and goose fat and splinting the leg tightly with the bandages from her pack.

Feeling the drink's analgesic effects, Megabyzus had insisted on trying to mount a horse in spite of Jemmah's vehement objections, a decision that had almost landed him on his head if not for Irda's quick reactions.

Jemmah rubbed her face with a tired hand. "Those men's friends are likely to come looking for them eventually. We can't remain here. Even with the rain, there are enough tracks to lead them to this place."

Aryasb nodded. "We must move on." He rolled out the map on a piece of oiled leather and studied the trails. "This is the path we must take."

Jemmah studied the route for a moment. "We could use a diversion to buy time." She hunkered down close to the map. "Aryasb, could you take the Median soldiers' horses and ride to the west, along this trail?" Using a stick, she pointed carefully to a narrow line on the map. "Those who come looking for their comrades are bound to follow your tracks, believing they will lead them to their friends. Do you see this cross path here?" She tapped her stick on a tiny line. "It looks to be no more than a footpath. You will have to walk. But it will intersect our path here in the east. We will wait there until you join us."

Aryasb considered the map. "It makes for a good diversion. We will be long gone by the time our pursuers discover they have fallen for a trick. Though it galls me to leave all those lovely horses behind."

"That leaves us with Megabyzus. Any ideas?"

"We must build a litter. You will have to carry him between two horses."

"Too slow. Too awkward." Zarina frowned. "We'll never make it to the Median outpost in time to intercept Keren."

"You don't have to carry him all the way to the outpost. You can hide Megabyzus. Here." He pointed his finger at a spot no more than an hour's ride away. "Then we ride to the outpost to free Mistress Keren. We can fetch Megabyzus on our way back. If all goes well, he need only wait a day or two. Should be safe enough."

Jemmah swallowed hard. "And if we have to go on to Ecbatana?"

"In that case, we must separate. Someone will return to fetch Megabyzus home. The rest will go on."

Jemmah's mouth turned dry. She could only hope that there would be no need for such an eventuality. They were down two men already. Another would reduce their numbers to a mere three. Four, she reminded herself, if she counted Cyrus's spy in Ecbatana. Four against a walled city and Astyages's entire squadron of personal guards. She shook the horse blanket she had spread on the ground and dropped it on the broad back of her placid mare.

"I am ready," Aryasb called, breaking into the stream of her thoughts. He mounted the Median officer's stallion and pulled on the line he had rigged that brought the other horses trotting behind him. Within moments, the rest of the companions had packed and restored the place to its natural order. Jemmah entered the cave where they had left their prisoners.

"I am leaving you a skin of water and some bread, lest your companions do not find you soon. Enough time and effort, and you should be able to remove your gags." She was uncertain what the loud mumbling that followed her out of the cave might have meant. Were they cursing her or expressing their appreciation? A little of both, she decided.

Irda and Zarina had slung Megabyzus on a blanket between their horses and now proceeded slowly in the direction Aryasb had indicated. Jemmah painstakingly cleared their tracks behind them, using an evergreen branch. In spite of their best efforts, poor Megabyzus suffered a most unpleasant ride, especially once Irda and Zarina were forced to dismount, thanks to the narrowness of the path, and carry the Immortal bumping and thumping between them.

Even in the frosty air, Megabyzus's face shone with sweat by the time they arrived at the hidden curve of rocks Aryasb had chosen as a good hiding place. Jemmah could see why. It remained invisible from the road, and the boulders formed a heavy ledge, shielding the injured man from both sun and rain, offering as safe a shelter as they could provide outside an actual house.

Jemmah knelt beside Megabyzus. "There is food here and water. Your favorite wine, too."

"Go on, mistress. I can last a couple of days without your tender care."

"I shall take that as a promise."

*　*　*

Their pace turned painstakingly slow once Aryasb rejoined the group. Hoping to avoid detection, they left the path in favor of barely distinguishable tracks. The further north they traveled, the more the terrain changed, rocky outcrops turning into sprawling fields and pastures. Come spring, the place would be a sea of green, clover and hay growing tall and verdant, a haven of rich pasture for the elegant Median horses valued the world over.

Now, yellow grasses and barren soil ran into copses of trees, Persian ironwood mixed with sycamores and evergreens. Upon occasion, they rode parallel to the boundaries of mature orchards, pruned apple and pomegranate trees standing in precise rows, looking like a battalion of soldiers ready to march.

Except for the tired plodding of horses' hooves, no other sound broke the grim silence. They all felt too weary to speak. Bleak possibilities tormented Jemmah. Trying to rid herself of her mounting anxiety was like trying to dry herself under a waterfall. No sooner did she wipe away one thought than another took its place. If Megabyzus was found by the Medians, he would be defenseless in his condition. Her mother would fare no better. If they did not arrive at the outpost soon, she would be gone. Lost in Astyages's maze of hidden prisons. Or worse.

Relief mingled with anxiety when they finally arrived at the Median outpost. Securing the horses in a copse of trees several minutes' walk away, they crept toward the settlement on foot.

A high wall surrounded the ramshackle buildings, its only gate closed and guarded. They circled to the back, where Aryasb climbed the wall with ease, fingers clinging to the top as he drew himself up so he could observe the scene within.

"I only saw half a dozen men." Aryasb wiped his dusty tunic as he gave his report. "Two narrow buildings and a large wooden stable. No sign of Mistress Keren. Likely they are holding her in one of those buildings."

"Did you recognize any of the men you fought when they took her?" Jemmah asked. "Or their horses?" If the men who had attacked her mother were within the outpost, then chances remained good that they still held her mother prisoner within those walls.

"No. But that means little. They could be inside one of the buildings. And they would have changed horses before this, as we did."

Jemmah hunkered down. "Draw us a map. We have to get inside those buildings."

Irda stared at Aryasb's simple drawing in the dirt. "We need a big distraction at the north wall, here, where the gate is. I have an idea that will draw the soldiers away while two of you climb over the south wall and get into those buildings to look for Keren. It won't take long if the windows are open."

"I'll go in with Aryasb," Zarina said.

No one could deny Zarina was the best climber in their midst, better even than the Immortal. Jemmah grimaced. "Very well. But if you find her, leave the fighting to Aryasb. I will stand guard over the south wall. Aryasb and Zarina will be blind once they are inside the buildings. Irda, can you manage your distraction alone?"

Irda nodded once and grinned wildly before slipping into the long afternoon shadows cast by the wall. A moment later, Jemmah heard a short, strangled warning from one of the soldiers inside. Irda's distraction had arrived in the form of a hail of fiery arrows, setting small fires to a bale of hay, followed by the shingled roof of a shed. The smoking fires drew the soldiers away from the buildings in a welter of confused action. Taking advantage of their turmoil, Zarina and Aryasb climbed the south wall in catlike silence, lending a hand to Jemmah so she could straddle the lip of the wall, lying flat to watch over their progress.

The southern portion of the compound seemed gratifyingly

empty as Zarina and Aryasb made their way down. Holding close to the shadows, they converged on the first building. Jemmah saw, with relief, that the window had been left open. Aryasb slid through, motioning for Zarina to wait.

The wooden shutter in the window of the second building stood likewise open. These Medians did not seem too concerned with a possible rescue attempt of their valuable hostage. Disquiet shivered down Jemmah's spine. Their progress seemed too easy. She expanded her scrutiny from the obvious walkways, looking for anything that might hint at a trap.

There! In the shadows between the two buildings, she detected a small movement. Shimmying down the wall as fast as her scrabbling fingers allowed, she managed to land in a dark corner. Just then, Jemmah saw the shadow move, serpent-fast, toward Zarina.

Jemmah had her bow at the ready. The arrow flew, hitting solid flesh with a sickening twang. A man groaned. Jemmah gave Zarina a swift nod as she ran toward the injured man. At the sight of her, he cried out weakly, trying to alert his comrades. Her arrow had found its mark in the man's shoulder, leaving him dazed from the wound but conscious. Jemmah shoved her hand over his mouth to silence his next cry, hoping the noise of the commotion on the other side of the building had covered the sound. Zarina had arrived at her side, and together, they managed to gag and bind him, tucking him into the corner of a chimney shaft.

"Aryasb is taking too long searching the first building." Zarina pointed to the second building. "We have to see if Keren is in there."

Jemmah followed Zarina's quick steps. They pushed the shutters wider and peered within. Inhaling sharply, Jemmah took a hasty step back. Inside, the room was tomb-like, dark and enclosed, with a low ceiling. She felt the cloying stickiness of sweat break out over her skin.

"Look!" Zarina pointed to the corner. Keren was sitting on the ground with her back to them, hands and feet tied before her.

Jemmah's heart slammed against her chest, relief bringing sudden tears to her eyes. Zarina climbed inside the window, legs and arms moving in rapid, graceful harmony. Jemmah took a step closer and braced a trembling hand inside the window frame. The simple touch made her queasy.

She turned her gaze to her mother, sitting there with her back to them, hoping the sight of her would release her from her sick paralysis. The image wavered for a moment. She gulped a breath, then narrowed her eyes, staring harder at the woman. Something was wrong. She was wearing her mother's tunic. Her mother's torn blue shawl hung from her neck. But something about the curve of the shoulders, the loop of the hair, the thickness of the waist was awry.

"Zarina, stop!"

The urgency in her tone brought Zarina to a halt, two short steps away from the woman. Curiously, she looked at Jemmah over her shoulder.

"It's not her."

Zarina turned, brow arched. She took a cautious half step forward, her body's posture changing from eagerness to battle ready. The woman jumped to her feet, her bonds flying loose with a snap of muscular arms, and turned to face them. She had large eyes in a moon-round face and full, pursed lips that made her look like a guppy.

A complete stranger.

A decoy, placed there to help capture them.

In her haste to come to Zarina's aid, Jemmah heedlessly thrust one leg through the window, then froze, straddling the window frame, one leg hanging uselessly outside. She tried to pull herself all the way into the dark chamber. Her world shrank. Wrenching terror curled through her, turning her muscles into lead.

Fear—unreasoning, overwhelming fear—held her hostage. She watched helplessly as the woman leapt toward Zarina. Still Jemmah felt unable to move, unable to pull herself through the window without losing her frail hold on consciousness.

In the chamber, the woman reached Zarina. In her mind, Jemmah's monsters held her in their fierce grip. She sat in the open window, ashamed of her impotence, and watched as the Median woman curled a fist into Zarina's hair and pulled.

CHAPTER NINE

O LORD, there is none like you to help,
between the mighty and the weak.
2 Chronicles 14:11

───────────── ASHER ─────────────

Asher lurched to his knees, dizzy from his latest beating. He had landed on his face when the guards had flung him back inside his cell. He wanted simply to remain prone on the ground and not move a muscle. But aware that the guards reported his every move to the king, he refused to give in to the pain. Reeling from the fresh onslaught on his body, he barely managed to sit up, treating the guards to a bloody grin. He suspected it emerged more as a grimace.

"My thanks for the lift," he said with a cheery wave. "Do you think you could have the laundress wash my robes? They begin to stink of Astyages's torturer. His reek is more excruciating than his pummeling."

They slammed the door in his face and clapped down the bar noisily.

He spat out a mouthful of blood and watched it sink into the dirt floor. Drawing a tentative hand over his jaw and the delicate bones around his eyes, Asher winced. Everything hurt. He did not think the bones of his face broken, though his eye had already swollen shut, and he would be more colorful than a grape soon. Other than a few cracked ribs and a lot of nasty bruising, he doubted he had sustained any permanent damage. Presumably Astyages wanted to keep him alive and conscious enough to share his secrets. Miserable with pain, terrified of more torture, but sufficiently aware to draw the chariot plans.

He closed his eyes and tried to think of something other than the intense pain in his face. Something lovely. Like food. He thought of his favorite dish, roast lamb served with a side of wild asparagus. His stomach growled. His mouth watered as he pictured a piece of steaming hot bread, freshly baked in a stone oven, piled high with eggplants fried with garlic and onions, and garnished with dried mint and saffron. Hunger pangs only added to his other aches and pains, doing nothing to bring him relief.

He snapped his good eye open when the door rattled. Were they back so soon? He ground his teeth, trying to prepare himself for another bout of torment. Impotent rage snaked through him. Caged like a little rabbit, he had no power to protect himself.

But instead of dragging him out, the guards hauled in another prisoner and dropped her against the wall before withdrawing. Asher studied her with interest. He had wondered if the king would send in a spy. But it had not occurred to him that he would send in a woman. She was dressed in a ragged tunic a few sizes too big and wore only one shoe. Save for a small bruise on one cheek and rope burns around wrists and ankles, she seemed in good health. Under the generous layer of gray dirt that covered every scrap of visible skin, she was rather beautiful in a modest, understated way. Tall and slim, she appeared to be in her early thirties, though something about her carriage and the steady gaze with which she scrutinized him made her seem older. In that steady gaze, Asher sensed fear, though she reined it in well.

"If you are here to spy on me," he said by way of introduction, "you are wasting your time."

"Same to you," she said, leaning her back against the wall.

That made him smile. She was good. Convincing. Then again, Astyages would not have sent her if she weren't the best at her trade. Whatever that was.

Asher scuttled away to the opposite side of the cell and, lying down, closed his eyes again. He must have slept, though he could not say for how long. When he opened his good eye, he saw that the woman had not moved from her corner, though she now sat with her knees raised tight against her chest and her face planted on top like a squashed lily.

A dozen bruises and scrapes screamed in protest as Asher turned. He felt an old scab open on his back. Swallowing a groan, he drew his legs up into his belly, trying to find a bit of warmth. He froze at the sound of voices outside the door. Since he had been brought here, he had only ever heard two guards at one time. Now he could hear the sound of several feet. Soldiers marching.

The woman lifted her head and stared at the door with dread. Asher forced himself to sit up. The effort made him queasy, and he swallowed bile.

Someone scraped the bar loose on the other side and the door opened with a groan. At first, Asher did not see him, surrounded as he was by members of his personal guard. Then they parted, like the famed sea of his mother's people, and Astyages stepped through. Bejeweled and bewigged, smelling of a dozen sweet perfumes, he jangled his way into the cell.

He bent over Asher. "Still alive?"

Asher waved him away. "You smell like a perfumer's shop. It offends my nose."

"You smell like a baboon's behind."

Asher tried to smile, but his bloodied lips would not cooperate. "I think you will find that it is your jail you smell."

Astyages ignored him and turned his attention to the woman. "Enjoying my hospitality?"

"It is no less than I would have expected from you."

The king arched an eyebrow. "No? It could be much worse, let me assure you." He delivered a vicious kick into Asher's side. A puff of air escaped Asher's lips, though he managed to swallow his cry of pain.

"Do you see this swollen, purplish lump under my foot?" Astyages delivered another kick, though Asher managed to evade most of its force by curling into himself. "This is my son, or so his mother claimed, and I have no reason to doubt her. Look you well, Keren. If I treat my own flesh like this to get what I want, what do you think I will do to you? Cyrus's chief scribe? I hold your little neck in my hand." He closed his fist and pressed hard as if already feeling the delicate bones breaking in his grasp. "Think on that tonight. I will give you that long before I come to question you."

The woman's lips flattened. "You waste your time, Your Majesty."

She spoke Median fluently. Still, Asher detected a mild accent. Something about the cadence of it felt familiar. Astyages had called her Keren. Cyrus's scribe. He had heard of the woman, of course. She had become something of a legend in the quiet back rooms of the Median kingdom. The woman who had saved the Persian prince's life and defeated Astyages's plans so long ago.

Could this willowy, dirt-encrusted woman truly be Cyrus's chief scribe? How had Astyages managed to land such a plump morsel?

The thick wooden door slammed shut behind the king and his well-armed cohort. The woman scuttled over to him. "I had heard rumors of you," she said, pinning him with her curious gaze.

It hit him, all of a sudden, that accent. Her intonations reminded him of his mother. The same Babylonian overtones, the same soft Judean music undergirding the syllables. And just like that, he believed her. Not Astyages's spy at all. But the famous Judean scribe, a Babylonian captive like his mother had once been. The woman who had helped the young Persian king run rings around Astyages for years.

"And I, you." He tried to collect himself, pulling the frayed edges of his disguise around him like a protective cloak. "Charmed to meet you, lady. Though I must deplore the circumstances under which I have the pleasure. My hair is usually more elegantly arranged." He made a half-hearted attempt at straightening his twisted sleeves. "I am sorry you have to meet me in these rags. Really. The king ought to be ashamed. He could have at least left me a fresh tunic."

She regarded him quizzically and laughed. Laughed! That shook him a little. Had his guise slipped so much? "Come now," she said. "You need not pretend with me. I had heard you were exceptionally fastidious. Some even call you delicate. Then one of the swords you forged came into my possession. It was one of your earlier works, done by your own hands. And already, my husband said, you could see the genius in it. Hardly the work of a man who does not like to sweat."

"Oh, that. I got rid of that filthy business as quickly as I could manage. It made me enough silver to live the life I desired."

She wagged a chiding finger in his face. "Astyages may have bought the myth you created about yourself. But you and I both know that you are no delicate slave to the latest fashion, following in the footsteps of shiftless young aristocrats." She pointed to his fingers. "You still have the calluses of a blacksmith."

He folded his fingers, making an annoyed fist.

She bent close and lowered her voice. "Your workshops have continued to produce excellent weapons, under your own supervision. We recognized your touch and followed up a few of your sales." She nodded. "I have kept a close eye on you, Asher."

The certainty in her voice blasted through him. He sensed the futility of denying what she obviously knew. She had spied on him over the years with far greater success than his own father had managed to do. Slowly he said, "I am glad Astyages did not pay me the same compliment."

She laughed again, this time at his expression. "Your work is worthy of attention. I couldn't afford your workmanship for our army. But a woman can dream."

He made a noncommittal sound in his throat. His lack of response did nothing to repress her enthusiastic monologue. "I must confess, I had never believed the rumors that you are Astyages's natural son. It seemed impossible, especially once you started hiding your wares from him. I assumed, if you had truly been his son, that you would have wanted to help him. Until just now, when he introduced you. Hard to deny the evidence of my own ears." She waved a hand toward his face. "And eyes. Your eyes, that is. The same green shade as your father's. You have that in common with Cyrus."

"Astyages sired me. That does not make him my father," he said, his voice wooden.

"No more than having sired Mandana makes him Cyrus's grandfather." She examined her hands, fingers twisting into one another. "But why not claim you? He has no other sons."

"My mother was a lowly slave who took his fancy for one night. But he considered her far too unworthy to keep. After he had his pleasure, he abandoned her like a crumpled piece of rubbish. In his eyes, I am no more royal than you." Asher pressed the bridge of his nose. He was starting to feel dizzy.

"That explains why we never found one of his soldiers armed with your weapons. You have been hiding them from him."

"Lady, you know entirely too much."

"I fear that is true." She threw a worried glance at the door. "You know why he has brought you here, into this cell?"

"To frighten me, of course. As he said, if he does not withhold his violence from his own flesh, what might he do to me?"

Asher frowned. "If he wanted to torture information out of you, he would have done so already."

Her lips rounded into a circle as his meaning dawned. "Is this—" she waved her fingers to indicate the cell—"an empty threat?"

"Astyages knows harming you would be like baiting a lion. He would only embolden Cyrus to storm harder against him. And that is an inconvenience he would rather avoid at the moment. Astyages would prefer to focus on keeping his territories safe from the Babylonian king's clutches. That war takes greater precedence in his mind."

Asher shifted, trying to find a more comfortable spot. "The Babylonian affair will not prevent him from coming against Cyrus, you understand? He has enough resources to buy a huge force of mercenary fighters from Saka tribes all the way to Lydia. He will attack your little king. But he would rather do it in his time. And harming you might force him into an earlier attack than he plans."

"So you think I am safe?"

Asher drew a hand through the tangle of his hair. "Safe? Hardly. Astyages is as unpredictable as a hungry Egyptian crocodile. He may not put your head on a pike yet. That does not mean he can't grow nasty. I hope you have a plan to get out of this place soon. Not that it will help you much. Your Cyrus is bold and clever. But you will find that is not enough against Astyages's superior forces. The Persian king simply lacks the resources to win his war. One way or another, you will find yourself crushed under Astyages's foot."

"You could help."

"You said yourself you cannot afford me."

She drew closer still. "Asher? I know that name. It belongs to one of the tribes of my people. Like your mother, I believe."

"That does not make you my auntie. And you still can't afford me."

"Did your mother ever tell you about the prophecies of our people?"

Asher slid against the wall and closed his eyes. His mother had, as it happened, though he did not know to which particular prophecy Keren alluded. "You have tired me out. I need a nap."

TEN

They are distressed, because they had been confident;
they arrive there, only to be disappointed.
Job 6:20, NIV

Zarina twisted the woman's arm, forcing her to loosen her hold on the fat braid hanging down her back. In two moves, she had tussled her to the ground. The Median fought like a feral cat, hissing and kicking and scratching.

Jemmah watched appalled as the woman landed a great fist in Zarina's face. Trying to crawl inside to lend Zarina a hand, she came to a staggering stop. Her vision narrowed as she pushed deeper into the darkness, and she began to feel like she could not breathe.

The punch barely slowed Zarina down. Within a moment, she had subdued the woman, squatting on her bucking chest and pinning her arms to the ground.

Jemmah sagged with relief against the window frame.

Zarina kept the flat of her hand on the guppy-round lips to prevent the woman from screaming. "You were right," she panted. "It's not Keren."

Jemmah gave a huff of soundless laughter. She turned to their captive. In Median, she said, "Where is the woman whose robes you stole?"

The woman mumbled under Zarina's hand and tried to take a bite out of the fleshy part of her palm. Zarina pressed her hand harder, neutralizing her sharp teeth.

"What did she say?"

"Something about us being fools and Keren never being here."

"They must have sent her clothes to the outpost but whisked her away directly to Ecbatana." Despair made her voice sharp. "They knew we would come here. They set this one up, hoping to capture us."

With deft moves, Zarina stuffed a fat woolen handkerchief into the woman's mouth and gagged her, before turning her attention to her wriggling wrists. Behind her Jemmah heard a sound. In a moment, her dagger was in her hand, poised.

"Aryasb!" She swallowed at the sight of the Immortal slipping into the chamber. "I thought you were one of the guards."

"Hurry," he said.

On his shoulder, under the flat of his hand, Jemmah saw a dark stain. "You're hurt!"

"It's not serious. But we must hurry. They had set up a trap in the other house. That's why it took me so long to come to you." He indicated the woman. "New friend?"

"Also a trap."

Zarina finished tying up the Median woman and, grabbing Keren's blue shawl from her neck, scrambled through the window. As soon as Jemmah stepped away from that dark chamber, she felt she could breathe again.

Aryasb was panting hard. Jemmah cast a worried glance at that spreading stain. She doubted the wound was as negligible as Aryasb had made it sound. Too much blood covered his clothing. In spite of help from Zarina and Jemmah, he barely managed the climb back up the wall. At the top, before Zarina slipped over to the other side, Jemmah pointed to the narrow latch that held the door of the stable closed.

"Can you hit that?" she asked. "I could never manage it. I think you might."

In answer, Zarina nocked an arrow. The latch flew open with one shot. Jemmah nodded in approval. "Now a few more into the barn. Enough to spook the horses."

Zarina landed the arrows at exactly the right angle to alarm the horses without harming any. A mare came cantering out, neighing in agitation, followed by two stallions. Soon, all the residents of the stable that had not been tied up securely came trotting out into the courtyard. The Medians would have their hands full trying to calm their precious mounts and restore order.

Helping Aryasb descend the wall, they crawled through dried grass and found their way back to where they had hidden their horses.

"Keren?" Irda pelted into the clearing, her breath coming in gasps.

Jemmah shook her head. "A decoy only. My mother never came through here. And Aryasb is injured."

There was no time for explanations. Vaulting on their mounts, they fled back toward the mountain track, hoping the fires they had set, along with the confusion of the loose horses, would give them the lead they needed to get away.

They rode soundlessly until Aryasb tilted on his horse and almost pitched on his head. Irda signaled a stop. "The horses need a break," she said.

"Let me see," Jemmah told Aryasb. A trail of blood had soaked the front of his tunic and spread like a bloody map down one arm and across his back. She shook her head. "He won't last all the way to Ecbatana. I can sew up the wound. But he needs to rest. Eat. Drink. Two days at least, before he can ride hard."

"I am sorry," Aryasb said, his head drooping.

Jemmah placed a hand on his shoulder. "This is no fault of yours. Twice you have been injured in your efforts to save my mother. Twice you have almost given your life. You have fought bravely. I am grateful, Aryasb. Now your part in this rescue is over." She looked at Irda. "We need to get Aryasb and Megabyzus home."

"I will help Megabyzus," Aryasb said quickly.

"I thank you for the offer. And you shall ride to Megabyzus. But you will need more help. Irda?"

She knelt on one knee next to Aryasb. "I will look after the Immortals, Jemmah. I will look after all of you. You will come to no harm."

Jemmah's eyes welled up. "I am not returning with you. I will go to Ecbatana to look for my mother."

Irda surged to her feet. "You must be mad. It is suicide! How shall I answer your father?"

Jemmah swallowed hard. Irda's reasoning was sound. She did not have the strength or expertise to save her mother. At best, going to Ecbatana would prove a useless endeavor. At worst, a reckless undertaking that would end in her own imprisonment or demise. Yet she felt a dagger-sharp conviction that she was meant to follow this path.

TESSA AFSHAR

Perhaps for the first time in her life she had begun to understand her parents' faith. To practice the trust that reached beyond her own puny ability and relied wholly on God for provision.

"Father will understand. I cannot abandon my mother."

"She would want you to, Jemmah! Do you think she would approve of you rushing headlong into Ecbatana all by yourself?"

"She will not be by herself," Zarina said quietly. "She will have me."

Jemmah hesitated. She understood Irda's agitation only too well, for she felt those same feelings about her sister's declaration.

Zarina placed a hand on Jemmah's shoulder. "Do you remember Eleazar?"

For a moment, Jemmah grasped at the name blankly. Then, in one sharp sweep, it came to her. "David's man of war. The one who fought in the plot of barley."

"Who is David?" Irda threw her hands up. "Who is Elcazar? And what do they have to do with you going to Ecbatana?"

Jemmah gave Irda an apologetic smile. "David was the greatest king of my people. One day, as he faced his enemies in a plot of barley, his warriors lost heart. To a man, they fled."

"They ran away?" Irda's voice was drenched with disgust.

"Except for one. Eleazar remained. He stayed by his king and fought until his grip froze around his sword and he could not open his fingers after the battle was done."

"He died a hero?"

Jemmah shook her head. "He lived a hero. He ought to have died, given the odds. But the Lord saved Eleazar. More. He gave him a great victory." She reached for Zarina's hand and clasped it tightly in her own. "This is our barley field, Irda. Our time to stand firm and not run. I do not know how to win a victory.

I have no clever plan. But I know I must try. And leave the rest to God."

"This is madness. How will you even find your mother, the two of you on your own, let alone rescue her?"

"We are not completely alone. We still have Prexaspes."

"The waste remover?"

"Perhaps it is not so much how high your position or how great your influence," Jemmah said slowly. "Perhaps what matters is whether you are a perfect fit in God's plan. A lowly profession can hide an exalted ability."

* * *

The city of Ecbatana stood guarded by seven concentric walls, each boasting battlements that had been painted in seven different colors. The last two, leading into the city, had been gilded with silver and gold, an impressive sight to any visitor approaching the ancient capital of the Medes.

At the foothills of all this glory, a large village had sprung up, where the peasantry and farming community had built their humble homes, close enough to commute into the city for ease of trade. Close enough, also, to find quick harbor within its walls in case of enemy attack.

The village, a haphazard assortment of mud huts and wooden structures housing animals and people, spread out in a disorderly jumble that had arisen out of need rather than good planning. Riding through it, Jemmah felt accosted by a myriad of loud sounds and powerful odors.

Before bidding Irda and Aryasb goodbye, they had changed into the modest Median garb they had brought along in their saddlebags in case of this eventuality. Earlier that morning, on their way to the Ecbatana village, they had stopped briefly at a farm on the intersection of the Khorasan Highway and the road leading south. Jemmah knew the old farmer from her mother's tales and remembered that he still considered himself Harpagus's man. Limping and ancient, the man had taken their horses without comment in exchange for a dilapidated cart and an aged, gray donkey. For rather a lot of silver, he sold them half a cartful of onions.

Now, two young Median farm girls approached the cheapest inn at Ecbatana's village and paid for a room. Jemmah did the talking. She spoke Median fluently, without an accent. The two languages, Persian and Median, had sprung from the same root and remained similar enough to learn with ease, but the intonation of certain words could prove tricky. Having learned it as a child, Jemmah had retained the knack of it.

In their room, they took the time to wash off the dirt that clung to every pore. Wending their way past the stables, they entered the common chamber of the inn and found a quiet corner with two wobbly stools. Jemmah asked the innkeeper for two bowls of the mutton stew she saw bubbling over a fire. She sighed with pleasure as she tasted a mouthful, the first hot meal she had eaten in over a week. As they ate, Jemmah complimented the innkeeper on his tasty stew, the generosity of his portions, his warm fire, and the sweetness of his wine. His grin grew wider with every compliment. Without being asked, he topped off their bowls and fetched a new hunk of warm, stone-baked bread.

Tearing off a piping hot piece and dipping it in her stew, Jemmah asked, "Do you know where I can find Prexaspes? The waste remover?" She did her best to keep her expression neutral, not revealing how desperately she wanted to know the answer.

The innkeeper made a face. "That one. He lives in the village, but he works in the city and only returns home just before the gates close. You will want a good bath if you come anywhere near him."

*   *   *

Prexaspes lived in a modest cottage at the outskirts of the village. Jemmah drove their onion cart to his door and fed the donkey wads of hay as she and Zarina waited for his arrival.

She had hidden Cyrus's tiny scroll in a loop of Zarina's braids. Now, undoing the loop gently, she retrieved the scroll with a furtive swipe of fingers and restored Zarina's hair as if she had been doing nothing more than a bit of pleasant hairdressing.

Prexaspes arrived as the sun slowly sank behind the mountains. He sat perched atop the seat of a wide cart with high sides. He hardly needed an introduction. The odor that permeated the air around him proved introduction enough.

"My friend sends you these onions in thanks for your service," Jemmah said in greeting, pointing to her cart.

Tiny black eyes sparkled with interest as he examined the small hill of tired-looking onions. "I have been paid worse," he said.

She handed him a large pink onion, the thin scroll pressed to its side. "They are not so bad as they seem."

His face remained impassive. She could see why he made a good spy. "What a terrible host I am. Let me fetch you both some water." He padded inside his cottage, onion clasped in the palm of his hand.

Returning, he handed them two chipped cups filled with clear spring water. "I think I know what my friend wants."

"Do you?"

"I thought he would send someone . . . bigger to fetch her home."

Jemmah's heart leapt into her throat. "We had bigger. This is what remains." She wanted to scream at Prexaspes to stop his spy game and speak plainly. Then again, there was a reason he had survived in his secret trade for over two decades. She took an excited step toward the man. "Do you know where she is? How?"

Prexaspes tapped a finger against a bony, bumpy nose. "I can't smell. Not a thing."

Jemmah blinked. "Pardon?" With something akin to despair, she wondered if the man had become unhinged. Perhaps the years of keeping secrets had affected his ability to reason properly.

As if reading her mind, he smiled. He had a sharp, long smile, like two thin pieces of string, showing a lot of teeth. "Help me bring the onions to my cellar," he said and spoke no more until they had hauled their load into a stone root cellar under the cottage.

"We can speak more freely here," he said.

"You saw my mother?"

He raised a thick brow. "Your mother, is it?" He studied Jemmah before nodding to himself. "Last I saw you, you were a bitty thing."

"Where is my mother?" Jemmah said, losing patience.

"In Astyages's prison. Where did you think she would be?"

"How could you have seen her if she is imprisoned?"

"I told you. My nose doesn't work."

Jemmah felt like stamping her foot. She glared at the man, beyond words.

He tapped his nose again. "I can't smell anything. The

soldiers can, you see? And they don't like it. They are supposed to bring the prisoners' waste to me, while I wait outside in the courtyard. But they never do. Instead, they let me go in with one of them and collect it from the cells myself.

"That's how I came to see her. Your mother. Recognized her right away, from all those years ago, when we met in Ecbatana."

Zarina grasped Jemmah's arm with bruising force. "She lives."

Jemmah swallowed. "Was she sick? Hurt?"

He shrugged a thick shoulder. "Seemed well enough for someone in Astyages's prison."

"Did she recognize you?"

"She thanked me very prettily for emptying the pot, but if she knew me, she kept it to herself. Then again, I hid my own surprise at finding her there. One of the guards had his beady eyes on me the whole time I remained inside that cell. Wouldn't do me any good if a prisoner were to seem too familiar. Your mother would know better than that." Pulling a small stool over, he sat down slowly.

"Can you help us rescue her?"

He crossed his arms. "Not without revealing who I am. I obtain information by getting into places no one else can. I am a ghost to most people. They don't see me. They only smell my cart. That's how I gather intelligence for Cyrus.

"I let him know the latest numbers in Media's army; I discover who is in prison, who has fallen into disfavor, who feels offended by the king. Information. That is my trade. If, somehow, I manage to help you with this rescue, it will be my last job in Ecbatana. Once I finish, I will have to clear out of this place. Because even if at first they don't suspect me, eventually it will dawn on them that I must have had a hand in it."

Jemmah pointed to Cyrus's bold seal depicting a Persian

prince wearing a fluted crown, carrying a sword in one hand, and in the other, holding a lion dangling by its leg. "Cyrus knew that when he put his seal on that letter. Yet he told us to seek you, Prexaspes. You know who she is. You know her value to him. Whatever the cost, he would consider the gain greater."

Jemmah held her breath, waiting for the man to respond. Without him, they had no hope of reaching her mother.

Prexaspes regarded her dispassionately, his expression closed. Abruptly his mouth widened into its thin, stretchy smile. "Ah, well. I was thinking of retiring, in any case. The waste business is beginning to stink."

CHAPTER

ELEVEN

Thus says the LORD to his anointed, to Cyrus,
whose right hand I have grasped,
to subdue nations before him
and to loose the belts of kings,
to open doors before him
that gates may not be closed.

Isaiah 45:1

―――――――――――― CYRUS ――――――――――――

The pulled muscle in his calf screamed with every weary step. Still Cyrus pressed on, determined to see to his men and to show them how proud he was of their courage. The battle had been ferocious that day, exacting a high price. They had won because he had surprised the enemy yet again and grabbed for himself the advantage of charging down from higher ground, his cavalry a wall of power as it formed the first rank of attack. But they had paid for that victory.

He frowned as he took in the haggard faces of his soldiers, their tattered clothing sticking to sweat-drenched bodies under insufficient armor, wrecked leather boots exposing blistered feet. Their weapons, if possible, were in even worse shape. They had managed to take a few swords and shields from Astyages's soldiers who had died on the battlefield. But their comrades had snatched away much more than they had left behind.

There would not be another campaign season if Cyrus could not manage to somehow arm his men properly.

"They fought bravely," Harpagus said at his elbow. Like all good generals, he had learned to mourn for the loss of his men without giving in to the sorrow.

Cyrus gave a single nod, putting his heart into the frugal motion. "They gave everything."

Harpagus bent to pick up a light-gray stone, painted scarlet by someone's blood. He twirled it in his palm, turning it over so that it showed now ash gray, now red. "You must pace yourself for this. For the many years ahead."

Cyrus whipped his head toward him. "What do you mean?"

"What do you think will happen when you defeat Astyages?"

Cyrus's smile was fierce. "I will enjoy it?"

"Undoubtedly. But beyond that?"

For so long, his entire mind had focused on winning this war. On beating Astyages and setting Persia free from the yoke of their mighty cousins, the Medes. He had rarely allowed himself to think past that moment. He shrugged. "Use our spoils to build Pasargadae. Give our people a better life."

"And?"

"And what?"

"What of Media? You cannot topple Astyages from his throne and leave that throne empty."

Cyrus swallowed. For the first time, he spoke the thought aloud. "I will sit upon it. My grandfather's throne will be my throne."

"Precisely. That one battle, the one that finally defeats Astyages, will be the one to make you king not of a kingdom, but of an empire. Which means this cannot be the end of your warfare. As soon as you sit upon that throne, every nation that owes your grandfather fealty will either try to untangle itself from you or, worse, turn against you and try to take from you what you have won."

It took only a moment for Cyrus's agile mind to capture the thread of Harpagus's reasoning. In the world he occupied, there was no room for a small independent kingdom. Small nations were swallowed up by greater powers. He either had to rule an empire or die trying. "More battles." A shudder went through him.

"Years of them."

Cyrus stared at the stone turning over and over in Harpagus's hand, now gray, now scarlet. Years of war. Could he live with that?

He had always felt that the Persian deity Ahura Mazda himself had selected him to rule. Believed that his kingship and the spiritual realm somehow collided, imbuing him with a responsibility to bring justice and truth to his people. Even Keren and Jared, neither of whom followed Ahura Mazda, believed that their own god had called him, though they had always skirted around what they meant by that calling.

He knew one thing. King of the Persians, the Medes, or whatever nation he came to hold under his scepter, he would do his best to bring good and order to the people he ruled. And he would give those who worshiped a different deity from his own, like his friends Keren and Jared, the right to follow their gods in freedom, without coercion or intimidation.

His heart burned at the thought of Keren. It had been some

days since he had received a message from the small coterie that had gone in search of her. Something twisted inside him at the thought of the horrors Astyages might have visited upon her. Though he was a man rich in friendships, he knew as a king that few came close to enjoying the degree of open trust he could lay at that woman's feet. Her family were his family. He fisted his hand and cursed the helplessness that bound him to this hillside. Bound his stretched resources to the next battle so that he could send so little to her aid.

He felt, with the rising of bitter bile, as though his heart were breaking. Resolutely, he bore the pain of it and took another step, and another, until he had covered the length and breadth of the field of men who called him king and laid their lives at his feet.

TWELVE

The LORD sets the prisoners free;
the LORD opens the eyes of the blind.
The LORD lifts up those who are bowed down;
the LORD loves the righteous.
Psalm 146:7-8

───────── ASHER ─────────

Asher watched dispassionately as Keren wrapped his ribs using a strip of cloth she had managed to tear from the bottom of her ragged robe. He had shared his cell with her for ten days. Oddly, he felt like he had known her for ten months. Like a protective mother, she had tended him patiently every time he returned from a fresh bout of beating, pouring her own share of water through his split lips, forcing him to eat her water-soaked bread so that his tender jaw could manage the simple act of chewing.

They had filled the hours with words. Keren had told him of her life in Babylon and mesmerized him with her story of how she had come to meet Cyrus. He had told her of his mother, of the faith that had sustained her through cold nights and sometimes called to him now, even though he had chosen to go his own way.

He refused the watery bean soup Keren offered him with a shake of his head and waved his hand to indicate she should eat it. She had grown thin and fragile over the past ten days. New bruises decorated her face, and a crust of dried blood clung under one nostril, courtesy of her latest questioning. Nothing to threaten her life, he told himself, though the sight of those bruises made him want to slowly pummel the men responsible.

One thing to torture him. From the moment he had begun the dangerous business of defying Astyages, he had known he was playing with fire and accepted that risk. He had wanted to pay the king back for the pain he had caused his mother. For the hard, endless shame that had dogged her life following Astyages's abandonment, and the unnecessary poverty that had swallowed her up one bite at a time. Bitterness had landed him in this cell. Bitterness and a steel-edged desire for justice.

But Keren had no business in a place like this. She was not some power-hungry courtier or callous man of war. She was a simple scribe, a woman of letters and learning. Staring at her damaged face, he laid another outrage at the feet of Astyages and felt his anger soar.

"Stop grinding your teeth," Keren said as she knotted the makeshift bandage. "There. Is that too tight?"

He filled his lungs with an experimental breath. "It feels better. My thanks."

She leaned against the wall. "What has you in so foul a mood?"

Wordlessly, he indicated the blood trail under her nose. In the past couple of days, Astyages's torturer had become bolder in his approach. He feared she had little time. If he could not somehow find a way out of here for them, Astyages might lose all patience with her and start crushing one bone at a time.

She shook her head. "That is for me to bear. Besides, I have a feeling we will not remain here long."

Asher gave her a pitying look but kept his skeptical words to himself. There was no point in taking away her empty hope. It would require a miracle to break out of this place. He heard footsteps outside, followed by the scraping of wood on wood as the bar on their door was lifted.

Every muscle in his body clenched. He had tried to tempt their guards with a series of outrageous bribes. Whether they were too afraid of Astyages or merely did not trust Asher to make good on his promise of riches, they simply ignored every enticing offer.

He could think of no other recourse save a wild bid for escape. He had considered the possibility a number of times and always felt the risk too great.

It dawned on him as he took in Keren's gaunt and colorful face that the risk of remaining surpassed that of an attempted escape. No time like the present, he decided abruptly. After all, his body was only growing weaker with each passing day. Less capable of defeating the guards in a physical altercation.

In an instant, he had sprung to his feet, fingers interlaced to form a hammer made of sinew and bone. The door slammed open. He bounded forward to hit the guard on the back of the neck. To his utter amazement, before he could make his move, the guard toppled over like an uprooted oak in a hurricane and landed face-first on the dirt floor. For a brief instant, he stood staring at the unconscious man at his feet.

Two young women rushed into the cell, forcing Asher to

leapfrog backward. He gaped as the women embraced Keren, a confusion of tears and laughter and words jumbling together so that he barely understood what was happening. He caught the word *Mother*, and it dawned on him that these were Keren's daughters. Not Cyrus's spies or soldiers of fortune sent to release the senior scribe from the king's prison, but untried girls come to rescue their mother. He did not know whether to applaud or to laugh. He could not begin to imagine the brazen courage needed to bring them this far.

"We must hurry," the taller girl said in Persian. Asher was familiar enough with the language to understand this simple exchange without difficulty. "We don't have much time."

Keren pointed at Asher. "He's coming with us."

The girl turned toward him. "Of course. We will set him free. We are opening the doors to all the cells."

"No. Asher is coming with us. Without help, he will simply be recaptured."

The girl threw him a narrow-eyed look. He saw the resemblance now. The shapely brows, the tall frame, the rounded chin. Her hair, escaping wildly from its braids, looked curly, though, and the eyes, so narrowly riveted on him, were a startling amber, more gold than brown. He felt an odd tug in the vicinity of his belly under that unshifting gaze and frowned.

"Mother, be reasonable!" she said. "He could be Astyages's spy."

"He is better than that, Jemmah," Keren said, smirking. "He is Astyages's son."

Asher felt a moment of raw satisfaction when Jemmah's mouth fell open wider than his cell door.

"He is coming with us," Keren repeated, her tone brooking no argument.

The younger girl ended the discussion by simply walking out the door. "No time for this haggling," she hissed.

As she walked through the outer hallway, she lifted bar after bar from the cells on her way. No more than half a dozen seemed occupied. Most of Astyages's prisoners did not last long, finding their way to the sharp edge of a sword within days of their arrival. But even six men were enough to cause a good deal of confusion.

The girl Keren had called Jemmah herded her mother to the back end of the hallway. Asher was about to take his chances with the guards in the courtyard when Keren snagged his arm, pulling him behind her in the opposite direction.

By now, the younger girl had reached the front door of the prison, which opened to the courtyard. Without hesitation, she let out a scream that might have shaken the rafters. "Treachery! Murder!" she cried. "The prisoners are free! Help! Help!"

Asher looked over his shoulder and watched her race back toward them. Sure-footed and agile, she wove through the confused hurtle of men who had been freed of their cells and now sought a way to escape. Beyond her, he could see three guards in the courtyard dropping a fat skin of wine and trying to press their way back inside. They found the door already closing in their faces by half a dozen desperate men who were in no humor to return to their captivity.

Asher hoped Keren's daughters had a plan beyond this audacious breakout. To his relief, he spied a large, open window at the back of the building as they turned a corner. Beyond it, a cart awaited. Not even the worst stench of the prison cells could compare with the miasma that assaulted his nose. There was no mistaking the source of it.

Just then, the man he assumed must be the driver rounded

the corner of the building and hurriedly lowered the rear hatch of the wagon. Keren's brow wrinkled. "Prexaspes! I thought that was you in my cell. But when you did not return, I feared I must have been mistaken."

"I only service the prison once a week. Had to wait before I could return." He made a showy bow. "All yours, mistress." Without even a twinge, he stuck his hand into the brown pile in the cart, revealing the end of a wooden pole, and with a flip, unfurled a clean blanket buried neatly underneath.

Keren's brow puckered. "What is that?"

"My own invention. There are poles sewn into the double layer of blankets. I only sprinkled the top with a strategic layer of—" he paused—"my 'wares' to hide it from view. You will hardly feel the weight of it. In you go."

"It is not the weight that concerns me." Keren gave Asher a wild look.

He shrugged. "Your chariot awaits."

"After you," she whispered.

Prexaspes handed each of them a long, hollow reed. "So you can breathe."

"I beg your pardon, Mother," the tall woman said. "We could think of no other way."

Keren gave a strained smile. "I am grateful to be out of that place, whatever the means."

Asher did not even bother to cover his nose. Steadying himself on the wooden side, he sprang into the middle of the blanket, trying to avoid the warm odorous piles surrounding him. Keren crawled next to him, a clean scarf firmly wrapped over her nose and mouth. He was oddly touched by the sight of that thick piece of wool, knowing Keren's daughters had tried to make this journey as bearable for her as humanly possible.

They had barely stuck the reeds in their lips, when without bothering with a warning, Prexaspes drew the top layer of the blanket over them. Asher screwed his eyes shut and tried not to gag. For an instant, he wondered if he might find himself asphyxiated before they arrived at their destination. Wherever that might be. Then he remembered to breathe through his mouth and, with relief, found sweet air pouring into his lungs through the reed.

In the foul-smelling darkness, Keren shivered next to him and somehow managed to find his hand and clutch at it. He tried to give it a comforting squeeze. Judging by the hasty pats on top of them, Prexaspes was readjusting the piles in the cart to once again hide the blanket. In another moment, the cart rolled forward, leaving the confines of the prison and palace complex without being challenged even once. The soldiers were too busy putting down an outbreak.

Sucking in a deep lungful of outside air through his reed, Asher decided this was one escape story he would never share with anyone.

CHAPTER

THIRTEEN

As one whom his mother comforts,
so I will comfort you.
Isaiah 66:13

Jemmah gripped the side of the wooden seat as the cart rattled down the orderly main street that ran through the center of Ecbatana. Luxurious villas made of dressed stone and embellished with carved columns dotted the landscape. They were not far from the first set of gates when a man hailed them loudly.

"Stop! You!"

Jemmah felt her heart catapult into her throat. She tried to swallow and found her mouth too dry. From the corner of her eye, she saw Zarina's hand clench the dagger she had hidden in the folds of her tunic.

Coolly, Prexaspes brought his donkey to a stop. The spy looked as if he hadn't a care in the world. Turning his stringy smile on the man who stood in the frame of an ornate door and waving vigorously, he said, "Master?"

"Our regular man did not show up. It's been a week. The house is starting to reck. Can you take our waste?"

Prexaspes adjusted his felt hat. "It would be my honor, master. But let me get rid of this lot first, before I return. Or else I would only add to the stench."

"See that you return quickly, then."

Jemmah drew a trembling hand over her mouth. The spy nudged the donkey, and the cart pulled ahead, making its plodding way toward the seven gates of the city. To her utter relief, the guards hastily waved them through with little fanfare. Nobody wanted them to linger too long, thanks to the stench of Prexaspes's cart. On the way out, Jemmah could not resist one final look at the city. Atop the highest hill, the domed roof of the king's palace glinted silver in the sun, its dove-gray stone walls adorned with scores of silver-and-gold colonnades. To Jemmah, it all seemed vapid and ugly. Even Prexaspes's odorous cart was more pleasant than Astyages's palace. She had seen with her own eyes what lay behind the palace compound—the long, narrow prison that housed a tiny fraction of the king's cruelty.

She would never forget the horror of the filthy cell where she had found her mother, bruised and skeletal, shivering with cold, nor the sight of the battered man who had shared that dank prison with her. Her head throbbed as she remembered that the same man now hid in their cart, lying silently next to her mother.

His skin a patchwork of scabs, he had more purple on him than a royal cloak did. In that bruised face, the green eyes had shone, unmistakably familiar, eerily reminiscent of Cyrus. It made sense, she supposed. If he was truly Astyages's offspring, that made him Cyrus's half uncle.

But fire and lightning! What were they doing carting off

Astyages's son with them? Any moment, she expected him to jump out of the wagon and cry for help.

But to her relief, he lay silent, never betraying his presence with a single twitch.

Prexaspes refused to stop the cart and let the prisoners loose from their horrible hiding place until he considered he had put enough distance between himself and the city. Eventually he drove them off the main road westward and rode on for an additional hour to ensure their privacy.

Pulling onto an abandoned field, he hid the cart behind a squat hillock and finally allowed his passengers out of their cloying blankets. Jemmah embraced her mother, holding her tightly, not quite able to take in the reality that after so many disappointments, they had truly managed to free her.

Her mother gathered both girls to her, kissing and caressing now one, now the other. Their tears and laughter mingled until Jemmah found her chest shaking with hiccups that made them all dissolve in half-hysterical giggles.

"Where is your father?" her mother asked finally, taking a tiny half step away. "Is he waiting at Prexaspes's hideout?"

Jemmah's laughter came to an abrupt stop. "He had to return home. He came down with a fever, though he insisted on riding with us at first. He would not hear of resting in bed. Not until he toppled from his horse could I convince him to return home."

Her mother went still. "Is he very ill?"

"The fever weakened him. But the physician assured me he would improve with rest. By now, he is probably fully recovered and pulling his hair out one at a time, wondering what has become of you. And us. We must send him a message as soon as we are able. He bid me tell you that his heart goes with you, though his body cannot."

Her mother's eyes filled with tears. "I miss that man. I feel as though I have lost a limb."

"Well, I brought you the next best thing." Zarina handed her the blue scarf.

She gasped and clutched at the bit of fabric. "I never thought to see this again. Where did you find it?"

Zarina grinned. "I wrestled for it."

"My clever girl! You must have such stories to tell me." She brought the shawl halfway to her shoulders and stopped. "On second thought, you best hold on to it for now. I must wash before I wear it."

"We found your bracelet, also," Jemmah said. "Father held on to that one. You can claim it when we return home."

Looking up, Jemmah caught Asher's gaze fixed upon her. For some reason, it brought heat to her cheeks. She dropped her eyes. By accident, they fell on Asher's boots. They had high heels, something she could not imagine anyone of her acquaintance wearing. And though for the most part the leather had been mired in so much grime it looked gray, a little spot showed through with the original color—the bright azure of a summer sky.

"Are your shoes dyed blue?" she blurted before thinking. In Persia, even the courtiers at the palace wore plain clothing. The thought of elevated heels or dyed leather would never enter a Persian man's head. Then again, the Median courtly fashions were far more embellished and dainty.

Asher proffered an elaborate bow, though he winced as he made it. "A glorious blue before it was so deplorably ruined," he confirmed. "You should have seen the embroidery on my tunic." He heaved a sigh. "What a savage we have in Astyages. Imagine ruining so dazzling a robe." He placed an outraged hand on his bosom. "To say nothing of my poor hair, which is doubtless in hopeless disarray."

Her mother turned on him with a pinched look. "Stop that at once, Asher. These are my daughters. They have risked their own necks to save your life every bit as much as mine. They deserve your trust."

Asher's expression turned to marble. "Just because you nursed me in prison does not give you the right to issue orders."

Jemmah looked from one to the other in confusion. Whatever tension lay between them broke when Prexaspes stepped forward. "You can reminisce about jail when we are safe. For now, we walk." He had unhitched the donkey and loaded the animal with the small bundle of their possessions. "We must be on our way," he said.

He led them along sheep tracks and through barren fields, setting so brisk a pace that none of them had breath for long speeches. Jemmah's mother walked between her girls, leaning first on one, then on the other. "My brave girls," she would murmur tiredly over and over again.

They stopped frequently to give Asher and her mother a chance to catch their breath. In the afternoon, they shared a few bites of bread, white cheese, and pickled cucumbers. But Prexaspes was in a hurry to bring them out of the open fields, which lay too close to the city for his comfort. His intention of pushing through the night was finally defeated by Asher's injuries and Keren's weakness. They had to stop for the night.

Spreading thin blankets under the protection of a stand of wild pear trees, they lay down, too tired to complain of the cold. At least the weather remained dry, sparing them the misery of soaking robes.

Relief, like a stimulant potion, buzzed through Jemmah's

veins, staving off sleep. Sitting up against the trunk of a pear tree and keeping watch, she did not dare remove her hand from her mother's shoulder, half-fearing she might disappear in the night.

They arose before dawn and, after a quick breakfast of more bread and cheese, followed the spy into the lea of expansive fields and plains, moving always toward the Zagros Mountains. An hour into their morning trek, Asher stopped abruptly and broke off the heels of his boots, throwing them into a tangle of winter vines. He borrowed Prexaspes's sharp knife and hacked at his long hair, leaving it a short snarl at his neck.

"Lice," he explained matter-of-factly.

This pragmatic, almost-cavalier treatment of his beloved shoes and hair seemed so at odds with his earlier behavior that Jemmah stared at him open-mouthed.

He seemed to enjoy her bewilderment. "Pleased to meet you. I am Asher," he offered.

The fastidious mannerisms were gone, as was the mincing speech. Even the way he stood underwent a transformation, so that he no longer appeared almost delicate. Abruptly she realized that he had broad shoulders, and although the deprivations of imprisonment had wasted his body, she could still see the power of well-trained muscles under his filthy tunic and wondered how she had missed them. Beneath the raggedly chopped hair and wild beard and crusting of dirt, it was hard to know quite what he looked like. But she realized she wanted to find out.

Prexaspes studied him quizzically. "Do we have another spy in our midst? Which side is he on?"

"My side," Asher said. "And I'm not a spy."

"No," Jemmah's mother said happily. "He is a weapons

manufacturer. Creates some of the best weaponry I have ever seen."

"Which you can't afford."

"True enough. Of course, my daughters did save your life."

He groaned. "I can see you are going to make a habit of reminding me." He gave Jemmah a sideways appraisal. "Speaking of which, how exactly did you manage that rescue? Why were the guards not in their assigned places?"

"As to that, you can thank Prexaspes." Jemmah tried to make sense of the new revelation that Asher made weapons. Who exactly was this man, this son of Astyages, who wore high heels and created weaponry so admired by her mother?

The spy's face remained impassive as he began to walk again, forcing the rest to follow. "Couldn't have managed it without the girls," he said, his breathing even in spite of the brisk pace he had set. "I did what I do once a week. I came to the prison to empty the prisoners' waste buckets. Usually they send me in with only one of the guards, while the other three gather in the courtyard so they can be spared the reek."

"Prexaspes told the guards Jemmah and I were his wife's nieces," Zarina added. "And that he had finally convinced her to allow us to work for him. Which meant we could empty the buckets while he drank wine in the courtyard with the guards."

The spy winked. "The soldiers would have objected if I had brought my 'nephews' along. But two young, pretty girls? They could hardly suspect them of foul play."

"They fell right in with our ploy like little lambs," Jemmah said with a smile.

"Everything else went as usual. I left my cart in the back of the prison, in deference to the guards' noses. I brought my skin

of wine to the courtyard to share with the boys. These two—"
he pointed his chin at Jemmah and Zarina— "took care of the
guard who escorted them inside. The rest, you know."

Asher pulled a hand through his jagged hair. "I begin to see
why Astyages has not managed to subdue Cyrus yet." He looked
at her. "What kind of name is Jemmah? I never heard a Judean
called that."

"My full name is Jemimah, for Job's eldest daughter. But
my twin brother, being precocious in all things, began speaking
before his mouth was ready for words. He could not say my full
name and instead called me Jemmah. The name stuck."

"And Zarina?"

"My father was a Saka prince in the north," she said. "He
named me for his mother."

Asher cast a confused glance toward Jemmah's mother.
"Zarina is my daughter," she explained. "But not by birth. Her
own mother was from a Saka tribe far to the east."

"Twins and a mixed Saka child. You certainly have an exotic
family."

"I have a beloved family."

"My mother would call you blessed." *Blessed.* A Hebrew
word. His mother must be an Israelite!

"Are you close to your siblings?" Jemmah asked.

"I have none."

"You have one, at the very least. Cyrus's mother, Mandana,
is your half sister." Jemmah stared at him curiously. Without
the boost of his heels, he stood a little shorter than she, though
since he had stopped playing the fop, he somehow appeared a
lot bigger. "So you are a prince?"

He gave a twisted smile. "A prince unrecognized and
unwanted is no prince at all." Pressing a hand to his side, he

grimaced. He was obviously in pain, though he had yet to complain of it.

"How far is it to this hideout of yours, Prexaspes?" she asked.

"A few more hours. We will make it there before nightfall. And then roasted mutton for everyone." He rubbed his hands together.

"And a bath?" Keren asked faintly.

"There is a river nearby, and lye enough to kill all your vermin."

Her mother and Asher sighed in perfect harmony.

CHAPTER

FOURTEEN

The son shall not suffer for the iniquity of the father,
nor the father suffer for the iniquity of the son.
Ezekiel 18:20

Prexaspes's bolt-hole turned out to be a cozy cottage tucked into woodlands that fringed the base of the Zagros Mountains. He had built the place cleverly so that it was not visible from either the road or the narrow track they had traveled upon. Jemmah thought it improbable that anyone who did not already know its location would be able to find it.

They arrived after nightfall and, in spite of rumbling bellies, found themselves too tired to think of cooking. Or bathing. Using dried applewood stored in his diminutive barn, Prexaspes built a fire in the pit behind his cottage, and after another meal of stale bread and cheese, augmented with dried nuts and raisins from the spy's stores, they decided to sleep outdoors for one more night. Prexaspes's sweet-smelling fire offered enough heat to ward off the chill. And they all agreed they would rather not bring their vermin into the spy's well-tended cottage.

For the first time since receiving news of her mother's abduction, that night Jemmah managed to sleep soundly, dreaming of apple trees and princes in blue boots. In the morning, Prexaspes built up the banked fire, and after hauling enough water from the well to fill the shallow wooden tub he kept in the barn, he handed a bag full of lye to Keren.

"Thank you, Prexaspes," Jemmah said. To her embarrassment, her voice trembled.

"For the lye?"

"For our lives."

"But the lye is almost as good," Asher drawled.

The spy shrugged. "Not as good as hot mutton. I am going to the small village that sits at the foot of the mountain. They know me there. I will return in a few hours with food and supplies." He took the donkey with him, whistling as he went.

Asher poked at the fire with a long stick, rearranging the wood to make it burn more efficiently. Turning to Keren, he said, "I'll take the river. You take the tub and the barn." Without further elaboration, he emptied some of the lye into a kerchief and headed for the river, a small bundle hanging over a shoulder.

Jemmah lugged a large iron pot from the cottage and filled it with the water Prexaspes had drawn from the well. "Hot baths for everyone!" she announced.

It took two baths before her mother's skin emerged pink and glowing, and the water stopped rinsing out gray. They had to burn her tunic, which had already been dirty when the Medians had given it to her. After her stint in prison, the ragged garment now crawled with an offensive infestation.

Wrapping themselves in the fresh blankets Prexaspes had

left for them, they washed the rest of their clothing, including the robes Jemmah and Zarina had stuffed into their modest baggage. Although a cool day, the sun shone brightly, and their lighter tunics proved dry enough to don. Jemmah gave her mother her spare riding tunic and trousers. No sooner had she put them on than Keren fell promptly asleep, already exhausted by the day's activities.

Jemmah was lounging by the fire, slowly combing her loose hair, when she caught sight of Asher strolling toward them. The hand that held the ivory comb froze in the air.

Asher had cut his own hair down to a mere scruff, thick and dark against his scalp. His beard, too, had been shaved, except for the merest shadow that darkened his chin. Instead of looking mangy and unappealing, the loss of hair merely accentuated the hollows of his cheeks and the sharp lines of his jaw. His lips, hidden before by the mass of his beard, were now revealed to be a thing of beauty, perfectly symmetrical, drawn with precision as if by a scribe's most exacting stylus. His nose—set improperly after a recent break in Astyages's prison, she guessed—was the only part of the face in any way imperfect. And yet, annoyingly, the small deviation added to the attraction of those splendid features.

Green eyes, edged by dark, curled lashes, twinkled with wicked amusement as he returned her unwitting perusal, as though aware of every thought that had wafted through her empty head like clouds in the wind.

Jemmah snapped to her feet and ran to the barn, breathlessly announcing that she would help Zarina empty the bath. The sound of his laughter, low and mocking, accompanied her steps. She found herself grinning. He must be accustomed to goggle-eyed perusals from young women.

Not long after, Prexaspes returned, his donkey's saddlebags bulging with fresh supplies. He had brought mutton as promised, and Jemmah, finding sea salt, wild onions, garlic, and several aromatic quinces in his sack, set to preparing *khorake*, meat braised slowly in a rich sauce. Zarina watched her preparations with alarm. She had an aversion to all domestic undertakings. With a sniff, she settled herself by the fire, cleaning and sharpening their swords and daggers, and tending to their well-used bows.

Jemmah was taken aback when Asher knelt next to her. "I found saffron in Prexaspes's saddlebags." He held out a small cedar box filled with the scarlet filaments.

"My thanks."

Jemmah's wonder increased as Asher grabbed an old knife from Prexaspes's supplies and set to chopping the onions and garlic with admirable skill. "You know how to cook?"

He shrugged. "Sometimes, when I was younger, I helped my mother."

She waited expectantly, hoping for more. She had started to find the man fascinating. A dispossessed prince. A half-Hebrew Median lord who had never known the privileges of palace life. Her mother had said that he was fabulously wealthy, and yet here he sat, chopping onions with the easy vigor of a household servant.

It was well past noon by the time the *khorake* had cooked. It would have tasted better with lamb, but they were blessed to have meat of any kind. Jemmah had managed to bake a few simple flatbreads from the rough wheat flour that Prexaspes had brought with him.

Her mother arose from her sleep, looking more like herself in spite of the lingering bruises on her face. "I see I am in time for lunch," she said. "How clever of me." Licking her fingers after taking a bite, she sighed with pleasure. "Delicious."

Jemmah had to agree. Still reeling from the relief of finding her mother safe, she found that the simple meal tasted better to her than the best spread offered in Anshan's royal palace. "Asher helped me cook," she said, not wanting to claim all the credit.

"He is a talented man."

"Are you sure you're not a spy?" Prexaspes shoved a huge piece of bread stuffed with mutton and quince into his mouth. "You seem to possess all the tricks."

Asher's lips tipped sideways. "I'm sure."

"Pity. Could use a man like you." Prexaspes turned to Jemmah's mother. "I heard some bad news in the village. Astyages has already sealed shut all the paths into Persian territory. Even the shepherds said they were searched when they took their flocks to southern pastures." He took another bite of bread and sighed. "You can't travel to Persia, that's for certain. I welcome you to spend the winter in my hut."

Keren shook her head. "Then what? Come spring, we would still be stuck here, with no way home. Astyages will be moving his armies south as soon as the passes open. That would mean travel for us would become even more fatal. My thanks, Prexaspes. But I think not. We need to cross the mountains and head west to Babylonia. We have friends there."

Prexaspes held up his hand. "You will have to avoid the main passes there too, and you won't survive such a trek without help. Not this time of year. I myself am not familiar with the territory. I could inquire at the village for a guide. There are a few men who might know their way through the secondary passes. But I doubt any will volunteer. A month earlier, perhaps. Now?" He shrugged. "They prefer to spend the winter cozy at home, with their families."

Asher stirred the banked fire. "I might be able to take you through."

Everyone grew still. "You know the way?" Jemmah asked.

"I am familiar with it. And I know where the guards are stationed. Astyages has had those paths well-guarded since his border war with Babylon began. They can only patrol near where the Medians have built small bunkers. We can go around those areas." He tore a piece of bread and dipped it into the rich sauce. "I dreamed of this when I was in prison, you know."

"Of taking us across the mountains?"

"Of quince stew. But I can take you through the passes. One of my workshops is on the way. We can break our journey there and restock our supplies."

"Excellent!" The spy rubbed his hands together. "Now that's settled, I will be on my way come morning."

Jemmah tried to keep the concern out of her voice. "You are not returning to Ecbatana? By now they will surely suspect you of aiding in the prison break."

"Not to Ecbatana, no. I told you that if I helped release your mother, my work there would come to an end."

"Why not come to Babylon with us?"

"Cyrus already has men working for him in that court. No, I am headed north. If I can't gather information in Ecbatana, then I will go to Lydia."

To Jemmah's surprise, her mother nodded her head in understanding. "Not as good as your intelligence from Ecbatana, of course. But we are likely to need eyes and ears in Lydia soon enough."

Asher whistled. "No wonder you want my weapons. Just how ambitious is this Cyrus of yours?"

Keren gave him a sweet smile. "Ambitious enough to set our people free from their captivity."

* * *

Time nipped at their heels. Every hour they delayed was an hour lost to worsening weather and approaching storms. Delay meant they might run aground somewhere in the mountains and be unable to make it into Babylon. A few hours could be the difference between life and death.

By sunrise, they were already dressed and packed for the journey. Asher had put on a thick wool tunic belonging to the spy. Tight in the Median fashion, the slits on the sides revealed his own trousers, which he had washed with obvious zeal, leaving them threadbare in places.

Again she became aware of the pull of him. The simple clothing exaggerated the narrow waist and the wide lines of his shoulders.

Jemmah swallowed, trying not to stare. "How is it you know the routes that avoid Astyages's guards, Asher?"

"I grew up in a nomadic tribe. They have their own particular routes they travel every year, finding pasture for their cattle." He rearranged the blanket he was rolling into his bag. "It may be hard to believe looking at those forbidding peaks. But hidden within them, there are small plains and rivers. Enough to support their herds as they make the trek to the other side of the mountains, where they settle for the cold winter months."

Jemmah was familiar with such nomadic tribes and had visited a few as they traveled through the plains of southern Persia.

Originally, the Medes and Persians had all been nomads. Over centuries, most had settled into cities and villages, preferring the comforts of a rooted life. Some, however, maintained the old traditions of a traveling life.

Of these, many smaller clans lived a poor and hard existence. But amongst them, a dozen tribes had grown extensively, and their leaders, like Gaubaruva, her mother's friend, had become powerful cattle lords, wielding substantial wealth and influence, their favor sought by kings and merchants alike.

"I thought your mother was a Judean? How came you to live with nomads?" she asked.

"My mother was amongst those taken by Nebuchadnezzar in the siege of Jerusalem. Both her parents had died in the first wave of Babylonian slaughter, and my mother was carried into Babylon and sold as a slave. The chief of our tribe had brought horses to sell at Babylon's market that day. He noticed my mother. She was the same age as his daughter, and at her request, he purchased my mother as a companion for her. He had ten sons and only one girl. He did not want her to grow up lonely."

"My mother's parents were captured in the same siege. The family managed to stay together in Babylon, except for my mother, who went to work as a servant in the home of a distant cousin."

Asher stopped working. "*Keren?* A servant?"

Jemmah grinned. "Apparently she was appalling at every task they set for her."

He laughed. "Now I know you are jesting. Your mother has not been appalling at anything in her life."

"I speak true. She will tell you herself."

"Then how did she become so knowledgeable a scribe?"

"As to that, her grandfather had been a scribe in Jerusalem. He began training her as a little girl. Her master discovered that although she had no talent for domestic service, she made an exceptional scribe."

He returned his attention to his pack. "You surprise me."

"You thought perhaps that she came from an affluent family?"

He gave a short nod.

"If it makes you feel better, my father's father was a minor prince in Judah. A terrible man, as I understand. I never met him, thankfully. He disowned my father before I was born."

Asher stopped again and stared.

Jemmah laughed merrily. "Did you think you were the only one with an evil father? Or a poor mother?"

Beyond them, the door of the cottage clattered open. Jemmah gasped as she beheld the man emerging.

The creature before her was curled and perfumed, beard neatly combed, hair cut short and artfully arranged in the Ionian fashion. He was wearing the Greek costume of the Lydians and looked so tidy in his folds of wool that Jemmah blinked. *"Prexaspes?"*

Zarina had sprung to her feet, knife in hand, thinking some stranger had infiltrated their hiding place. "Is it him?" Slowly she allowed the knifepoint to flop downward.

The man gave a courtly bow. "Sandanis the merchant, at your service."

Asher grinned. "What happened to the waste remover?"

"King Croesus has displayed a deep interest in commercial matters. Only recently he funded the building of the temple of Artemis in Ephesus. He means to turn it into one of the wonders of the world. Which is why a merchant with valuable connections around the world will find an open invitation at the court. Sandanis is a better fit for Lydia."

"Well, you certainly smell better," Zarina said.

The spy frowned. "Too much? I cannot smell perfume any more than I can the stink of excrement."

"It will fade by the time you arrive in Lydia," Asher said dryly. He pointed to the packed donkey. "Your friend there might object to the dizzying array of fragrances you have rubbed into your skin. Don't go near his hindquarters for a fortnight or you might find yourself the object of a vexed kick."

The spy snorted. "His nose is no better than mine, for he never balked at carrying waste." He adjusted the folds of his cloak. "I suppose I better take my leave of you. I wish you all a safe journey."

Jemmah took a step toward him and shocked the man by throwing her arms around the thick shoulders. "I will forever be grateful to you for your aid, Prexaspes. If that is your name. Whatever you call yourself, I am your friend. Should you ever find you need help, call on me and my family. We owe you much."

He gave her a startled glance, then cleared his throat awkwardly. "Well," he said. "Well. This perfume must be better than I realized."

She stepped away, offering him a bland smile. "It's not a man's smell that makes him worthy of friendship. It is his heart."

"Don't worry. I will charge Cyrus an enormous sum for this last escapade." But Jemmah could see by the bright flush on his cheeks that he was pleased by her words. She supposed that as a spy, he had few opportunities for true friendship.

Keren handed Prexaspes two letters, one for Cyrus and another for Jemmah's father. Prexaspes added to them his own message for the Persian king and hid them in a secret compartment in his sack. They had written everything in a language so general, the content could hardly raise any brows. Keren had made no mention of Asher at all. The man's life was in enough danger without Astyages discovering his new connection to Media's enemy.

Jemmah hoped Cyrus and her father would be able to understand all the hints and hidden messages contained in those baffling missives.

* * *

Letter to Cyrus, King of Anshan
From Sandanis, merchant of antiquities
  Regretfully, I must inform you of the death of the waste remover. He lived a good life and died serving his betters. He spent his final hours removing excrement from a difficult location. As sometimes happens, he managed to find something of value in the waste. This, I hope, he has sent safely your way.
  Should you require any merchandise from Lydia, let your servant know.

Letter to Cyrus, King of Anshan
From his old tutor
  My king, I hope you have not forgotten your servant after this long while. I have traveled far since we last met and found myself enjoying the warm hospitality of an old acquaintance. But my daughters discovered me and insisted that I leave the abode of my charming host so that I might accompany them on a new adventure. It was an

invitation I did not wish to refuse, in spite of my host's desire to detain me.

Sadly, I shall not see you soon. My daughters and I have other friends we long to see before winter comes. I wish you health and remain, as ever, your servant.

Letter to my husband
From your faithful wife

How I long to see your beloved face. Our daughters tell me you managed to make yourself sick with a fever. You better be recovered by the time we return from our travels, or else you will have me to contend with.

I am well and enjoying the fresh outdoors. No matter how welcoming one's host or how charming his dwelling, nothing equals the bracing air of the mountains.

It shall be a cold winter without you. I pray I will bring good news upon my return. Until then, I will miss you every hour.

FIFTEEN

For the traitors have betrayed,
with betrayal the traitors have betrayed.
Isaiah 24:16

———————— ASHER ————————

Not long after the departure of the spy, the small troop started their own journey, heading west toward the Zagros Mountains. Asher instructed the women to remove all jewelry and to tuck their knives away, for the metal would glimmer in the high passes, drawing unwanted attention from patrols who might be close enough to notice.

He pressed his aching body on, ignoring the shooting pain of his cracked ribs. The dull ache radiating from dozens of cuts and contusions reminded him that he needed time to heal. But he did not have the luxury of time.

The impending snows were not the only threat that hastened his steps up this timeworn path. He had a mole in his organization. Someone who had betrayed him to Astyages. He needed to discover the identity of the man who had sold him out. His whole enterprise remained in danger of being discovered and confiscated by the king as long as that nameless betrayer remained free.

Unwittingly, Asher's father had given him enough information to know which workshop had bred this treachery. Astyages had only mentioned swords and the new chariot. Over the years, as Asher's business had grown from one small blacksmith's shop into multiple workshops, he had learned to separate his stock, keeping the manufacture of each weapon tied to a particular location. As an additional layer of safety, he kept the existence of each workshop secret from those working in other locations.

The mountain workshop was the only one that produced swords.

His closest friend had charge of the place. Asher and Phraortes—whom everyone called Phray—had grown up together like brothers. Asher would stake his life on the man's loyalty. And yet he could not deny the evidence of his own cracked bones. No one in the workshop had seen the drawings of that chariot save Phray. Asher tamped down his disquiet. He refused to blame Phray until he had a chance to speak to him.

It would be a bitter day if he discovered that his closest friend was the wellspring of this betrayal.

One thing still puzzled Asher. If Phray had indeed sold him out, why did Astyages not know the location of the workshop? This question, as much as the betrayal itself, pushed him onward, though every breath he took burned as it made its way into his lungs.

They had been climbing for two days, gaining elevation with every step. Tomorrow they would descend, only to climb again. It was a hard journey, one etched in his mind from his childhood.

He knew the exact spot where he wanted to make camp for the night. It required another hour at their present pace. Zarina could have made it in half that time. But the best Asher could offer at the present was one step. And another beyond that.

Jemmah studied him when she thought he was distracted. He could sense her concern, which bounced back and forth—like a child's exuberant ball—between him and Keren. That girl had too much heart. It was as if she could pour herself out like water from an endless spring over everyone she saw. Asher had even detected a suspicious moistening in the spy's little dark eyes after she had bid him an affectionate farewell. Under the weight of her kindness, that hardened granite of a man had found himself all soft and dewy.

The girl was a menace. He had better watch himself lest he turn soft and dewy like the spy. That would be a good jest on him, after escaping the machinations of numerous fathers and the not-so-subtle hints of hopeful mothers, to now find himself caught at the end of a Hebrew girl's hook. In spite of the severe lectures he delivered himself, he still found his feet maneuvering to step alongside hers whenever the trail allowed two people to walk side by side.

By the time they arrived at the smoke-stained firepit built long ago by members of his tribe, the sun had started to sink, disappearing quickly behind the jagged peaks to the west. Dropping his pack, Asher found the cache of dry wood, which had been stored on an elevated rack. Though crude, the simple rack with its stone foundation kept the wood safe from dampness and vermin.

He hefted a couple of logs to the firepit and knelt to arrange them. He could fall asleep like this, with his head on one of the logs, and forget about the fire. As if she had read his mind, Jemmah fetched smaller pieces of wood from the rack and word-lessly made a pile of shavings with her knife. Within moments, the flames burned, hot and bright.

He liked that about her, he decided. The quiet habit she had of lending a hand at the right moment, without waiting to be asked. With a sigh, Asher lingered over the flames, warming his cold fingertips.

"Anything to hunt around here?" Zarina asked.

"Not in the dark."

"We are going to run out of food soon."

Without a donkey to carry supplies, they had been forced to pare down their packs, bringing only the barest necessities. Their food would not last long. Then again, the mountains were no place to prowl about after sunset. "There are bears, wolves, and lions in these mountains. Not to mention gorges you could fall into. Besides, hunting requires time, which we do not have."

"I don't mind a few hunger pangs," Keren said, holding her hands out to the flames. "Less ferocious than bears."

Jemmah drew out several flatbreads rolled up around a lump of white cheese. "This is all I have left."

Keren produced a bag of flour and a pot of butter. "We have these as well."

"And this." Asher spread a kerchief filled with shelled almonds and tiny raisins.

Zarina knelt closer to the fire. "Except for salt and a handful of chickpeas, my share of food ran out this morning. I packed a couple of extra knives. They took up more space than I realized."

"They will come in handy." Jemmah set aside half the bread

and put the rest away in her pack. "How far to your workshop, Asher?"

He liked the sound of his name on her lips. She pronounced it the Hebrew way, with the stress on the second syllable. Shaking his head, he tried to clear it from the ridiculous fascination he seemed to be forming with her lips, especially when they pronounced his name.

"Three days. If the weather holds."

"I definitely foresee hunger pangs." Zarina took the knife Jemmah had used to make woodchips and began to sharpen it against her flint.

"Not necessarily," Asher said. "Tomorrow we will pass a small river. We might be able to catch a trout or two."

"How will we manage that?" Zarina examined the edge of the knife. "We packed no nets."

Asher held up his hands. "With these."

Jemmah passed him half a loaf of flatbread with a tiny lump of cheese in the middle. "You have some very odd skills."

"Thank you. I might say the same of you."

"It's a good thing you did not grow up in Astyages's palace. The result is much more interesting."

Asher sat up straighter. "You think I'm interesting?"

"I think your mother was."

Asher choked on his bread. The girl's grin flashed brighter than the flames. He wagged a finger in her direction. "You are a dangerous woman."

"Thank you. Speaking of your mother, how did she meet the king?"

"Nosy, aren't you?"

"Sometimes you make it quite evident that you did not grow up in the court," she said with a sniff.

Oddly, the barb hurt. He shrugged. "It's no secret. Astyages had called all the Median chiefs to an official gathering in the plains outside Ecbatana. While speaking with the cattle lords at their camp, he caught sight of my mother at the well. He must have enjoyed what he saw." Grabbing a long branch, he played with the logs in the pit. "That night, when he went to his sumptuous royal tent, he asked the chief to send my mother to him."

"And the chief agreed?" She sounded outraged. He liked that. A good friend knew when to be outraged on your behalf.

"He had little choice. Astyages had already started showing himself a despot. He had increased his demands upon the tribal chiefs, treating them as vassals rather than as brother chieftains, which is the Median way. Our tribe had suffered a number of setbacks. We had lost many cattle to a recent plague. The chief was in no position to antagonize the king. Certainly not over a slave girl."

"And after? Astyages never took her to his palace? Never acknowledged her as his concubine? Never provided for her needs?"

He shoved the branch roughly at a smoldering log. "He considered her beneath his dignity. A Hebrew slave with no influential ties. She was a moment's pastime to him. No more."

"And yet you are his only son."

He laughed. The sound of it reverberated bitterly in his own ears. "He did not know that at the time I came into the world. I suspect he always assumed he would sire a boy upon one of the highborn princesses in his harem. Likely he still cherishes those hopes in spite of his advanced years. He forgets his mortality quite frequently. In any case, by the time he might have felt an interest, I had grown too old. My education had been neglected.

I came with none of the elegance and training of a lord. Worse, I refused to offer him my unquestioning obedience. I would never lick his boots and he knew it. Astyages could never forgive me that."

"You are in good company," Jemmah said. "He could never forgive Cyrus for the same failing."

CHAPTER SIXTEEN

Be merciful to me, O God, be merciful to me,
for in you my soul takes refuge;
in the shadow of your wings I will take refuge,
till the storms of destruction pass by.
Psalm 57:1

Asher's voice held no emotion as he shared his mother's story. To listen to him, you might believe the whole episode meant less to him than a scribe's list of palace rations. Jemmah was not fooled. The tight line of his shoulders and the angry little jabs he gave the fire with a twisted branch told their own story. It was not the lack of feeling that made his tone flat. On the contrary, in his attempt to hide the surfeit of emotion, he had reined in every inflection lest he give his heart away.

It dawned on her that he wove veil after veil to shield himself from the world. Layer upon layer of subterfuge and misdirection. He would be a hard man to draw close to. She suspected few had ever glimpsed the true Asher. Even with the high heels gone and the long hair cut and the fastidious manners vanished, what he revealed of himself was the barest shadow of the real man.

She tried to imagine the little boy who had grown up fatherless. His mother had remained a slave all her life, though for the sake of his royal blood, Asher had been born free. And yet the life of a child unclaimed amongst a proud and at times harsh people must have been especially difficult.

It made her appreciate his accomplishments all the more. As they traveled together, she had sensed a leashed energy to Asher, as if every moment must be expended on some useful task. Every hour accounted for by some worthy deed. Even in pain, he drove himself. She wondered if that restless drive found its roots in his thorny childhood.

The moon sat high in the star-punctured sky. It must be past midnight. And here she lay by the dimming fire, still thinking of the man. Still trying to put the pieces together. Her fascination with him had grown to alarming proportions. This had to stop. Immediately. But she drifted off to sleep with a foolish grin on her face, Asher's disgruntled words the last thing she remembered. *You are a dangerous woman.*

* * *

The next day's trek proved no easier for being downhill. When the sun had moved all the way to the middle of the sky, Asher came to a stop. "Astyages has a small fort a short distance away. The soldiers have a habit of coming to the river to fish. We'll be able to see them as we approach since we have the high ground. But prepare to move quickly should we spot them. If they happen to be by the river, we'll have to find a hiding place swiftly before they notice us." He dropped his voice to a whisper. "Sound carries in the mountains. We best keep silent as we go now."

They traveled for another hour with no sound for company save the occasional shriek of a golden eagle and, once, the sweet trilling song of a male rock thrush. The wind whistled and the gravel crunched under their feet. The tension increased with every stride, as the reality that they might encounter the enemy at any moment cast a shadow over each step.

Jemmah came to an abrupt stop when, without warning, the track seemed to disappear over a ridge. Asher motioned for them to drop to the ground and creep to the edge. Jemmah saw that her perception of the track ending had been a trick of the eye. It continued on after a sharp drop, coiling its way into the valley below, where it stretched as far as the eye could see.

A narrow river snaked through the floor of the valley. Its water ran clear as glass so that the smooth stones covering the shallow bottom remained visible even from this height. Pale-blue water twinkled against the gray gravel of the narrow beach, frothing white where the currents broke against rocks protruding out of the riverbed. On the hilly embankments, short, scruffy vegetation held on stubbornly to a motley collection of green leaves in spite of the cold.

Jemmah exhaled, enchanted. For a moment, she forgot the weariness of her muscles and the pesky blisters on her feet. She even forgot the nagging awareness of the danger that followed them in this hostile, enemy-infested territory.

"It's beautiful," she whispered.

"Looks clear," Asher said. "Let's go."

Zarina led as they headed down the sharp incline, her hand on Keren's arm to keep her from slipping on the unstable gravel that covered the surface of the ground. Asher went next, using a thick staff he had picked up at the camp to keep his gait steady. Jemmah brought up the rear, distracted by the glorious scene below, falling further behind with every step.

Ahead, Zarina came to a sudden stop. She lifted her arm. "Hold!"

They all froze where they stood. "Down!" Asher hissed, and everyone dropped flat onto the ground. Below them, on a wide path that intersected the river from the south, a group of Median soldiers were laughing as they walked into view. Jemmah counted a half-dozen men.

Asher whispered something to Zarina and pointed to a spot above them. Zarina nodded and positioned herself alongside Keren like a shield. Together, they crawled off the narrow track until they reached the wall of the mountain where a boulder protruded out at a sharp angle. Jemmah saw with relief that the vertical shelf would shield anyone standing behind it from those who occupied the valley below.

As Keren was about to rise, her foot caught a rock, causing it to roll noisily. She flattened her body against the ground as the gaze of a curly-haired soldier turned in their direction.

Jemmah held her breath. As long as they lay flat on the ground, she did not believe they could be seen from the valley floor.

Still, the soldier pointed in their direction and barked something to a couple of the men. He must be their commander, Jemmah realized, as obediently two men peeled away from the rest and headed to where the track began to climb into the mountains.

How long before they arrived up here? Perhaps a quarter of an hour? Perhaps less. Abruptly the gap between her and the rest of her companions seemed as wide as a canyon. Why had she allowed herself to fall so far behind? She tried to close the distance between them, dragging herself downhill as fast as she could, stomach hugging the ground tightly.

To her dismay, her body's movement caused a small gravel slide. Looking alarmed, Asher signaled her to stop. Not only could a gravel slide cause her to tumble dangerously close to the gorge, it might also draw the attention of the rest of the soldiers, who had now reached the riverbank and were settling themselves on the shore.

Abandoning his staff, Asher began to crawl up the trail, every movement torturously slow. Jemmah's gaze shifted from him to Zarina and her mother. They had managed to come to their feet and had begun to climb the rock face. The section of the mountain where they had been trapped offered easy hand-holds, making their ascent thankfully simple. Soon they had disappeared behind a cleft where the jutting edge of a boulder hid them from Jemmah's view.

It took Asher several tense moments to arrive at her side. "We have to get off this trail," he whispered. "We are too exposed here. They will see us by the time they are halfway up the track." He pointed at the silver band holding back the coil of her hair. "Tuck that away. If the sun shines on the metal, the reflection will draw their attention."

Jemmah reddened. She had forgotten about this small ornament. Hastily, she covered the ornament with the palm of her hand, pulling it off carefully, without exposing the metal.

Asher pointed toward the rocks. "We need to crawl up the pass until we can get behind those boulders. There are small caves scattered in those rocks where we can find refuge. Zarina and Keren will have found one already. But they are too far from here. We must find a different one closer to us."

At the mention of a small cave, Jemmah's eyes widened. She shook her head. "No caves."

Asher frowned. "This is no time to be squeamish. We have to get out of sight."

"Why can't we hide amongst the boulders?"

"Because from the valley below, most of those rocks are visible. Come, Jemmah. We must go. We can be easily spotted on this track, and those soldiers will be upon us soon." Not waiting to argue further, Asher began to crawl uphill, before cutting across toward the mountain wall. When he reached the edge, he came to his feet quickly and began to climb. The rock face, she saw with relief, was pocked with cracks and fissures, providing plenty of footholds.

Jemmah lay flat for a beat, watching Asher. She knew she had no option. She could not remain on the track, as much as she wished it. The more she delayed, the more likely she was to be caught by the approaching soldiers. If she lingered another moment, Asher would feel obliged to come and fetch her, which would place him in even greater danger than he was in already.

She angled her body toward the mountain and began to drag herself along the ground in an excruciatingly slow crawl, trying to keep the gravel from shifting. Sweat trickled down her brow in spite of the cold temperature. The sharp stones scraping her skin, the gravel slithering with every movement, the imposing rock face she would have to climb, the laughing soldiers ascending from the valley below all seemed like child's play compared to what awaited her at the end of this slippery climb.

A dark, narrow cave.

She forced her mind away from that thought.

As soon as she reached the rock face, she anchored her foot in the first foothold and, grabbing a slab, pulled herself up.

Clinging to the sharp edge of an overhang with her palm, she moved up to the next ledge, ignoring the flash of pain that came as she cut her hand against the jagged limestone. Her toes found a tiny hole and pressed in. Again, she anchored her fingers above and pulled herself upward until she stood just below Asher. Leaning down, he held a hand toward her.

Strong fingers gripped her wrist, tendons and bones holding on relentlessly. She felt her body fly for a brief moment, and then her feet found a ledge to stand on. He gave her a brief reassuring nod and began to climb again, this time behind a protruding crag. Jemmah stayed close, taking the hand he offered every time he found a secure hold. They were both panting by now, and still they had to climb.

Finally they came to a spot where the ledge widened, expanding into a broad natural terrace with room enough for them to walk on. "This will do," Asher whispered. She followed his pointing finger and paled. The cave was no more than a hole in the side of the mountain. She would have to clamber on her hands and knees to get inside.

"You go. I'll stay here," she said, her voice thinning.

"Don't be a fool. Move!" She followed two steps without thinking, until she came to the mouth of the cave. Then the horror hit her in earnest. The dark maw of that hole, the devouring tightness of it.

"I'm not going in there," she hissed.

"You are," he hissed back.

"I . . . I have a condition."

"What? You like being caught and tortured by Median soldiers? Get in there, woman!"

"Can't."

He stared at her, lips pressed flat, eyes glittering with anger.

Something in her expression must have gotten through to him. His face softened. "Are you scared?"

She thought about that. "Something worse than that. I can't do it, Asher."

"All right. All right." He brushed a hand over his short hair. "Then I will stay here with you."

That was when she knew. She had to do this. She had to crawl in there somehow. Monsters or no monsters. She could not risk Asher's life. "I'll go." Her voice trembled. "That is, I will try. If I stop, push me in. And don't be alarmed if I faint. I'll survive."

"You? Faint? I don't believe it." He bent down and entered the tight crevice, his fingers wrapped tight around Jemmah's wrist like a manacle.

She stopped breathing. The world went black, and still, somehow, she could see dark spots dancing before her eyes. Her knees were on the ground. If she reached up, she could touch the damp, cold ceiling.

In an instant she was back at the bottom of the well. Cold. Wet. Death pressing in on her, bloated and ugly, its stench unbearable. From a distance she heard a voice whispering her name. Again and again. Arms wrapped about her. Vaguely she could feel herself moving, half-dragged, half-carried. The walls remained too close, unbearably tight. But the ceiling seemed to rise higher, and arms lifted her to her feet. It made no difference. Kneeling or standing. The monster awaited.

CHAPTER

SEVENTEEN

You have captivated my heart, my sister, my bride;
you have captivated my heart.
Song of Solomon 4:9

—————— ASHER ——————

Asher tugged on Jemmah's wrist, drawing her behind him into the dark cave. She stumbled along. He could feel the tension of her arm beneath his fingers, her tendons and muscles unnaturally rigid.

What ailed the woman? She had faced the deadly dangers of a prison break, risking her neck to save her mother; she had marched into treacherous mountains, trudging with a hungry belly for days on end without a twitch. Why had a little cave defeated her?

They had dropped to their knees in order to enter the cave. She began to shiver violently as soon as they left the daylight behind and entered the full confines of the cave. Without warning, she froze, one foot still outside, digging into the stone. Gingerly, he released her wrist to put an arm around her back.

"Jemmah?"

Beneath the uncontrollable trembling of her body, she seemed to have turned to iron. Was she even breathing?

Ignoring propriety, he pulled her into his arms and held her tight. "Jemmah. Jemmah. I'm here. I'll look after you."

Sweat had drenched her skin. But she was ice-cold to his touch. Was she ill? Feverish? Fear blunted his thinking. He could not unravel the mystery of her plight. What had she said before he had forced her into this place? That she had a condition.

For a moment he considered dragging her back outside. She was tormented—he could sense that. He could not bear her suffering. Just as he flexed his knees to gain better traction before lifting her, he heard the voices of the soldiers. They were grumbling about having to miss the fishing, chasing after nothing. One laughed at their commander's overzealous wariness, accusing him of being nothing but an old woman.

They were close. Near to where Zarina and Keren had left the track, he suspected. Too late to do anything but hide in this hole now.

He shifted Jemmah's body against him. His vision had grown accustomed to the dark, and he perceived that behind them, the cave widened a little.

"Jemmah, I am going to move you, all right?" he whispered close to her ear. "The ceiling is higher a few steps away."

If she understood him, she gave no sign. He could feel her shivering as he moved them deeper into the darkness. Instinctively he pulled her closer to him once they were able to stand and, feeling the violence of her quavering body, wrapped his arms around her.

"Come, now," he whispered. "I won't let anyone harm you. You are safe with me."

She moaned softly.

"Jemmah? Can you hear me?"

She slumped against him. Whatever slight hold consciousness had on her finally snapped, and she slipped away from him. He put one arm under her legs and, adjusting the one behind her back, swung her up, careful not to bash her feet into the walls. Her deadweight and his bruised ribs made for bad companions. With a huff, he sat down, leaning his back against the damp, rocky wall.

He moved her head gently so that it could rest against his shoulder and hoped he was not giving her a crook in her neck. From his pack, he extracted a skin of water and carefully poured a few drops between her lips. Then splashing a thin dribble into his palm, he wet her cheeks. When she remained insensible, he gently slapped her cheeks.

She gasped. Her eyes snapped open. The shivering began all over. "Jemmah. Jemmah! I'm here. You aren't alone."

For a moment, she seemed to hear him. "Asher?"

"Yes. Yes. It's Asher. You're with me. You're safe."

But the flash of coherence did not last. For several agonized moments, she tried to break free, her arms flailing weakly. He felt a brute, forcing her to remain in this forsaken cave. Then he heard the soldiers, closer than before, and knew he had no choice. To keep her alive, he had to subject her to whatever torment she was battling. As gently as he could, he tried to subdue her resisting body, holding tight until she stopped twisting against him.

"Jemmah, Jemmah. I am sorry."

She lost consciousness again, her long arms and legs a

desperate tangle against him. He felt like a beast. In his younger years, when he had for a short stint served as a mercenary, he had killed more than once. But this felt worse. It felt more brutal to hold her here against her will and watch her twist in some agony of soul he could not understand.

"God, if you are there, help her!" He said the prayer aloud, whispered against her cold forehead, his lips sealing the words against her skin. "Help her, Lord, I am begging. And forgive me."

It was the first time he had spoken to God since his mother had died. The first time he had asked for forgiveness since before that.

The next time she awoke, the shivers came again, followed by the merciless wide-eyed terror in her twisting limbs. That was when it finally dawned on him. She had come into this oppressive hole for his sake. To keep him safe. She had known she would face this horror if she crawled inside this cave. But she had come. Willingly. To save him.

In that sliver of a moment Asher truly understood Jemmah. With her quivering in terror and out of her mind from some nightmare, his arms helpless to bring her comfort.

That horrifying moment of pain and contrition became the moment that Asher lost his heart completely.

As he sat stunned, holding Jemmah's limp body in hands that shook, he realized that this was God's answer to his prayer. Not her healing or ease. Not a lifting of his guilt. But this ridiculous, agonizing insight into her and into himself. Using this hour of anguish, God had revealed to him Jemmah's heart in a way he never would have grasped in a hundred days.

Jemmah knew how to love, body and soul. She did not shy away from the sacrifices of devotion. The measure of her love would always exceed her fears. She would always crawl into the caves of life if it meant protecting another.

It was as if his whole soul leapt up, like a man dying of thirst who saw a chalice of cold spring water. All his life, he had longed for this. He had not believed in it. He had stopped looking for it a long time ago. And now he found it, with Astyages's soldiers at his heels and an unconscious girl in his arms.

He gave a tired laugh, the sound a huff echoing in the tiny cave. He wondered what her devout Judean parents would think of him as a suitor for their sweet girl. Astyages's illegitimate son. A mercenary. A maker of weapons, a seller of warfare, a man with a bitter heart. He dropped his head until it rested against Jemmah's forehead and, for the second time in years, whispered a prayer.

CHAPTER

EIGHTEEN

The LORD your God will clear away these nations before you little
by little. You may not make an end of them at once.

Deuteronomy 7:22

The next time Jemmah opened her eyes, her mind remained clear for long minutes. Asher's arms held her so tightly, it made the cave feel wider somehow. Safer.

"Asher?" Her voice emerged a croak.

"I'm here, Jemmah." His voice seemed to hold a world of reassurance.

She swallowed painfully. Her throat felt as if she had been screaming for hours, though she knew she had made little sound. "Leave now?" She could not string together a full sentence. Disjointed words and thoughts were all she felt capable of. Though her mind remained in this present time, in this particular cave, a parallel world awaited in the shadows. A world of stinking, bloating death. She pushed at the memory, trying to cling to this reality.

"Soon," Asher promised. "I heard the soldiers talking in the pass below. I think they are headed back to the river. As soon as they are far enough, I will bring you out. I promise." She felt him shift her, elevating her head. "Thirsty?"

"Yes."

A few drops of cool water wet her dry lips before the trickle increased. She gulped once and choked. To drown the sound of her coughs, she pressed her face against his chest. He held her against him, gently tapping her back. She found an odd tenderness in the gesture. When the spasms of the coughing fit finally came to a stop, she tried to sit up. The walls were starting to close in again. Her belly roiled.

"Oh, go away. Go away," she moaned as the other darkness, the one haunted by monsters, crowded in. "Stop tormenting me!"

"Who, beloved? Who is tormenting you?"

But she was beyond answers and explanations now. The well swallowed her. Rainwater drowned her one handful at a time. Then *she* came, bumping and grotesque, needing help and finding none from Jemmah. She struggled to get away from that bloated, cold touch. Weakly, she flailed . . . and found no escape.

* * *

Shafts of light, warm and bright, made an odd dance against her lids. Light! Jemmah snapped her eyes open and found herself lying on the rock shelf, with the blessed sky stretched over her and no walls closing in, trying to suffocate her. She gulped in one breath after another and rose up on her elbows. There was no sign of Asher. He had covered her in his cloak, rested her head on her pack, and disappeared.

A vague recollection of his arms holding her protectively brought the sharp sting of heat to her cheeks. What a fool he must think her. What a sniveling coward, fainting at the sight of a few walls.

The sun had moved in a deep arc to the west. They must have been in that cursed cave for over an hour. No wonder Asher had disappeared. He was probably disgusted with her. A wave of shame swept over her.

Once, when she had been fifteen, she had entered a tiny alcove in the palace with a group of young aristocrats. They were playing some game, and Jemmah had been swept inside before she could make an excuse. By the time someone had thought to drag her out of the stifling confines of the tomb-like chamber, she had put on quite an entertaining display. The sound of quiet sniggers had awakened her. Her companions did not bother to hide their derision. Ever after, they seemed to regard her as lacking, somehow, as if every time they saw her, it was through the frame of that memory.

The thought of Asher feeling that way brought the prick of hot tears. She felt, with sudden conviction, that she could not bear the weight of his disdain. She groped to find a barb of humor as she always did when her condition shamed her before others. But laughter evaded her.

Flipping on her belly, she crawled to the edge of the shelf and examined the horizon. On the valley below, it seemed the soldiers were coming to the end of their afternoon hiatus. They were busy collecting their fish and wrapping up their nets. Strolling toward them were the two men the commander had sent up into the pass.

Jemmah exhaled. Thanks to Asher's quick thinking, they had managed to escape detection. Soon, they would be able to resume their journey. Behind her a tiny sound made her jump. Turning over, she saw Asher crawling toward her.

"You're awake." His eyes seemed to take in every detail of her face, boring into her with a strange intensity.

She pulled self-conscious fingers through her tangled braids, feeling the curls sticking out at haphazard angles. "Next time, shall we stay and wrestle the Median soldiers? I bet it would be a lot easier than wrestling me."

He did not crack a smile. "How do you feel?"

She decided to tell the truth. "Like a fool."

He frowned, the shapely brows dipping into a furrow. "There is nothing to feel foolish about." He seemed to find sudden interest in a couple of shapeless clouds. With some difficulty he pulled his gaze back to her. "Forgive me."

"Forgive you? For what?"

"For dragging you into that place. And for keeping you inside it." He swallowed convulsively. The whole of winter seemed to weigh on him. "You did it for me, didn't you? You crawled inside to keep me safe."

She offered him a weak grin. "I might answer you with your own words. You did it for me, held me inside the cave to keep me safe. Nothing to forgive." Confused by the compassion in his voice, she changed the subject. "Where did you go?"

"To search for a different track. Jemmah, do you want to rest here for the night? We can make camp after I fetch Zarina and Keren."

"We should push ahead while we have light. I feel well now. Shall we put the whole incident behind us? Forget it ever happened?"

"If you want."

"More than you can imagine."

He gave her a troubled look. "For now."

She pointed at the soldiers leaving the river valley. "We can start soon, I think."

Asher's gaze lingered on her for a long moment. Her throat ran dry under the weight of that look. Trying to cover her embarrassment, she said, "Do we resume where we left off on the track?"

His lips lifted, the slight movement filled with irony. "No. I will fetch Keren and Zarina to us. We ought to bypass the direct path to the valley in case we run into more soldiers."

"Yes, that could prove awkward. But how do we avoid them once we reach the valley?"

"The route we were taking forks further down this incline. One path goes directly to the river, which is how the soldiers managed to get to us so quickly. The other trail would have disgorged us further down the river. The soldiers avoid that area. For one thing, it is a long walk from their bunker. For another, the main pass that they use is blocked by an old rockslide. Climbing it means a long delay for them, so they never bother. Not while they have this stretch of beach easily accessible.

"I had not counted on them noticing us this far up. It's best if we leave the path altogether now. That commander seemed a little too attentive for my liking. He might have decided to set up sentries where we can't see them."

"How will we get down to the valley, then?"

"I found a goat track that connects with the right path. It's not smooth walking, but we ought to remain safe enough." He cleared his throat. "If you are certain you wish to continue, you better rest while I go to fetch Zarina and Keren."

As she huddled against the wall of rock, wrapped up in her cloak and feeling more alone than she had in a long time, a clear memory of her father came to her. He had sat next to her bed, where she had gone to hide after her companions had laughed at her for fainting in the alcove.

He had held her hand without words for a long time. "Why won't God heal me?" she had wailed. "Why does he not take this ugly thing away?"

He had thought about his answer. "I understand your longing, my girl." He fiddled with his eye patch. "I have asked similar questions of God, myself." He leaned a little closer. "Sometimes his answer is *little by little*. Like when his people were about to enter the Promised Land, longing to end their wanderings, longing to settle down and be at peace. But Moses told them that God would make a way for them *little by little*, that he might not provide the desire of their hearts *at once*. Our aching hearts always long for the *at once* answers of God. We want the pain gone all at once. We want to have relief, at once. Instead, God chooses a *little by little* answer.

"You think God has not healed you. I see it differently. Every year, you take a little step closer to healing. A little more understanding. A little more patience with yourself. A little more trust in God. Little by little, my girl. God's healing for you is coming in the *little by little*s of grace."

Jemmah thought of the hours in the cave. Of the final time she had opened her eyes and clung to Asher, able to speak a few words. For a moment, able to feel . . . safe. That had never happened before. She wondered what had made it possible now and knew the answer instinctively. Because Asher had remained with her, not only in body, but somehow all of him occupying that darkness with her.

A little by little gift from God. Feeling safe in that cave for a moment. What a price she had paid for it! For there could not have been a breakthrough if there had not first been a cave.

Over the ledge, she saw her mother's head as she scrambled toward her ahead of Zarina and Asher. She ran to Jemmah's side. "Did you have to hide in a cave like us?"

Jemmah hooked her finger over her shoulder. She had avoided looking at that gaping maw since she had been carried out of it.

"In there?" Her mother's voice emerged strangled. Without another word, she enfolded Jemmah in a fierce embrace. "How did you bear it?"

"I did not. Not well, that is. Asher cared for me."

Her mother beamed at him.

He rubbed his neck. "I ask your pardon, Keren. I could think of no other way to protect us from the soldiers. I fear I caused her great anguish."

Jemmah snapped to her feet. "Shall we move from here? If Asher adds any more undeserved guilt into that pack he carries, he is sure to fall flat on his face, and then where shall we be?" To Jemmah's relief, everyone laughed, even Asher.

The little goat track reminded her of some of the Persian paths they had traveled upon at the start of their journey, when they had feared they would never see her mother again. The thought cheered her. They had accomplished the impossible. They had rescued her mother. No cave could rob her from the joy of that reunion.

The new path proved narrow and uneven, curling into the mountain, now bringing them to the precipice of a deep gorge, now shielding them behind high walls. At another time, without the threat of ill weather and Median soldiers, she would have enjoyed the brisk march through the majestic Zagros Mountains.

The sun had dipped below the horizon when they arrived at the tapered valley floor. Another regular stopping spot for Asher's tribe, they found a well-tended firepit and tidy wood-pile. But Asher said they had best not light the fire in case the light drew the attention of soldiers. Instead, they sat around the cold firepit and made short work of the last of their bread and cheese, with a miserly handful of nuts and raisins, their stomachs still growling hungrily after they had finished. The women laid out their thin blankets close to one another to share their bodies' heat in the cooling night, while Asher insisted on taking the first watch.

Jemmah could hear the murmur of the river a few steps away as it wended its way past them in the shadows. They had escaped Astyages's soldiers. And she had survived her monsters.

As she fell asleep, she heard the echo of Asher's voice in her ear. *Who, beloved? Who is tormenting you?* Her brow furrowed. What an odd thing to have imagined! As if he would ever have called her that.

Beloved.

And yet, for some reason she could not fathom, she clung to the word the way a drowning man clings to broken flotsam.

* * *

Morning arrived too soon, the sun turning its weak light upon them while sleep wanted to linger. Asher had forbidden them from speaking aloud, forcing them into a solemn quiet, broken only with an occasional whisper. Until he took them fishing.

He waded into the edge of the frigid water, his fingers search-ing beneath the shadowy rocks on the riverbed. The first time he found what he wanted, his body grew very still. A moment later he pulled out his hands, cupped firmly around a wriggling rainbow trout. Jemmah gasped. He had caught the fish with his bare hands.

He held up the fish, his smile flashing proudly. Turning, he moved toward them. His foot must have caught on a river stone. For a moment he teetered and let go of the trout in order to regain his equilibrium. The fish swam away gaily. With both arms outflung, Asher still could not gain his balance. Abruptly he sprawled in the river, water saturating his clothes.

Jemmah stuffed a hand over her mouth. Behind her, Zarina had shoved her whole head into her cloak, trying to stifle the sound of her laughter. Her mother managed to keep a straight face for a moment or two. Then she dissolved.

Asher rose, dripping volumes of cold water. His expression turned fierce. "That was practice." He shoved his hands under the rocks again and remained still as a statue.

"Ha!" he shouted and showed them another wriggling trout, bigger even than the last one. He managed to hold on to this one securely.

The women loaned him their cloaks when he waded to the shore so that he could dry his drenched tunic and trousers without freezing half to death. Since it was daylight, they lit a small fire, using aged wood to keep it from smoking.

Roasted on the fire, its belly filled with the wild onions they found growing nearby, the salted trout was ready by the time they made bread from the last of Keren's flour. The warm meal and the suppressed laughter that still burst upon her every time her eyes fell upon Asher's wet tunic cast out the lingering shade of Jemmah's monsters.

"You look better," Asher whispered in her ear.

"You look wetter," she retorted.

He grinned. "But I caught my prey." He leaned away, pulling the folds of his cloak tighter about him. "Let that be a lesson to you."

She felt an odd flip in her belly at the way he said those words, as if he had stopped talking about the trout and landed on something entirely different.

Before she could ask him what he meant, he strode away to a copse of trees and cut down three sturdy branches. He spent the next hour whittling away bark and twigs and smoothing the ends. By the evening, he had made three rugged walking sticks.

"The way ahead can be rough," he said, handing each woman her own walking stick. "These will help you navigate the path."

When Jemmah tried hers, she discovered he had cut it at exactly the right height. "How thoughtful. My thanks."

"You look like a proper nomad now," he said.

NINETEEN

My companion stretched out his hand against his friends;
he violated his covenant.
Psalm 55:20

ASHER

The workshop, a plain mud structure in the shape of a bent elbow, sat hidden in the lee of an enormous boulder. Asher had picked the spot because it lay close to the path his tribe took every autumn on what they called *kuuch*, their seasonal decampment and journey from one plain to another on the opposite side of the Zagros. This proximity meant that he knew every handsbreadth of the place. At the same time, the desolate location protected it from prying eyes, a key factor in selecting the site for all his workshops.

Asher and Phray had built the cylindrical towerlike smelting furnace first, before digging the foundation of the workshop. Phray's brother had joined in to help erect the walls and install the rafters. Inside, the long part of the structure housed a smaller furnace, a container for charcoal, and another for ore, with a wide stone worktable in the middle. On the walls hung the various tools of their trade. The shorter portion of the structure, which sat perpendicular to the workshop, served as Asher's private chamber where he could enjoy a cozy retreat whenever he stayed at the place.

He had been unable to alert Phray of his coming. No messenger would have arrived any faster than he had. Besides, now he could gauge his friend's reaction to his unannounced arrival. He had barely pulled the thick door open when Phray leapt to his feet, hand already on the hilt of the dagger hanging at his side. But at the sight of Asher, his face split into a wide grin.

"Asher, my brother! Where have you been? I have not received a message from you for an age! I was starting to worry."

Asher's gaze never slipped from that face, its smile as open and guileless as ever. Not a shadow of dismay had passed over those hawkish, brown features. Asher felt his tense shoulders loosen. There was no treachery to be found here. No man on earth could prove so good an actor. Asher should know. He had engaged in his fair share of playacting.

Phray arched an eyebrow. "What happened to you? Did you run into a door?"

Asher ran a finger down his nose, feeling the new bump at its ridge. Ten days of traipsing in the mountains had given his face time to heal. Most of the bruises had vanished or faded to a sickly yellow. But enough scabs and cuts lingered on his abused skin to hint at his unpleasant adventures.

"I ran into a king."

"Astyages? What happened?"

"All in good time." He scraped his fingers against his rough cheek. "First, you must meet my friends." Asher had asked the women to wait outside while he assessed the possibility of danger within. He opened the door a crack and waved them in.

"This is Keren and her daughters, Jemmah and Zarina." He laughed at Phray's astonished expression. He had never brought a stranger here. The location of the workshop remained hidden even from family and friends. This had always been his private dominion, guarded jealously against violation of every kind.

Phray looked from one to the other, his face twisting with bewilderment. "You . . . you . . . you are in our workshop."

"We certainly are," Jemmah confirmed. "And an agreeable place it is too. I especially appreciate the heat emanating from your furnace. I've been cold for weeks."

"But what are you doing here?"

"Don't be rude, Phray," Asher drawled, enjoying his friend's confusion. "These are my friends. They saved me from Astyages's prison. They have walked a long way and are no doubt longing for a good rest. We best make them welcome."

"Of course. Of course. I will go and apprise the men of your arrival. They are in the barn. We will slaughter a sheep and have a hot meal ready for you in a few hours."

"Wait a little and we shall go together." He turned to the women. "Come. My chamber is at your disposal." Opening the door to his private room, he stood aside, watching Jemmah's face as she entered.

Her lips parted with wonder. She turned a slow revolution, taking in every detail. He felt an odd welling of pride at her reaction. This chamber was a glimpse into his personal world. His place of rest. The closest he came to a home. It meant something to see that she understood the charm of it, although he supposed that after the brutal harshness of the mountain passes, any four walls would be a vast improvement whether or not they offered painted plaster and sculpted shelves.

"There is something restful about this chamber," she observed. "Like a tiny oasis of peace."

He was astounded that she understood, precisely, what he had wanted to create.

"How exquisite!" She studied the crimson-red carpet that covered almost the entire floor of the chamber.

"It's from Bijar, a small village northeast of here. The artisans who live there are famed for their superb work, passing down their craft from generation to generation. Each rug is unique." He pointed at the complex hexagon pattern in the center. "Amongst my people, these are known as iron rugs and are highly sought after."

"Why iron rugs?"

"They are almost indestructible. After tying each row of knots, the weavers add a strand of wet wool as an extra weft into the carpet. They pound that wool down into the knots to create a heavier foundation than other carpets, allowing for longer wear."

From a chest, he pulled out a bundle of tunics and hunting trousers. "See if you find anything here to serve you. In the chest over by that wall, you will find clean blankets and pillows. Tonight you will sleep well. I will heat water so you can wash before you rest. We must have something to eat stashed about the place. Later this evening, there will be a proper feast, with roast mutton and fresh bread."

"Thank the Lord!" Zarina cried.

"Indeed," Jemmah said. "Zarina's stomach has been growling louder than a mountain lion."

Zarina bunched up her shawl and tossed it at her sister. "That *was* a mountain lion."

Jemmah laughed and sank onto a fat cushion. "Feathers!" she said. "Bliss. I may never rise again."

Asher carried a cauldron full of hot water into the chamber, followed by a tray heaped with stacks of bread left over from the men's morning meal, and a small bowl of yogurt. Before leaving, he took a moment to examine the contents of a small chest, hidden behind a curtained alcove. Finding everything exactly as he had left it, he closed the chamber door softly behind him and sat down for a quiet chat with Phray.

"What on earth are they doing here, Asher?" his friend burst out.

"I told you. They're friends." He gave a short account of his capture and escape, leaving out some of the details.

"I wondered why I had not heard from you!" Phray cried. "But how did Astyages know about the swords?"

"I have been asking the very same question."

"And?"

"And it grows worse. He knew about the chariot, Phray."

Phray went still. "Your new chariot? But that is impossible!"

"So I believed, until Astyages himself told me about it." Tiredly, Asher came to his feet. "Let us go greet the men. Are they both here?"

Besides Phray, two men served in this workshop. Phray's brother, Deioces, and their childhood companion, Spitamas. Phray, Dei, and Amas had been with him since the beginning of this enterprise, long before any of them could have imagined its eventual success.

"They are in the barn, cleaning the swords. I thought the

metal could use polishing. We had expected to ship them before now."

"We would have, if I had not found myself enjoying the hospitality of my sire."

Outside the barn door, Phray hesitated. "Asher, you do not suspect Amas or Dei, do you? Or me, for that matter?"

Asher put his hand on Phray's shoulder. "Do not concern yourself, my friend. We will soon come to the bottom of this mystery."

Asher walked into the barn first, wanting to see the men's unalloyed expressions. As with Phray, they ran toward him, smiling their welcome, showing no hint of unease.

"Where have you been hiding yourself?" Amas asked, his scarred face flushed with obvious relief. "You were due weeks ago."

"You will never believe it." Phray sat on the edge of a bale of hay and stretched his legs before him. "Not only does he show up late, but he has brought guests! Three women."

"Women!" Dei whistled.

Amas's jaw came loose. "You jest."

At the age of seventeen, Amas had been thrown from a spooked horse into a shallow river, which had left his face a ruin of fat scars from the sharp rocks that had cut into him. The girl he had loved had taken one look at him, her expression congealed with revulsion, and turned away. Now Amas preferred to remain hidden away in the mountains, spending his time working in the workshop and avoiding people, especially of the female persuasion.

Dei grinned. "Have you finally found yourself a girl who will have you, Asher?"

In spite of himself, Asher felt a flush crawl up his cheeks. "They helped me escape from Astyages's prison."

"Prison?" Amas sank down onto an old stool. "That's even worse than women."

Dei's grin widened. "Only marginally."

Once again, Asher told his story. He had never shown the chariot design to anyone in this workshop, save Phray. His instinctive reserve rather than a lack of trust in his oldest friends had long since made him reticent when it came to his ideas.

He was aware, nonetheless, that they could have over-heard him speak of the chariot to Phray. The plans appeared untouched in their hiding place. Then again, that did not mean clever eyes could not have found a way to examine them. No one here was above suspicion. One of them must have told Astyages about his work.

But why this betrayal? To what end? What could it have gained them? Asher had always been generous with the profits. As far as he knew, each of the men had managed to amass a small fortune. If, for some inexplicable reason, they had need of more silver, they knew they only needed to ask.

When he revealed the king's demand for the swords, a shocked silence filled the barn.

Amas sprang to his feet, scars standing out starkly against his white skin. "He knows where we are?"

"No. That is the odd thing. He knew I had this workshop. Knew about the stockpile of swords. Knew even about the latest design I have been working on. But he did not know the location of any of it."

Amas began to pace. "Do you think we are still safe here?"

"I cannot be certain of that until I discover who betrayed me."

The silence that met this pronouncement bore a different

kind of weight. Asher slapped his hands against his thighs and rose. "I need a bath, a shave, and food. A lot of food. Let's slaughter that fat sheep Phray told me about. We can sort out the rest later. On a full stomach." His friends agreed readily, but he could see by their troubled expressions that they were not fooled by his easygoing manner.

* * *

Asher was impressed by the women's healthy appetites. In the evening, they all gorged themselves on roasted mutton served on hot flatbread that soaked up the butter, garlic, and onion-infused juices of the meat. His guests, who seemed able to keep up with him bite for bite, poured lavish praises upon his friends for their culinary skill.

Asher sipped water flavored with honey and vinegar syrup and reached for the dessert, a tiny sweet made from chickpea flour and pistachios, spiced with cardamom and rose water and sweetened with honey. He sighed as the complex tastes melted on his tongue. He took another bite and closed his eyes, savoring the luscious pleasure.

"Did one of you make these?" Keren asked. "They could grace a royal table and not be ashamed."

"Phray's wife," Dei said, shoving two in his mouth at the same time. "Stateira sent them to the workshop with my brother the last time he visited home."

Of the four friends, only Phray was married. In the summers, he split his time between the workshop and the tribal camp. Winter brought with it the closing of the passes. Asher usually took over the running of the workshop, allowing Phray to spend the winter months with his family. The delay resulting from his imprisonment must have caused his friend considerable concern lest he found himself trapped in the workshop for months.

Asher popped another exquisite sweet into his mouth. "How is Stateira?"

His friend's smile seemed to diminish. "All right."

Dei stretched contentedly and sighed. "Grumpy is what he means."

Concluding that Phray must be in trouble with his wife for not joining her earlier, Asher said, "You shall leave for home tomorrow. Stateira will forgive your delay once she discovers you had good reason."

"It's not that." Phray took a long-suffering breath. "She wants to leave the tribal life and settle down."

Asher raised a brow. More and more, he heard of families amongst the nomadic tribes who chose to abandon the old ways and settle permanently in villages and towns. The nomad's manner of life could prove hard. The constant travel wore on body and soul. Wealthier members enjoyed many advantages. The affluence that came from large herds meant that their tents, like Phray's, were as luxurious and well-furnished as a house. But these riches did not entirely diminish the discomforts of an unsettled life. A growing number of nomads longed for the ease of a permanent home and cultivated land.

Phray had never been amongst them. He reveled in the freedom of a traveling life, in the growing number of his cattle and the tight community of his tribe.

"Where does Stateira want to move?"

"Ecbatana."

"The capital?" That surprised him. Most nomads settled in villages, finding life in congested cities too overwhelming. Even those who chose to put down roots within the protection of walled towns avoided crowded cities like Ecbatana.

Dei, never too shy to put in his oar, smirked. "It's Stateira, after all."

Asher bit his lip. In fairness, Stateira had never been a commonplace tribal wife. He had always thought she would do better in a palace somewhere, living as a princess. Phray had fallen for her wild beauty, thinking his newfound wealth enough to satisfy her. A memory of her, petulant lips pulled down and sulky, filled his mind. That one did not know her way to contentment. There would always be something more she wanted, no matter how much silver Phray placed at her disposal.

Phray waved his brother's comments away. "She dreams her dreams as always. She understands it is impossible."

Asher sipped his syrupy water. Stateira must be dreaming, indeed, if she believed her complaints would ever convince Phray to move to a city. As well ask the man to hang a bell around his neck and moo in the fields on four legs. Phray could never fit into life in Ecbatana.

Midway to his lips, the cup in Asher's hand froze. He sat up slowly. The pieces fell together in one smooth, perfect fluctuation of thought. He had found his mole.

He came to his feet. "Shall we seek our beds? Tomorrow is a long day."

He offered to walk the women to his chamber. Jemmah thanked him sweetly for the meal, for the bed linens and the cushions and the carpet, and even for the ill-fitting clothes on her back. With Stateira so recently on his mind, he could not help comparing the two and admiring the differences in Jemmah. Having grown up close to royalty, welcomed in and out of palaces, she seemed little impressed by them or the life they offered. Instead, she knew how to appreciate the small things, to find joy in the comfort of one fluffy cushion rather than miss the hundred luxuries that she had given up in order to rescue her mother.

After the incident of the cave, while making their way to his workshop, Asher had found himself opening up to her, laying bare parts of his life that he usually kept jealously guarded. Reluctantly at first, and then more freely, he had told her about his childhood years. He had an odd sense that she had come to know him the way an old friend knows you to the bone and that she truly liked him, even the murky bits he tried hard to keep hidden.

His disguise had fallen apart under her confused scrutiny by the second day of their journey. Now he found the rest of him breaking open. With a mixture of relief and horror, he discovered that he could not pull himself back inside, neatly curled and concealed as before.

That anguished moment of realization in the cave had left him undone in her presence.

The irony of it did not escape him. He, well-known amongst friend and foe for his taciturn manner, had opened the door of his heart a crack, only to take it off its hinges, while she continued to hold tightly to her secret. She never told him the story behind her terror in the cave. He recognized that he could not demand it from her. Trust did not work like that. It was not an even exchange. He had offered his past to her freely. She would have to do the same for him if ever she felt safe enough with him.

What was he supposed to do now? he wondered. She would hardly be impressed by his wealth, the way Stateira had been by

Phray's. He could not ask her to share this unsettled, danger-filled life. Ask her to throw her happiness on the burning pyre of his bitterness toward his father. Jemmah deserved a man who could offer her a proper home. Offer all the things he did not have to give. His mouth turned dry. With a wordless bow, he left her at her door before returning to the deepening shadows of the barn.

*　*　*

He waited until the steady rhythm of his friends' breathing told him they slept. Wordlessly, he shook Phray awake and gestured to the door. They slipped out quietly, Phray not questioning his request. Asher's heart contracted with pain at the thought of this easy camaraderie. At the imminent loss of it.

"You told her about the chariot." He said the words without preamble when they were far enough away not to be overheard. "Stateira knew."

Phray stood for a moment, his head bowed. "You believe it was Stateira who betrayed you to Astyages. I knew it as soon as I saw your face." He swallowed. "I tried to deny it. To shake that terrible thought. But I knew you were right."

"She must have thought it would force you to move to Ecbatana, if Astyages were to take away the workshop. Or perhaps he promised to move the production to the capital and set you at the head of it." Asher shrugged. "Who knows what temptations she faced. Or what Astyages's men promised when she approached them."

"I never thought she would betray us, Asher. Betray *me*. She had been complaining about life with the tribe. About its dirty, dusty inconvenience. That was nothing new. Then she changed tack and began griping about my work. How deplorable it was. How unworthy. Without thinking, I told her of your chariot. The brilliance of it. The way it could change warfare. I did not mean to betray you." He sighed. "I only meant to impress my own wife. She already knew about the swords, though she had never been to the workshop. I thought no harm would come of it."

"I know, Phray." Asher put a hand on his friend's shoulder. "I know."

"It's over, isn't it? My work for you?"

Asher exhaled, feeling a part of him loosen and leave with that breath. A part he feared he would never gain back. "Go and sort out your home. I will close down this workshop. It will not be safe now. All Astyages's men have to do is to follow one of us from the camp when we come to visit."

"I am sorry, Asher. Truly, I am."

Asher's smile was bittersweet. "It's only that I will miss you, you son of a dog."

Phray wiped a hand over his eyes. "And I you." He took a deep breath. "I will tell the boys."

"No need. This can stay between you and me."

"Best they know. In case Stateira tries her wiles on them." He pulled a hand through his hair. "What will you do with the swords now? Or do you not wish to tell me? I would not blame you if your trust in me was broken beyond repair."

"One moment of indiscretion can hardly do that. I cannot blame you for trusting your wife. I plan to ask Dei and Amas to stash our stockpile in my hideaway for now, until I can arrange to move them."

Phray nodded. "Nabonidus will be glad enough to have them."

"I will forge a formal deal with the Babylonian king. It is fortuitous that I must head to Babylon, in any case. My Persian friends need my help to make the journey. That is a debt I must pay, since thanks to them, I found my way out of Astyages's prison."

Phray looked pained. "For that, more than anything, I owe you."

"My arrest is not your doing, Phray. Clearly Stateira had already decided to sell me out to Astyages. With or without the chariot, she had enough information to rile Astyages. She knew I was still running the workshop." Asher shrugged. "Like you, I thought I could trust her. Enough to reveal that much to her, at least."

Phray's expression darkened. "She has shattered my trust."

"But not your love," Asher observed sadly.

CHAPTER

TWENTY

I am the LORD, and there is no other,
besides me there is no God;
I equip you, though you do not know me,
that people may know, from the rising of the sun
and from the west, that there is none besides me;
I am the LORD, and there is no other.

Isaiah 45:5-6

——————————— CYRUS ———————————

The winds in the highlands had blown fierce all day, bringing with them a sharp blast of cold that made the joints ache.
Cyrus's army had fought the last battle of the season. The
Medes, having suffered several defeats, had packed up their
carts and headed for home. Like all armies, the great challenge
of moving a large force over mountainous terrains meant that,
with the approach of colder weather and imminent snows to
the north, they had to give up the fight or risk being trapped
in enemy territory. Their cavalry had decamped the day before,
followed by the infantry earlier that morning.

Cyrus exhaled. At the start of the war, he had imagined he

could penetrate deep into Median territory and coerce Astyages into a quick head-on campaign. But for two years, his grand-father's forces had pressed south instead, and after several hard reverses, Cyrus had had to settle for a strong defense rather than the decisive offensive he had dreamed of.

Astyages, whose goal in attacking Cyrus was to gain Persian territory, would no doubt feel the sting of this loss. After eight months of fighting, he had had to lick his wounds and retreat with nothing to show for his expensive attack.

In spite of his victory, Cyrus felt his own loss. The Persians had repelled the Median army, true. But they had failed to gain a palpable military foothold in Median lands. Two years of war, and he had made little significant gain.

After Cyrus had watched the lumbering march of the Medians snaking in long columns up the main highway at dawn, he had spent the rest of the morning inspecting his own leftover supplies. The relief of his small victory came smashing against the shock of his army's deficient supplies.

His men had never been well-equipped. Persian bows were constructed from simple wood and cord, lacking the power of the compound bows used by the Scythian archers Astyages employed. Under their wool-padded tunics, most Persian soldiers could not afford to wear scale armor, and instead of helmets, they had cloth hats that served to keep their ears warm in winter months and offered little else by way of protection. His infantry fought their enemy while standing utterly vulnerable to the heavy volleys of bronze-tipped arrows sent their way, protected by nothing except their round wicker and leather shields.

Over a full season of war, they had spent every last arrow in their quivers. Likewise, his cavalry had thrown the full store of their javelins and spears, until most of them were left with barely anything to fight with save for their bare hands.

This disastrous state of lack had come about because Astyages's men had quickly learned to gather arrows and spears from their comrades' injured and dying bodies even as they retreated from the battlefield, leaving little behind for Cyrus to reclaim. Every battle won had also been a battle lost. They had gained a sliver of territory and lost all their weaponry.

In spite of the long odds, Cyrus had managed to win by dividing his cavalry into two and setting each half to flank his archers. They might lack the composite bows of the Scythians, but his men attacked with the deadly accuracy of long practice. The cavalry's javelins followed immediately with head-spinning speed. The strategy had been his own invention, one that sent Astyages's generals into a tailspin they could not recover from. Day after day, their battalions were forced into retreat. But they had learned to hold out long enough to strip the dead of armor and weapons. Astyages waged a war of attrition, which, though costly, he could easily afford. Most of the men dying were not even Medes, but mercenaries lured into battle by the promise of the king's silver.

Come next spring, Astyages would be at his door again, better equipped than before, with more men at his back. The Median king had the riches of old Assyria, which his father had helped to conquer, still jangling in his coffers. He could buy anything he wanted. Mercenaries, horses, perfectly fashioned armor, spears, swords, shields, bows, and an endless supply of arrows.

Cyrus had scraped the bottom of his own treasury to see him through this year. He would have enough to feed his men next year. But he had no way of supplying them with much-needed weaponry. He did not even have the iron or bronze to fashion his own arrow tips.

Time to return home. Somehow he would try to unravel the knot that lay before him.

A messenger ran up to him, carrying a dusty leather cylinder under his arm. Wordlessly, Cyrus held out a hand. It took him a mere moment to read it. A slow smile spread across his face.

"My horse!" he cried.

Harpagus, never too far, appeared at his side. "Going somewhere?"

"Pasargadae."

"I thought you were headed for Anshan in the morning?"

Cyrus's wife, Cassandane, and his little boy, whom he had named for his father Cambyses, awaited him in the palace at Anshan. He longed to see them, to hold his wife's hand in his, to laugh at his boy's antics. To forget the war for a moment. "I have something more important to do first." He handed the missive to Harpagus.

The general gave a hearty laugh when he read the message. "Trust Keren to survive Astyages's prison. I wish I had been there when they told the old king she had escaped right under his nose."

Cyrus grinned. "That would have been an enjoyable sight."

"Why do you head to Pasargadae?"

"That is where Jared awaits news. He will not have heard yet."

"Go home, man. Send a messenger. They will probably ride faster than you." Harpagus pointed at the bandage around Cyrus's arm.

Cyrus flicked the short tail of linen that hung from the

binding around his wound. "This little scratch won't slow me." He rolled the message and stuffed it back within the leather cylinder. "Besides, I want to bear the news to Jared myself."

"I suppose that is why your men lay down their lives for you so readily. This impulsive largesse. Go then, if you must. But have a care. You are more tired than you realize."

"I was." He tapped the scroll. "This revived me."

He had felt the burden of Keren's capture through every hour of the past few weeks. Felt it weigh on him like a grinding stone, growing heavier still when he heard of the rescue party's unsuccessful return, leaving only Keren's daughters to help.

Jared must have been stone-cold with fear every hour of those weeks. Cyrus wanted to look into his friend's face when he brought the good news.

Tired as he was, he did not wait to refresh himself. Instead, with no more than half a dozen Immortals at his back, he rode hard for Pasargadae, stopping for the night under the rough shelter of an overhanging rock and taking to the road again before sunrise.

Jared must have seen the horses coming. He awaited them in the yard, his face a stony mask, hiding the ice-cold dread that likely spiked at the sight of them. Cyrus grinned at him, holding the cylinder aloft. Jared's eye closed slowly.

"They are well, my friend. All of them. Your girls succeeded. They rescued their mother."

"Come in, my lord. Come and refresh yourself." Jared sent a servant to the Immortals, who, gray with dust and weariness, still had the discipline to stand at formal attention behind their king. "Feed those men well," he cried over his shoulder.

They entered Jared's modest receiving chamber, where Johanan was busy working upon a wax tablet. The sight of an owl sitting comfortably on a wooden perch next to the young scholar brought Cyrus to a surprised stop.

Detecting the new visitor, the owl bobbled its head from side to side, yellow eyes studying Cyrus with interest. The king returned the scrutiny with equal curiosity. "Have you hired a new assistant?"

Johanan, lost in his work, sprang to his feet. "My lord! We were not expecting you."

"I bring fair tidings. They are all safe."

"Where are they?" Jared showed Cyrus to a comfortable chair.

With a sigh, he took his seat, grateful that it was not the back of another horse. "Prexaspes sent the message from his hiding place near the Zagros Mountains. They will have left there by now. According to him, they were headed for Babylon."

Cyrus motioned for Jared to take a seat across from him. With relief he noticed the color returning to his friend's white face.

"How did they manage to escape Astyages?" Jared asked.

Cyrus handed him the scroll. "It's brief. But you can fill in the details for yourself."

Cyrus rested his head against the back of his chair while Jared read the report from Prexaspes. He pointed at the speckled bird. "That looks more like a friend of Jemmah's than yours, Johanan."

"Jemmah rescued him when Zarina brought him home with a wounded wing," Johanan explained. "I was supposed to set him free after he recovered from his injury. But he refused to go." He shrugged and, donning a thick falconry glove, held out his arm for the bird, who perched upon it readily. "Meet Gilead."

"You *named* him? It becomes evident why he would not leave."

"I don't know how I will explain it to Jemmah. She gave me strict instructions to return him to the wild."

Cyrus laughed. "I daresay after being away from home for so long, she will be in a forgiving mood."

"A waste cart?" Jared murmured.

"What did you say, Father?"

"That is how they escaped. In a waste cart."

Johanan's mouth tipped up. "Jemmah forced Mother to hide in that? That's much worse than keeping the owl."

Jared clutched the scroll of papyrus against his chest. "They are safe, thank the Lord." He turned to Cyrus. "You are kind to deliver this in person. I received news of your victory a few hours ago. The Medes have left?"

"Gone with their tails between their legs. For now, at least."

Jared gave him a warm smile. "Another man could not have succeeded, not with those odds."

Cyrus rapped his fingers on the table, making the owl jump. "It's not much of a success, Jared, if I cannot finish what I started. My men are tired, hungry, injured. I have pushed them beyond their limits. Now I have no weapons to give them come spring and no money with which to buy what I need. I expect Astyages will grow tired of sending his generals and come down in person to put me in my place. He knows that after two years of war, I am running out of resources. He will seek to crush me while I am at my weakest."

Jared nodded solemnly. "A sound plan. Pity for him it will not succeed."

"Will it not?" Cyrus came to his feet and walked restlessly to the table where a servant had left them chalices of wine. He savored a mouthful. The wine, silky smooth, washed away the taste of dust, and with a sigh, he took another mouthful. "I have no way of defeating his armies. He will have too many men, each one well-armed."

Jared tented his fingers. "I think it is time I told you something. Wait for me a moment, if you would."

He returned from an inner chamber, bearing in his hands a curious cylinder of silver filigree. Opening a small catch, he extracted a scroll. "You know, lord, that my nation was defeated by Nebuchadnezzar over fifty years ago, and twenty years after that, his army utterly destroyed the city of Jerusalem and our glorious Temple. The Babylonians took our people captive and carried them back to their own cities."

Cyrus nodded in sympathy.

"What Keren and I have never told you is that our prophets foretold that our captivity would come to an end."

"I am certain it will, my friend."

Jared's smile had an odd quality about it. An intense animation that made Cyrus set down his goblet.

"Amongst those prophecies, there is one about a man whom God calls his Shepherd. The one who will rebuild Jerusalem and its Temple. He is named by the prophet. His name is Cyrus."

Cyrus stared. "What did you say?"

"His name is Cyrus. And God promises to go before him, to remove the obstacles in his path, to level the mountains and smash down gates of bronze."

Cyrus had known Jared for years. More than once, this man had helped to save his life. There was a quiet wisdom in him that Cyrus trusted. But in this, he must be mistaken. "Jared, I am no Judean," he said gently. "I am a follower of Ahura Mazda. I do not serve your god, though I respect him for your sake. I doubt he will want a Persian to play shepherd to his people."

"On the contrary, my king. Our God is willing to bless you, to help you and open doors before you for the sake of his children, though we are often wayward."

"Come now, my friend."

"In the prophecy, the Lord says to Cyrus, *I have equipped you for battle, though you don't even know me.*"

"Equipped you for battle?"

"Precisely."

Cyrus sank slowly into the chair. "You think your god will equip me for the war against Astyages? Help me win that impossible battle? Why? How would that change anything for your people in Babylon?"

Jared held out his scroll. "According to another prophet, the Lord will inspire the kings of the Medes to march against Babylon and destroy her. It is a Median king that sets the Judeans free from bondage."

It took Cyrus only a moment to understand the juxtaposition of these prophecies. A man called Cyrus would one day set the Judeans free from their captivity to Babylon. This Cyrus would help restore their city and rebuild their Temple. But if the two prophecies described the same man, then one more crucial fact about him emerged. "The Cyrus who accomplishes these things will be a king of the Medes."

Jared gave a jerk of his chin, his expression solemn. "The Medes shall one day have a king named Cyrus."

Cyrus leaned back. If he was the king described in these prophecies, as Jared clearly believed, then the throne of Astyages would come to him. The Lord, the god of the Judeans, had chosen him as his champion.

In his own way, Cyrus was a man of faith. He believed in the battle of light against darkness. He believed Jared's god to be part of that light. If Ahura Mazda had chosen him to be a champion of the Persians, why could he not also be a champion for the Judeans?

He grinned, forgetting the weariness of his body. "Well, if your god wishes to equip me for battle, I hope he knows his way around a miracle or two."

Jared's teeth flashed white. "You might say that is his specialty, my king."

TWENTY-ONE

We do not know what to do, but our eyes are on you.
2 Chronicles 20:12

Jemmah was puzzled by the somber tenor of Asher's farewells. The four friends seemed shrouded in a strange gloom, far deeper than their temporary separation would warrant. The laughing faces of the previous night had vanished. Some gray malady of the soul had robbed the sparkle from their eyes. There were no more jests and teasing, no more mock threats and cheerful promises. Nothing save downcast glances and monosyllabic goodbyes.

Asher remained silent as he led them up the timeworn track that carried them west, toward Babylon. When the track allowed, Jemmah maneuvered her steps next to him. "We are traveling uphill again," she observed.

"We will continue to ascend for two, perhaps three days,

depending on the weather, before the path begins to descend again."

"Is that why you are preoccupied? The weather?"

"I didn't realize I was preoccupied."

She gave an emphatic nod. "I can tell from this line right here." She pointed to the spot above the bridge of his nose.

"It's not polite to point out people's wrinkles."

Jemmah flushed. "It isn't a wrinkle. You only get this line when you brood."

"In other words, all the time?"

He came to a sudden stop. Abruptly she found herself crashing against him. His arm shot forward to wrap around her, bringing her to a stop. Blood beat against her eardrums. She was surrounded by a fortress of muscle, hard as the iron he shaped. Her pulse exploded as Asher exhaled slowly.

In a calm voice she asked what was wrong. At least, that was her intention. What emerged instead turned into an incomprehensible collection of vowels strung up in no particular order.

He took a hasty step away. "Pardon! You were about to trip on that rock. See it sticking out from the path?"

"Oh."

Asher took to the trail like a hound on the scent, leaving Jemmah scrambling to keep up. "Thank you for saving me from a bad fall."

He looked at her over his shoulder. "I am closing the workshop."

"What? Why? My mother practically salivated over your swords and daggers. Surely that is a profitable enterprise."

"Astyages knows about it. It is only a matter of time before his spies find the location." He shrugged. "We have a leak."

Jemmah gasped. "Not one of your friends, surely!"

"No."

"I am sorry, Asher. It must be a loss to you."

"I have others."

"But this is your favorite."

His step faltered. "How do you know?"

"It was the first place you built. I saw a handprint in the mud, at the base of the wall. It must have belonged to you or one of your friends. You poured something of yourself into that place. Before you found all the success you now enjoy, you honed your talent in the fires of that furnace. That workshop is the birthplace of your dreams."

"Yes," he admitted. "It's hard to lose it." Weaving through the simple words, she heard a faint echo of the grief he had swallowed when he left at dawn. The workshop would be empty and abandoned the next time he walked this path, its forge cold.

Without thinking, she reached out and squeezed his hand. For an instant his grip tightened around her fingers. Then the track narrowed, and hastily she dropped back to avoid smashing against the shelf of rock that stuck out like a wide blade into her path.

* * *

That night, they slept again under the stars, huddled beneath blankets that felt too thin in the dipping mountain temperatures. By dawn, they were walking again, uphill—always uphill in the thinning air—until gasping with every step, Jemmah felt her lungs might simply give in. It became the pattern of their days, the sunrise walks, the grinding climb, the icy nights. On the fifth day, the wind began, at first a mere nuisance, then picking up until it howled and shrieked its way inside their padded clothing and chapped their skin to shreds.

The track had brought them to the edge of a precipice. Jemmah grasped her walking stick until her knuckles turned white. The views would have been breathtaking if not for the wind, which made them stagger like men with too much wine under their belt, now smashing against the rock wall and now lurching too close to the sheer drop.

Just before they stopped for lunch, when Jemmah was hazily wondering whether she ought to serve bread and cheese or the last of Amas's lentils, a terrifying crack rent through the air. Like the sound of a hundred bones breaking, it echoed so ominously that the howling wind became a kitten's sleepy growl in comparison. An instant later, a boulder came tumbling from nowhere, a giant rock that tore off the cliff face, loosened by the ice and snow of years, severed from the cliff by the force of the blowing gusts.

It narrowly missed Asher. Jemmah only had time to let go of her stick and throw herself to the ground. She slid backward, down the rocky incline, nails digging uselessly into the soil until they bled. Her pack went flying into the gorge, taking with it her blanket and all the food she carried.

In the same spinning motion, the edge of the boulder caught Jemmah's mother in the shoulder, knocking her breathless to her knees. But it was Zarina who took the brunt of it. She spun about, dragged by some projection in the rock to the edge of the precipice.

And went flying over.

Several things happened at once. Jemmah's mother screamed. With great force, the rock hit the side of the mountain somewhere below them, causing a cloud of dust to rise, blinding them. Ignoring the noise and the choking dust, Asher dove after Zarina with the agility of a hunting cat until he came to the edge of the precipice where she had gone over.

Jemmah scrambled after Asher, looking over the edge, fearful of what she might find. As the dust settled, she saw Zarina, face covered in blood, holding on to a fistful of deep-rooted scrub, dangling over the precipice by one hand.

Next to her, her mother gasped. "Zarina! Hold on, my girl! Hold on."

Asher scrambled so far forward that for a moment Jemmah feared he would go hurtling over the edge himself. She fell upon his legs, trying to play ballast to his suspended body.

It must have only taken an instant. The length of a kiss between friends. To Jemmah, it stretched to a century. Whole seasons passed.

Then Asher wrapped his fingers about Zarina's wrist. The cords in his neck stood out as he pulled her up, his hands finding purchase on her arms. Without warning, she slipped from his grasp and slid down like a slippery eel. The pack she had strapped to her back fell tumbling and twirling into the void of the gorge below. At the last moment, Asher managed to tighten his grip, his fingers holding on to hers, both groaning from the crushing pain of holding on.

Zarina, dazed from the bleeding wound on her temple, somehow managed to jam her toes inside a narrow fissure of rock, steadying her swinging body enough to give Asher the stability he needed to pull her up. Her body came, at last, flying over the edge so that Asher lost his balance and fell sideways, with Zarina over him and Jemmah still clinging to his legs.

For a moment they lay, the four of them tangled together, Asher half-buried under Zarina's body and her mother gripping her youngest child in an iron hold. No one said a word. The tortured sound of their gasping inhalations mingled with the noise of the wind.

Asher broke the silence. "I am glad Lord Jared cannot walk in upon us at this precise moment. I am not sure how I would explain myself."

Jemmah sat up enough to see the picture they presented, legs and arms tangled together, Asher lying at the center like a conquering king with his harem. She huffed a laugh, which turned into a sob.

Gingerly Asher sat up. "Let's move away from this edge, shall we?" He supported Zarina as she stood unsteadily, and motioned toward an indentation in the rock a small way up the path. "That might provide us with some shelter from the wind."

Jemmah helped her mother, seeing for the first time the pallor in her face and the odd angle of the arm she held against her side. Zarina staggered a few steps with Asher's help. When she collapsed, he gathered her against him and led the way to the sheltered spot.

Jemmah washed her sister's blood-soaked face, wondering if Zarina had fainted from blood loss or from the shock and pain of dangling over the side of a mountain. Or whether something worse ailed her. Head injuries could be complicated.

The bleeding gash was deep enough to leave a scar, not that Zarina would care. Jemmah's needle and bandages, as well as her small package of medicinal herbs, had gone into the gorge with her pack. She would have preferred to suture the cut, but the injury did not seem life-threatening and would close up even without stitching. Yet Zarina remained unconscious.

"How is she?" her mother asked.

Jemmah used a strip of cloth from her mother's spare tunic to create a bandage around Zarina's head. "The cut itself is not bad. You can see the bleeding has almost stopped. The bruising and swelling around it might indicate a worse injury beneath the surface. I know little about such wounds." She bit her lip. "It will be a good sign if she awakens soon." She noticed her mother's chattering teeth and white face. "Let me see that arm," she said.

Her mother lowered her cloak. "You will have to cut the tunic."

Asher handed her a short, vicious-looking knife. By the time Jemmah had cut the sleeve away, she thought her mother might join Zarina in a faint. A fine film of perspiration covered her pale face. Jemmah forced herself to do a thorough examination, knowing that her prodding only added to her mother's discomfort.

She wiped her fingers on a scrap of cloth and sat back. "The bone in the upper arm is broken." Jemmah had read enough Egyptian medical texts to know theoretically how to treat the fracture. But she had never actually set a human bone.

"It will be painful," she said, looking anxiously into her mother's eyes.

"So I have already gathered. Do what you must, Daughter."

"The Egyptians call what I am about to do reduction by traction. You might call it torture."

"I see. Perhaps we should pray?"

"Please!" Asher said with feeling.

Jemmah pushed back the wave of tears that burned her eyes. *"God, we do not know what to do, but our eyes are on you."* The prayer of King Jehoshaphat sprang to her lips, perfect for this desperate hour. She swallowed. "Please guide my hands that I may attend my mother's arm. Set her bones, God. Do what I cannot accomplish with my meager knowledge."

Asher held up a half-empty skin of wine to Keren. "May not fix your bone. But if we get enough into you, you will not care."

Keren smiled weakly. "A timely remedy."

Giving the wine time to do its work, Jemmah returned her attention to her sister. In spite of her best efforts, she could not rouse Zarina from her deep sleep.

"How's she?" Her mother's words came a little slurred.

"Her breathing is even and strong. A favorable sign." Jemmah could not help grinning at her mother's slack-jawed expression. "I see you are ready for me. First, let me help you lie down. Asher, please make more bandages from that spare tunic."

While Asher cut strips of wool, Jemmah folded her cloak to create a stout bolster. She tucked it between her mother's shoulder blades. Once the bandages were ready, she instructed Asher to hold her mother while she tugged on the injured arm. This process of lengthening should allow the bone to fall into place. At least that was what the Egyptian physicians claimed.

Her mother screamed once. The sound, high-pitched and redolent with pain, pierced Jemmah like the point of a honed dagger. Still, she did not loosen her grip. She pulled the arm, one hand feeling to see if the bone had settled into place while Asher held her mother down.

Finally, when she was satisfied that she had set the bone properly, she sat back and pushed her hair away from her face with a shaking hand. "Now we will bind the arm. I have no alum to spread on the cloth. Do we have honey?"

"In my pack," Asher said, sounding strained.

Jemmah applied the honey to the bandage and tied the strips

of cloth firmly about the limb to keep it immobile. "In a week, we can add splints. For now, we will change the bandage daily."

Asher blinked when a soft snore was followed by another. "Did she fall asleep?"

Jemmah nodded. "Must be the relief from the pain I inflicted."

He tipped up her chin. "You managed that masterfully. Not once did you lose your nerve."

She felt that odd flip in her stomach. "I fooled you, then."

"I am not easy to fool. How is Keren's arm?"

"I think she will recover full use of it. I could not feel any bone fragments under the swelling, which is a good sign. But I am no expert."

"You did better than many physicians I have seen. Can Keren and Zarina be ready to move soon?"

Jemmah rubbed her arms. "If Zarina wakes up, I think so. But either way, we should remain here for the rest of today and tomorrow, at least. Give them a chance to regain their strength."

Asher ran a restless hand through his hair. "We lost two packs, which means our supplies have been cut in half. Two blankets, only, and it grows colder every day. We still have at least another five days of travel ahead of us before we arrive at the outpost on the other side of the mountains. Zarina's and Keren's injuries will slow our pace, so probably longer."

Jemmah gulped. "Can we survive, do you think?"

"As long as we don't have another boulder land on our heads or get caught in an early squall. I can feed us, and there is water aplenty in these peaks."

"Are there any more soldiers we need be wary of?"

"Astyages has a small fort two days' walk from here. I know how to circle around it. They will not find us." He pressed a hand on her shoulder. She felt something warm and reassuring travel through his touch into the marrow of her bones. "Try not to worry," he said.

When he looked at her like that, she had no difficulty following his advice. But when the hours arced ahead, the sun chased away by a thrifty moon with no sign of Zarina gaining consciousness, Jemmah felt the cold hand of anxiety return once again, refusing to budge no matter how hard she prayed.

TWENTY-TWO

Vengeance is mine, and recompense,
for the time when their foot shall slip;
for the day of their calamity is at hand,
and their doom comes swiftly.
Deuteronomy 32:35

Jemmah huddled in her cloak next to Zarina and watched her sister's chest rise and fall in a reassuring rhythm. Why would she not open her eyes? Jemmah had managed to drip a bit of water through her sister's chapped lips before Zarina had choked, forcing Jemmah to give up trying.

A slight rustle nearby made her turn her head. Asher crouched next to her. "I will watch her for a few hours. You must sleep."

"I can't."

"You can. Leave her to me. I will wake you if I see any change."

"I need to stay with her," she whispered.

"Then lie down next to her and close your eyes. You can hold her hand while you rest."

She opened her mouth to argue. He held up his palm, forestalling her objections. "This is not a request, Jemmah. I am in charge of our safe passage. It is my responsibility to deliver you and your family to Babylonia, preferably in one piece. Or at least no more pieces than we already have. To succeed, I need you physically strong. Once we resume our journey, you and I have to help your mother and sister navigate this hard terrain. You will not be able to do that if you are staggering with exhaustion. I will get us to safety, Jemmah. But I cannot do it alone. I need you."

Jemmah knew he was right. She caressed Zarina's cheek. "Don't sleep too long, lazybones," she whispered. "I'll see you soon."

A narrow spot lay cold and hard between Zarina's blanket-covered figure and the bluff. She stretched out tiredly. Turning to Asher, she said, "Are you certain you can bear the deprivation of my scintillating conversation?"

His teeth flashed white in the dark. "I will endeavor to survive it."

In spite of the bitter cold that nipped at her chilled flesh and her concern for Zarina, Jemmah fell almost instantly into a dreamless sleep. She snapped awake when Asher whispered her name.

"She woke up briefly!" he said with a grin. "I think the sight of my handsome face must have proven too much for her, though." He scratched his scruffy beard. "She seems to have fallen asleep again."

Jemmah rolled up so quickly, she almost strangled herself by stepping on the hem of her tunic. "Did she speak?"

"No. But she waved at me."

In the predawn light, a tinge of color tinted Zarina's cheeks. "Zarina?" Jemmah called softly, tapping the side of her face.

Thick eyelashes fluttered. "What?"

Jemmah sighed with relief. "How do you feel?"

"Fine."

Jemmah shook her head. "The truth. How do you feel?"

"Like I was hit on the head."

Jemmah laughed. "You were. By a big boulder."

Zarina opened her eyes. "Poor boulder."

"Can you remember what happened?"

Zarina frowned. "Bits and pieces."

"You've been asleep since before lunch yesterday. Had me worried."

"You always worry." Gingerly she felt the bandage around her head. "Did you have to sew it up?"

"I lost my needle. Went over the side with the pack. All I could do was bandage it to stop the bleeding. You will have a nice, fat scar."

"Always wanted one," Zarina croaked. "Something to drink?"

Asher handed Jemmah their only cup, half-filled with water. Thirstily, Zarina gulped it down. "Breakfast?"

"You're hungry?"

"Starved."

Asher arched an eyebrow. "Something as negligible as hanging down the side of a mountain isn't going to ruin her appetite."

Jemmah noticed for the first time that he was stirring a pot over the small fire he had built. "Oh, excellent. Look, Asher is cooking. What have you made?"

In answer, Asher filled a bowl from the steaming contents of the pot and handed it over. Jemmah sniffed the nondescript white porridge and shrugged, shoving a spoonful in Zarina's direction.

Zarina swallowed it and made a face. "Fire and lightning! I thought you could cook."

"We lost the butter over the side and need the honey for your mother's bandage. Besides, you are sick. Bland food is part of your treatment."

Zarina swallowed another spoonful. "Why does Keren need bandages?"

Asher rubbed his eyes tiredly. "Broke her arm."

"Fire and lightning! Any other bad news you want to share?"

Jemmah shoved more porridge in Zarina's direction, hoping to forestall the next volley of questions. "You have to be on your feet by tomorrow, or Asher is going to carry you."

Zarina fixed Asher with her exotic eyes. "I'll walk."

"You have my gratitude." Asher came to his feet. "I am going hunting. If we have to remain here for the day, I might as well put the time to good use."

Zarina grumbled under her breath. "You are doing that on purpose."

"What?"

"Going hunting when I can't join you."

The green eyes sparkled. "Life is very arduous."

Two hours later, Asher returned with a small mountain goat, which he had already skinned and gutted. Within moments, he had set up three roasting spits over the fire, the goat meat skewered at just the right height to cook without charring.

Soon the smell of roasted game tantalized their empty bellies while Keren, roused from her exhausted sleep, sat next to Zarina and quietly spoke to her.

"Time to change your bandage," Jemmah told her mother.

The patient bore Jemmah's unpleasant ministrations without a sound, though she turned pale, her lips drawn into a tight line.

"It looks like it's mending well," Jemmah said with satisfaction. She pointed to the blue-black skin, which bore no sign of contagion. "That's a bit of heaven, right there. I could not have done that without God's help."

* * *

After lunch, Zarina and her mother fell into the worn-out sleep of invalids. Jemmah cleaned the knife Asher had loaned her, examining its sparse, elegant lines as she did so. "One of yours?" she asked, returning the weapon to him.

"My first." He flipped it nimbly in the air before returning it to its scabbard. "The secret is to sustain the right temperature during the smelting of the ore."

"No doubt the process is more complicated than that."

"True."

"How did you embark on this business?"

"By accident. I had no notion of making weapons when I first began. Our tribe had grown poor under Astyages's rule. Before his time, the kings of Media treated their tribal leaders with respect. They considered them brothers in arms. Rulers together. Astyages changed all that. He made the heads of the tribes subservient to him. Some were wealthy enough to survive his demands for an outrageous share of their wealth. But our tribe did not.

"As our poverty grew, so did my mother's suffering. A slave in a poor tribe." He shrugged. "Her work doubled while her food diminished. She grew weak and sickened. I was young yet.

But I knew I had to find a job. I lied about my age so I could join Astyages's personal guards."

Jemmah leaned forward, surprised by the revelation. "You served Astyages?"

"The foolishness of youth." He arranged more wood in the fire, his movements precise. "At first, I hoped I could win his sympathy for my mother. Though he had never raised a hand to help us, I thought he would show compassion for the woman who had borne his son if he learned of her predicament. It would not have taken much to help her. For the cost of one of his royal robes, he could have fed and housed her for years."

"He refused you?"

"Astyages had me thrown out of the guards for daring to speak to him. It had taken me a year to gain an audience. By then, I had served him long enough to learn how his army operated. After that, I hired myself out as a mercenary to the Lydians and, a few months later, to the Babylonians."

"A mercenary? That is hard work."

"It pays well. Enough to look after my mother's needs."

She thought of the life he must have led, traveling from one bloody battlefield to another, and felt choked by a sudden fist in her throat.

"Every time I served a different army, I learned something new about weapons. What they could do well and what needed improvement. I realized quickly that the swords they provided us were of poor quality and liable to get you killed in combat. I had worked in a blacksmith's shop as a boy. I knew the rudiments of metalwork. After a particularly bloody battle, we camped not far from that blacksmith's workshop. I paid him a visit, and for a bit of coin, he helped me make this." He tapped the knife at his side.

"I found I had a knack for it. When the campaign season came to an end, I returned to the blacksmith and learned everything I could from him about forging steel. I had managed to save a little of my pay from my three years of service. With that, I set up my first workshop." His hand clenched against his rib in a way he had not done for days, as if the old pain had returned to haunt him.

"My mother never saw it. She died that winter, before I could provide the life I had always dreamed of giving her." The hurt of a boy bled into his voice.

"She would have been proud of you, Asher," Jemmah said, instinctively knowing the truth of her words.

The green eyes clouded. "Perhaps."

"It seems you succeeded to spite Astyages."

"I succeeded to *beat* Astyages. My years as a soldier gave me an advantage. I knew what soldiers need. The range, the balance, the quality of metal that could withstand the shock of repeated strikes. Once I mastered swords and daggers, I branched out to other weapons. I have made my fortune by selling most of my wares to Astyages's enemies."

Jemmah grew still. She felt as though he had allowed her a glimpse into the most secret chamber of his being. The impetus behind every endeavor. The crowning objective of his life.

To beat Astyages.

In an odd way, Jemmah had been surrounded since childhood by those who wanted to vanquish the Median king. Cyrus. Harpagus. Even her parents. But for all of them, beating Astyages was merely a means to something better. Something more noble. Cyrus wanted freedom for his people. He wanted to offer them a just and stable rule. Her parents wanted to see God's promises fulfilled. They longed to restore their people to their homeland. Even Harpagus, who fought against his own army and his own king, did so because he felt the Medes deserved a better king.

But for Asher, beating Astyages had become the end. It had turned into the goal. His life was consumed by this singular purpose.

She thought of the ancient wound that still bled, ruling his life, shaping every decision. It dawned on her that this revelation had not been a casual slip of the tongue. Asher had chosen to show her the honed blade of his bitterness. He had stripped back the curtains that usually veiled his heart and allowed her a glimpse.

She remembered the way his eyes had clouded when she had told him his mother would be proud of him. *Perhaps,* he had said, not sounding convinced. *Perhaps,* because he knew his mother would not have wanted him to waste his days on the cause of bitterness.

And yet he could not let it go.

Little wonder he refused to sell weapons to Cyrus! It was not more silver he craved. He simply did not believe Cyrus was powerful enough to beat Astyages.

Everything in Asher, every plan, every last drop of ability, the mighty tempest of energy that gave him such a restless air, *everything* had been harnessed into the service of this one thing. This need to beat his father.

He could not free himself from that need. Though somewhere inside him, he doubted the worthiness of such a purpose, he could not walk away from it. He had wanted her to know this about him. This glimpse into his heart had been a warning, she realized. His heart already had a mistress. Her name was vengeance.

"I lived through an earthquake once," she said thoughtfully. "It lasted no more than a handful of moments. I remember I wanted desperately to move from where I stood, next to a heaving cypress tree that looked as though it would topple on top of me at any moment. But the earth seemed to grab me with a force I could not resist. My feet were glued to that spot, and I shook and heaved along with the tree, unable to escape.

"Life can be like that. Something grabs hold of you, and you can't move away from it, much as you try."

Asher nodded slowly.

She held his gaze and knew, for the first time since she had crawled out of that well a decade earlier, that she wanted to share her story. She wanted him to know she understood how it felt to be caught in the grip of something that twisted your life and would not let go.

CHAPTER

TWENTY-THREE

*And you saw how the LORD your God cared for you all along the
way as you traveled through the wilderness, just as a father cares
for his child. Now he has brought you to this place.*

Deuteronomy 1:31, NLT

"Before moving to Pasargadae, my family lived in Anshan,"
Jemmah began. She halted for a brief moment, unable to make
her tongue form the words. At length, she found her voice
again. "Our garden bordered on the property of one of Cyrus's
generals. His daughter, Lanunu, and I became inseparable by
the time we were three. Except for the years my family was in
Ecbatana, I spent every free hour with Lanunu."

The memory of that laughing face rose up, teasing, incorrigible, full of life. "We sometimes called her the Little General,
because she was as fearless as her father. Like everyone who
knew her, I adored Lanunu."

Jemmah drew her knees into her chest. "Together, we managed to find more trouble than a dozen boys our age. Without

Lanunu, I would probably have lived a quiet life. Boring and predictable. But she turned the world into one long adventure. And wherever she led, I followed.

"By the time we turned ten, my brother had already sped ahead of me in his studies. His mind is extraordinary. Which is why I began studying with Lanunu instead. She was refreshingly normal in her grasp of sums and languages. This alone endeared her to me. Being the only ordinary person in a family populated by brilliant minds is not always easy. With Lanunu, I felt at home."

Jemmah wove her fingers together to try to keep them from trembling.

Asher leaned in to rest the tips of two fingers on the back of her hand. "We are coming to your earthquake?" he guessed. "The thing that you can't leave behind?"

Mouth dry, she nodded. Those two fingertips, so small and unremarkable, seemed to carry some magic strength within them. She felt the twisting tension loosen.

"You don't have to tell me," he said, his voice soft.

"I want to."

He straightened, tucking his hands inside the warmth of his sleeves. But his eyes never left her face.

"One afternoon, when we were meant to be studying, Lanunu and I sneaked out of her house. She had discovered a fox's den outside the city walls and wanted to show it to me. I remember the clouds gathering, growing thick and gray as we ran through the tall grasses of a wild field.

"Lanunu was holding my hand, running fast, while I trailed behind, trying to keep up. Then, in a blink, she disappeared! Before I had time to stop or scream, the momentum of her hand wrapped around mine pitched me in right after.

"I found myself flying through the air. My shoulder hit something slimy and cold, and then I landed hard. For a moment the breath was knocked out of me. At first, I could see nothing. Except for the small circle of light high above me, everything was covered in darkness. I could hear Lanunu moaning. I called her name. But she could not answer." For a moment she found it impossible to go on.

"Where were you?"

"It took me some time to discover the answer to that question. Once I blindly felt about me, I saw that we had landed in a dank pit at the bottom of a long stone shaft. I was sitting in a shallow pool of stinking water."

"An old well?" Asher guessed.

"Yes. Left over from ancient times, when men would dig a pit wide enough to fit two workers at once. The wooden cover had rotted with time, and the grass had hidden it from our eyes. If Lanunu had let go of my hand when she fell, I would have been able to run for help. As it was, I found myself trapped with her.

"Lanunu lay next to me, groaning with pain. I tried to rouse her. She never responded. The only thing issuing from her lips was a tortured sound. An endless, excruciating groan. For hours. She could not seem to stop."

The sound of her nightmares. The sound that still haunted her daylight hours. "I screamed for help until my voice grew hoarse, and still I screamed. It was useless, of course. We were in a deserted field. Later, I discovered that shepherds would sometimes bring their flocks there. None came that day.

"We had never told anyone where we were headed. We had sneaked out of a window and run to find the den. No one knew where to look for us.

"As my eyes adjusted to the darkness, I saw, dimly, the outline of rough steps cut into the stones of the well. They ended high above me. A grown man might have been able to reach them. Pull himself up by the fingertips until his feet gained enough purchase in the rough stones to draw himself to the first step. I could not, though I tried over and over.

"Slowly, in spite of all my effort, I saw the light disappear overhead."

Asher winced. "You had to spend the night in there?"

"I spent three nights there. The first night, I drew Lanunu's head onto my lap and tried to offer what comfort I could. As the night grew cool, I took off my summer tunic and covered her with its inadequate warmth. I had no food to offer her, nor water even though we were trapped in a well. What little water had collected down there smelled foul. I suspected it would do her more harm than good if I tried to give it to her."

"She never spoke?"

"Not one word. Sometimes she would jerk and convulse in my arms, choking. Sometimes she lay motionless, moaning that endless, eerie sound. Then, as the sky above us began to lighten, she stopped moaning. I sensed something change in her body. She grew heavier somehow. More still. I could not hear the sound of her tortured breathing any longer. Even so, I cradled her to my chest, unable to accept that she was gone."

Asher's voice was warm with sympathy. "You were very brave."

"You will find you are wrong." She leaned away. "In the morning, I began hollering for help again. As the light grew brighter, I pulled on my tunic and tried to climb the walls to reach the steps. I only managed to bruise myself as I slipped on the slimy stones and fell, over and over. That whole time I prayed, begging God to allow me to reach the steps. I never did.

"Then the rain began. Later, they would tell me that it was the worst storm in living memory, pouring more rain in two days than we normally received all spring.

"At first, the rain was a blessing, alleviating my terrible thirst. I tried to wash Lanunu's face. Finding it ice-cold and swelling, I leapt away from her. I finally had to accept that she was gone. My friend, my lively, sparkling companion, who could make me laugh on the darkest day, had left me."

Jemmah inhaled. "I renewed my efforts to climb to the steps. I scrabbled, I clambered, I bounced and jounced to no avail. The stairs remained out of reach. Time stretched before me, an unending landscape of terror. No one heard my pleading.

"The rain, at first a friend, now added to my misery. Wet and hungry, I could find no comfort. The well, made to collect water, gathered every drop to itself and the waters rose. First to my ankles, then to my knees. I could not sleep for fear of drowning."

Her voice deserted her for a moment. This part of the nightmare she had never shared with anyone. Not even her family. "Lanunu's body began to float. Bloated, cold, hard, it kept knocking into me. Once my hands fell upon her misshapen face. It was a thing of horrors! My friend was now a monster, hounding me at the bottom of the well. It would not allow me a moment's peace. In the tight space of the well, it continued to chase me, harass me, until I thought I should go mad.

"In my terror, I came to hate it, that thing, which had once been my friend. Guilt and terror mingled, for I felt I ought to look after Lanunu, though only her body remained. She would have been kind to me even in death. But I could not manage it. I became convinced that I would drown in that pit of darkness, next to my friend's rotting body."

She shuddered as the old ghost rose up in her mind, sullen, angry, betrayed. "That's why I cannot leave Lanunu behind. Year after year, she chases me. Chastises me. Her exuberant, laughing face, once warm with friendship, now accuses. Her bloated body now follows me into every confined space, an indictment against me. I cannot leave the terror of it behind.

"Perhaps if I had been able to cling to God in the midst of the terror, I would have been comforted, but he seemed absent to me. In that well, as the waters rose, I started to doubt him. To believe he had abandoned me. I thought, not that he had lied about his faithfulness, but that he *was* a lie, because I could not imagine the faithful God of my childhood allowing such a horror. I had grown up in a home filled with faith. God was in the air we breathed. He seemed as real to me as my own father. But in that well, I lost him."

Jemmah reached frozen fingers toward the embers of the fire. "Did your mother ever pray over you, Asher?"

He nodded. "It's one of my clearest childhood memories. Her hand resting on my head as she prayed. She loved to speak snatches of the Psalms over me. She still remembered them from her early years in Jerusalem."

"My parents, also. I think I am here today because of those prayers. I should have been dead, a pile of bleached bones at the bottom of that well. Instead, God blessed me with a miracle."

"How did you escape?"

"A strange thing happened. The very rain that ground down my faith and stole my hope saved me. As the waters rose, so did my body, until, in the morning of the fourth day, I found I could finally reach the steps carved into the stones of the well. I had prayed for God to take away the rain, thinking that would save me from death. Instead, it was the rain that became my salvation.

"It took an unprecedented storm to rescue me. A miraculous rainfall not seen in Anshan for over a hundred years." She still felt awed at the thought.

"A shepherd found me half-conscious in the field and carried me home. After some days, when my body had recovered from its ordeal, I began to understand the significance of that deluge. God had appeared absent in the rain. Instead, he had been with me through every hour, working toward a miracle. The whole time I accused him of faithlessness, he was busy raising me up so I could escape."

She came to her feet, unable to stay still. "The truth is God never abandoned me in that well. I was the one who abandoned God."

She lifted her heavy braid and turned her back to him so that he could see the hunk of silver hair at the base of her head. "When I awoke safe in my bed, I had this. It was as if those days and nights in the well swallowed up my childhood." She dropped her braid, hiding the silver hair, and faced him. "In a way, I became an old woman at ten."

She fell silent, allowing the words to settle between them like a wall of bricks. She expected him to look differently upon her now that he knew the full truth. Expected him to take a half step away, his lips turning flat and cold.

Instead he wrapped his fingers around her wrist and pulled until she tumbled against his chest. She gasped as his arms tightened around her, at once gentle and firm, as if he could not bear to let her go. His lips whispered something against her neck.

She could not make out the words. But she felt a warm comfort in them. A softness that sank soul-deep.

She was not sure if it was the compassion in his voice or the strength of his arms that loosed the tears. They came in a torrent, sudden as the mountain winds, heaving and violent, carrying with them the bitter recrimination of years.

Through it, Asher held her, unperturbed by the ugly, silent sobs, his hands soothing as they caressed her back, her hair, her cheeks. Spent, she finally took a shaking breath and stepped away.

With the corner of her cloak, she wiped the trail of tears and other unladylike traces from her face. "That did not work out as I had planned," she said shyly.

"What had you planned?"

"To comfort you."

"To comfort *me*?"

"About your father. About being caught in your bitterness and not feeling that you could free yourself from it. I wanted you to know I understood. I may not be shackled by resentment. But I understand what it's like to be caught." She pressed a hand to her chest. "In here."

Asher paled. "You keep doing that."

"What?" she asked, confused.

His lips twisted. "You would have preferred to spare yourself the pain of reliving that nightmare. But you chose not to, for my sake."

She shrugged.

His irises had turned a deep green, more summer than spring. "You keep surprising me."

"I do?" She thought of herself as the most ordinary of people. She lived, after all, with exceptional people, whose gifting and accomplishments made her seem utterly drab in comparison. She could not imagine surprising a man like Asher.

"When I first met you, I thought you were sweet and unspoiled. I told myself that someone like you, cosseted and loved from birth, would never be able to comprehend my life. The deprivations I have had to swallow. In a way, I suppose that is true. Our lives have been very different." He pulled gentle fingers through a curl that had sprung free from her braid. "And yet you have proven me utterly wrong, too. You know what it is to suffer. To feel caught in something bitter and agonizing, like a bird in a hunter's net."

Her throat turned dry at the casual touch. He had held her much more intimately before, pressed her against him, his warmth sinking into her with the caress of his hands. But she had known instinctively that every touch had been meant for comfort. A quieting of her overwrought emotions.

This simple caress, his finger brushing a curl, felt entirely different. This was the touch of a man for a woman.

He must have felt it too. The shift in himself. He sprang back, increasing the distance between them. His arms crossed over his chest, fingers tucked under. "I . . . I had better tend the fire."

She swallowed the laughter that bubbled up her throat along with the desire to tell him that he had already tended the fires very proficiently, thank you.

CHAPTER

TWENTY-FOUR

The rain and snow come down from the heavens
and stay on the ground to water the earth.
They cause the grain to grow,
producing seed for the farmer
and bread for the hungry.
Isaiah 55:10, NLT

Three days later, they awoke to gray clouds that sat ominously low over the mountains. They had run out of food the night before, and their forecast of a five-day trek had now stretched to seven thanks to short but fierce squalls that forced them to seek refuge under whatever cover they could find.

In that time, there had been no opportunities for more revelations or personal conversations had Asher or Jemmah wanted them. And the closed expression on Asher's face made it clear that something in their earlier exchange had made him crawl back inside his shell.

"We are approaching one of my tribe's stopping places." Asher rubbed red, swollen fingers together. "We will find food there."

The stopping place, when they arrived, had nothing but a pasture with dried grass and a clutch of oak trees. Asher knelt near the base of the largest tree and, using the trowel from his pack, began to dig.

"Are you expecting us to die of hunger?" Zarina drawled. "Because it looks like you are digging a grave." In spite of the arduous trek, she had regained some of her strength and, with it, her acerbic humor.

"Not quite. We will need a fire, if you please, Zarina. The wood is stored over that way." Asher pointed beyond the oaks to the remains of an old stone pit.

While Zarina and her mother went to start the fire, Jemmah lingered to watch Asher. Soon Asher's trowel revealed a layer of carefully laid out oak branches, under which someone had spread an old piece of felted cloth. When Asher removed this, she saw a pit filled with green acorns, each one as long as a finger.

"We're going to eat those?"

"I will roast them first and grind them into flour."

Jemmah grimaced. "I did not realize they were fit for human consumption. Won't they be bitter?"

Asher began emptying the pit, piling the acorns on top of the felt covering. "Not after resting in the pit for a few months as they have been. The earth leaches the bitterness out of them. Now, beyond these trees, you should find a patch of wild vines. This time of year, there are often raisins that have dried on the vine. You may even be able to find some on the ground."

Jemmah followed Asher's directions and found the yellowed clumps of wild grapevines. As he had predicted, some of the grapes had turned into raisins on the vine, which she gathered carefully into her sack. She was heading back to their camp when a large shrub caught her attention.

"Pomegranates!" she gasped. Small and mostly cracked, the wild fruit would still provide a satisfying snack for four hungry people who had not had enough to eat for days. She used her walking stick to draw the branches within reach and, wrapping her fingers in her scarf to avoid the nasty prick of large thorns that protected the fruit, picked enough pomegranates to fill her sack.

Cheered with her unexpected discovery, she returned to find Asher removing acorn cupules and shells with a knife. He made it look easy, but when Jemmah attempted to help him, she found the process more complicated than it seemed.

"Careful!" he warned. "You can cut yourself badly holding the knife like that." Wrapping his fingers around hers, he demonstrated how to hold the long acorn and how to cut into the shell with rapid longitudinal strips. Jemmah barely noticed the tutorial. All she felt was the heat of his skin on hers, an odd fire that seemed to travel up her arm and into her chest, until she could barely breathe.

Without warning, Asher dropped her hand and leapt away. "Well, you have the idea."

She had an idea, certainly, though it had little to do with acorns.

After that, they shelled the acorns in silence, each occupied with his own thoughts. Once the acorns were ready, Asher showed her how to scrape off the brown testa, the thin layer of skin that covered the pale fruit beneath, though he did so from a safe distance.

"The skin is bitter," he explained. "As is the tip. So we shall cut that off as well."

By the time the heap of acorns was ready, Zarina and her mother had managed to build a large fire. A small rabbit hopped close to the periphery of their camp. Zarina reached for her bow.

"That is unclean, beloved," her mother said, amused. "We cannot eat it."

Zarina groaned. "Sometimes I feel my Saka blood more hotly than my Judean upbringing." She flung her bow aside.

Jemmah studied the girl who had become her sister. Zarina's father, a blond, blue-eyed northern Saka prince, had given her his pale skin and passion for hunting. Her mother, a woman from a Saka tribe much further east, had imparted high cheekbones, straight blue-black hair, and exotic eyes to her daughter, though their color, a light gray, was uniquely Zarina's. No one would take that face for a Judean. No one would take her for northern Saka or Persian or eastern Saka, either. Like her eyes, Zarina was entirely unique. And sometimes that made her chafe against the boundaries of one people or another.

"The food regulations are not only about Judean law, you know, Zarina." Jemmah plopped down next to her adopted sister.

"No?"

"Of course, it is the Law. But I think it's about something broader, too. It's about Eden. Where we all once belonged, before we were Saka or Israel or Judah or Persia."

Zarina's gaze became interested. "What has Eden to do with eating hares?"

"God had few rules in Eden. Few boundaries. You shall not eat, you shall not touch, yes. But only one thing remained out of the reach of the first man and woman. And even then, we failed.

"Living beyond Eden in this thorny world, we need to learn better boundaries. We need to learn to honor God's you-shall-nots. The only way to learn that kind of obedience is to practice it continuously. Practice it in our everyday choices, like what we eat and what we touch."

"I have to stay hungry because I am not in Eden?"

"You have to stay hungry because your desire to obey God outweighs your desire for food."

Zarina sighed. "Sometimes I prefer food." But the tight line of her shoulders relaxed.

"I don't even know where you put it all. You are made out of one big muscle."

"That has not been hard, trudging through these mountains." Zarina picked up a handful of fat wild garlic. "Look what Keren found. They would have been perfect in rabbit stew," she said morosely.

"We can roast those." Asher, who had been listening quietly to this conversation, placed the heads of garlic next to the acorns on hot stones.

While they waited for the acorns to roast, they munched on the tangy wild raisins and sweet pomegranates Jemmah had found. When Asher deemed the acorns ready, he transferred them onto a flat stone he had washed earlier. With quick, deft motions, he ground the roasted acorns into a rough, oat-colored flour.

Mixing a bit of water with the flour, he kneaded the mashed garlic cloves into the sticky dough. Using a piece of tree trunk from which Zarina had scraped off the bark, Asher then rolled out the acorn dough into thin, round loaves. Jemmah's mouth watered as she watched the loaves cook on hot, flat stones in the firepit.

Within moments, a pile of wafer-thin golden loaves was stacked up and ready to eat. Jemmah bit into the delicate acorn bread gingerly, expecting a trace of bitterness, and found none.

A slightly sweet, nutty flavor blended perfectly with the roasted garlic. She closed her eyes and sighed.

"You're not so bad a cook after all," Zarina said to Asher, waving her piece of bread in the air.

"I am certainly an improvement to death by starvation."

Jemmah leaned back and sighed with pleasure, replete for the first time in days. Asher handed her a cup filled with a beverage he had made using acorns that he had left in the fire for a longer roast. The aromatic drink warmed Jemmah down to her toes, proving the perfect ending to a memorable meal.

Her mother sighed and leaned against the trunk of an oak. "Well, Asher. You have saved my daughter from tumbling down a gorge. You have guided us through winter squalls. You have made bread from acorns and delivered us from Zarina's growling belly."

Zarina's head snapped up. "Hold, now! Last night I woke up thinking a bear had sprung in our midst, only to find it was merely Asher's stomach."

"What I wish to know," her mother said, ignoring Zarina's outburst, "is what you plan next. When we arrive in Babylon, I mean."

"On the other side of the mountain, when we cross into Babylonian land, I happen to have a little hideout."

"Of course you do."

"We can rest there for a day or two."

"Bathe?"

"With as much hot water, lye, and perfumed oil as you desire."

"Never mind bathing. Will there be food?" Zarina asked.

Asher grinned. "A lot of food. Heaps of food. Mountains of it."

"Let's not mention mountains for a while." Jemmah leaned forward. "And after that? What will you do after we rest and bathe and gorge our bellies?"

"After that, I plan to purchase four horses and accompany you into Babylon, where I will personally deliver you to your friends' door."

"Ah." Her mother seemed to relax. "Excellent. In that case, I should like to invite you to remain with us for as long as you wish."

Asher's gaze slid toward Jemmah. "I may take you up on that invitation."

Jemmah could not help the toothy smile that spread over her face.

"I have business at the palace," Asher added. "I will be in Babylon for some days, in any case."

Jemmah and her mother frowned at the same time, though for entirely different reasons.

CHAPTER

TWENTY-FIVE

Babylon was a golden cup in the LORD's hand,
making all the earth drunken;
the nations drank of her wine;
therefore the nations went mad.

Jeremiah 51:7

Jemmah was momentarily blinded by the bright afternoon sun reflecting off the shiny sapphire-blue bricks of the Ishtar Gate. Edged with golden-yellow tiles and ornamented with fantastical animals, the gate and its surrounding high walls had been designed to leave the visitor breathless with amazement. Jemmah guided her spirited mare the last few steps down the grand processional way toward the imposing gate, appreciating the splendor of the scene before her.

The wonder of the known world, Babylon had the distinction of being the largest city created by any civilization. Astoundingly wealthy, the capital of the Babylonians housed one quarter of a million men, women, and children in its cosmopolitan bosom. No one had ever seen the likes of this sprawling center, at once stupefying in its breadth and dazzling in its architecture.

Her father had once told Jemmah that the old Babylon, the one erected in the same spot over a thousand years ago, had been captured and defaced by the Assyrians and, before them, the Hittites. By the time Nebuchadnezzar followed his father to the throne, he had inherited nothing more than a tired, scarred city with a few new buildings, which his conquering father had managed to erect before dying.

Nebuchadnezzar had transformed the city. Its crenelated walls, encircled by moats, stood so wide in places that a chariot could be driven over them. From the Hanging Gardens that boasted broad, leafy trees and colorful bushes rising up from the rooftop of one of the royal palaces, to the seven-story ziggurat which housed the bejeweled temple of Marduk at its summit, Babylon left its visitors dazed with its inconceivable wonders.

It had been two years since Jemmah had visited the city, and she felt disoriented by its noisy congestion. After the silence of the Zagros passes, Babylon hit her like a blast in the chest.

She had forgotten the city's overt sensuality. Passing by a house with open windows, she caught sight of several women, half-tumbling out of their sheer tunics, singing lewd songs as loudly as the men. Asher caught her staring and grinned, making her turn the color of cooked beets. He had not looked at her once for hours, the vexing man. He had to go and pick that moment to turn her way.

She thought of the previous afternoon, when he had sought her out in the tiny courtyard of his house. The memory of it brought a different kind of color to her face, and she blew out a breath in exasperation. She seemed destined to spend life flushing and blushing with Asher around.

For the hundredth time that day, she relived that unexpected exchange. The four of them had finished a late luncheon, and Zarina and her mother had fallen asleep. Restless, Jemmah had slipped into the tiny courtyard to enjoy the calm, sunny day, which in comparison to the chill of the high elevations, felt almost balmy.

A rustle behind her made her whirl in alarm.

"Did I startle you?" Like the rest of them, Asher had bathed and changed into Babylonian robes, a long, formal tunic with loose sleeves and a short, golden fringe at the hem that made him seem unfamiliar somehow.

The attentions of a barber had transformed his trail-rough face into something more civilized, though no less tame for all its neatness. She found her attention fastened on the sharp lines of his perfectly symmetrical lips and turned away to hide her mortification.

"I startle too easily these days," she said.

He came to stand near her, leaving only a small wall of air between them. Her skin prickled in response to that proximity—the almost-but-not-quite touch of his shoulder against hers.

"I have been thinking about what you told me. About your time in the well, I mean." He kept his face averted as he spoke, seemingly fascinated by a rosebush flowering in a profusion of late-autumn buds.

Her stomach caved like a sinkhole.

"We never had time to really speak of it," he added.

"Not much to speak of."

"On that, we disagree."

She shrugged.

"Do you know how I think of you now?"

Broken? Odd? Undesirable? She shrugged again.

"The silver girl. I think of you as the silver girl."

She threw him a horrified glance. What had possessed her to show him that peculiar patch of silver hair? Now that was all he saw when he thought of her.

He held up a hand. "It's a compliment. The silver girl, because silver is refined in a furnace. It is purified in affliction. It becomes more . . . beautiful by it."

Jemmah felt the breath hitch in her chest. *Beautiful?* That was definitely better than odd.

Asher reached out to play with the pink petals of a half-open blossom. "You think yourself ordinary because you do not grasp languages with the same facility as your brother and do not have the natural talent of your sister with weaponry or the brilliance of your father in administration . . ."

"Is there a point to this long discourse on all that I do not do well?"

He grinned. "I am arriving there." The smile faded as his expression grew thoughtful. "Jemmah, I have only known you for weeks, and it is clear, even to me, how extraordinary you are. Your days in the well only made you more so."

Jemmah laughed. "After your speech on how unremarkable I am, your conclusion sounds faulty."

He waved a hand in the air as if sweeping away her objection. "Do you know why you blame yourself for what happened in that well?"

"I believe I do."

He ignored her answer and the side helping of sarcasm with which she had served it. "Because for once in your life you feared more than you loved. Once! The rest of us mortals struggle every day to place love above our fears and fail with painful regularity.

"You do not understand how remarkable you are! Like when you decided to crawl into that cave to keep me safe. Me! The son of your enemy.

"As if that was not enough, you chose to tell me your story even though in the telling you turned white as marble and had to sit on your fingers to keep them from shaking. And why did you rip your heart open? To offer me a bit of comfort. The strange part is that you succeeded. As if you knew exactly what to say. As if you understood me better than I did myself.

"You are like that with everyone. It astounds me that you do not see how remarkable that is. You cannot grasp how extraordinary you are."

He lifted his face and finally looked at her. The dark, charcoal-gray circles around the emerald irises had contracted, and his eyes were molten and bright. "In that well, you had a glimpse of how the rest of us feel. How we sometimes cannot bear to pay the price of love. To offer the sacrifices it requires of us."

He reached for her hand and held it for the briefest moment. "Never call yourself ordinary again, Silver Girl. It's the last thing you are. That well didn't ruin you. It softened your heart even more than it was already."

She gaped at him. For years her parents had called her sweet and loving. It had not meant much. She had never thought of these things as a valuable talent, the way sums or languages or athleticism could be. Asher made her sound rare and precious. She felt a little like she had believed herself a sparrow all her life only to be told she was a peacock. She had fooled him somehow. Made him believe she was better than she was.

She opened her mouth to tell him so. But he had walked away without giving her a chance to speak, as if knowing her response would be a deflection. An objection he did not wish to hear. She had stared after him, slack-jawed.

He had kept to himself since then, barely looking at her, addressing her only when practical circumstances made it necessary.

Jemmah sighed. A large pile of garbage in her path forced her out of her reverie so that she could bring her dancing mare back under control. In spite of its wondrous monuments, the residents of Babylon had a habit of throwing their rubbish into the street without thought for the inconvenience it caused.

The companions made their way down a broad street, riding two abreast without difficulty. The central avenues of Babylon were laid out in a careful grid pattern, intercepted by narrow alleys that wove through the city in labyrinthine fashion, a curious juxtaposition of ancient Babylon's haphazard neighborhoods against the meticulously planned new city.

They crossed over a bridge that spanned one of Babylon's many canals and entered a narrow, unpaved road. If not for her mother's native knowledge, Jemmah would have been lost as soon as they left the central street.

Her mother wobbled in her seat for a moment. Jemmah cried a warning. Before she could maneuver to her side, Zarina had nudged her horse forward to ride shoulder to shoulder with Keren, physically supporting her until she managed to regain her equilibrium.

Even after spending two nights in Asher's hideout on the outskirts of a small town in Babylonia, they were all still weak from their grueling trek in the mountains.

They had spent most of their time in Asher's house resting and eating lavish meals of a gratifying variety: roasts, stews, breads, vegetables, fruitcakes, and date-sweetened pastries served with Babylonian beer and expensive Median wine. In spite of long stretches of sleep on comfortable, feather-filled mattresses and their new rich diet, they all remained painfully thin. The Zagros Mountains had taken their toll on their bodies.

Jemmah's mother had fared the worst of them and seemed on the point of collapse. Kidnapped, jailed, beaten, starved, and injured, she had grown alarmingly frail. Although her broken arm had finally been treated with alum-smeared bandages and stabilized with splints thanks to the services of a proper physician, Keren appeared pale and fragile.

She had picked at her food and tried valiantly to hide her pain. She would need a long convalescence once they arrived at Daniel's house. Her traveling days were over for at least a month, according to the physician.

Jemmah sighed with relief as they neared Daniel's residence. Against all odds, they had managed to reach safety. They had saved her mother and escaped Astyages's mad pursuit. After over a month of being away from home, she could think of nothing so pleasant as enjoying a long, monotonous stretch of days that held no more excitement than the conversation of friends and family.

It dawned on her then, like one of the icy showers in the passes that would drench them in a moment and suck out every fragment of warmth from their flesh, that her season of rest and security would also mean saying goodbye to Asher.

Intent on destroying Astyages, Asher would never sit still for weeks. Likely he would drop them off at Daniel's house and head to one of his workshops, where he could harness his restless energy in the service of revenge. Something inside her caved at the thought. Perversely, she found herself wishing she could return to the harsh mountain passes. At least there, Asher never left her side.

* * *

Along with messages to Cyrus and her father, they had dispatched a letter to Lord Daniel as soon as they had reached Asher's hideout, apprising him of their imminent arrival. Daniel, who had once served as governor over the province of Babylon, was a distant kinsman of Jemmah's mother. In her youth, Keren had served him as a bond servant, though the household treated her more like a beloved family member.

Her mother's great scribal knowledge had been honed in Daniel's household. She had been tutored at a tablet house, the private school Daniel had set up in his home for his sons and Jemmah's father. That was how her parents had met and fallen in love, sitting in that tablet house and making goggle eyes at each other over Akkadian poetry.

Jemmah had enjoyed many a holiday in Babylon, most of which they had spent at Daniel's house. Her grandparents' home, tiny by comparison and filled with grandchildren, rarely had enough room for them. Besides, Daniel's wife, Mahlah, would not hear of them staying anywhere else.

Finally Daniel's three-story house with its whitewashed brick walls came into view. Before they had a chance to knock, Mahlah pulled open the sumptuous cedar doors to welcome them.

Though no longer young, Daniel's wife still exuded elegance with her perfectly arranged and ornamented hair, a mint-green fringed shawl draped diagonally across one shoulder.

The curved lips that dipped into a deep wedge at the center

tipped up subtly at the edges. "Welcome, my dears." A stranger would not recognize the change in the inscrutable face, but Jemmah noted the shift in the brown eyes, the slight deepening of the lines at the corners of them, and grinned. For Mahlah, this was like a shout of joy.

Their hostess held Keren for a long beat, careful of her bandaged arm. "I will need to fatten you up, child."

It tickled Jemmah to hear her mother called a child. Within moments, a servant had taken charge of their horses, and Mahlah had ensconced them in a cool dining room.

"Daniel will be home soon," Mahlah assured them. "And this evening, your family is joining us for supper, Keren."

Her mother's smile might have lit up all of Babylon.

CHAPTER TWENTY-SIX

Remember the days of old;
consider the years of many generations;
ask your father, and he will show you,
your elders, and they will tell you.

Deuteronomy 32:7

— ASHER —

Asher studied the large chamber with interest. A partitioned case made of cedar spanned the length of one wall. Clay tablets and cylinders occupied every cubby, while in one corner, stacks of papyrus scrolls lay in orderly piles. In front of this treasure trove of documents stood a neat table, also of old cedar, oiled to a golden patina.

His host, Lord Daniel, a dignified man with silver wings at his temples and deep grooves radiating from warm brown eyes, sat on the edge of the table. Years of navigating the delicate dance of court diplomacy had given him an air of competence, an invisible authority that seemed at odds with his gentle demeanor.

"Keren has told me a little about you." His voice had a deep, pleasant timbre. "I understand you wish to meet with the king."

Asher bowed his head. "If you can arrange the meeting, I would be grateful."

Daniel smiled. "We both know you are capable of arranging such a meeting yourself, young man."

"Not as quickly as you can, perhaps."

"In a hurry?"

"I don't like wasting time."

Daniel sipped from his cup. "In the matter of meeting with the king, it is impossible for us both, as it happens. Nabonidus has not visited Babylon for these two years."

Asher arched a brow. "The rumors are true, then? He does not live in Babylon?"

"He spends his time in the north, at Harran."

"That seems unusual for a Babylonian king."

"King Nabonidus was born in Harran and believes the region should belong to Babylonia. Astyages swooped down to swallow that portion of the kingdom after Nebuchadnezzar's death, when the nation experienced a period of instability."

"Astyages is good at swooping down."

Daniel chuckled. "Nabonidus might have let the matter drop, if not for the Ehulhul temple. He is a devoted follower of the moon god Sin and harbors deep concerns for the fate of that temple under current Median rule. Nabonidus's mother once served as priestess of Sin, which gives the king a personal interest in Ehulhul. He finds it an offense that the Medes have conquered the province and have allowed the temple to fall into ruin."

"I see." Asher's mouth tightened in frustration. "I had not realized he had quit Babylon altogether."

"The king has moved his residence near Harran in order to keep a close eye on the battle."

"It is concerning those battles that I seek a royal audience."

"I can arrange a meeting with the Crown Prince Belshazzar instead, if you wish. In the absence of his father, the prince rules Babylon."

"Can he purchase weapons in his name?"

The genial brown gaze grew sharp. "If you wish to sell them to Babylon."

"I do."

"I will see what I can arrange." Daniel set his cup on the table. "I met your grandfather a few times, you know. When I was still a boy. I remember him as a gracious man with a ready laugh."

Accustomed to people's eager observations about his royal heritage, Asher was nonetheless taken aback by this warm depiction of Astyages's father. Although he had never met Cyaxares himself, this quaint description of one of Media's greatest kings, a conqueror of Assyria and Lydia, hardly seemed apt. "Indeed?" he said with polite interest. "I had never heard that of Cyaxares."

Daniel smiled. "I was speaking of your mother's father."

Asher blinked. "You knew my maternal grandfather?"

"Beriah the goldsmith, Keren said?"

Asher's mouth turned dry. Growing up in Media meant he had had little contact with his mother's people. "You knew him?"

"Not well, you understand. I met him three times. On the occasion of my thirteenth birthday, my father commissioned a set of matching rings from Beriah the goldsmith, one for me and another for himself. That would have been the year before Nebuchadnezzar conquered Judah for the first time."

The year before Daniel had been carried to Babylon as a captive.

Daniel twisted the gold ring on his finger. "Beriah came to our house to take the order. He would have been about thirty at the time. I remember he made my father laugh aloud. Not an easy task. My father was a somber man by nature."

Asher took a step toward Daniel, curiosity piqued. "Are you certain you have the right man?"

Daniel smiled. "Well, let us see. He had the right name and the right profession. But the true test would come from his lineage. The people of Judah set great store by their ancestors. Did your mother perchance tell you the name of your grandfather's father?"

"Beriah, son of Malchiel."

Without a word, Daniel pulled off the ring from his fourth finger and handed it to Asher. The gold had been shaped into two lion heads facing each other. A skilled hand had molded each tiny beast with exquisite detail, mouths open in a fierce roar, four obsidians shimmering in the tiny eye sockets.

Inside the wide band of gold, Asher discovered a small stamp. "I cannot read it."

Daniel took the ring and surveyed the stamp. "It is Hebrew, the language of your mother's people, though many of your generation have forgotten it. We all speak Aramaic now. It says, *Beriah ben Malchiel.*" He gave the ring back to Asher.

"Beriah, son of Malchiel," Asher translated. His fingers closed about the jewel. "My grandfather made this?"

Daniel nodded. "Nebuchadnezzar had the treasurers return it to me as a reward for a service I once provided." He leaned back on his table. "Like you, your grandfather was a skillful worker of metal. You have that in common. I visited his shop once, when my father sent me to collect the rings. Would you like to see where it was located?"

"Please." Asher's voice sounded hoarse in his own ears.

Daniel withdrew a large papyrus scroll from the cedar case and spread it over his table, anchoring opposite corners with two marble weights. "This is a map of the city of Jerusalem before it was destroyed by the armies of Babylon thirty-five years ago.

"Here, to the north, is the Sheep Gate. Entering through that gate, to your right you would see the glorious Temple that Solomon built. To the left stood the royal palace. My family's house was not far from it. On a warm night, when we slept on the roof, we could see the lights of the palace complex, so bright they competed with the stars."

Using a reed stylus, Daniel traced a line on the map, traveling south. "This is the City of David. The old Jerusalem. Here lies King Hezekiah's tunnel, which he built when threatened by an imminent attack from Assyria. He had it built so that in case of a siege, they could carry water from the Gihon Spring to the pool of Siloam."

Asher bent closer to study the squiggly line of the tunnel. "My mother told me that story. The stonecutters worked from both ends to maximize the speed of construction. It's amazing they managed to find each other in the middle."

"They used the sound of the hammers to locate one another. Your grandfather's shop was not far from the Siloam pool." He pointed his stylus to an expansive area west of the City of David. "This was the market area. Beriah's shop was toward the southern tip, here."

Asher felt a sudden yearning to know more about this grandfather he had assumed lost to him forever. "What . . . what did he look like?"

"Not very tall, as I recall. Pleasing to look at, with a warm smile. His wit is what I remember best—and his booming laugh, which was so hearty, it made you laugh right along."

Asher studied the seal hidden at the base of the ring. "My mother used to laugh like that, before illness and hunger robbed her of it."

"Your mother had not been born when I met Beriah. Your grandparents were still childless then. I remember because when he handed me the rings, he commented on the joy of having a son to share such memorials with and lamented that he had no children of his own to leave his shop to. Your mother's birth must have been a great blessing to them."

"She had happy memories of her childhood." A dozen images of his mother recounting those sweet years crowded his mind. "Her father used to take her to the shop and allow her to play with his goldsmithing tools."

"It was a lovely place, rivaling the best establishments in Babylon today. The shop itself occupied a space larger than this chamber, with an extensive workshop behind it. Your grandfather had built quite a reputation by then. My father ordered a number of pieces from him. Although young at the time, Beriah was already famed for the quality of his creations. You can see for yourself." He pointed at the ring. "Mahlah tells me she fancies she can almost hear those lions roar."

Asher studied the golden beasts more closely and nodded before returning the ring to Daniel. "Thank you for showing it to me."

He blinked several times, shocked at the moisture that had gathered in his eyes. The lion-headed ring had sparked something deep within him. Looking at Daniel's map—following the roads of old Jerusalem, seeing the very spot his grandfather had once worked—had made his mother's world come to vivid life for him.

It was as if in the span of a short hour he had gained a whole family.

Having grown up with a slave as a mother, Asher had always felt as if he had no people. His mother's stories had sounded like tall tales from a different world. A world made dust and ash in the aftermath of a brutal war. Her childlike memories had little to do with reality. Or with him.

Here, standing in Daniel's neat chamber, holding the bright gold his own grandfather had smelted and shaped, touching the letters of his name, hearing his words, learning about his shop, the tale had turned into reality.

For the first time since his mother's death, Asher realized he was not a rootless wanderer. He belonged somewhere. He had a people.

* * *

Keren's family were . . . noisy. Asher had spent his formative years amongst nomadic people. He knew the clamor of a crowd. Lacking family, he had forged deep friendships, a brotherhood built on loyalty and mutual interest.

But this boisterous, affectionate tribe was different. They shared long roots. They shared impossible dreams. And to his bewilderment, they pulled him right in as if he were one of them. In his tribe, he had always been the son of Rachel, the slave. The illegitimate son of Astyages, the king. But he had never been one of them.

Keren's family adopted him on sight. He had no other description for their warm reception, the affectionate embraces, the jests, the pokes, the welcome. Hearing he had guided Keren and her girls across the mountains, they showered him with gratitude. When they discovered that he was the son of Rachel and grandson of Beriah ben Malchiel, a goldsmith of Jerusalem, they doted on him.

They did not care that Beriah and his wife had fallen victim to a plague. That their store was ashes and their home pillaged. They did not care that Rachel had been made a slave and died in her servitude. To them, he was a son of their people, one of the few from the tribe of Asher who had abandoned the northern kingdom of Israel and settled in Judah at the time of Jeroboam's uprising.

It became increasingly clear to Asher that he had found his people. Here, he was no stranger. He was one of them. A Judean.

For the first time in twenty-seven years, he tasted what it felt like to truly belong. Without effort. Without achievement. These people accepted him as he was. More. They offered him his own history. A history he had lost before his birth.

"Of course I remember Beriah's shop in Jerusalem!" Keren's father, a tall man with snow-bright hair, waved a hand in the air, too excited to sit still. "I stood outside his window and stared at his dazzling merchandise often enough. I could never afford any of it. Too many mouths to feed at home. I dreamed of buying a pretty bauble for my lovely wife more than once, though."

The lovely wife jabbed an elbow in his side. "He would come home and describe a bracelet or necklace. *Imagine it around your neck, beloved,* he would say. And like a fool, I did! Somehow, knowing Asa wished to purchase it for me felt as good as owning it."

Asher watched the teasing exchange between the white-haired couple and felt his gut twist with a sharp pain.

He had never pursued marriage. Never sought to have a family. He spent so much time traveling from one workshop to the next, bent over his furnace, striking new deals, always on the run from Astyages's spies, that the thought of a family had seemed untenable. If ever he became a father, he wanted to watch his children grow. To watch their first steps and celebrate their first words. He wanted to be everything that Astyages had never been.

But the life he led made such dreams impossible. He had avoided the very thought of marriage. It did not fit into his plans.

Now looking at this simple family, neither rich nor important in the eyes of the world, Asher felt something loosen inside him. Almost like a broken string, he felt the rupture of it.

He stared at faces creased with the passing of years and felt swept away by yearning. He wanted what they had. This simple love. This unconditional belonging. This long road together. This noise. This laughter. He wanted it all.

But he also wanted to defeat Astyages. He wanted to wrest the power from the man who had forced him to live a powerless life. And these two desires would not mesh. He could have one or the other. He could not have both.

* * *

A tall mulberry tree occupied the center of Daniel's courtyard. Asher set down his clay lamp and spread the thick, felted blanket. The smell of burning sesame oil in the lamp mixed with the lingering aromas wafting from the kitchen: cardamom, butter, and baked dough.

He sighed, enjoying the stillness of the courtyard, and laid his head against the smooth bark. He felt as though he had been hit on the head with Zarina's mountain rock. Confused and disoriented, he tried to recover the equilibrium he had left somewhere in Daniel's dining room. No. If he was honest with himself, he had lost it before that. Lost it on the floor of a dark cave in the Zagros Mountains.

As if summoned by his thoughts, Jemmah slipped out of the house and, spotting him, waved. "Mahlah wants to know if you lack anything in your chamber."

"She has provided all I need. My thanks."

She drew closer and crouched to face him. Her proximity played havoc with his calm, heating his blood. He reached a hand and pulled on a curl that had escaped her complicated Babylonian hairdo. He sensed the rhythm of her breathing change and felt a sudden kick of satisfaction.

In spite of the stern lecture he had given himself only moments before, reminding himself that she had no place in his plans, he realized with tooth-grinding frustration that he wanted her company more than he wanted good sense.

TWENTY-SEVEN

*With him is an arm of flesh, but with us is the L*ORD
our God, to help us and to fight our battles.
2 *Chronicles 32:8*

"You look very elegant," Asher said, his voice sounding husky. "I suppose this is how you dress every day when you are at home."

Shifting, Jemmah settled herself next to him on the blanket, not waiting for an invitation.

"Like this? Fire and lightning! It took Mahlah almost an hour to arrange my hair. I would go mad if I had to go through that every day."

"How do you dress, then?" he asked, sounding fascinated.

"Since we moved to Pasargadae, life has become very informal. The whole place is one massive construction site. On most days, you will find me wearing riding gear."

"And when you go to Anshan?"

"Cyrus's court is not nearly so dignified as the one in Ecbatana. His courtiers are men of war. Nobody wears blue leather boots with elevated heels." She gave him a cheeky grin.

His gaze seemed to fasten on her lips. Jemmah's heart beat like a war drum in her chest.

He glanced away. "I like your family."

"They like you. My grandmother says she might adopt you."

"What did your grandfather say to that?"

"He said he has no objections so long as she does not change her mind and choose to marry you instead."

Asher laughed. The silence stretched for a beat. She sensed he was working up to something and gave him room to form the words.

He adjusted the wick in the lamp to stop it smoking. "Daniel showed me a ring my grandfather had made."

"No! What does it look like?"

"Two lion heads roaring at each other."

"I remember seeing that ring on his finger. Your grandfather made that?"

He nodded.

"It's beautiful." That unexpected discovery must have astonished him. Must have found its way into some aching places. Perhaps that was why he had sneaked out to the dark solitude of the courtyard. "You have lost so much," she said. "Family. Security. Your mother. But all the hardship and loss has not managed to destroy you."

"I suppose not." He did not sound impressed.

"You remind me of that lovely carpet in your chamber. The bijar."

His back stiffened. "I am not sure I like being compared to something people walk on."

"You told me the bijar is called the iron rug."

"True. It endures like no other."

"But its strength does not come from gentle treatment. You

said the carpet's resilience comes from the extra wool weft that is pounded into each row of knots. The weft and the pounding strengthen the foundation.

"You can't make an iron rug without a mallet, without some savage beating, all the way at the core of the carpet."

He made no answer.

"Asher, as long as God is the one who controls the pounding, you are safe, because it is not the mallet that shapes you. It is the hand behind it. The mallet Astyages wielded against your life can be used by God for good. And I think it already has been. When I see you, I see strength. Resilience. I see a glorious bijar."

His mouth tipped up. "Well. In that case, you may call me a carpet."

She came to her feet. "Morning comes early around here. You better head for your chamber soon, or you will yawn through Daniel's morning blessings."

"Morning blessings?"

"We gather in Daniel's chamber first thing in the morning for a word of encouragement. It turns the whole day right side up." She smiled. "Good night, Bijar."

"Good night, Silver Girl."

Jemmah slipped into her chamber, expecting to find Zarina asleep. Instead, she lay sprawled on her bed, engrossed in a scroll.

"What are you reading?"

"A discourse on the benefits of compound bows."

"Of course you are. Where did it come from?"

"Keren found it amongst Daniel's scrolls. It was misfiled apparently. Daniel says he has never managed to recover proper order in his study since your parents left."

"I thought Mother would be in bed by now."

Zarina pointed at a scroll resting on a small table. "That arrived after dinner. She said we could read it. I wanted to wait for you."

Jemmah recognized the broken seal. "From Cyrus. He must have sent it before receiving our latest letter." In his personal communications, Cyrus tended to be brief, skipping the long, formal introductions of royal letters. After a quick perusal, she read the missive aloud so Zarina could hear it:

"Cyrus, King of Anshan, to Keren, my scribe and friend,
All peace. If you read this, you have made your way
through the Zagros Mountains safely. Know, then, that we
have been victorious in battle. The army Astyages sent to
our borders has returned home without conquering a single
field.

Now we need to prepare for the coming spring. You
know what we lack. While in Babylon, endeavor to find us
that which we need most urgently. Return to us soon. Your
place is empty."

Zarina dropped her scroll on the blanket and sat up. "He means weapons, of course. They were stretched at the start of the campaign. By now, they must be scraping the last of their supplies." She pulled her knees into her chest. "Have you ever thought that this war is madness? Lack of weapons is the least of Cyrus's problems. He has half the army of Astyages and cannot pay for merceneries. His treasury is almost empty. One good drought and we will all starve."

Jemmah dropped to the edge of her narrow bed, facing Zarina. "It would be madness if you were to forget that our God is the Lord of hosts and the God of armies."

Zarina rolled her eyes. "Surely he needs something to work with. You can't expect him to carve a victory out of nothing. Do you not consider that false hope?"

"You ask that after we managed to spring Mother out of Astyages's prison? The two of us, alone, and a waste remover?"

"That was different."

"Why?"

"Because we happened to have exactly the right people to hand. In a way, we were better suited to that job than a whole battalion of Immortals."

Jemmah quirked an eyebrow. "And who arranged that? It's not as if we were so brilliant that we actually planned it."

"What's happened to you? You sound like Keren and Jared."

"Do I?" Jemmah asked, taken aback. Had she changed so much? Had the hardships of the past couple of months forced her to lean into her faith? To trust deeper in God?

Zarina waved the end of her braid in the air like a prince's scepter. "You think we will win this war? Without weapons, without manpower, without supplies? You think we will smash Astyages's defenses and take down one of the world's most powerful nations? One tiny, impoverished kingdom of peasants and farmers who have spent the past century paying tribute to those stronger than us? You think we will succeed when the great nation of Lydia had to concede defeat and bow the knee to Astyages?"

"It does sound far-fetched when you put it that way." Jemmah leaned against a pile of cushions. "Of course, our mother did happen to find herself imprisoned with the most brilliant weapons expert of our time. And he does occupy the chamber down the hall at this very moment."

"You believe Asher will help us?"

Jemmah's smile faded. "Not unless his heart is freed." A desperate hope. An unlikely eventuality that consumed too much of her thoughts these days. And not solely for the sake of Persia or out of concern for Judea.

She had become hopelessly entangled with the green-eyed son of Astyages. And she was afraid—she was very much afraid—that her heart cared a great deal more for him than for his weapons.

She thought of the look in his eyes when she had called him a glorious bijar. An odd interweaving of disbelief and hope, despair and desire. She had wanted to pull him into her arms and hold him until the stiffness melted out of his spine and the rigid lines of his jaw softened.

She had wanted to hold him until he gave in and held her back.

She reached for the walking stick he had carved for her. She had managed to hold on to it through squalls and storms and kept it close wherever she went. Somehow, knowing that Asher had carved it for her, had shaped it to suit her height and grip exactly, made the simple walking stick precious. She cradled the weathered staff to her chest, wishing it could steady her listing heart with the same ease as it steadied her shaking legs on mountainous trails.

TWENTY-EIGHT

So shall my word be that goes out from my mouth;
it shall not return to me empty,
but it shall accomplish that which I purpose,
and shall succeed in the thing for which I sent it.
Isaiah 55:11

ASHER

Asher felt like a part of him left with Jemmah as she returned indoors. Leaning against the mulberry tree, he stared moodily into the dark after her. Without warning, Keren materialized beside him.

He blinked in surprise. "You move silently for an old, injured woman."

"You startle easily for a young, strapping man." She gave him a sly look. "She looks ravishing in her finery, my daughter. Doesn't she?"

"She looks ravishing in a tattered riding tunic." He indicated her bandaged arm. "Ought you not be in bed?"

"I have something more important." She settled herself next to him on the blanket.

It seemed rather than providing a private spot for reflection, the old mulberry tree was the crossroads of Babylon. He sniffed. "Make yourself comfortable."

"I will try, though it is difficult with this contraption wrapped around one arm." She dropped several fat scrolls between them. "It is time we speak of prophecy."

"Not this again! I thought you gave up trying to cook my brains with your prophetic foreshadowing while we were in prison."

"I gave up because I realized it was not the right time. Now you know who you are. Not only the son of Astyages. You are Asher ben Rachel bat Beriah ben Malchiel. Judah is in your blood. You are finally ready to understand why Cyrus matters." She looked at him. "Shall we go inside? Even your sharp eyes will not be able to see these scrolls in the dim light of one clay lamp."

"Then why did you drag them out here?"

"To win your interest." She huffed as she rose. "Would you carry the scrolls, please? It is a chore with only one arm."

Asher gathered her precious prophecies in his arms and followed in her steps. "It is a chore with two."

She ignored the complaint.

He kicked a small stone out of his way with unnecessary force. "You are irksome, Keren bat Asa."

"You are intrigued, Asher ben Beriah."

To his annoyance, he could not refute that charge.

* * *

Long before dawn, Asher slipped into Daniel's chamber. Thanks to a sleepless night, he had managed to arrive first at what Jemmah had called Daniel's morning blessing. Two lamps burned on a side table, casting their weak light into the predawn darkness.

With a sigh, Asher lowered himself onto one of the chairs that faced Daniel's table. He had half succumbed to the lure of sleep when the door opened softly and his host stepped in, attired in a dark-blue formal robe, his beard curled and perfumed.

Asher came to his feet. "Lord Daniel."

"I shall not ask if you slept well. Those are impressive circles under your eyes. Keren spoke to you, I expect?"

"She came well-armed with stacks of your scrolls."

Daniel gestured to the chair and Asher took his seat again.

"You belong to a dispossessed people," he said, sitting across from Asher. "A people without a home. Without a Temple. Without a palace or a king. Even our language is fading from our memories."

Asher's smile was drenched in irony. "Perhaps being the son of Astyages is not so bad after all."

"Ah, but we have a promise. A promise for our future. A promise that one day, not too long from this very hour, a man will set us free. One anointed to restore us to our homeland. The name of that man is Cyrus. Cyrus, king of the Medes. Not Astyages. Cyrus."

Asher's brows knotted. "So Keren tells me."

"You must understand, Asher ben Beriah, it is not only for the sake of Judea that I speak to you. Our people were meant to be a blessing to the nations. Salvation shall one day come from the children of Abraham. We were created to be the light of the Gentiles.

"Our freedom, our nation, our worship—these things are not merely a matter of national independence or personal convenience. God's plans for the world are somehow entwined with Judah's destiny. Which makes God's plans for Cyrus crucial to the fate of the world."

Asher felt like a squirming fish under Daniel's spear-sharp gaze. He decided to abandon the veneer of good manners in favor of honesty, even if his forthrightness verged on rudeness.

"Let us assume your prophecies are true. A great assumption from where I sit. How can you be certain it is this Cyrus to which they point? Perhaps your prophets had another man in mind, many generations from today."

"A Median king with a Persian name?" Daniel leaned toward him. "You know how unlikely that would be. Besides, our prophets gave us a timeline. Seventy years from the time Nebuchadnezzar rode into Judea and carried away the first captives. About a dozen years from now. You see why Keren believes Cyrus will defeat your father?"

"Prophecies do not win wars, Lord Daniel."

"On that, we agree. Our Scriptures are filled with prophetic words. Hundreds of them. Do you know how many miracles are needed for one of those words to be fulfilled? How many men and women have to walk in obedience in order for one of the smallest intentions of God to come to pass? None of us can even begin to estimate the threads of God at work in history throughout generations. Our minds cannot fathom the intricacy of his design.

"And yet he chooses to include us in his plans. Use us. Often in tiny intangible ways that we shall never comprehend. Upon occasion, a few of us are given the opportunity to make a greater mark. You can be one such, if you choose."

"You want me to give my swords to Cyrus?"

"It is not what I want that matters."

"As you wish, then. *God* wants me to give my stockpile of swords to Cyrus."

"Is that all you have?"

Asher's head whipped back as though slapped. "Of course not."

Daniel studied him unblinkingly.

"You think God wants me to give up everything? Cyrus will lose the lot to Astyages come next spring. He will molder in a Median jail while my life's work lies rusting in some field."

Daniel said nothing.

Asher flopped back in his chair. How had this man become Babylon's governor? How had he gained a reputation as a man of preeminent wisdom? "You are mad!" he murmured.

"Faith can sometimes seem mad, I agree. But let me ask you a question. Would you rather lose everything in an attempt to help your people, to bless the entire world, even? Or would you prefer to hold on to what you have merely so that you can prove you are not powerless?"

Asher's eyes widened.

"Which seems the madder course? To sacrifice all that you have in the cause of good or to hold on to it in the cause of bitterness?"

Daniel came to his feet. "How do you think you found yourself sharing a prison cell with Cyrus's senior scribe? How many threads lead to that eventuality? How many choices, necessities, exigencies had to intersect so that the two of you could meet? Do you think these things a coincidence? Or did a hand masterfully set each thread in motion?"

"The same masterful hand that refused to save his faithful daughter from a lifetime of slavery?" Asher crossed his arms over his chest until they ached. "If God has the power to free nations, how is it that he could not free one lonely woman? If he could not win my mother's freedom, how can he win the freedom of a whole people?"

"Your mother served as a slave. She worked as a slave. She suffered the poverty of a slave. But from what you have told me of her, she was not a slave." Daniel sat down, pulling his chair closer to Asher. "My young friend, I know something about captivity. Living half a century in Babylon has taught me many things about slavery."

Asher flushed.

"One thing I have learned through those years. Through death threats and impossible choices. Through times my heart was anxious and my spirit troubled. True slavery is here." He rested a hand against his chest. "Tell me. Do you think your mother was a slave in her heart?"

A memory of his mother's wild belly laugh flashed in Asher's mind. She had known joy, that woman. Known how to bring it to others. Until the end, when she had grown sick and frail, his mother had lived freer than the chief of their tribe, who lived always in fear of one loss or another.

"No," he said. The acknowledgment came as a shock. "Not in her heart."

Daniel nodded. "Because of God. Her trust in God gave her a freedom that no slaver's bill of sales could rob." His expression grew troubled. "She ought never to have borne the hardships of slavery, Asher. But do you not see? There are thousands like her in this very land. It is for them that you would sacrifice everything."

His host retreated behind his desk, his eyes far away. His very silence quieted the room. "After all these years," he said, "I still find it strange that the Lord chooses to speak to us. It is not as though we are good listeners. Still, his whispers comfort us. His counsel guides us. His wisdom directs us. And sometimes his arrangements turn our lives upside down."

His smile had a sad edge. "You seem to have tumbled into a world I know too well and have occupied these many years."

Without a word, he removed the lion ring from his finger and placed it before Asher. "This is for you. To remind you of who you are."

"I cannot take that. It is a gift from your father."

"I carry my father here." He laid a hand over his chest. "You need this more than I do. To remind you of a beautiful shop you never visited and a smiling man who would have loved you with every fiber of his being."

Asher clutched the ring silently and sat stupefied as the others trickled into the chamber. He heard nothing of Daniel's morning blessing. It was as if between the time it took for deep darkness to turn into the gray predawn light, his world had been ripped into pieces.

Like an unerring surgeon, Daniel had slashed his way into the suppurating wounds of Asher's heart. *Would you prefer to hold on to what you have merely so that you can prove you are not powerless?*

Was that what he had been doing? Proving that he was no longer powerless? Did his expanding workshops, his endless hours of labor, his constant drive to succeed, his urge to win all come to this? This crack in his soul?

He had known for some time that the trajectory of his life had become unworthy. Wrong. Yet he had felt unable to free himself from the need that drove him. Perhaps that was partly because he had nothing better to run to.

Which seems the madder course? Daniel's question rang in his mind, making him dizzy.

TWENTY-NINE

Because, as surely as the LORD lives, you are safe;
there is no danger.
1 Samuel 20:21, NIV

Asher had disappeared. Jemmah awoke to discover he had ridden off without leaving a message for any of them. She ran to the gate and stared anxiously into the road, hoping for a sign of him. Her mother followed, her steps more measured.

"Do you think he is gone?" Jemmah's voice emerged thin with anxiety. "Forever?"

"It is possible." Leaning against the whitewashed brick wall, she crumpled the trailing end of her blue scarf in a twitching hand. "Of course, he may have gone to the palace to make a deal with Belshazzar, the crown prince. Or perhaps he is merely enjoying a pleasant ride."

"For three hours?"

"He had a lot to think about." Her mother released her stranglehold on the scarf. "If it helps ease your mind, I believe he will return. He has unfinished business here."

"What unfinished business?"

Her mother walked back inside, forcing Jemmah to follow. "He said you look ravishing in a tattered riding tunic," she said over her shoulder.

Jemmah blinked. "He said that? On his own? Voluntarily? You did not trip him into saying it?"

"Well. Perhaps I led him by the hand a little. That does not signify he wasn't earnest in the sentiment."

"You think I am his unfinished business?"

"Of course."

Jemmah dropped her head. "I hope you are right."

"I know, beloved."

Before Jemmah could think of a response, a knock sounded on the gate. Not waiting for the servant, she ran to open it.

"Asher! Asher!" Her relief at discovering he had not departed for parts unknown had apparently caused her to misplace all coherent words.

"Still remember my name, I see."

"Where have you been? I thought you might have left us."

"And face Mahlah's wrath?" He shuddered.

"I am glad you came back."

He pushed a hand through his hair, a gold ring sparkling on his fourth finger. Recognizing it, Jemmah gasped. "Is that Daniel's ring?"

"It was. Our good host gave it to me this morning."

"He honors you greatly. That is a generous gift."

Asher grimaced. "Gift? The most expensive piece of jewelry a man ever bought, if I choose to pay his price."

"What price?"

The shapely lips twisted. "Don't pretend you don't know. They must have told you what they planned." Before Jemmah could respond, he strode inside, leaving her gaping after him like the trout he had caught in the mountain river. Forgetting her joy at his return, she crossed her arms and stomped indoors, only to run into her mother.

"What happened?" her mother said. "Asher marched past me, looking like he had swallowed an unripe quince."

"I wish he had! It would be less than he deserves."

"What did he say?"

"That absurd man had the gall to accuse me of colluding with you and Daniel. Apparently you have some evil plan I know about."

"Ah. I should have foreseen this."

"What? You don't have an evil plan, have you?"

"Of course not." Her mother led the way to the empty reception room, where they could speak without interruption.

"Mother, what is this about?"

Her mother smoothed her tunic. "As you know, we need those weapons of his. But there is only one way Cyrus could pay Asher. If he wins the war against the Medes. If he loses, Asher will receive nothing. Not one silver shekel. Most of Asher's wealth is invested in that stockpile. If the weapons are lost, the fortune he has worked so hard to build will be gone.

"He has lost a country already. After escaping Astyages's prison, he cannot return to Media. He has no home. And if he does as we ask, he may be left with no fortune, either."

"That's why he is angry with me? He thinks I am trying to help you and Lord Daniel press him into taking a gamble on Cyrus? But I have never even broached the subject with him!"

"No."

"He can't blame me for what you and Daniel ask of him."

"True."

Jemmah threw her hands in the air. "I don't understand."

"Beloved girl, did I not tell you that he called you ravishing? In a tattered riding tunic?"

"He also thinks a glowing lump of red-hot iron extracted from a furnace is ravishing. It means nothing."

"What if it does?"

It took her a moment to understand. "Fire and lightning."

* * *

Jemmah found Asher in Daniel's chamber. Sprawled on a stout cushion, he seemed engrossed in some Aramaic document. She sank onto the cushion next to him and gently pushed the scroll aside. "Daniel and my mother do not keep me in their confidence," she said without preamble. "I can guess what they want from you. It's no secret you have the means to help Persia."

Asher's expression remained impassive.

"But I have not been toying with your heart in order to secure those weapons. Everything I feel for you is genuine, Asher."

Some of the chill drained from his face. "Everything you feel for me? And what might that be?"

She felt her face turn lava hot. "Isn't it your job to declare that?"

The corner of his mouth tipped up. "It would be if you did not want my stockpile of arms so badly."

Jemmah pressed an unsteady hand against her lips. "You are the most annoying man ever born. Also, exceedingly frustrating. And sometimes quite unreasonable."

"Not a noble start, Silver Girl."

"You ought to trust me, Bijar."

"I am not skilled in that area."

"I had noticed." She inhaled. "You want to know how I feel about you? Remember in the cave, when I opened my eyes and spoke a few words? For a moment, I was able to feel . . . safe. That had never happened before. The only reason I had those moments of peace was because you remained with me. Not only in body, you understand? Somehow all of you occupied that darkness with me. Without judgment. Without derision.

"You made me feel safe where I have never felt safe."

"That is all? I make you feel safe?"

She stiffened. "It's more than you deserve considering you thought I would feign friendship to manipulate you."

Asher pulled agitated fingers through his hair. "Forgive me, Jemmah."

"With all my heart." She offered him a smile. "Now, Mahlah has promised to serve her famous Babylonian lamb stew, cooked according to Israel's dietary law, without milk."

He sprang to his feet. "We better hasten, or Zarina is sure to eat my portion."

Dinner held a Babylonian touch that evening, with musicians playing the eleven-string lyre and flutes in the background as the family ate. Jemmah sat next to Asher on a narrow bench as servants set down platters of food on the long, claw-footed dining table. There was barley bread baked with milk and butter, roasted partridge sprinkled with vinegar and rubbed with salt and crushed mint, and Jemmah's favorite, lamb cooked with Persian shallots, leek, and garlic.

Although Babylonians simmered this dish in milk, Mahlah had adjusted the recipe so that the meal would not violate Israel's dietary laws by mixing dairy and meat.

Jemmah passed Asher a cup of beer, served with a straw to keep the hulls floating on top from getting stuck in one's teeth.

Babylonia's soil, unsuitable for grapes and the production of wine, nourished barley with greater ease, making beer the preferred choice in the land and wine an expense few considered worth indulging in.

"What are those?" he asked, leaning over to whisper in her ear. She felt hard muscles against her arm. The faint fragrance of cypress made her want to press her nose against his neck. She coughed and took a long sip of water. He had a self-satisfied grin on his face when she stole a glance at him.

She kicked his foot under the table. It was his turn to cough.

"Pardon. My foot slipped. Water?" She batted her eyelashes.

Asher dabbed his lips with a napkin. "I was inquiring about those crispy things before I was so rudely assaulted."

"They are crackers. You are supposed to dip them in the juice of the lamb stew. They are called *risnatu*. Mahlah's cook makes the best in Babylon. Try one."

Asher took two before passing the basket to Zarina.

"You actually left some for me. It's a miracle." Zarina grabbed three crispy crackers. "So where did you take yourself off to this morning? You had half the household spinning around in circles, looking for you."

"Only half? I am insulted. Who looked hardest?" Asher stole a piece of Zarina's cracker before she could stop him.

Zarina choked on a spoonful of stew. "You shameless thief!"

"That's what you get for asking impertinent questions."

Without pausing, Zarina took a large chunk of lamb out of Asher's bowl and stuffed it in her mouth. "Well?"

"What? I am not going to force that out of your gullet."

She waved the suggestion away. "Not that! Where did you disappear to this morning?"

Asher sighed. "I feel like a hare being chased by a hungry

wolf. I went for a ride, if you must know. I had not seen the new section of moat completed last year. So I decided to enjoy a bit of sightseeing."

"The new moat?" Daniel arched an inquiring brow. "West of the Euphrates?"

Asher smiled. "That's the one. The opposite side of town from where the royal palace is."

* * *

The next morning dawned unseasonably warm, and after Daniel left for the palace, the rest of the household decided to spread a few blankets in the courtyard and enjoy the cool breeze.

Asher waved away a lazy fly before shifting restlessly on the blanket. It was unusual for him to lounge about, and he seemed at a loss with himself. He blew out a breath. "I have a lot of questions for Cyrus."

Jemmah's mother sent him a shrewd glance. "Have you?"

"If I am going to lay my life's work at the man's feet, I need to know he is not a fool. If he has some kind of plan, I would like to know it."

"A sensible request."

"Which is why I must travel to Persia."

Jemmah had known that he would not be content to sit back and while the time away without forming a plan. Over the hours that she had spent tossing and turning in her bed the night before, this very possibility had occurred to her. Deep down she had sensed that he would make this demand. Which had driven her to a conclusion of her own. "I will go with you," she said.

Asher snapped to his feet. "Don't be ridiculous."

"He is right, Jemmah." Her mother cradled her injured arm as though it ached. "There are no safe roads. My kidnapping has proven that."

Jemmah crossed her arms. "You are both overlooking an important fact. Mother, you have never made mention of Asher in your letters to Cyrus." They had all known that Astyages would leave no stone unturned in his search for them if for one moment he believed that his weapons-forging son was making an alliance with his enemy. He would intensify his search, sending spies even into the bowels of Babylon itself. They had not dared refer to Asher in any correspondence that might land in the wrong hands. "Cyrus has no idea Asher helped us. Do you expect him to receive a son of Astyages as a welcomed guest?"

Her mother fidgeted. "Not at first, perhaps."

"You think he will trust Asher merely because he comes with a promise of weapons? Can you see Cyrus answering any of Asher's questions? Likely our king will pitch him into a dank cell and call him a spy."

Her mother frowned. "I will write him a letter of introduction. Cyrus will trust my word."

"What can you write that will not give too much information to Astyages if his agents catch Asher? Your very seal would doom him, even if they do not recognize him. This meeting requires a personal introduction."

Jemmah's mother dropped her forehead in a thin hand. "Then I will go with him."

Jemmah knelt next to her. "A brave offer. Of course, you cannot even walk to the end of Zababa Street without wobbling, let alone cross the mountains into Persia. You know the physician said you need at least a month of convalescence."

"This is absurd." Asher took a half-turn around the court-yard. "I will go alone. I can convince Cyrus I am no friend to Astyages regardless of our relationship." He pointed a finger at Jemmah. "Under no circumstances will you accompany me on another dangerous journey."

THIRTY

It is the LORD who goes before you. He will be with you; he will
not leave you or forsake you. Do not fear or be dismayed.
Deuteronomy 31:8

───────────── ASHER ─────────────

They rode east on the main highway out of Babylon, crossing
over the Tigris River. The road brought them back into the
Zagros Mountains, this time far south of the route they had
taken from Ecbatana. Though cold, there was not yet any sign
of snow in these southern elevations, and they traveled with
relative ease.

Still Asher sensed Jemmah lagging and slowed his pace to
accommodate her flagging strength. Unaccustomed to the rigors
of rough travel, she had barely recovered from their harrowing
escape from Media. He clenched his jaw. He still was not certain
how she had managed to insert herself into his plans. Yet here
she was, and here she would stay.

He supposed it was a sign of Keren's trust in him to send her daughter alone and unaccompanied with him on this journey. No doubt it was also a sign of the desperate times they inhabited. Normal rules of propriety had to be shelved when the exigencies of war intruded. In the end, Keren had chosen trust over tradition. She knew Asher would do all in his power to keep her daughter safe.

His stallion pranced a few steps, objecting to the way Asher had tightened his hold on the reins. He sighed and brought the horse under control. If only his own heart could be so easily subdued.

The annoying truth was that part of Asher had wanted Jemmah's company. Had longed for it. The idea of leaving her behind for weeks had bored a hole inside him that he could not seem to fill with reason.

For years he had traveled from one end of the world to another without feeling pinned to any one place or person. He had a genuine affection for his friends. But they did not hold him down. Now this long-legged woman with her big, lambent eyes and wide, incandescent smile had wormed her way inside his head. Inside his heart. And he could not seem to free himself from her hold.

He barely understood himself anymore. Here he was on his way to Anshan. Anshan! Where the treasury sat empty and farmers and bricklayers and blacksmiths made up most of the army. What did he expect to find there but empty dreams and failure?

He shook his head and kept his stallion headed west instead of turning it right around like any sane man would do. Finally the highway brought them to the gates of the old and venerated city of Susa.

Once the capital of the ancient Elamites and an independent city, Susa had been leveled by the Assyrian king, Ashurbanipal, a hundred years earlier, only to rise out of its ashes and rebuild. These days, the Babylonians governed the city, having helped to restore it, if not to its former glory, then certainly into a comfortable residence for those who lived within its walls.

Asher, familiar with the city from his frequent visits, chose a small, clean inn with a wide porch that ran the length of the front wall.

The respectable-looking innkeeper's wife greeted them with a smile. "Welcome, lord. I am Manzat. Do you wish to stay in the public house this evening?"

He shook his head. "I will take two of your private chambers adjacent to one another, if you please."

She gave a gap-toothed smile. "I have just the thing."

"And fodder and water for our horses. We have ridden them hard."

The innkeeper took their horses to a tidy barn made of fresh lumber while Manzat guided them to a shaded yard in the back of the square house. A row of single rooms had been built against the left wall.

She gave them a peek into a diminutive chamber with unpainted mud-brick walls. "This here door has a bar on the inside," she said.

Asher nodded his approval. "That one for the lady."

"The chamber next to it only has a curtain."

"I will manage. And fresh sheets if you please, Manzat."

The apple-cheeked woman rubbed work-roughened hands together. "Of course. Of course. Cost extra, mind."

Wordlessly, Asher handed her a silver shekel. She beamed her approval at him and within moments had made up the pallets in each room with clean linens that still carried the scent of sunshine.

Jemmah collapsed on her neatly made-up mattress. "This is a pleasant improvement to sleeping outdoors."

"Enjoy it. It will be the last inn until we arrive at Anshan."

"You seem familiar with these parts."

Asher leaned against the wall. "I have a workshop not far from here."

Jemmah grinned.

"What?"

"I was waiting to see if you would faint after sharing such sensitive information."

Asher straightened, trying to conceal how that cheeky smile charmed him. "Bar the door behind me. I am going to faint in the privacy of my own chamber."

He stopped at the small rectangular pool in the middle of the yard to rinse his face and hands. The water was colder than it looked, making him gasp as it drippled down his chin. He would have to warn Jemmah about that.

The girl had started to haunt his every thought! He could no longer deny the pull she had on him. Sometimes, when she drew near, his heart welled up until he could barely breathe.

Where would these feelings lead? He threw his arms in the air. If he chose to deny Cyrus, would she still want him? Would she still offer him that sparkling grin and call him Bijar?

And if he chose to give up his arsenal to the Persian king, to burn everything on the pyre of God's promise, what then? Over the years he had sunk most of his silver back into the business. If he delivered all his resources to Cyrus and the Persians lost the war as they doubtless would, where would that leave him?

He might not become destitute, but he would certainly not be rich either.

Would Jemmah want such a man? Homeless, landless, and with no great means to recommend him?

Whichever path he followed, he could not see Jemmah wanting to follow it with him. Wanting to be his. Wanting to hold his hand until their hair turned gray and their grandchildren played at their feet.

Because Asher wanted no less than that. He had acceded the victory to his heart.

* * *

The following morning, they picked up the highway that wound its way southeast toward Anshan, stretching long and narrow at the foothills of the Zagros Mountains just after noon. They crossed into Persian territory, passing a few sparse villages on the way where they could rest the horses and replenish their supplies.

Unlike the verdant terrain which occupied the northern Zagros scenery, the dry southern climate gave rise to a barren landscape. The Persians had learned to pull their water out of the very rocks of the ground, discovering hidden springs in the bowels of the earth. Underground tunnels called qanats conducted the water into their settlements. Wherever these qanats poured their riches into waiting reservoirs, the desert had turned green, sustaining life and agriculture. The rest of the land bore the harsh marks of its arid weather.

The journey from Susa to Anshan would require eight days, barring bad weather and unforeseen complications. Asher had set a steady pace that would not exhaust Jemmah. Posing as a young married couple, they attracted little attention from the few travelers they ran into. On the sixth afternoon, the sky turned overcast, iron-gray clouds portending a severe downpour, forcing them to stop early.

It was only by chance that Asher saw the men, though Daniel would have given it another name. The old governor had spoken to angels and seen wonders. Such experiences had meant that Daniel occupied the spirit realm the way anyone else occupied a chair.

Asher considered himself an ordinary man without such sight, thank heaven. He had tied the horses to a bare tree branch and obeyed the sudden urge to walk to the top of a rocky hill merely to stretch his legs. No angels had appeared to guide his steps. Those steps had saved their lives, nonetheless.

In the shallow valley below, he saw them, four men gathered around a fire, their mounts tied securely behind them. He threw himself to the ground before he could be spotted. A brief survey made him exclaim under his breath.

His trained eyes picked up the glint of metal under a gaping vest. Armor, hidden beneath homespun tunics. The men were dressed in Persian riding clothes, their beards clipped short in the Persian manner. But amongst Cyrus's soldiers, few could afford armor. Those who did would do so openly while traveling in their own territory.

When he detected a sword's pommel peeking from under a discarded cloak, Asher withdrew silently from his hiding spot, slithering back down the hill.

"Company," he hissed at Jemmah, pointing beyond the hill he had just vacated. She made no objection when he grasped hold of her hand, pulling her behind him in a half run toward the horses.

"They are sure to hear us if we ride." He grabbed the reins of both mounts in his free hand. "We must find a place to hide the beasts."

Jemmah tugged his hand. "This way." She guided him up a narrow track and took a sharp turn to the left. "I came upon this while you were gone."

This turned out to be the wide opening to a cave. Asher gaped. "You jest. I am not taking you into another cave."

"Not for us. For the horses. It seems large enough."

Asher felt the knot in his neck loosen. "I will see. Wait here." He guided the beasts inside the cave and breathed with relief when he discovered the high ceiling of the cavern, which allowed a tiny shaft of light from an unseen opening. He tied the horses and left them with a whole sack of hay for company.

"I think they will be calm enough there. Well spotted, Jemmah," he said. "The hay I left should keep them quiet."

He studied the terrain around them and decided that the higher elevations would offer the best cover. Small rocks slipped in tiny rivulets under their leather boots as they ascended.

Behind him, Jemma panted with exertion. "Where are we going?"

He pointed. "Over that ledge. If that curve is not a dead end, it will likely provide a nice cleft where we can take cover."

Asher heaved a sigh of relief when they pulled themselves onto the shelf and followed the rock wall. As he had hoped, the boulder's curving edges fashioned a small cleft that kept them hidden from a casual observer below, while leaving enough open space to accommodate Jemmah.

"We'll have to wait them out." He settled down against the wall and exhaled.

"Who are they?" Jemmah sat next to him. In the tight space,

their shoulders touched. Asher felt a ridiculous urge to draw her closer.

"Median spies would be my guess."

"Like the ones who took my mother hostage?"

Asher nodded and explained what he had seen. "We almost walked into them."

"Thank the Lord you spotted them. We would have been hapless flies caught in a spider's web." She fisted her hand. "Can't we capture them? They cause a lot of trouble, those bands."

Asher's lips tipped up. "You take three. I will handle the runt."

She grinned. "I was thinking I would cheer you from here and you take all four."

"I think we best sit this fight out."

"If you insist."

Asher put a finger to his lips when he heard the echo of voices.

"Fire and lightning!" Jemma hissed. She sprang to her feet and tried to look past the curve of rock. "They are coming this way."

Alarmed, he pulled her back. "Stay away!"

He could make out their words now. "I heard a horse, I tell you," one said, sounding belligerent. And close. Asher pulled Jemmah all the way under the rock overhang, hoping the cleft would keep them hidden from view.

He felt her body tremble against his and realized that with the rocks surrounding them and the overhang above, she would soon dissolve into panic. He tugged her chin. "Jemmah. Look at me. Look. I am right here."

She stared at him, eyes wide.

"I make you feel safe, remember?"

Her mouth wobbled.

He cursed under his breath. Roughly he pulled her into his arms and did the only thing he could think of. He kissed her.

At the first touch of his lips, she startled. But the look of terror faded from her eyes.

His mouth softened over hers, slipping from comfort into something entirely different. A man's kiss. A kiss of longing. She melted into him, panic forgotten, soft curves yielding, molding. He deepened the kiss, pulling her closer still.

He was mad! Astyages's men were roaming out there looking for their horses, looking for them. And here he stood wrapped around Keren's daughter, forgetting all sense.

The thought of Keren abruptly doused the fire in his blood. With a gasp, he sprang half a step away from Jemmah. She stood temptingly close. There was nothing to be done about that. Putting more distance between them would bring him out of the protective shelter of the cleft and expose him to the soldiers rambling below.

With effort, he managed to bring his breathing under control. "Pardon." The single word emerged raspy, making him sound like a frog with a mouthful of water.

She nodded as if beyond words. They stood awkwardly, facing each other, eyes downcast, staring at their boots, at the gravel beneath their feet, at the twin blades of grass that had managed to cling to the side of the rock wall. Time dragged. Finally, when he sneaked a look over the curving rock face, he saw the soldiers withdrawing toward their camp.

"I'll follow them to see if they are planning to spend the night here."

Jemmah made a sound between a croak and a squeak. "Spend the night?"

Asher pointed to the ominous sky. "Perhaps, like us, they are stopping early."

Jemmah slid down the wall and sat abruptly. "Fire and lightning."

"I hope not." He did not relish being stuck in that tiny cleft in the midst of a storm. "Stay here. I will be back as soon as I discover their intentions."

CHAPTER

THIRTY-ONE

Yours, O LORD, is the greatness and the power and the glory and the victory
and the majesty, for all that is in the heavens and in the earth is yours.
Yours is the kingdom, O LORD, and you are exalted as head above all.
1 Chronicles 29:11

Stunned, Jemmah relived Asher's kiss in detail. What *was* that? Had it been a mere diversion? If so, it had succeeded spectacularly.

It had managed to banish every trace of Lanunu's ghost. The dank well had faded away as if it had never held her in its grip. The initial shock of that soft kiss had hauled her out of the old memory.

But it hadn't stopped there. It had morphed. For her, at least, the kiss had quickly spun into something far more captivating than a diversion.

Asher had sprung away from her, his blanched face congealed in dismay, the lips that had traced hers only moments before frozen with dread. He must have sensed the transformation in her. The utter enchantment. Was that why he had broken the kiss?

What did Asher feel for her, after all? She knew he liked her. Admired her, even. But he had never confessed to love her. She laid her head on her knees. The kiss, in all likelihood, was merely an attempt to keep her from sinking into another endless bout of panic. No more than that.

She felt like weeping.

The sound of scrambling footsteps forced her to her feet. Peeking over the edge, she saw Asher climbing toward her. "They are gone," he panted. "Packed up their camp and left."

Jemmah pasted a smile on her lips. "That's a relief."

They chose a flat spot outside the cave to make a fire. Asher spread out his bedroll and sat in the center. "I'll keep watch tonight. In case they return."

"I will take over at midnight."

When Jemmah awoke, the moon had dipped low in the western horizon. She sprang up. "I have slept too long. Why did you not wake me?"

"You were snoring so musically. Seemed a pity."

"I do not snore!"

"I beg pardon. Must have been the thunder."

Jemmah threw a twig at him. It landed against his chest before falling to the ground. He slapped a hand against his heart. "Impressive aim."

"My aim is only average. You are sitting an arm's length away. A turnip could have hit you dead-on."

His lips twitched. "You might as well go back to sleep. I am not tired. If the Medians return, I can always find a turnip to help me."

She sat up. "I'm not sleepy anymore." The breeze shifted the clouds. "It never rained," she said in wonder.

"Not one drop."

"It goes to show that sometimes the terrible storms you expect don't materialize."

"And sometimes they do." He flung the twig she had thrown at him into the fire. His expression grew somber. "If I do this, Jemmah, if I give all my weapons to Cyrus and he loses the war—which he undoubtedly will, let us not fool ourselves—I will have squandered most of my fortune."

She made a sympathetic sound. "It's a great sacrifice."

"Without the income to run them, I would lose the workshops. You might as well call me homeless."

She had always known that helping Cyrus could prove a costly endeavor to Asher. But hearing him put it in plain terms made something in her melt. "A daunting possibility."

He let the silence stretch. "Phray's wife, Stateira."

"Yes?"

"She would never put up with that. Settle for a man without a home. Without a fortune."

"Then Stateira is a fool."

"You would accept such a man?"

She stopped breathing. He turned to study her, his expression unreadable. Moonlight filtered through translucent clouds, lighting his face. Jemmah's blood thrummed in her ears. "I would."

"What if I choose to keep my weapons? What if I decide that Cyrus does not deserve to have them?"

"Tell me, Asher. Do you believe in the God of Israel? The one who reveals mysteries and cares for orphans and widows? The one who is exalted above all?"

Asher twisted the gold lion ring around his finger. "More now than I did before I landed in Astyages's jail with your mother. Perhaps that is why he allowed me to find my way into that lice-infested hole. But, Jemmah, that is not the same thing as believing I should hand my whole arsenal over to some young king who is hanging on to his kingdom by an unraveling thread." He cleared his throat. "What if in the end I choose not to make this sacrifice? Could you accept such a man?"

Jemmah's mind raced. She could answer that question so many ways. Give him half-truths and prevarications. Or she could be valiant. She could offer him everything. "I could love such a man," she whispered, because what she felt for him far outweighed what he could do for her.

He seemed thunderstruck. A myriad of expressions flitted across his features. Doubt. Disbelief. And something she could not discern, like a kind of leashed hunger. It took a long time before he moved. Leaning across her bedroll, he traced the line of her cheek, her jaw, her lips with an unsteady finger. "I could love such a woman."

Her heart leapt in great pounding beats. Heat followed where his finger traveled. She frowned. He had not exactly said he loved her. Had he? "Such a woman?" she asked, fishing for a little more.

"Hmm." He leaned closer, his breath tickling her ear. "One who is not Stateira." Falling back on an elbow, he smirked. "As you see, I don't have very high standards."

She bit her lip. "That works in my favor, I reckon."

He laughed. Without warning, he shifted, leaving his bedroll to sit next to her. "You exceed my every expectation, Silver Girl," he whispered.

"You exceed mine, Bijar."

Jemmah turned until their faces almost touched. Their breaths mingled. Asher's eyes widened, fixed on her lips as they parted.

Asher jumped to his feet as if chased by a hungry leopard. Grabbing his bedroll under one arm, he carried it to the opposite side of the fire before spreading it. "You better stay on your side, Silver Girl. I can explain away the kiss in the rock cleft if I try hard. But any more kisses, and your mother will make me long for Astyages's prison and his torturer's gentle hands."

* * *

Built by the Elamites, the ancient city of Anshan had been ruled by the Persians for over a hundred years. Cyrus's engineers and gardeners had managed to turn this dry southern landscape into a garden, though the orchards and vineyards were barren this time of year.

Jemmah led the way to Cyrus's palace, navigating newly paved roads along which contemporary villas had sprouted next to antique houses. They arrived still garbed in their riding gear. Under a brown cloak, Asher was dressed in a short linen under-tunic and a green woolen overtunic with bands of blue embroi-dery and tight brown trousers tucked into his long leather boots.

He wiped his face with a folded kerchief. "Will the king not mind us arriving covered in dust?"

"Once we take our cloaks off, we won't look so begrimed. Besides, this is not Astyages's court. Cyrus is accustomed to visi-tors in casual garb."

"I can like that much about him at least."

The guards at the gate recognized Jemmah and waved her through. Though the palace at Anshan was modest in compari-son to Astyages's residence in Ecbatana or the royal palaces of Babylon, there was a charm to the limestone building with its turquoise-blue tiles and shallow pools.

They stopped at one of the pools to rinse their faces and hands and to wipe their boots before approaching the Immortals who stood at attention in the waiting chamber outside the royal reception hall.

"I am Jemmah, daughter of Jared ben Hanamel, the king's administrator in Pasargadae. We seek an audience with the king."

"I recognize you, lady." The Immortal strode into the audience hall to carry her message.

A few moments later, it was not Cyrus who strode toward her with long, rapid steps. "Father!" she cried and ran into his outstretched arms.

He enfolded her against his chest, resting his chin atop her head. "My girl!" he rasped. "My girl! How I missed you! But what are you doing here?"

"I was going to ask the same of you." She sniffed happily, overcome with joy at the sight of his beloved face. "You look well, thank the Lord. Are you quite recovered?"

He nodded. "I was coming to Babylon to see all of you. I merely stopped for a final audience with Cyrus before setting out in the morning. Your mother isn't with you, is she? And Zarina?"

"No. Mother is growing stronger by the hour. But her broken arm would make travel difficult."

"So she told me in her letter, which is why I am headed to Lord Daniel's house. What brings you to Anshan? I expected you to remain with your mother."

"I have brought a friend to meet Cyrus." She waved at Asher.

"Oh?" Father's brows rose all the way to his hairline.

"Father, this is Asher ben Rachel bat Beriah."

Her father studied Asher quietly. He had not missed the oddity of that introduction, through the mother's line rather than the father's, as was proper.

Asher flushed under her father's open scrutiny and bowed his head. "Lord Jared."

"That is an Israelite name?"

"Judean."

"Asher was Mother's companion in Astyages's jail. It is thanks to him that we were able to find our passage safely through the Zagros passes."

"It seems I owe you a great debt, young man."

"I owed the debt first. Your daughters set me free from Astyages's prison and helped me escape."

"I had not realized your mother had a cellmate in Ecbatana."

"We could not write you of him, for fear the letter would fall into the wrong hands." Jemmah wrapped her hand around her father's. "Can you join us when we meet with Cyrus? That way you will both hear our story at the same time."

"With pleasure."

Jemmah could sense her father's curiosity pulsing through him as they approached the throne room. It was not every day that she asked for an audience with the king. She supposed her father must have realized by now that she had traveled alone with a man all the way from Babylon. A man who was a complete stranger to him.

Asher's face had grown expressionless. He had grown increasingly quiet since two nights earlier when he had almost told her that he loved her. Almost. *I could love such a woman,* he had said. A repetition of her own words.

Did he regret that confession? He had certainly not expanded upon it. He had not told her simply, without spiral phrases, that he loved her. If anything, he had maintained his distance, keeping well apart from her.

Looking at his inscrutable features, she felt a shiver of dread go through her.

THIRTY-TWO

Thus says the LORD, your Redeemer . . .
"I am the LORD . . .
who says of Cyrus, 'He is my shepherd,
and he shall fulfill all my purpose';
saying of Jerusalem, 'She shall be built,'
and of the temple, 'Your foundation shall be laid.'"
Isaiah 44:24, 28

ASHER

Asher trailed behind Jemmah and her father as they processed down Cyrus's rectangular audience hall. Upon a plain dais, Cyrus sat at the edge of a carved wood throne, studying a clay document, a scribe waiting at his elbow.

He was a handsome man, hawkish in visage with the powerful build of a natural athlete. His eyes, when he glanced up at the sound of their approach, had the look of a man who had not slept well. Seeing Jemmah, he handed the tablet to the scribe and sprang to his feet.

"Couldn't stay away?" He kissed her twice on the cheeks like a favorite uncle and grinned.

Jemmah offered him a bow, graceful as any court-bred princess. This was the side of her Asher had not seen in the mountain passes or even in Daniel's house. Comfortable with court civilities.

"How fares your mother?"

"She grows stronger every day, my lord."

"I am relieved to hear it. The letters Keren sent me were thin on details. You must tell me of your adventures. I take it you had to cross the Zagros in foul weather."

"We did."

"How did you manage to evade Astyages's soldiers?" The question might have sounded casual. But Cyrus's intent expression belonged to a military leader interested in uncovering every advantage that came his way.

"We found our way through the mountain passes thanks to a friend." She turned to give Cyrus a full view of Asher. "My lord, may I present Asher."

Green locked with green, two sets of irises almost identical in color.

"Do I know you?" Cyrus frowned.

Asher smiled with ironic amusement. "We have never met, Your Majesty."

"You speak with a Median accent."

"I was raised in a nomadic tribe in Media."

"How do you know Jemmah?"

"I was in jail with her mother."

Cyrus went still. With a wave he dismissed the scribe and returned to his throne. "I sense an intriguing story." His tone sounded friendly, but a curtain had been drawn over the handsome features. The two Immortals standing behind him stepped closer.

Asher understood. He had felt the same way when Keren had first been dragged into his cell.

Astyages's plant. A spy.

"I better explain," Jemmah said. "Asher makes weapons. My mother has told you of his workshops. She said to tell you this is the man who made your sword."

Cyrus came to his feet. From its scabbard, he withdrew a well-worn sword. "This is your work?"

Asher took the weapon from him and studied it with a practiced eye. "One of the ones I cast with my own hands. I don't do that as much anymore. The workshops have grown too large. Now I design the prototypes and train my men to do the smelting." He felt a thrill of pride at the honored place his blade had found with the king. A king's sword stood for more than a convenient weapon. To Medians and Persians alike, a king's sword was endued with inherent power. And Cyrus had chosen the blade Asher had smelted with his own hands to serve as his personal weapon.

Cyrus's face grew animated. "It is a work of genius."

Asher shrugged. "It is a good weapon."

"How did you land in Astyages's prison?"

"I refused to tell him the location of my stockpile."

"Ah. My grandfather would not like that."

Asher was beginning to like this man. "He did not."

Cyrus crossed his arms. "I do not understand. Astyages is usually generous with his assets. He knows how to oil the right wheels."

"He is generous. It so happens that I do not wish to sell my weapons to him."

"An odd choice for a man who makes his livelihood selling arms."

"I suppose it is."

"How is it that my senior scribe happened to land in your jail cell?"

"Astyages wished to make an object lesson of me." He touched his slightly bent nose. "This used to be straight."

Next to him, Jared stiffened. "Object lesson?"

"He wanted to frighten her. Beating me up was supposed to demonstrate what he would be willing to do to her if she refused to cooperate. She never did give him the information he sought. With Prexaspes's help, your daughters rescued us before Astyages grew too impatient and resorted to hard torture."

Cyrus studied the glint of sunlight on the blade of his sword. "Some things do not align here."

"It might help if I tell you that Astyages is my father."

Cyrus froze. "My grandfather has no sons."

"That is true enough. He sired me. But he never acknowledged me." Asher carefully avoided Jared's scrutiny. When he had imagined this scene, he had never assumed that Jemmah's father would be standing next to him as he revealed his secrets.

"My mother was a Judean slave who had been purchased by the chieftain of a nomadic tribe. Astyages saw her one night and took her. He considered her beneath him, of course, and never claimed her. Not even after I was born."

Cyrus sank slowly onto the edge of his throne. "You are my uncle!"

"By blood only."

"What other way is there?"

"By attachment? By covenant? By law? You and I happen to share the blood of an old man. That hardly makes us relatives."

Cyrus handed the sword he had laid across his lap to one of the Immortals. Gripping the carved handrests of his throne, he leaned forward. "You are the son of my greatest enemy. Tell me why I should not put you in chains right now."

"My lord!" Jemmah stepped closer. "My mother trusts this man."

Asher motioned her to be still. "Because you are the grandson of *my* greatest enemy."

Cyrus gave him a narrow-eyed stare, looking more like a hawk than ever.

"You ask why I do not wish to sell my weapons to a king who would pay me well. Because that king caused the death of my mother. He used her and abandoned her with less thought than he would give the rubbish he discards on a heap. He is an evil man who should be defeated. Astyages will have no weapons forged by my hands."

Jared frowned. "Your Majesty, do you recall the reports on Asher's workshops? That he had sold them? Then Keren found new weapons that were clearly his work."

"She told me she did not believe he had sold the workshops at all."

Asher crossed his arms. "She is annoyingly accurate with her information. I fooled Astyages well enough. But Keren caught my trail. She told me that your people recognized my touch and followed up a few of my sales."

Cyrus nodded. "I remember."

"My king, surely this supports Asher's claim," Jared said. "Why hide his workshops from Astyages unless he wanted to avoid helping the Median king?"

"If you are who you claim," Cyrus said, "what brings you to my door?"

Asher lifted his chin. "When I arrived in Babylon, I intended to sell my stockpile to King Nabonidus. He has a treasury full of silver and an army large enough to stand up to Astyages."

"He could pay you generously and strike Astyages a hard blow at the same time."

"My thought exactly. Instead, your senior scribe convinced me I should meet with you first."

Cyrus's lips twitched. "Keren can be very persuasive."

"She had help." Asher twisted the lion ring around his fingers. "I have made no decision on the matter. I will not waste my stockpile on your war if you have no chance of winning."

Cyrus leaned forward. "But you are considering selling your weapons to me?"

Asher arched a brow. "Can you afford them?"

"Not at present. No doubt Keren informed you of that. I would be able to pay you at the conclusion of the war."

"Only if you win."

Cyrus smiled. "I daresay I hardly seem a sure bet from where you stand."

"You are not." Asher scowled. "Nor am I convinced you are the man to whom I should entrust my life's work."

"And yet here you stand. You traveled a long way merely to growl your disapproval at me."

Asher took off his ring and held it aloft for Cyrus to inspect. "My grandfather made that. He was a goldsmith in Jerusalem before the destruction of the city. This is my heritage. These are my people. Here is my true lineage. A bloodline not belonging to Astyages."

"I understand. I too am the son of Cambyses, not the grandson of Astyages."

"And your name, son of Cambyses, is in our prophecies. Of Nabonidus there is no mention."

Cyrus glanced at Jared. "I have heard of this prophecy."

"Then you know what brings me to your door."

A strange look passed over Cyrus's features. Under his breath he whispered, *"I have equipped you for battle!"* He rose from the throne. "Well, Jared. It seems your god may have a miracle or two up his sleeves, as you claimed."

He lifted a hand toward Asher. "Come. Come and meet my men. Most of the militia has gone home to their families. The standing army is here, of course; and some members of the militia who live in Anshan still come to the armory to practice."

Asher followed the king outside the dainty palace. He was surprised by the dearth of pomp and circumstance in the wake of this king, who strode about more as a warrior accompanied by a couple of his Immortals rather than a ruler trailed by courtiers. Outside the armory, they came upon a group of men throwing spears at wicker targets. The distances were almost epic. Cyrus came to a stop before one. "How is that toothache, Hydarnes?"

The man took off his felt cap and bowed. "It is gone, lord, as is my tooth." He grinned, showing a gap at the back of his mouth.

"Pity you could not save it."

"That's what my wife said. I am so pleased to be rid of that pain, I don't even miss it."

Cyrus smiled and walked on. He lingered to watch a young man practice archery. His arrow landed a little left of the mark. "Try again, but bring your right leg further back," the king said. "Your anchor point is slightly off." He treated the man more as a comrade than a subject, even though his clothing marked him a peasant.

The young man made the adjustments to his posture and loosed the arrow. It landed dead center. Cyrus clapped as if the archer had achieved some great feat. The man's face turned red, his dark eyes sparkling with pride.

Again and again, Cyrus stopped to speak to his men. He knew them by name, peasant or aristocrat, knew their circumstances, remembered their children's names.

In the armory, they stood aside to watch two of the Immortals fight, muscles rippling, skin shining with sweat. They moved like cats, sinuous and fast. Asher watched, fascinated as one twisted his wooden practice dagger in an arc that ought to have been impossible before it landed against his opponent's throat.

"They are good," he said.

"They are the best."

As Asher continued to watch the soldiers around him, he realized that Cyrus's words were no empty boast. A sword fight captured his attention. He grinned as the smaller man slithered under the arm of his opponent and brought his sword down all in one motion, holding it to the larger man's belly. Asher blinked. "That's a woman!"

"You have spotted Panteah, I see."

"Your women fight?"

"Those who have a talent and desire for it. We are a small nation. Every hand counts. Panteah is a particularly gifted fighter. But she is also a good strategist. She'll go far."

"Is she married?"

"To Aryasb. The man who lost the fight."

"Does he mind?"

"Losing? None of us like that. But he is proud of her."

After the tour, Cyrus arranged for an intimate luncheon with Asher, Jemmah, and her father as his only guests. They dined in a diminutive chamber whose walls and floors had been covered in a thousand square tiles, glazed in various shades of turquoise blue.

Crimson-red wine filled their glass goblets. A servant brought them thick slabs of wheat bread hot from stone ovens, served with creamy yogurt spiced with Persian shallots and garnished with fresh mint. The main meal was a hearty soup made with mutton shank broth, onions, garlic, beans, and chickpeas. Asher copied his host, who cut up his bread and dropped the pieces into the broth to soak.

The meal, though rich in flavor, was surprisingly simple. This king ate no better than his soldiers, though his food came in fancier serving platters.

Cyrus spoke of his childhood in Media and his narrow escape from Astyages's plans. Charm flowed from his speech like a natural spring out of a deep well rather than a manufactured pool. It was an unconscious part of him, like the color of his eyes. Though he had intended to stay on his guard, Asher found himself warming to this man who ate bread and cheese and wore a crown. Like Asher, he had once lived as a peasant and had managed to retain the simplicity of his early life in spite of the honors that came with his royal title.

"You will pardon me if I hold my strategies for future battles to myself." Cyrus smiled apologetically, taking a small sip from his goblet. "But I can tell you how I have managed to hold my own against the superior forces of Astyages thus far."

He spread a map between them and showed, step by fascinating step, how he used the very terrain against his enemies. Cyrus wasted nothing. Not a single opportunity nor a single man. What Asher saw, as he heard story after story of battles won and territory saved, was that Cyrus's men loved him.

Astyages bought his men with Assyrian gold. He instilled fear in them. He threatened and bribed his way to power.

Cyrus won them with love.

His men laid their lives at his feet. They faced foul weather and hunger, blistered feet and muddy battlefields, sleepless nights and exhaustion, because they trusted Cyrus utterly. High general or lowly militia, he had conquered them all, heart, soul, and body.

That was Cyrus's true genius. The weapon Astyages had never wielded.

Cyrus's greatness was not a trick of fat jewels and gaudy surroundings. It flowed from his soul and went to a person's head like the wine in their glass goblet. He was a man made to become a legend. A legend that could never be as great as the man.

In one fell swoop, it all came together: Keren's prophecies, Daniel's exhortations, Cyrus's hidden power, like dough mixing perfectly under kneading hands. For weeks, he had been agonizing about this decision. Here, at Cyrus's simple table, listening to the man describe how another hopeless battle turned into a victory, Asher knew his answer.

Nabonidus was a shadow compared to this peasant king.

"I will give you my storehouses," he said by the end of their humble repast, eaten as they sat around a mud-spattered map. "You can have my weapons."

Cyrus grew still. His smile, when it came, was almost painful to watch. "Everything?"

"You can have every last piece from my stockpile."

Cyrus glowed, bright as a seven-branched lamp. "How soon can you fetch them?"

"Ah. There we have a problem."

"I wondered about that."

"Three of my workshops are in Median land. They produce swords, daggers, and spearheads. All the things you need. But Astyages has the roads closed as tight as the doors to his women's quarters. It will require a magician to transport those weapons here."

CHAPTER

THIRTY-THREE

Pray that the LORD your God will tell us
where we should go and what we should do.
Jeremiah 42:3, NIV

Like a wave, Asher's declaration crashed over the blue-tiled chamber, turning it as silent as the bottom of the sea.

His quiet agreement to give all his weapons to Cyrus had shocked Jemmah into dumb wonder. Given the way he had squirmed under the weight of that decision for weeks, she had expected him to need days to make a final decision. Who knew that one morning in Cyrus's company could settle his mind so completely?

But weapons stuck in a workshop were useless in war. Asher's decision, unless it could be followed through by action, meant little.

Cyrus traced the lines of the Zagros Mountains on the map. "The mountain passes you used to cross into Babylon when you were running from Astyages—can you not use them?"

Asher shook his head. "By now, the snowfall will have closed most of the secondary passes. Only the main road remains open, and that is manned by Astyages's soldiers. Even that will be blocked in a month or two. The weather is unpredictable that far to the north, and winter arrives hard and early."

They discussed an alternative passage. It soon became clear that moving the large stockpile of weapons from Median territory would be impossible until spring, when the secondary passes opened.

Cyrus rubbed his temple. "It might be too late. Astyages will take the highway south as soon as the main roads can be navigated by a lumbering army. Assuming you start at the same time, you will have to travel the back roads out of Media into Babylon, find a way south without being detected, and once again cross the mountains into Persia. It will delay you by several weeks."

"I have two other workshops I can access." Asher made a list of the weapons and armor in his hideouts.

Cyrus studied the contents. "This is good."

"But you need the rest."

Jemmah, who had been listening intently to this exchange, tapped her finger on the main route between Ecbatana and Babylon. "Did you not capture a food merchant a while back? One who traveled this route?"

Cyrus glanced casually at the map before returning to his study of Asher's list. "Food merchant?"

Her father sat up straight. "Cyrus! She is right! The food merchant who carried provisions from Harran."

Cyrus dropped the list on the table. "Fire and lightning! I should have thought of that. Well done, Jemmah."

Asher gave Jemmah a questioning look. "Why are we excited about a food merchant?"

"Because he had an interesting arrangement with the Medians," Jemmah said. "Astyages's soldiers at Harran have developed a taste for Babylonian specialties such as beer and dates. They take the stuff home with them when they go on leave and share them with friends and family. There is quite a market for such Babylonian delicacies in Ecbatana these days."

"I am aware of that. Even our small tribe began clamoring for beer." Asher frowned. "I don't see how that helps us."

"A sly Babylonian merchant saw the potential in the situation and, not being too particular about which king he served, obtained Astyages's permission to carry specialty foods to Ecbatana."

"Sadly he ran into some trouble before he made his first delivery." Cyrus's eyes twinkled.

"You captured the man?"

Cyrus rubbed his hands together. "Not only the man. We also have Astyages's sealed letter giving him permission to bring goods into Ecbatana from Babylon."

Asher arched a brow. "You have agents operating in Harran, with Babylon on one side and Ecbatana on the other? It's a wonder they aren't crushed between the two."

"My men are wily."

"I see that." Asher grew thoughtful. "I take it the Median border guards do not know this merchant by sight?"

"We caught him before he made his first crossing."

"That letter will help me get into Ecbatana. But how do I get out of it with the weapons?"

Jemmah grinned at him. "You underestimate the genius of the good merchant. He did not want a wasted journey back home. So he also wheedled permission from Astyages to carry Median foods back to the soldiers in the battlefront at Harran. They miss their wine and fruits, you see."

"You have a letter with Astyages's seal allowing passage to and from Ecbatana?"

She nodded happily. "With big carts full of merchandise."

Asher took a sip from his glass goblet. "I see I am about to change profession."

Jemmah's mind was two steps ahead of his. "As am I. I will serve as your most humble servant."

Three pairs of astonished eyes swiveled her way.

Asher's lips turned flat. "You can forget that idea."

Her father cleared his throat. "He is right, my girl. This journey is not for you."

Cyrus tapped a finger against his chin. "You have proven more useful than three Immortals in the past couple of months, Jemmah. If not for you, Keren—not to mention Asher—would likely still be stuck in that prison cell. And of course, the very idea we are about to implement came from you. I am most grateful to you. But it is time for you to enjoy a respite. With your father headed to Babylon, I could use you in Pasargadae. Johanan will be happy for your help."

Jemmah wilted. The three of them banded together, every spine straight with implacable intention, crushed any hope she had of bringing them to her way of thinking.

*　*　*

Peace, like a coquettish lover, refused to be her companion. Jemmah had thought she had let go of the desire to accompany Asher. Like her brother, she had learned acceptance in the war years. She had gained the hard discipline of obedience.

But when she prayed in her chamber that night, peace would not come. She felt convinced that she was meant to go on this journey. That somehow Asher would come to need her. The harder she prayed, the more convinced she became.

She tried to broach the subject with her father and found him immovable on his decision. Over two months had passed since he had seen her. Two months of anxiety. She understood why he was unprepared to let her traipse off into danger again.

She even agreed with him.

None of that good reasoning shook off this growing conviction, however. God wanted her on this journey. She had a role to play.

Sleepless, she stared at the dark walls of her chamber. Could she disobey her father and her king? What would Asher say if he found himself saddled with the responsibility of protecting her again?

Was it pride that pressed her into this untenable path? Could she be deceiving herself into doing exactly as she liked in the name of God? That question more than any tormented her through the night. She stared it squarely in the face. Parsed the threads of her heart one by one: desire, obstinacy, pride, and defiance. But after she picked at each thread, the call remained.

Go with Asher.

* * *

Astyages's sealed letter gave permission for passage from Harran into Ecbatana through the Zagros Mountains. This meant that Asher would once again have to cross west into Babylonian land and navigate his way back into Media rather than travel directly north, which would have been the faster route. They had already found the merchant's cart and a few of his casks of beer in Cyrus's warehouse, providing a perfect cover.

Racing against time, Asher had decided to leave with Jemmah's father since they would both be traveling to Babylon. By dawn, the men were ready.

Though nothing about her plan was guaranteed, Jemmah now felt the peace that had evaded her the evening before. If God wanted her on this journey, he would open the way.

She took leave of her father first, hoping the predawn darkness covered the shamed flush staining her cheeks. Turning to Asher, she said, "God go with you, Asher."

"And with you," he said. An odd expression passed over his face like a wave. "I will come back, Silver Girl."

"I hope so, Bijar."

The men walked away, distracted by a mule that had turned lame. No one watched the cart. Jemmah scrambled in and found a convenient hiding spot behind the wooden casks of beer, pulling the blanket that covered the back of the cart more securely over her head. She had already tucked food and water in one corner.

The idea had come to her from Zarina, who at seven had managed to hide in her father's war cart for days. Of course she had been much smaller. Jemmah folded and refolded her long legs and arms to find a comfortable position.

The cart lurched forward. No going back now.

The first day proved the hardest. She lived in dread of discovery, afraid to scratch the itch on her nose, to cough, to sneeze. When the daylight hours faded and they stopped for the evening, she took her first easy breath in hours. She had done it! She had stayed hidden. While the men slept, Jemmah sneaked out to stretch her cramped muscles and see to her body's needs, scrambling into the cart before sunrise.

Five days passed without incident. Then six. The rumbling

cart made for an uncomfortable ride, the wooden sides poking into her back no matter how she squirmed. The worst part of her secret conveyance proved to be boredom. Asher and her father passed the time conversing, but their words were swallowed by the clangor of the wheels.

Though she was never alone, the silence of the cart turned into loneliness, irksome like a blister rubbing against a shoe, growing more painful with the passing hours.

The monotony of her hours lulled her into a false sense of security. She thought she would ride like this all the way into Ecbatana. But on the seventh day, everything changed.

The men had planned to stop at Asher's workshop outside Susa to arrange for the transport of a large shipment of compound bows and arrows to Anshan. A few hours before arriving at their destination, they stopped at a modest oasis with a single well and a handful of crooked trees to water the animals.

Her father had unhitched the mules and was leading them to the trough. Asher sauntered to the back of the cart to fetch his cloak. He turned, distracted by something her father was telling him. Through the narrow spaces between the wooden casks, Jemmah had a clear view of his laughing profile.

And of the man who stepped out furtively from behind a tree trunk, dagger raised, aimed at Asher's back.

"Behind you!" Her warning came too late. Asher would never be able to turn in time to deflect the attack.

Why did she always find herself in these unwholesome situations? No time to pray. To plan. To consider.

In one smooth motion, Jemmah grabbed her walking stick and, coming up in a crouch, thrust it forward like a battle staff, past Asher's turning body, and straight into the man's chest. She executed the thrust so perfectly even Irda would have approved.

The knife tip went flying into the air. The man stumbled backward, regained his balance, and lunged at Asher. This time he was ready for his attacker. The series of defensive moves came so swift, Jemmah did not even see half of them. A moment later, the man lay on the ground, unconscious.

No one said a word.

Her father studied the prone body in the sand and bent to pick up the abandoned knife. As if in one long-rehearsed motion, he and Asher turned together to stare at her, still crouching under the cover of the blanket.

She swallowed. Her limbs were shaking. She shoved aside the blanket and straightened. Her father's face was turning red, while Asher had grown pale. Both of them looked like they wanted to strangle her.

She clutched her walking stick and wove her way past the beer casks to the edge of the cart, where the wooden gate hung open. "Would this be a good time to point out that I saved Asher's life?"

THIRTY-FOUR

Our God is a God of salvation,
and to GOD, the Lord, belong deliverances from death.
Psalm 68:20

ASHER

It took a long while for Asher to find his tongue. "What are you doing here, Jemmah?"

She pointed at the unconscious man. "I came to help."

Asher fought the violent desire to shake the woman until her teeth rattled. Did she not understand the danger she had faced? "We agreed that you would return to Pasargadae."

"I know. I ask your pardon. I could not do it."

"I would have expected such a stunt from Zarina," Lord Jared said, tight-lipped. "She is young and impetuous. You know better."

Jemmah dropped her head. "I am sorry."

The man on the ground moaned. Asher put his booted heel on his back, holding him secure to ensure he did not create further mischief. "You lied to us. You said goodbye, all dewy-eyed with pretend grief, knowing the whole time that you intended to hide in there."

She drew herself up. "I was not sure I would manage to stow away. My goodbyes were sincere."

"Why?" Lord Jared took a long step toward her. "Why did you defy the king? Why did you disobey me?"

She winced. "I had every intention of obeying you. But that night I could not sleep. I had a sense that I was to come. That I was needed."

Lord Jared grew still. "What sense?"

"Father, I prayed. For hours. I could not shake the feeling that I should accompany you." She pointed to the man stirring under Asher's boot. "It's a good thing I did, wouldn't you say? Asher would be dead if I had not been hiding in the cart."

Her hands were shaking. She wasn't nearly as composed as she wanted them to believe. Asher cursed under his breath. Striding forward, he grasped her about the waist and pulled her out of the cart. She tumbled into him, not quite steady, her curves soft and warm, pressing against his chest. He let out an explosive breath.

"Sit down," he snapped, his voice tight. "Sit down before you fall."

She obeyed him, leaning against a tree, her hand wrapped about her stick as if it could hold her up while she sat.

Asher turned his attention to the fool who had tried to kill him. He was stirring in earnest now, eyes blinking dazedly. Asher turned him over and pressed the point of his dagger against the thick neck. "Who are you? Spit it out and be quick."

The man stumbled over his words. "Be merciful, lord! Be merciful."

"I did not notice you offering mercy when you pointed your rusty knife at my back. I want to know why."

"I . . . well, I wanted the beer, see."

"Are you alone?"

The rheumy eyes took on a sly look. "Very alone."

"You thought to take two men all by yourself?"

"Well, your companion would hardly want to come against me with my blade at your back, would he? I could have succeeded if that fiend had not attacked me from her hiding place in the cart. It's not womanly, I say, to bash a man with no warning."

Asher pressed the dagger point deeper into the jiggly skin of his throat. "Never mind her. I want the truth. Now."

The man stared into the trees. "I had a friend. He must have scarpered when you beat me, curse the coward."

Without a word, Lord Jared slipped into the trees.

"Your name?"

"In these parts, they know me as Huban."

Asher frowned. "I've heard of you."

Huban grinned, brown teeth foul with an unearthly stench. "I'm famous."

"As a common thief. When did you expand your business to murder?"

The lumpy face turned shifty. "I did not mean to murder. Just the threat of a knife to make you friendly. I wanted the beer, is all. No harm done, young lord, eh? Why not let me go my way and I let you go yours?"

Jemmah jumped to her feet. "He is lying! That knife was no mere threat. He intended to use it. I saw it in his eyes, in the bulge of his muscles, the lift of his arm. He meant to shove that blade all the way in."

Asher ground his teeth. "Sit down before you fall over." She looked too pale, all trace of color washed out of her face.

"But, Asher, I am telling you . . ."

"I know, woman. Now sit and keep your peace." He did not doubt Jemmah's word. She had saved his life. Of that he was certain.

He ground his boot into the thief's belly. "Who paid you to kill me?"

"Pay me to kill you? No one. I said I wanted your beer."

Asher pressed the knife deeper until a few drops of blood welled up at the sunburned throat. "I am losing patience."

Huban sputtered. "Young lord, watch that blade! It's sharp as a demon's tooth. I am only a thief. You said so yourself."

The knife went in deeper. Blood flowed more freely. The thief cried out. "Stop, stop! I will tell you."

Asher eased the pressure on his blade. "Well?"

"A Mede came sniffing around, looking for the man who made weapons hereabouts. He offered a reward for any man who found you."

"What reward?"

"A bag of gold to find your workshop. Another for your head."

Jemmah gasped and turned her stick until it sat in her palm like a battle staff, her expression thunderous. For some reason, her fierce I-will-annihilate-you-if-you-try expression made Asher smile. He jiggled his boot in the thief's belly. "Go on."

Huban licked dry lips. "I had seen you once, driving a cartful of apples with one of your men. Only they weren't apples. Underneath, the cart was full of iron-tipped arrows."

"And how would you know that?"

"I am partial to apples, see? I meant to take a few. But when I stuck my hand in, I nearly sliced off my thumb on a sharp arrow tip." He wiggled his thumb. Under the thick crusting of dirt ran a shiny white scar. "I made my escape right quick. Didn't think it was good for my health to tangle with you."

"You were wiser back then, it seems."

"When the Mede came seeking a man who made weapons, I knew it must be you. I've been keeping an eye out since, hoping to run into you again. This morning I spotted you some ways back down the road. I recognized you, though your hair is shorter. I followed you to this here oasis."

"Why didn't you wait until I made my way to my workshop? Then you would have had two bags of gold."

"I am not a greedy man, lord. Who knew where you were headed? I saw my chance when you turned your back and decided one bag would be plenty."

"One bag of gold and a cartload of Babylonian beer," Asher said, amused. "You couldn't resist the temptation."

So Astyages had discovered he had a workshop in this neighborhood. At least he had not found the location yet. But his pincers were tightening. Were other criminals sniffing around, looking for him, emboldened by the promise of gold? In spite of all his caution, Huban had managed to finger him. How many others would find their way to his door?

If he had not decided to give all his armament to Cyrus, he might have lost the lot to Astyages sooner or later.

He trussed up Huban like a piglet, arms and legs bound together in unbreakable knots while the thief cried his protest and wriggled like an eel. Lord Jared strode into the oasis, frog-marching a skinny, pimpled youth in front of him.

"Found him running down the road," he said, panting. "He's fast for a runt."

Asher told him what he had discovered from the thief while they bound his skinny accomplice.

Lord Jared crouched next to Huban, looking grave. "Where is this Mede?"

"I cannot say, master."

"How were you to contact him to claim your bag of gold?"

Huban stuttered. Asher twisted the rope around his wrists, making him squeal. "In Susa, master!"

Lord Jared bent his head closer to the man's face. "More specific, please. Susa is a big place."

Huban refused to say more. With a sigh, Asher pressed the edge of his blade to his bleeding throat again. "I thought we had an understanding."

The skinny boy cried out. "Don't hurt him! The Mede waits at the tavern. The one across from the persimmon fountain. He is there most evenings."

Asher studied the boy's face. "Is this fool your father?"

"Yes, lord."

"Well, you cannot help that." He sauntered to the cart and emptied a bit of beer into a cup and carried it to the boy.

Huban twisted his body, pinning Asher with greedy eyes. "What about me?"

"You don't deserve any." He studied the thieves. "What are we to do with these exemplary citizens?"

"I have an idea." Lord Jared fetched his writing implements from the cart. "You cannot be married to Keren for over twenty years and travel without these." Asher watched with interest as he wrote two signs on scraps of papyrus. The first read *Huban the Thief*, and the other, *Huban's Accomplice*.

He crouched by the pimply youth. "Listen to me, boy. Your father's fate is sealed. He is a thief and a murderer, too, but for my daughter's quick actions. He will face the judgment due him. To you, I give a choice. You can accompany him. In which case, I will tuck this sign under your ropes and drop you off at the gates of Susa with him. Do you know what it says?"

The boy shook his head, wide-eyed. "I cannot read, master."

"It says, *Huban's Accomplice*. You can stay with your father and be judged alongside him. Or you can part from him and choose a different path. An honest life. If you wish it, I will make that possible."

The boy started to snivel, great globs of tears mixing with mucus. "I cannot leave him! I have no one else."

Huban, slithery snake that he was, still seemed to have some thin thread of fatherly affection left in him. "An idiot as always," he said with a sniff. "Resist being such a fool for once and do as the man says. I don't want you anywhere near me."

"But, Father!"

"I said I don't want you!" Huban addressed Jared. "He is no son of mine. You can take him."

Lord Jared nodded. "Boy, do you agree?"

The boy's dribbling response emerged in hushed misery. "Yes, lord."

"Now what?" Asher asked.

"Now we make a new plan."

Lord Jared waited until they had walked far enough to speak without being overheard. "I cannot go to Babylon given what we have discovered. I must pursue this agent of Astyages. He poses too great a danger to you. If he finds your trail, he will pursue you. Even if you manage to evade him, he may hear about your new disguise and send that information to Ecbatana."

"I imagine my reception will not prove too warm if he does." Given that Astyages had ordered his death, his disguise would be the only thing standing between him and a sharp blade.

Lord Jared pressed a hand against Asher's arm. "I will ensure that he is removed as soon as possible."

Asher frowned. "You will go alone? What if he has an accomplice?"

"Cyrus has a man in Susa. I will seek him out. We will try to capture Astyages's spy alive if we can. No doubt he will prove a fount of useful information." He adjusted his leather eye patch. "The most important thing is to keep you safe so you can go on to Ecbatana and fetch your weapons. Agreed?"

"Agreed." Asher thought for a moment. "I will close down the workshop here when I send my men to Cyrus with the weapons."

"Good plan. Even if I capture Astyages's agent, they have already come too close for the workshop to remain safe."

"What will you do with the boy?"

"I know a family in Susa who will take him in for my sake. They are good people. Without his father's bad influence, he will have a chance at a new life."

Asher cocked his head to one side. "Do you show grace to all your enemies?"

"When possible. Do you object?"

"On the contrary. I wish there were more men like you."

The single hazel eye bored into Asher. "There is another matter we must discuss."

"Jemmah." The name tasted bittersweet on his lips.

Lord Jared bowed his head. "Whether she comes with me or goes with you, she will face danger now."

Asher pursed his lips. Jemmah had saved his life. He supposed he ought to feel grateful. Instead, a torrent of anger bubbled out of him. "She lied to me." He was shocked by the vehemence that burst out with those words.

"And to me. I have never known her to practice deception before. Which makes me wonder why she resorted to such means in order to accompany us." He raised a placating hand. "I am not defending her actions, you understand. I merely wonder what drove her to it."

"In the end, a lie is a lie."

Lord Jared nodded, acceding the point. "She should have told me of her prayer."

"Would you have let her come if she had?"

"I would have considered it."

"I would not."

"Which may be why she did not speak. No matter. While I do not approve her methods, we are here. She is with us. We must decide what to do with her. Does she come with me or go with you? I must know your mind before I make my decision."

Asher shook his head. "It's an impossible situation. She should not have placed herself in so much danger."

Lord Jared's smile was tinged with sadness. "My daughter was raised in the midst of war. Lest you forget, she helped set you free from Astyages's heavily guarded prison. And she saved your life just now. She is not helpless."

"Yes." The admission came begrudgingly. He wondered why he could not shake his anger the way Lord Jared had. Why he could not reason through it.

She had betrayed him! Taken advantage of his trust to do what she wanted. How could he trust her now? How could he be sure that every soft word was not a manipulation?

Asher hesitated. He had missed her through every hour of the past seven interminable days. The only thing that had made her absence tolerable had been the knowledge that she was tucked away in the safety of Pasargadae. He saw no safety now. She either had to accompany him back through the Zagros Mountains or tail her father to Susa in search of Astyages's spy. He winced at the choices before him.

She had been so certain that God had wanted her to come. He could not deny he would now be lying in a pool of his own blood if she had not been hiding in his cart. He drew a tired hand over his face. "Let the choice be hers."

* * *

An hour later, they dropped three men outside the gates of Susa. One bound up in ropes with a scrap of papyrus declaring him a thief, another wearing a leather eye patch, dressed in the neat robes of a scribe, accompanied by a bumbling, skinny servant. Before striding away, Lord Jared lingered next to the cart.

"My wife trusted you with my daughter. I assume I can do the same?"

Asher's chin jerked down, the small movement a solemn promise. Lord Jared nodded in return, accepting the promise.

Asher did not say a single word to Jemmah for the two hours it took to navigate their way to his workshop. The last half hour, as they left the packed dirt of the main road, the track became rough. Bump after bump jarred their bones. Once Jemmah lost her hold on the side of the cart, and her body catapulted against his. He steadied her with one arm, holding on to the reins with the other.

"Pardon," she said. And although he ignored her, he could not extinguish the thrill of satisfaction he felt at the flush that crept up her throat and stained her cheeks.

It was a relief to finally arrive. He had five men working for him in this location, each one an old hand at his business. Though surprised by the news that they must abandon the place, they wasted no time with making objections. They had always known the end might come without warning.

By dawn they had packed their whole inventory into carts. The casual observer watching the small caravan only saw carts full of cheap rugs and mats being driven by stodgy merchants whose loose robes hid the bulging muscles of men who worked a forge. They would hire extra guards in Susa for safety before setting out for Anshan.

"Time to become a Babylonian food merchant," Asher said.

CHAPTER

THIRTY-FIVE

Behold, how good and pleasant it is
when brothers dwell in unity!
It is like the precious oil on the head,
running down on the beard.
Psalm 133:1-2

Jemmah followed Asher into the workshop as he carried the hefty wooden chest that had belonged to the merchant Cyrus's spies had intercepted. He tugged open its expensive iron clasp and rummaged through the contents. Holding out an armful of items, he said, "I am going to change." They were the first words he had spoken to her in hours.

"You will not wait until we are closer to the border?"

"My transformation must begin today. Since there is a price on my head, the earlier I change my identity, the safer we will be." He waved a hand toward her. "Have you brought anything apart from your Persian riding gear? You will not convince anyone you are my servant dressed like this."

"I paid one of Cyrus's servants for her old robes." The girl had squawked like a goose when she had seen the coins Jemmah was willing to pay for her threadbare clothing.

Asher indicated the room off the workshop. "You can change in there. I will remain here."

The chamber had been stripped of all his personal effects, leaving it bare except for a wide table and a leather-backed chair. Jemmah discarded her grubby riding outfit with relief and indulged in the first luxury she had enjoyed in a week. She scrubbed her body clean thanks to the bowl of water and lye Asher had provided.

She donned her own clean loincloth and undertunic before putting on the simple brown robe she had purchased from the palace maid. She twisted her hair into the braids popular amongst Babylonian women and threw on the thick felt cloak the girl had given her. The gray fabric settled above her ankles, its ragged edge hanging crooked. She examined herself one last time and decided she would pass for a Babylonian servant.

She opened the door to the workshop and froze when she came face-to-face with a bearded stranger. "Fire and lightning!" An irresistible urge to giggle welled up in her chest. It required all her will to keep her face straight.

"If you laugh, I will leave you here."

She clapped a hand over her mouth. Asher had donned a flowing wool robe embroidered with colorful flowers, held in place with a purple belt. Over a long, elaborately curled wig, he wore a purple-and-blue turban on his head. But the most exotic thing about him, and the cause of the bubbling giggles she could not swallow, was the false beard. Reaching his chest, the blunt-edged bush had rounded curls clipped at regular intervals with golden rings.

"You look . . . resplendent."

"I look like Kandalanu the merchant. Babylonian courtiers are mad for wigs and false beards, and the wealthy merchants follow in their footsteps. If I discard this frippery, I am sure to be suspected as an imposter."

"I see why you came over to Cyrus's side. The Persians are too poor to afford all this false hair."

Asher pulled himself up with dignity. "What matters is that the guards believe I am Kandalanu when we cross into Median land."

"I believe you will find no problem there. You look more like Kandalanu than Kandalanu."

"One more word and you can walk to Media."

Jemmah bowed, a humble servant who knew when to keep her mouth shut.

Asher took a moment to write a short missive. "In case one of Astyages's spies finds the place," he said, head bent to his strip of papyrus. Jemmah caught a glimpse of the message on their way out:

> To Astyages, king-for-the-moment
> From one you sired but never fathered
>   You gave me nothing. I return your favor.

* * *

Riding next to Asher ought to have been more comfortable than her journey to Susa, hidden behind the creaky casks of beer. Asher's tense silence, however, made every hour crawl. She had hoped after their humorous exchange about his disguise that his reserve had melted. But he was clearly determined to maintain the distance between them.

After three days, Jemmah found his reticence intolerable. "For your own sanity you ought to speak to me. Think of the endless hours stretched ahead of you. You will explode from boredom."

"I like my own company."

The cart dropped into a large pothole, throwing Jemmah sideways. She grabbed the handrail to straighten herself. "I like your company too."

Asher ignored her.

"You are angry that I deceived you. I ask your pardon. I should not have done it."

He flicked the reins, signaling the mules to go faster.

"You feel you cannot trust me."

Another pothole sent her flying into the air before landing painfully on her backside.

He smiled.

She rubbed a hand against her bruised hip. "What you cannot believe, Asher, is that my decision was an aberration. An exception. I never behave that way."

He flashed a furious look her way. "And how am I to know that?"

"You will learn it in time, if you stay my friend."

"I would have to be an idiot to trust you again."

Her head drooped. "Asher, do you know why my father forgave me so quickly? Because he knew that deception does not come to me naturally. But if I had to do it again, I would, because it saved your life."

He huffed an exasperated breath. "You speak from both sides of your mouth. You ask my pardon yet admit you would do it again. I don't believe you are sorry at all."

"I *am* sorry. Sorry I lied. I am not sorry that in coming, I saved your life. What I mean to say is that I did not trick you lightly. In fact, the only thing that would induce me to do such a thing is the conviction that I was somehow needed. Urgently, absolutely needed. That is what you can trust."

He did not respond. But the next time they came to a rut in the road, he slowed the cart so that her teeth did not jar in her head as they passed over it. And an hour later, when he signaled for the mules to pull over into a field, he walked around and, before she could hop down, helped her alight, his hands wrapped around her waist.

"There is a well here. I will water the mules and fill our bags," he said. "You go see to your business. There are some straggling trees behind you. They will provide some privacy."

If he had given her an armful of wildflowers that he had picked personally, she would not have found it more winsome than this present thoughtfulness. She bestowed her brightest smile upon him and skipped into the tree line.

A truce settled between them after that. Though still somewhat stiff in manner, he had clearly lowered the high wall of offense he had set between them.

The following morning, the breeze that had accompanied them for several days turned into a blasting wind. Violent gusts picked up the dry surface dirt and drove a thousand sand particles into their faces. Jemmah coughed, half-blinded by dust. Asher pulled the cart over.

"Where is your scarf?" He had to yell to be heard over the roaring gusts.

"I did not bring one."

His comment got swallowed by the wind. A good thing, since it was not likely to be a compliment.

Asher searched in his chest and drew out a long square of

fabric. "Turn your face toward me," he ordered. In a few quick twists, he wrapped the fabric across her nose and mouth and over her head, until nothing showed except a slit for her eyes. It was the first time he had touched her face so intimately since his caresses by the fire. Jemmah's heart did a somersault.

Asher leaned back. For a moment he stared at her, eyes narrowed, before turning away to loosen a fold of his turban. He wrapped the trailing linen over his nose and mouth, securing it under the turban.

When he took up the reins, Jemmah grabbed the handrail. "You want to drive in this?"

"If we are to make it through the Zagros passes into Media and back before they grow impassable, we cannot be overcome by a flimsy dust storm."

"You call this flimsy?"

He waved a hand in the air. "This is nothing. You should experience a proper sandstorm in late spring."

"I think this is proper enough for me."

By the time they stopped for the evening, dust had wormed its way into every crevice of her body. In spite of the protection of Asher's scarf, her mouth tasted like dirt. Her head itched, her scalp grainy with grit. She felt as if she might never be clean again.

But one look at Asher's decorative beard had her doubled over with laughter. The tight, oiled curls had absorbed every particle of dust that had swirled near their vicinity, turning the beard a putty color that made Asher look like an old man.

"This is not amusing."

"Not at all." She tried to keep a straight face and failed.

"It's a serious problem."

Her shoulders shook. "It must weigh as much as a melon. Doesn't your neck hurt?"

He pulled himself up. "If we don't fix it, my disguise is ruined. I don't have time to go shopping, you know."

"It's not so bad. You merely look . . ."

He glared.

"Like you are carrying the weight of the world. Not on your shoulders. In your beard."

"I am disappointed that you cannot appreciate the gravity of the situation." One corner of his mouth twitched. "You should see your own hair. You could pose as a statue."

He reached out and undid the knot at her ear, pulling off the scarf she had loosened. Softly, his fingers brushed the crown of her head. Her throat went dry for a whole new reason besides dust.

"There is a pond down that hill." He gestured with his head. "Let's see if we have it to ourselves."

The pond, greenish and calm, seemed deserted. "You can bathe first," Asher offered, pulling off the wig and beard with a sigh of relief as he turned to walk back up the hill.

Jemmah squealed as she stepped into the pond. The water was cold as honed steel. She exhaled and forced herself to walk deeper. Her teeth chattered as she stripped off her robes, rinsing them with numb fingers. Her skin had turned blue by the time she washed her hair, her legs jiggling like mutton jelly as she walked to the shore.

Asher had given her a clean blanket to use as a towel. She snuggled into its folds, pulling one corner over her dripping hair.

"You haven't drowned, have you?" he cried through the trees.

"No. But I may have frozen."

"I have a fire going. Come up."

She hefted the blanket more firmly around her and hiked up the hill. A cheerful fire burned at the center of the camp

Asher had set up. She dropped to her knees next to the flames. "You might reconsider that dip when I tell you how chilly the water is."

"It won't be my first cold swim. I grew up traveling through snowy mountains."

Jemmah pulled on her riding clothes while Asher bathed, spreading her wet tunic and cloak on a few bushes to dry. By the time Asher returned, she had combed the tangles out of her hair and was finally starting to feel warm.

Asher returned looking invigorated rather than blue with cold. He had changed into a spare tunic, but like her, he had washed the clothes he had been wearing when the wind whipped up and spread them next to hers to dry.

"Your supper is ready, Master Kandalanu," she said. She gestured to the bread she had warmed and gave him a plate of venison jerky and cheese.

He folded his body next to the fire. "You make a tolerable servant." After they finished eating, he pulled the wig and false beard out of the bag where he had stuffed them and gazed at them dolefully. They looked like a couple of dead squirrels. "I think they're ruined."

Jemmah snagged the hairy objects from him and, holding them at arm's length, shook them vigorously. A cloud of dust puffed into the air. "Do you have any perfume?"

"Kandalanu does." Asher rummaged through the wooden chest and extracted a small alabaster jar and held it out to her.

Jemmah sniffed the oil cautiously. "Juniper and myrtle." The merchant had good taste in some things, at least. She filled a large bowl with water. "We can experiment with the wig. If it goes wrong, your turban will cover the worst."

Gently she swished the wig in the water until most of the

dust washed out. Some poor woman had sold her long hair to a wigmaker to create these false tresses. She toweled the dripping water from the hair and with careful, patient strokes, combed out the tangles until they were partly dry.

She rubbed in the oiled perfume until the hair shone. Using the reeds she had gathered for the purpose, she curled locks around each rounded stalk until the whole wig was wrapped up in her makeshift curlers.

"By morning when the wig dries, Kandalanu should have his curls back."

Asher examined her work. "Did I say you were a tolerable servant? I take that back. You make a splendid servant."

She narrowed her eyes. "Is that supposed to be a compliment?"

"You make a splendid spy?"

"I will accept that, Bijar."

"That's Lord Kandalanu to you."

"Next time, I get to be the lady and you get to be the servant."

Asher wagged his eyebrows. "The present arrangement suits me very well, Silver Girl."

"You best beware, Master Merchant. I still have your beard to tend to."

Said object proved more demanding than she had hoped. After two hours, Jemmah's eyes were strained and her back aching. But she had managed to make adequate repairs to Kandalanu's bedraggled beard.

She held it out to Asher. "I suggest you keep that safely tucked in the merchant's chest until we are closer to the border. For now, you can pull the loose end of your turban over your face to keep your identity secret."

Asher scratched his chin. "I suppose you coming along on this journey has not proven to be a great disaster so far."

CHAPTER

THIRTY-SIX

Be strong and courageous. Do not be frightened, and do not be dismayed,
for the LORD your God is with you wherever you go.
Joshua 1:9

Asher set a hard pace, stopping at villages on their way to change the mules frequently so that they could press through with unrelenting speed. By the time they reached his hideout in northern Babylonia, Jemmah felt her bones might become unstrung. She was so desperate for sleep that she did not make a single objection when he told her in peremptory tones that she must remain in the house and rest. She barely kept her eyes open long enough to watch him leave for his workshop. Stretching on Asher's feather-filled mattress, she was asleep before she had taken her boots off.

He returned several hours later, a fresh team of mules and a bulging bag of supplies in tow. The beard came out of Kandalanu's chest. "I suppose I must bear with this torture device again. We will be at Astyages's main checkpoint in a day."

Jemmah grinned. "How fortunate I am to gaze upon your splendor once more."

"I hope there are a lot of potholes on the road."

She made a face at him. "You have bounced me enough already."

He rubbed the back of his neck, looking contrite. "I ask your pardon. It has been a rough journey."

"Asher, I can bear a little discomfort."

He stepped toward her, moving like a languid jungle cat, all liquid grace and bunched-up muscles. He lifted her chin. "You look spent," he said, his voice husky.

Her mouth fell open.

He bent his head lower. "And pale." His thumb traveled up her chin and flicked back and forth over her lip.

Her eyes widened.

"So I will try to avoid all potholes."

"Oh."

"Forgot your words?"

"Every single one."

He laughed. In a flash, his expression changed, growing serious. "I don't want to stay your friend."

"What?"

"You said I would get to know who you really are if I stayed your friend. But that's not what I want."

Jemmah's heart dropped like a Babylonian glazed brick. "What do you want?"

His hand traveled from her chin to her cheek. "I want more."

The corners of her mouth lifted with hope. "How much more?"

"I might tell you one day." His hand dropped to his side, leaving a cold spot on her cheek.

She crossed her arms, trying to hide her disappointment. He felt something. Wanted something more than friendship, but not enough to commit his heart openly. "One day I might return the favor."

His lips twitched. "The mules are waiting."

"So is your beard."

* * *

Jemmah clutched her walking stick to her belly until her fingers turned white. Four Median soldiers in full armor barred their way as they approached. Next to her, Asher sat with legs sprawled, looking confident in his expectation of a warm reception.

Reining in the mules, he held out the letter bearing the royal seal. "Kandalanu the merchant at your service."

Their commander perused the letter and studied the seal carefully. "What do you have in the cart?"

"Babylonian beer."

The soldiers grinned at each other. "You will have to open one for me to examine," the commander said.

Kandalanu scowled. "You can see I have the king's own seal to travel this road. You better not damage anything, or his senior scribe will hear of it."

The commander hesitated. He handed the letter back. "Open a cask, merchant."

Kandalanu sighed. "As you wish." He hopped to the ground and drew the smallest cask toward him. "Would you like a taste?"

The soldiers grinned. The commander's face did not crack. "Just open it."

Kandalanu obliged. Examining the contents, the commander passed to the next cask and shook it to ensure it contained nothing other than beer. One by one, he put each cask to the test. Jemmah's stomach twisted. If the soldiers subjected them to this minute search on the way back, they would certainly discover the weapons.

Kandalanu sighed as he waited, tapping his feet. "Now, Commander, I must tell you that I will return this way after I have dropped these casks off with the king's agent. This first crossing is an experiment to see if the import and export of goods between our two nations might prove profitable to both sides. If the king is pleased, I will have many more carts with me on the way back. If you choose to search every wine cask and pot of raisin or honey with the same overabundance of caution you have displayed today, I will be delayed by hours and more likely to be caught in the first winter snows. Which means I will be unable to cross into Harran, where your soldiers await with bated breath for the arrival of my imports from their country. I would hate to disappoint them, wouldn't you?"

The commander dipped his finger into the small cask he had opened earlier and tasted the beer. "What do you suggest?"

"Ah. Since we have already opened this cask, why not take it as a token of my gratitude?"

The commander hefted the cask off the cart and passed it to his waiting soldiers. "Now that I have ensured you are who you claim to be, we can see to it that your return passage is faster."

Kandalanu bowed. "I will be sure to write His Magnificence the senior scribe of your good service upon my return."

Jemmah hopped off the cart and bent low to loop her hands for the merchant. She grunted as Kandalanu put the tip of his boot into her waiting hands, and boosted him into his seat.

"Well, don't dawdle, girl," he said, looking down at her. "Move those lazy feet. Can't you see how late it grows?"

"Yes, master." The mules were flying before she had settled all the way into her seat. Behind them, the Median soldiers whooped and hollered as they had the first taste of their Babylonian beer.

She dropped her face into her hand, faint with relief. That had gone better than she had feared. Remembering Asher's last comment, her head snapped up. "You are enjoying this business of being my master a little too much."

"Can't deny that. You are proving to be a very obliging servant. The way you held your hands for my boot was inspired."

"The things I do for Persia."

"And here I thought it was for me, lest I get my little booties dirty."

* * *

Jemmah shivered as they walked into Asher's workshop in the mountains. So much had changed since they had last stayed here weeks ago. The smelting furnaces stood cold and shuttered. In the middle of the workshop, the empty stone table looked forlorn. The tools on the walls had been carried off, their hooks vacant save for spiderwebs and dust.

Asher stripped off his disguise and knelt to light a fire. "I asked the men to leave my private chamber untouched," he said when he noticed Jemmah blowing into her hands to keep them warm. "You will find blankets there."

Relieved to find the beautiful room as inviting as before, Jemmah wrapped herself in the folds of a felted blanket and fetched another for Asher. She returned to find the fire in the furnace already casting its welcome heat into the room. Carrying water from the well, she set it to boil while Asher chopped onions and garlic for stew.

She hunkered by the fire to stir lentils and salt into the water. "These should be cooked within the hour."

"As soon as we eat, I am going to retrieve the swords from their hideaway and see if my friends will agree to help us. I cannot drive all those carts by myself."

"I will get ready to leave."

"I am going alone," Asher said, his voice curt. "I intend to use a shortcut, which will save a whole day's journey. It's a hard climb, Jemmah, and this time of year, icy. I will travel faster without you."

"I understand. I wouldn't dream of slowing you down." She had sensed a different kind of chill in the air that morning and wondered if snow was not far-off. "The sooner we leave, the better our chances of getting out of these mountains."

He seemed relieved, as though he had expected an argument from her.

She drew the blanket closer about her shoulders. "How long will you be gone?"

"Three days. After meeting with Phray and Amas, I need to arrange for the packing of my last workshop north of here to ensure they are ready in time to join us on the pass."

"What do they make?"

"Short spears, mostly. The kind used by infantry."

"Don't forget to purchase enough food and wine to hide the weapons under."

"The village will have all the supplies I need. Hopefully we gained the trust of the commander on the way in. Even a cursory search would unearth the weapons."

"As long as you offer them a cask of wine, those guards will be amenable to a quick passage. You will be a familiar face this time."

He threaded his fingers through his hair, making little tufts stand on end. His hair had grown since he had sheared it to get rid of the prison lice, and now lay in a silky flop over his forehead. She had to squelch an odd longing to comb her fingers through it. "When do you think we will leave?"

"I hope we can head back to Babylonia in four days. We need to wait for all the carts to arrive. The ones from the northern workshop won't make that journey in less than three days."

"Will they manage to navigate those icy northern tracks?"

"The carts will be heavy. That will help stabilize the wheels. My men are used to these conditions. They can drive anything until the passes are completely blocked by snow. And the main pass is much easier to navigate than the tracks we took when we traveled on foot."

She watched him pack his Kandalanu disguise along with a heavy cloak. "Are you going to the village dressed as the merchant?" she asked in surprise.

"I will have to. Astyages had men loitering around the last time we were here. And there is Stateira to consider."

"You think she will betray you?"

He shrugged. "I cannot take a chance. Too much rides on it."

"What will you tell Astyages's men if they ask what such a fine merchant is doing in the backwaters of Media when he is supposed to be heading to Ecbatana?"

"I will say I am there to purchase honey for the soldiers at Harran. The village is known for the quality of its hives."

He crouched next to her. "Will you be all right while I am gone?"

The last time she had spent three days and nights alone, she had been trapped at the bottom of a well. She suppressed a shudder. Asher's workshop was nothing like that. "I will be fine."

"I don't like leaving you alone."

She forced a smile on her lips. "It's better than climbing up an icy rock face."

"My thought exactly. You will be safe and warm here."

"That's my plan."

He must have heard the tiny tremor in her voice. Without a word, he pulled her into him and held her for a long moment.

"The lentils are boiling over," she said, worried that if she stayed in his arms much longer, she might shame herself by bursting into tears.

He turned away from her to attend the sputtering pot, mumbling something under his breath. It sounded like *It's not the only thing*. But that made no sense. They were cooking nothing else besides the lentils.

Before leaving, Asher pointed to the carved chest that sat in one corner of his chamber. "You will find more blankets and extra tunics in there. Whatever I have is at your disposal."

"That's a dangerous offer."

"I mean it." He rummaged through the chest and exclaimed with satisfaction when he discovered a faded scroll. "You can read this while I am gone."

Curiously she unrolled the delicate papyrus. "It's the book of Joshua! How did you come by this?"

"Years ago, after my mother died, I ran across an old Judean priest in Babylon. He had once served at the Temple in Jerusalem. He sold me this Aramaic translation of the book." Silky hair flopped over one eye. "You can avail yourself of its comforts while I am gone."

Jemmah cradled the scroll. "You leave me in good company."

"I wish I didn't have to leave you at all."

*   *   *

After watching Asher disappear in the distance, Jemmah returned indoors to close the wooden shutters and bar the door as he had instructed. The utter silence felt eerie. Unfamiliar noises that she had barely noticed before now sounded sinister. She was a grown woman. She had faced men armed with arrows and knives. She ought to be able to face three nights alone in the mountains.

Before barring the door, Jemmah had fetched several jars of water from the well. If she was going to be stuck here, she might as well put the time to good use. This might be her only opportunity to launder clothes in days. She scoured through her pack and pulled out every article of clothing she had brought along. The servant's tunic she wore also needed a good scrub. Finding Asher's extra riding tunic and trousers, she decided to wash those alongside her own.

In Asher's chest, she found a long, forest-green linen tunic, soft from use. Stripping off her clothes, she donned Asher's tunic. Since he was almost of the same height as her, the hem hung perfectly at her ankles, though the shoulders were far too wide. She heated the water and scrubbed everything with lye.

In a corner of the workshop, she discovered a long loop of unused rope. Stringing it from empty hooks on opposite walls, she allowed the excess to drop to the floor and hung everything to dry. It was late by the time she finished. She ate the last of the lentil stew with cold bread. Nothing left but to retire.

She eyed Asher's bed with dread. While she had kept busy, it had been easier to forget that she was all alone in an abandoned building in the bowels of a mountain. She crawled under the blankets without blowing out the lamp.

An odd noise made her jump. She exhaled when she realized it was only a tree branch scraping against the walls. She pressed her face into Asher's pillow and pulled the blanket over her head. The faint spicy fragrance of cypress and man tickled her senses. Asher's scent. It reminded her that she was tucked in his bed, resting on his pillow. The thought made him seem closer somehow. She felt the agitated rhythm of her heart calm.

Enfolded in the man's blankets and shivering with fear, she finally stopped skirting around the truth and admitted it to herself.

She loved Asher.

She loved him the way her mother loved her father. The way you loved when you built a whole life together. The way you loved when the very thought of someone changed the rhythm of your heart and quieted your fears.

She sat straight up in bed. Fire and lightning! There was no going back from this! She loved the green-eyed son of Astyages.

And Asher had always danced around his feelings for her. He had made it clear that he was not indifferent. Then again, he had never declared his intention toward her.

He had once told her that a prince unrecognized and unwanted was no prince at all. She wished she could make him understand that he was anything but unrecognized and unwanted, because she recognized the wonder of him. The sheer joy that was Asher ben Rachel. And she wanted him all the way to the marrow of her bones.

She dropped her head in her hands and recited her favorite prayer. *"We do not know what to do, but our eyes are on you."* Still sleepless, she began reading aloud through the book of Joshua.

"Be strong and courageous," she read. *"Do not be frightened, and do not be dismayed, for the Lord your God is with you wherever you go."*

Verse after verse she read until her soul was no longer anchored to the lonely emptiness of the chamber, nor to the aching wound of unrequited feelings, but to promises that surpassed time and nation. In her own strength she was indeed frightened and dismayed. She had no courage. God's promises helped her become other than she was, and the woman who trembled on her lonely bed grew valiant.

THIRTY-SEVEN

They were glad when it grew calm,
and he guided them to their desired haven.
Psalm 107:30, NIV

On the second evening, the snow began in fits and starts. Jemmah exhaled with relief when by the next morning nothing remained of the storm save a few dancing flakes. A blanket of white lace covered everything. Jemmah pushed her hand into the powdery snow to measure its depth and discovered that it only reached her wrist. Not enough to close the passes.

The sun emerged from behind the heavy curtain of clouds an hour later, bringing an end to the storm but no warmth. Just when Jemmah started to exhale, the wind began. The squall picked up the flakes and created blinding spirals, rendering visibility near impossible.

Jemmah's heart sank. Asher was returning that day. He would have to climb down an icy rock face through this. She paced from one end of the workshop to the other. She prayed. She paced more.

Time trickled like cold honey. He should have arrived by now.

Unable to stand the wait another moment, she untied the rope from its hooks, and donning her riding clothes under her warmest cloak, she pulled a felt hat over her head and ventured out, gripping her walking stick in convulsive fingers. Whirls of snow flew into her face, their icy blasts making her gasp. She trudged to the barn, fighting the wind with every step.

Next to the barn door, she found an iron ring used for tying up horses. She tied one end of the rope into the ring. Holding on to the rope, she walked down the track. Within a few steps, the barn and workshop had disappeared.

She was grateful to have the safety of the rope. But that tether also meant she could only go so far. When she came to the end of the rope, she had to stop, knowing she would be unable to return home without its guidance. She stared into the dizzying whiteness, hoping to see Asher, but saw no sign of him.

She cried his name. Again and again she called for him. No one answered save the wind. Finally, as her fingers and toes went numb, she decided to return to the workshop. Inside, she stripped off her cloak and held her aching limbs to the fire. As soon as she had drunk enough hot water to feel her shivering subside, she returned to the barn and her rope.

Three times she went outside, calling for Asher until her voice grew hoarse. The third time, a creeping dread made her stay longer even though her toes screamed with agony. Just when she was about to give up and return, she heard a weak sound.

"Asher!" Her voice reverberated in the wind.

Silence.

No! No! She had not imagined that sound. "Asher ben Rachel, you answer me right now!"

It came again, that sound, a weak but unmistakable cry.

Jemmah pressed the balls of her hands into her eyes. He was alive! "Asher, can you hear me?"

He responded, though she could not make out his words.

"Asher, keep talking. I am going to walk toward the sound of your voice."

He probably could not make out her words any more than she could his. But he answered, and that was enough. She hefted a rock from the ground and dropped it on the end of her rope to prevent it from flying away in the wind. Untying her long, striped belt, she wrapped it tightly around the rock and watched the wind swirl the ends in the air like drunken temple dancers. She nodded with satisfaction. Even from a distance she ought to be able to spot that when there was a break in the squall.

She remembered with sudden clarity the story of King Hezekiah's tunnel. The builders had found their way to each other by the sound of their hammers striking the rock. She prayed for the same ability to be given to her now as she fought against the blinding whirls of snow. She could only hope that the noise of the wind would not confuse her.

She cried out Asher's name every few steps and stumbled toward the sound of his voice when he responded. For an instant, the wind died down, like a curtain parting, making the world almost visible. She spotted him then, huddled by the rock face, and sprinted.

A trickle of blood dribbled from his nose over swollen lips. Deep cuts ran down one palm. But apparently his injuries had not tamed his temper. He snarled at her. "Didn't you hear me telling you to turn back?"

"I could not understand what you were saying with all this wind. Are you hurt badly?"

He ignored her question. "You must have lost your mind. What are you doing out in this squall?"

"I came to find you."

"I was fine without your help."

She crossed her arms. "I can see that."

"You think getting yourself killed will help me?"

"No. But I think getting you home to a warm fire might help both of us."

"And how will you do that? We will both get lost as soon as we leave the rock face."

Jemmah watched for a break in the wind. "There!" She pointed to the dancing ends of her belt.

"What is that?"

"I tied a length of rope to the barn door and stretched it as far as it would go. We only need to make it that far. The rope will lead us the rest of the way."

His eyes widened. "Not bad."

She grinned. "High praise from you, Prince Grump."

"I am not a prince."

"As much as I am enjoying this riveting conversation, we need to get you inside. Can you walk, Asher?"

He made a face. "I'm not certain. My ankle twisted hard when I fell."

She wrapped an arm around him. "Lean on me."

He hissed as he came to his feet. Jemmah handed her walking stick to him. "You still have this thing?" he asked.

"Of course. It was your gift."

"This battered thing? Doesn't count."

"It counts to me. And if it helps us make our way safely to

the workshop, I might cover it in gold and hang it from my wall."

"You're definitely not Stateira."

"That's the nicest thing you've ever said to me."

Her breath came in gasps as she bore Asher's weight. They found her marker to the rope, and after that, it was just a matter of keeping their heads down and pushing onward, one tiny, unsteady step at a time.

Asher exhaled when they crossed the threshold into the workshop. He wobbled and almost fell before she managed to get him to the bed. "Let's see what damage you've caused," she said.

"It's barely a scratch. If the weather had not turned, I would have made it home with ease."

She examined his bruised nose. "I don't think you broke it again. And all your teeth are still in your mouth, although they are a ghastly sight covered in blood like that." She made him rinse his mouth as she examined the cuts on his arm and hand.

"Some of these cuts need to be stitched."

"You will find needle and thread in my chest."

She raised her brows and he shrugged. "You are not the only one with hidden talents. When you live this far from a physician, you learn to make do."

He bore her ministrations with aplomb. But when she turned to his swollen ankle, he pushed her away. "You don't have to be so rough."

"I have to determine if it's broken. That means I have to poke and prod."

He scowled. "You hurt worse than the injury."

She swallowed a smile. "Likely true. Especially since it's not broken. Just a nasty sprain."

"I told you it wasn't bad." He leaned back into the pillows.

"Thank you for coming for me, Silver Girl. I might have frozen out there without your help."

Her eyes widened. "Did you just admit to being wrong?"

"I admitted to being grateful." With a sigh, he leaned deeper into the pillows. "But I suppose I must also acknowledge that I was wrong about you coming along. You have saved my life twice, washed my wig, saved my beard, cupped your pretty hands for my manly boots, and walked through a life-threatening squall to save my sorry neck."

"And I laundered your extra hunting tunic while you were gone."

"No!"

"Indeed. Now before you dissolve into a paroxysm of gratitude, tell me how your journey went. Were you able to make all the arrangements?"

"Everything is in place. By tomorrow the carts should arrive. We will meet them on the main pass."

* * *

The last of the storm moved out by dawn. Phray, Amas, and Dei were amongst the men who drove the carts to the pass the next afternoon, though Phray was not staying. "I have left Stateira to her own company for too many years," he said, his eyes dark. "I told myself it was for her sake that I spent so many hours away. That a small fortune would make her happy. I fooled myself. A wife needs her husband's attention more than his wealth."

Jemmah pressed his hand. "I pray she will appreciate your sacrifice."

His shoulders drooped. "Likely not. Then again, I could not live with myself if I did not give this marriage my all."

He turned to tease Asher about cramming his linens, pillows, tapestries, and carpet into the carts, calling him a true son of nomads. But when they embraced, every teasing word melted away, and the two men stood with arms wrapped around each other for a long moment. They both knew this might be their last goodbye.

Amas and Dei had decided to accompany Asher all the way to Persia. "You think we are going to allow you to hog all the fun to yourselves?" Dei said when Jemmah thanked them for coming to their aid. "For years I have watched this son of Astyages travel the four corners of the world. It's time I shared in the adventure."

Amas stretched as he took his seat back on the cart and picked up the reins. "I don't know about fun. He is likely to get us killed."

"Or worse," Asher said, climbing into the cart Phray had vacated. "Convince you to join the Persian army."

"How is that any different from getting killed?"

"Well, there are women in the Persian army."

Amas looked horrified. "That is worse."

Everyone was laughing when the line of carts began lumbering down the narrow pass. Jemmah leaned over to take the reins from Asher's bandaged hand. "You best let me drive."

He gave her a dubious glance. "Do you know how?"

"I've been watching you. Doesn't seem hard."

He grabbed for the reins. She evaded his reach. "Calm yourself. I knew how to ride before I learned to walk. And I can drive a team of mules in my sleep."

"I should have known." He drew the false beard out of its bag. "Prepare to be dazzled."

Behind them, six men whistled and cheered and clapped

as Asher completed his transformation by placing his impressive turban over his head. He rose in the seat to offer a magnificent bow to his friends, lurching dangerously when the cart stumbled over a pothole. His friends' cheers grew louder.

"I thought you said you can drive in your sleep," he said, falling back into his seat.

"Yes, but sometimes I have nightmares. I see a giant beard on legs and I forget everything I know."

The cheerful atmosphere grew hushed by the next day when they approached the main checkpoint. Jemmah's jaw clenched as two soldiers ran to the middle of the road to stop their passage. But as she had hoped, they recognized the merchant and gave him no trouble after he offered them two bulging skins of wine.

Once again, Jemmah hopped down to fold her hands into a boost for the merchant's wet boots. Behind them, Dei made a choking sound. Kandalanu addressed him sourly. "You've been at my wine again, I see. I have a mind to leave you here to walk all the way to Harran."

Alarmed, Dei held up his hands in surrender. "Mercy, master. I never tasted a drop, I swear."

Kandalanu settled himself in the cart and addressed the commander, whose lips were twitching. "Thieves, the lot of them. But carts can't drive themselves."

"When will you return this way, Master Kandalanu?" the commander asked.

"By spring, if all goes to plan. And I will come with gifts for you all."

THIRTY-EIGHT

Let him kiss me with the kisses of his mouth!
For your love is better than wine.
Song of Solomon 1:2

ASHER

Cyrus went through every cart, examining the contents with his generals in tow. His eyes glittered with wild joy. "You have pulled off a miracle, Asher, and given me the means to fight this war. I owe you great thanks."

"I could not have done it without some divine help." Asher twisted his ring about his finger. "Nor without my friends."

"I hear Jemmah saved your life."

"Twice. It's very annoying, not to mention humbling, especially after I yelled at her for coming against my wishes."

Cyrus pressed a finger to his chin. "I don't suppose she can tempt you to remain with us permanently? We could use a man like you."

Asher kept his face impassive. "Do you think she wants to tempt me?"

"I am better at strategies and tactics on a battlefield. But if the way she gazes at you is anything to go by, I would say you are well-positioned to receive heaps of temptation." He placed a hand on Asher's shoulder. "That woman is like a niece to me. She owns a bit of my heart. If you do not love her, Asher, then leave." His arm dropped.

Asher's voice emerged gravelly as he said the words aloud. "I do love Jemmah. I love her more than I thought I knew how to love." He dropped his head. "But I might leave anyway."

* * *

Jemmah's family had made their way back from Babylon, choosing to remain in Anshan to await Jemmah's arrival from the mountains. Asher knew he could not face them yet. Taking his horse out of Cyrus's stables, he left the city walls in search of a vigorous ride. It had been a while since he had ridden a horse, and he urged the stallion into a wild gallop as soon as the land stretched out into an expansive plain. The mount answered the reins, his gait smooth as a calm sea. Asher pressed on until they were both panting with exertion.

He slowed the stallion to a walk to cool him and brought him to a stop near a narrow stream. Even after the exercise, he felt restless and meandered aimlessly by the sluggish water.

Confessing his love for Jemmah to another human had brought the ache of it to the forefront of his thoughts. All the fears attached to that love came tumbling out. What if, in spite of what she claimed, Jemmah only wanted him for the advantage his money and weapons could bring? What if the drive beneath her feelings was the desire to help Judah? To fulfill her parents' dreams? What if he lost his charm for her after a while, the way Phray had lost Stateira's affections?

He hurled himself down on the bank, stretching his legs before him. Gathering a pile of smooth, flat stones, he began throwing them, twirling and whirling, into the stream.

No one could answer these questions. No one could assuage his doubts. Because there could be no assurance deep enough to cover the risk of love. He would either have to take Jemmah at her word or walk away in fear.

He remembered the woman in the cave, writhing with horror, there merely to keep him safe. That was Jemmah. That was her love. Her loyalty. Her grace.

If he could not trust these things in her, then he could not trust anything in life.

He had given up so much control since his imprisonment. He had given up control of his workshops, his wealth, his destiny. By giving his weapons to Cyrus, he had even given up control of his plans to defeat his father. Now he needed to give up control over this final bit of his heart.

He laughed, the sound making a sparrow take flight. What a fool he had been. His heart already belonged to Jemmah. Asher conjured an image of Jemmah walking through a blinding squall in search of him; Jemmah cupping her hands for his boots; Jemmah washing his filthy clothes; Jemmah kissing him, body and soul poured into her touch; Jemmah facing his wrath; Jemmah saving him from a murderer's knife; Jemmah cooking next to him; Jemmah laughing at his stupid jests.

How the Lord had blessed him with that woman.

He would have waved the flag of total surrender sooner if he had not been so embroiled in one danger after another, too preoccupied to sit and parse his feelings.

He loved Jemmah, no matter the cost. And it was time he told her so.

He gulped past a rock in his throat. Time also to face her parents.

* * *

Asher decided to bathe after his ride. Some faceless servant had already delivered his chest to his chamber in the palace. He rummaged for some respectable clothing and had to settle for tight indigo-blue trousers and a short Median tunic of the same color with silver embroidery. At least he had trimmed his beard and anointed his hair with a bit of oil that smelled like a fresh cypress tree. Pulling on clean leather boots, he decided he looked as civilized as he could manage with his hair still unfashionably short and his coffers too woefully empty to allow him the purchase of Persian-style clothing.

Lord Jared's villa in Anshan was located a short distance from the palace. Asher squared his shoulders as he stood before the iron-studded doors and knocked. He had expected a servant. Instead, Jemmah pulled the door open.

Asher felt his belly flip at the sight of that wide smile and thought he would never grow used to the way the brightness of it tugged at something deep inside him. He opened his mouth to greet her, just a casual salute. Instead, the words that spilled out left them both rooted to the spot.

"I love you, Jemmah."

Her eyes rounded. "What did you say?"

He shrugged and decided to wade in all the way. "I love you with all my heart and strength, Silver Girl."

She leapt into his arms, hands twined behind his neck. He grinned against her lips. "As nice as this is, some words would be reassuring."

She drew her head back. "Did I forget to say? I love you, Asher ben Rachel. I have been dying to tell you."

He pulled her against him, her body locked tight against his, for a moment beyond speech. He kissed her quickly and hard, forcing himself to set her aside. "I need to speak to your parents."

She laughed. "You should see your face."

He frowned at her. "It's no laughing matter."

Taking a step away, she gazed at him. "You are serious. But they love you."

Asher pulled agitated fingers through his cypress-scented hair. "We shall see."

Keren, whom he had not seen since leaving Daniel's house, gave a short cry at the sight of him. Before he could react, he found himself being squashed in her arms like a long-lost son. He blinked, disconcerted to find his eyes were not quite dry.

"You rascal." She gave him a couple of taps on the cheek. "I missed that handsome face."

"You only say that because I emptied all my workshops and poured the contents into Cyrus's lap."

She smiled. "Well, it certainly adds to your charms."

Zarina walked in and gave him a curt nod. "Don't expect any of that exuberance from me," she said, pointing to her mother's arm that was still wrapped around his waist.

"I would be scared if you tried."

She gave him a knife-sharp grin.

"I was hoping to speak to you and Lord Jared," Asher told Keren.

"I thought you might." Jemmah's father beckoned him into an inner chamber. "Come."

Asher gave Jemmah's hand a desperate squeeze before walking into the chamber, followed closely by Keren.

"Wine?" Lord Jared offered.

Asher shook his head. He might choke if he tried to swallow.

The older man sat at the edge of his desk. "Jemmah has been regaling us with your adventures in the mountains. She says she wants to embalm Kandalanu's beard."

"She would." Asher grimaced. He felt a drop of sweat trickle down his back. "Lord Jared. Lady Keren."

"Ooh, he called me lady. This must be serious," Keren said.

"Hush, beloved. He is trying to make a good impression." Lord Jared pulled on Keren's hand until she settled next to him and gave Asher an expectant look.

Asher ran a hand down his face. "I *am* trying to make a good impression. But it might be a hopeless case."

"Well, don't give up just yet, son."

"I love your daughter, you see."

Lord Jared nodded sagely. "Keren said you thought Jemmah looks ravishing in a tattered riding tunic."

"Pardon?"

Keren waved. "Never mind. Go on."

"I . . . well, I want to marry her."

"That's usually how these things work," Lord Jared said.

Asher rubbed the back of his neck. "But you might not want that for her."

"You aren't already married, are you?"

"Of course not." He looked at his feet. "But my father

never married my mother. Never took her as concubine. An old Judean priest once told me that no one born of a forbidden union may enter the assembly of the Lord."

Lord Jared straightened. "Is that what worries you? But, my boy, right underneath that Scripture it says no Moabite may enter the assembly of the Lord, either, even unto the tenth generation. And Ruth certainly partook of all the Lord's blessings. Her great-grandson David is our most beloved king and a significant part of the assembly of the Lord. More, from his lineage shall come our promised Messiah."

He slashed a hand in the air. "When faith abounds, grace shapes the Law."

"You do not find me . . ." The words snagged in Asher's throat. He took a deep breath and forced them out. "You do not find me unworthy?"

Lord Jared stepped close, gentle, strong arms opening to take him into a warm embrace. "I find you perfect."

Asher blinked, trying to push the tears away and failing. He had a strange inkling that this was how it felt to be fathered.

* * *

"I have no home to offer you," Asher said.

Jemmah was sitting tucked against his side in the sunny reception chamber. For the moment the whole family had left them to their own devices.

"I know," she said happily.

"Where do you want to live?"

She considered his question. "How about Pasargadae? Everyone will be building homes there after the war."

He gave a slow nod. "If we win."

She shrugged. "The world is a big place. As long as we have each other, I don't mind where we go."

He felt his stomach tighten. This woman could turn his world right side up with one little word. "I don't want to marry until after the war."

"Why?"

"Because according to Israel's law, a newly married man cannot go to battle. And Cyrus needs every able-bodied man to stand with him come spring."

She dropped her gaze to her lap. "Our happiness has so many shadows over it."

Asher tipped up her chin. His kiss was gentle at first, full of promise. Her lips opened against his, turning his blood to lava. Without thinking, he fit her more tightly against him. "Don't think of shadows. Think of this."

She took a shaky breath when he lifted his head. "Maybe you should start wearing your false beard, Bijar. I am finding you a little too irresistible."

He gave a husky laugh. "Maybe *you* should start wearing it. I don't know how I am going to wait so long."

Without warning, Zarina dropped between them, forcing them apart by dint of her wriggling limbs. "Don't worry. I will help."

"So will I," Jemmah's twin brother announced. His yellow-eyed owl wobbled its head and hooted. "And Gilead wants to lend a talon to the cause."

Asher dropped his head. It was going to be a long few months.

THIRTY-NINE

Thus says the LORD to you . . . "Stand firm, hold your position, and see the salvation of the LORD on your behalf, O Judah and Jerusalem." Do not be afraid and do not be dismayed. Tomorrow go out against them, and the LORD will be with you.

2 Chronicles 20:15, 17

CYRUS

Cyrus's spies began trickling back into Anshan as soon as the worst of the snows melted. They brought reports of a terrifying army that far outnumbered the Persians. Astyages had conscripted every man who could walk straight and pull the string on a bow, supplementing them with an auxiliary division of Scythian and Saka mercenaries, wild fighters who had honed their skills over a lifetime on various battlefields.

Leaving nothing to chance, the king had also mobilized the full force of Media's standing army, a hardened professional military core made up of deadly spearmen, archers, and cavalry.

Most telling of all, Astyages's royal tent was being made ready for travel. The Median king went nowhere without ensuring his comfort. Which meant that, as Cyrus had suspected, his grandfather intended to personally conduct this war. He intended to crush Cyrus and the Persian army with one swift stroke and show the world what he would do to every upstart who dared stand up to him.

Cyrus spread his maps over a massive table. He stood surrounded by his top generals and advisors, including the chief among them, Harpagus, Oebaras, and Jared. He had also asked Asher to join this war council, impressed by the man's ingenuity in getting twenty-five cartloads of top-quality weapons into his hands, managing to sneak some of them from right under Astyages's veiny nose.

"My grandfather never takes the field without bringing along his chefs, musicians, and dancing girls. The size and opulence of Astyages's army give us one advantage. It will take him a month, at least, to wend that lumbering force all the way here. That gives us time to prepare."

He put his finger on the map where the main highway south snaked through the plains of the Zagros. "The Median forces will enter Persia here."

Harpagus studied the location. "Is that where you want to engage them?"

Cyrus shook his head and indicated a spot further south. "This fortified town will give us an advantage. I can use its walls as part of our defense. We will draw them to us here."

Jared frowned at the map. "There are towns and villages between their entry point and where you mean to take a stand. Astyages is sure to demolish everything in his path. He is here to deliver a message, and he will do it best by wrecking every unprotected bit of land he steps on."

Cyrus nodded. "Oebaras, you will need to move those populations into walled cities that can be defended. The people who are able to travel further can take shelter in Pasargadae. Can you accomplish that task in time to lead a battalion in the war?"

Cyrus had befriended Oebaras as a young man. Over the years, he had proven both his loyalty and his genius and risen to become Cyrus's greatest general alongside Harpagus.

Oebaras bowed his head. "You can depend on me."

No empty words, Cyrus knew. "We can do nothing about Media's superior forces," he said. "But our battalions have the advantage of speed. We are not weighed down by heavy armor and lumbering carts. Astyages is depending on his might. But by choosing to come into our territory, he has given up the advantage of familiarity. Even with the aid of his spies, he cannot know these mountains half as well as we do. That will also serve us."

He caught Asher watching him, a deep groove between the dark brows. He could guess the young man's thoughts. Speed and familiarity were no match for the sheer numbers that Astyages had gathered to him. Cyrus would need more than one miracle to pull off a victory.

* * *

From atop a high cliff, Cyrus watched the Median forces pour into the Persian heartland like a swelling tidal wave falling on a vulnerable shoreline. At first, all he could see on the highway below was a cloud of dust. Then the cavalry broke through covered in white armor, the tips of their bronze spears flashing in the sun. Behind them, in tight rectangular formations, came the infantry, carrying wooden shields that reached their ankles. Scythian archers followed in dense, neat rows, vicious-looking bows slung over their shoulders. The most eerie battalion belonged to the northern Saka, their tattooed arms and legs gleaming with wild patterns, conical, pointed hats covering their ears.

The spearmen marched next, twenty thousand of them, stepping in perfect harmony. Like a living wall, they protected the king, who rode in the center, his golden armor shimmering like a mirror.

The carts came at the end, carrying tents, pots, pans, food, wine, musicians, harlots, physicians, spare clothing, blankets, and fodder for the animals. The line of Astyages's army extended so far along the road that it seemed endless. Cyrus exhaled. It was worse than he had expected, the sight of this hungry host seeking to plunder his land.

Astyages signaled a contingent of men to destroy the first village on their way. Even though Cyrus knew Oebaras had emptied it of its inhabitants, he ground his teeth as huts were ravaged by battering rams and wooden beams put to the fire. The homes of his people gone in a flash.

He clambered down to where his army waited. In quick, compact movements, they withdrew into the gorges of the mountain to the fortified town that sat protected by towering peaks. There they waited in tense silence, knowing they would soon face the most devastating fight of their lives.

Johanan sprinted to Cyrus, handing him a message. Instead of using him in combat, Cyrus had decided to place the young man in charge of the couriers, ensuring that information traveled speedily between the nerve centers of his army. "Astyages is planning to attack in relays," Cyrus said, perusing the message from his scouts.

Harpagus's mouth tightened. "That will keep their men fresh regardless of the length of battle."

Cyrus studied the walls of the city. They would not be enough to protect his flank against that huge force. "Send the women and children who have remained in town to Pasargadae," he commanded.

He decided to divide his forces, placing a smaller contingent inside the city to safeguard their rear, with the rest arrayed outside the wall, where they would face the deadly volley of the initial attack.

Another courier ran to hand Johanan a message. "They're on the move," he said.

"Is Astyages with them?"

Johanan shook his head. "Astyages watches the fight from his throne, surrounded by his spearmen."

Cyrus's lips twisted. "I should have known. He is good at sending men to their deaths but not eager to face it himself."

The battle arrived sudden and brutal. His men held off the Medes, fighting for hours while Astyages replenished his forces by sending in a continuous flow of fresh men. Around him, Cyrus was vaguely aware of his generals engaged in furious combat, Jared and Harpagus back-to-back, while Oebaras led a large company to their west.

"Hold fast!" Cyrus held up his sword for his men to see, a symbol of power, of stability. "Hold your positions!" And they did. By dint of sweat and bloody courage, they fought off the superior forces facing them.

Cyrus heard a commotion behind him. Instinctively he knew what was happening in his flank before he received the message. Astyages had done what Cyrus himself would have. He had sent a detachment of forces to the back of the city, and they had breached the walls, too rapid for his messengers to carry a warning.

His whole army was now caught between two enemy forces.

"Push through," he cried and threw himself into the melee, fighting with new desperation to carve out an exit for his men. His generals, grasping his new strategy, gathered the men out of the walls of the city and fought with every last bit of their strength.

So unearthly their fervor that the Medians gave way long enough for the Persians to make their escape. That was the first miracle during those devastating days of endless battle. They should have been crushed between the two mighty forces Astyages had set upon them like an iron pincer. Yet somehow they made their way out of it, and while the Medes stayed to bury the dead, Cyrus led his men deeper into the mountains to regroup in a narrow pass that led the way to the valley of Pasargadae.

Again, Cyrus divided his forces, giving Oebaras charge over ten thousand infantrymen in the pass, while he led the bulk of his army into the valley. But Astyages's men followed over the mountains, converging upon them, forcing Oebaras out of the pass he could not defend.

Cyrus turned to Harpagus. "Report!"

"It's not good. If they come now, we are done for."

But Asher brought worse news. "I've been walking through the camp. Some men are inciting defection to Astyages."

Cyrus went still. His soldiers had begun to lose heart. If this fear spread, his defeat was sure.

Jared set down the sword he was whetting. "Do you want me to send out a few Immortals to root out the traitors?"

Cyrus pushed aside the initial horror at the news. "Perhaps we can use these men to our advantage."

Harpagus crossed his arms. "This I have to hear."

"Tell everyone I have an announcement."

Night had fallen, and the camp was lit with torches. Cyrus stood on a flat rock and faced his army. "My men. My friends. You have fought bravely for your homes. For your land. For your children. Do not lose heart now, for I bring joyful tidings. Thousands of reinforcements are about to join us. We are not the only nation unwilling to cede our rights to a despot. Others have left Astyages's side and have decided to unite with our cause. Hold strong. Our numbers are about to swell."

A mighty cheer met his announcement. Quietly he called Harpagus to his side. "Send men we trust to make torches and stand guard alongside the torchbearers."

"No reinforcements are arriving, are they?"

"None. But the additional torchbearers will make it look like they have come."

Harpagus's eyes narrowed as he stared into the distance. He pointed at several shadowy figures running out of the camp. "Those dogs! They are running to Astyages's camp." In a flash, he nocked an arrow and took aim.

"Stop."

He looked over his shoulder at Cyrus. "Stop?"

Cyrus's smile was razor-sharp. "We want them to tell Astyages our good news."

"Ah." Harpagus lowered his arm.

"It will buy us time to regroup. If they come tonight, with our lines in disarray and our hearts shaken, we are finished."

"You think Astyages will believe it?"

He shrugged. He did not really expect his ruse to work. His

grandfather would be a fool to delay sure victory on the strength of uncorroborated rumor. And Astyages was no fool.

To Cyrus's astonishment, Astyages's generals hesitated to pursue the enemy into a possible trap. They had already lost an unexpectedly large number of men. At the last moment, they erred on the side of caution and chose not to go after the weary Persians. By so doing, they lost the opportunity to defeat them in what would have been an easy victory. Cyrus recognized this unexpected reprieve as the second miracle of this impossible war.

He now had time to reposition his forces, creating a more effective defense by sending most of the men into rocky elevations, giving them the advantage of the higher ground. When the Median soldiers came, their advance was obstructed by the rugged terrain. Ringed by thickets of oak and olive trees on the ground, their every step became a fight against tree trunks and roots. From his hiding place behind a rocky projection, Cyrus watched with satisfaction as their careful formations broke up.

As Astyages's forces struggled to advance in chaotic clusters, Cyrus signaled his men. Now the Medians found themselves facing flying javelins, while great rocks came heaving down upon them from the heights. The Persians did not even spend their precious arrows. They used the bounty of the mountains to attack the enemy.

Cyrus knew that his strategy, though sound, could not in the end withstand the sheer numbers in Astyages's train. The valiant Persian resistance was simply not enough. When night fell, Cyrus could feel the heart of his men once again drain out of them. No reinforcements had arrived. In the morning, they faced a losing battle.

Persia desperately needed another miracle.

CHAPTER FORTY

*The LORD will cause your enemies who rise against you
to be defeated before you. They shall come out against
you one way and flee before you seven ways.*
Deuteronomy 28:7

Someone banged on the door with enough force to break it
down. It was the middle of the night, though none of them had
bothered to go to bed. They waited from hour to hour to hear
a snippet of news from the battlefront, which had now moved
to the valley surrounding Pasargadae. Jemmah sprinted to open
the door. "Irda!"

Irda hobbled inside, favoring one leg. Her dirty face wore a
grim expression. "We are losing," she said.

Jemmah's mother and Zarina came into the chamber in time
to hear the stark announcement.

Calmly her mother handed Irda a goblet of water. "Tell us
what has happened."

In jerky sentences, Irda described battle after battle. "Your
men were safe, last I saw them. Johanan runs relays between the
messengers. Jared and Asher keep close to Cyrus. But everyone

is tired. Worse. Our men have lost heart." She dropped her gaze. "Come morning, we will face defeat. I have only come to bring news. Then I will return to face our final battle."

Her mother, usually so skittish about swords, grabbed an old, dented one her father had left behind. She had finally had the bandages removed from her arm, and hefted the blade in both hands. "If the men have lost heart, then the women will give aid."

Zarina, who had been told by her parents that she was too young to participate in the melee, jumped in the air. "Finally! Someone speaks reason."

Jemmah's mouth dropped open. "Mother, you want us to join the battle?"

"I want the men to see us marching to their aid. Irda, gather the women of Pasargadae. Young and old. Tell them to wear their husbands' leather trousers. We are going to remind them how the Persians fight."

* * *

The men of Persia looked in stunned silence as their women, armed with old swords, homemade hunting bows, clubs, hammers, and axes, made their way into their camp. Under the bright moonlight, Jemmah could see bloodied faces, drooping shoulders, defeated expressions frozen in disbelief as they marched into their midst.

"They have come to fight," Irda announced, her voice flinty with pride.

If any of Cyrus's generals had an opinion about their new recruits, they kept it to themselves. They watched with fierce interest as the women lined up before the weary soldiers.

Jemmah steadied the woman who stumbled next to her, a

great-grandmother who had insisted on joining this unusual host. "Giving up?" she had said, her cracked voice indignant. "We'll see about that." Now she pulled herself up and hefted her cudgel. "We've come to show you how it's done!"

A wave of laughter went through the men. Zarina held up her knife. "You can't have all the fun to yourselves." More laughter.

The great-grandmother spoke up again. "Let it be forever proclaimed it was the women of Persia who beat Astyages. It was your mothers and grandmothers who shook him out of his pretty throne."

This proved too much. "Never!" a man shouted. Others joined in.

"No?" A young woman stepped forward, her voice challenging. "We hear you are ready to give up like little chicks. Too tired to fight for your children? If you want to lick Astyages's boots, then step aside. We will fight in your stead."

A grizzly soldier with a bandaged arm stepped forward. "Enough now. You have made your point. No need to shame us. Go home and let us do our work."

The army roared its approval.

The great-grandmother crossed her arms. "I better not wake up in my bed and see a Median soldier looking to ravish me."

Laughter exploded until eyes flat with despair began to sparkle.

The grizzly soldier held up his hand. "Grandmother, we will send those soldiers packing to Ecbatana. But you might have a line of Persian soldiers at your door, seeing there is obviously plenty of life left in you."

The woman pressed one hand behind her head and another to her waist, striking the flirtatious pose of a young girl vying for a man's attention. The men bent over and howled.

Jemmah felt a hand wrap around her wrist, pulling her backward until she fell against a hard chest. "What are you doing here?" Asher whispered in her ear.

"I came to help."

He turned her in his arms until they were face-to-face. "This is no place for you."

"It's no place for anybody." She glanced around. "Where is Cyrus?"

"He left around midnight to pray."

"That's good. It means he has come to the end of himself. I think God likes to step in when we finally tumble into that place."

Asher drew her closer. "Every man here found that place today. We all came to the end of ourselves. Spent the last dregs of our strength with our sweat and blood on the battlefield. But these women in their leather trousers have put iron in our backbones again."

Zarina sidled up to them. "I am staying."

Keren followed. "You are not."

Asher shot Jemmah an amused glance.

"These men need more than heart, Mother," Zarina said. "They need fresh fighters."

Keren's eyes widened. "What did you say?"

"I said they need fresh fighters."

"No. Before that. What did you call me?"

Zarina stretched like a cat. "Mother. What else am I going to call you?"

Keren made an odd sound in her chest and pulled the girl into her arms. "My girl." Her voice wavered, her eyes welling up with tears. She stepped away. "You are still not staying."

"Instead of arguing, why don't you join me? You aren't half-bad with that sword."

Jemmah stepped out of Asher's arms. "Zarina is right. I am no soldier. But neither are most of these men. They are farmers and shepherds, metalworkers and bricklayers, bakers and engineers. We have had as much training as them. And we are fighting for more than the boundaries of Persia. More even than the restoration of Judea."

Asher frowned. "Fire and lightning. You sound like Daniel."

"What do you mean?"

"He told me that our people were meant to be a blessing to the nations. That Judah's freedom and worship are not merely a matter of national independence. God's plans for the world are somehow entwined with Jerusalem's destiny. Which make God's plans for Cyrus crucial to the fate of the world."

Jemmah nodded. "I am fighting for that. I want to take my place in that promise. A thousand years from now, no one will remember my name. I will be no great hero, immortalized by poets. But I will be one of a long line of men and women who stood on God's promises and contended for this faith. I don't want to run just because it's hard."

Her mother wiped her tears. "I wish I did not have such greathearted children."

"I'm not greathearted," Zarina said. "I just want to pulverize Astyages's army."

Her father came running to their side. "What's wrong, Keren? Why are you crying?"

"Because she has such great children," Zarina said, smirking. "And because we are staying to help you fight, Father."

"What did you say?"

Zarina rolled her eyes. "Everyone has gone deaf today."

Asher drew Jemmah away from her family. "Jemmah, are you certain you want to stay? The odds are against us. I see no way of overcoming that horde out there. We will probably die on this mountain."

"In that case, you better kiss me. If I am going to perish, I would like to do so with the taste of your lips on mine."

Asher obliged her until she felt her bones melt. He was about to oblige her again when Cyrus walked into the clearing. His face had an eerie calm as he held up his arms. "A feast!" he shouted. "We are celebrating, for Ahura Mazda has promised me victory."

Before he had time to explain what he meant, Johanan ran to his side, waving a message. Asher grasped Jemmah's hand. "Come. Let us discover what is in that message."

Cyrus's smile was grim when he lifted his head from the scroll. "Astyages has started doing our work for us, it seems. He was so incensed when he discovered his generals botched the last attack by falling for our ruse that he had them executed."

* * *

When the sun crested the eastern peaks, Cyrus led his soldiers down the mountain while the Median host began to ascend. Jemmah stayed close to Asher, following in Zarina's footsteps, who descended sure-footed as a gazelle, their parents trying to hem her before and behind.

Later, she could never remember those hours with any clarity. They became a jumble of sounds and smells, arrows flying, swords and daggers thrusting, plunging, piercing. The noise grew deafening, men shouting, metal clanging, soldiers groaning.

Asher pushed her roughly aside at one point, narrowly missing the downward swing of a bronze-tipped axe. She prayed, snatches of words that tethered her to something beyond the horrors of this mountain, until her heaving lungs left no room for any sound save gasps.

How it happened, she could not say. But the Persians broke through the dense battle lines of the enemy, hurling them into utter confusion, unable to regroup. It was as if by their indomitable spirit they had wrenched out the backbone of the enemy. Later, it would be called a miracle. An impossibility. The routed enemy scurried before them, injuring themselves as they tried to leap out of their way, falling down deadly ravines and mountain gorges in their rush to get away.

At the foot of the mountain, a cry rent the air. Everyone froze at the incomprehensible sight that met their eyes.

Astyages, bound in chains, surrounded by his own officers.

One of them pushed the king to his knees. "Cyrus! Here is what you want. We have had enough of him, same as you. Let us stop this bloodshed."

Cyrus, sword gory with blood, stepped out from amongst his men. "Fire and lightning," he said beneath his breath.

The man who held his sword to Astyages's neck bowed his head. "He put to death our beloved generals. Good Medians who had served him faithfully. We have watched you fight at the head of your men while our king sits on his golden throne, sipping wine. We are done with him. Come and be our king."

Jemmah pressed her hands to her head. For a beat, shocked silence held the world still. Then a roar went up. Jemmah could feel the reverberation of it in the rocks beneath her feet.

Asher pulled her to him, hugging and twirling. Men danced. Immortals wept. And it finally dawned on Jemmah: she had witnessed another miracle.

FORTY-ONE

And all these blessings shall come upon you and overtake
you, if you obey the voice of the LORD your God.
Deuteronomy 28:2

───────────────── ASHER ─────────────────

The Persians had captured Astyages's royal tent and turned it
into Cyrus's headquarters. Asher pulled aside blue-and-scarlet
linen curtains as he entered the opulent pavilion to find Cyrus
hard at work behind his desk. Some things, it seemed, did not
change. Granted, the desk was bigger than the one he used for-
merly, inlaid with ivory and silver instead of dented wood. But
the distracted air and deep absorption of the man who occupied
it had not changed.

Earlier, Cyrus had appropriated his grandfather's purple
robe and golden scepter and sat in his bejeweled throne. To the
deafening cheers of his men, Oebaras had crowned him king of
the Medes and the Persians. The elaborate throne stood empty

now. Asher's jaw loosened as he noticed the man sprawled on cushions at its feet, a sour expression on his bruised face.

Astyages.

Hearing the rustle of the curtains, Cyrus lifted his head. "Ah, Asher. There you are."

Asher bowed his head. "Sire." He pointed his chin at the former Median monarch. "Shouldn't he be in fetters?"

"My grandfather has promised to be on his best behavior."

"You trust him?"

Cyrus shrugged and pointed to the muscle-bound Immortals that were trying to blend into the background. "I trust them."

"Feel better now, boy?" Astyages called from his pillow. "You have made slaves of your people so that you can have your revenge on me. I recognized your weapons in the hands of the Persians."

Asher studied Astyages for a frozen moment. Without his wig and false beard, he seemed shrunken, a florid old man, more guile than strength. Had he truly spent years of his life on the altar of his hatred for him? He felt the last of the old bonds loosening, unraveling. The resentment turned to ash.

He came down on one knee before the slumped figure. "I gave those weapons to the man who deserved them. A true king. Your name, old man, will be wiped from the earth, while his will live on."

"You turn your back on your father, pup?"

The old Asher, the one who had not been trapped in a cave with a loving woman, who had not worn his grandfather's ring, who had not recognized his enslaved mother's freedom, that Asher would have said, *You turned your back on your son.* Now he shook his head. "Tell me what you need, Astyages, and if it is not treason, I will do my best to secure it for you."

"Secure it for *me*? Who do you think you are? A nobody who belongs to no one."

Cyrus came to his feet. "If Asher is your son, that makes him my mother's brother and my uncle. He will always have a place in my court and in my life. He belongs to us."

Astyages leaned forward. "Your court. Ha! You are nothing but a boy playing king. You won't last on that throne more than a month, I wager. There are lions out there who will swallow you whole. True monarchs like Nabonidus in Babylon and my own brother-in-law, Croesus, in Lydia. You think they will let you stay on that throne? I held them back by my might. You believe because fortune smiled upon you out in that field, you are any match for such crafty rulers? They will crush you under their feet."

Cyrus grinned. "They can try. They will find, as you did, that it does not pay to underestimate me."

He beckoned one of the Immortals. "Find a comfortable tent for my grandfather's use. His company wears on me."

When Astyages had been escorted out, he waved a hand to the chair before him. "I believe I owe you a small payment."

"You can defer on that for a while, if you need."

Cyrus placed a plump bag full of gold before Asher. "Let me make a start at least." He tented his fingers before him. "We still have a few battles to win before we take Ecbatana."

"The bulk of Media's armed forces are here. I doubt you will find much resistance, not with Astyages's men sworn to serve you."

"I could still use a good weapons man. Astyages is right. Beyond Ecbatana, other battles await. Once we have captured Ecbatana, you can resume operations in your workshops."

Asher took out the scroll he had been sketching on over the

past few days. "As to that, you may find this chariot of help. It will be of no use to you in mountainous terrain like this. But on flatland, the steel scythes attached to the wheels will effectively disable rows of infantrymen, opening the way for your cavalry to break through. I have included all the design details. Any experienced chariot maker will be able to construct it."

Cyrus raised a brow. "Do you not intend to oversee its fabrication?"

Asher studied the chariot for a long moment. "My king, I do not." He pushed it toward Cyrus.

"And the workshops?"

"I have been a man of war since my youth. I find I have lost my taste for it."

"What do you intend to do?"

Asher felt the joy of his answer well up. "I intend to marry and do all in my power to make my wife happy. If God blesses us with children, I will watch them grow and love them with every last piece of my heart. You are building a royal city in Pasargadae. I hope to help you with that. Instead of weapons of warfare, I want to create tools for peace. Better farming implements, better devices for your engineers."

Cyrus rolled up the papyrus bearing the chariot design and set it carefully atop his pile of correspondence. "Your Jemmah will be a happy woman. Happier than my Cassandane, I believe."

* * *

Within weeks, the Persian army descended upon Ecbatana. The Sakas, who had officially transferred their allegiance from Astyages to Cyrus, followed in the wake of Cyrus's armed forces, a trailing column of Persian and Median fighters marching in neat formations, each one duly sworn to Cyrus. The resistance from the city proved negligible. Its nobles threw the doors open to the new king once they saw the old one displayed in chains.

The conquest of Ecbatana was more a political victory than a military one. Asher watched with fascination as Cyrus won over the Median nobles with the same velvet firmness that he reserved for his own lords.

He had expected to witness some of the famed Assyrian and Babylonian cruelty to be displayed by Cyrus also. After so many years of hard war and grinding poverty, he certainly had good reason to crush the enemy with a merciless arm. Instead, Cyrus called the Median nobles "my men" and allowed them to keep their homes and farms and shielded their wives and children from his soldiers' wrath.

"You have been the subjects of an unjust king long enough," he said. "Let us inaugurate a new rule." To prove his words, he freed most of his prisoners and kept none as slaves. He was no kitten, of course. Under that blinding charm, Cyrus had a steel-edged sense of justice that drove him to deal harshly with certain of his more dangerous captives.

Asher was oddly relieved to discover that Astyages was not amongst them. Cyrus grew in popularity by freeing his grand-father to live a princely life within his court. Astyages's freedom was somewhat curtailed by the constant company of Persian Immortals. Cyrus was no fool.

One of Cyrus's first acts was to take Ecbatana's treasury under Persian control, an enormous hoard that gave Cyrus and Persia limitless resources overnight. Keren and her scribes set to work, cataloging and dividing Media's riches with the kind of precise management that Asher had come to expect from Cyrus's administration.

By the end of the first week, the Persians had established themselves so perfectly in the Median capital that you would have barely noticed the city was under new management. Asher observed this smooth transition of power, his heart swelling with wonder. God had done this. God had blessed them with this impossible victory. And the same hand that had provided so many miraculous breakthroughs would in time complete the good work he had begun. He would fulfill his Word. One day, he would use Cyrus to set the Judean captives free and rebuild Jerusalem.

"Daniel was right," he told Keren one night over supper.

Keren set down her spoon. "He usually is. To which particular point are you referring?"

"He told me once that it required numberless miracles for each of God's promises to be fulfilled. Numberless men and women walking in obedience in order for the intentions of God to be established on earth. One thing I have seen with my own eyes over the past few months is the sheer complexity of God's plans on this earth. His majesty at work as he weaves a thousand different strands together. Each one of us was a tiny strand in his hands. Insignificant in ourselves. And yet he used the insignificant in order to bring about his glory."

On the first day of their second week in Ecbatana, Asher received a request to attend the king in his formal throne room. The last time he had passed through these ornate double doors, he had been in the company of two rather unfriendly guards. Now the guards treated him as a guest of honor as he walked down the long chamber with its gilded columns and high, domed silver ceiling.

Cyrus had donned royal robes and looked every bit a powerful Median monarch in his bejeweled throne. To Asher's surprise, Jemmah and her family were already present.

"Welcome, Asher," Cyrus said in the aristocratic Median accent he had learned from his mother.

Asher bowed, curious to see why he had been called to so formal an audience, especially given how busy the new king of Media found himself these days.

"I believe my senior scribe has a payment for you."

Keren approached, a guard trailing behind. At her signal, the guard placed a chest at Asher's feet. One glance showed him that it was brimming with gold and silver. Asher's brows rose to his hairline. "My king is generous."

"I have set aside five horses for you. I picked them myself, Nisaeans all."

The whole world clamored for Nisaean horses, a superior breed raised for centuries in Media's green pasturelands. Most men dreamed of owning one. To have five was riches indeed. "You honor me." Asher bowed. Knowing Cyrus's enthusiasm for horseflesh made this particular gift more personal. Cyrus had given him what he would have wanted to receive.

Another chest followed, larger this time, filled with rich textiles, embroidered fabrics, linens, silks, and wool so soft, it felt like downy feathers.

"A married man has certain needs," Cyrus said.

Asher sent a longing look at Jemmah. "I am not married yet, lord."

"No? And what are you waiting for?"

"We were waiting for the end of the war, my king."

"I have news for you. The war has ended. It is time to hold

a wedding." Cyrus spread a hand. "What do you think of my throne room?"

"It is glorious, lord."

"Yes, but it seems a little somber to me. We need an occasion to cheer the place up. I have a mind to hold a wedding here, Asher."

"A wedding?" Asher said, dazed.

"My grandfather never recognized you as his son. I aim to recognize you as my friend before the whole world."

Asher felt a knot lodge in his throat. Jemmah, who had been demurely standing next to her father, ran to his side. He hugged her to him, too overcome to speak. He felt as if God had taken all his crushed dreams, every crumb that lay wasted and ruined, and breathed new life into them.

"Jemmah?"

"Yes, my king?"

"Does tomorrow suit you for a wedding?"

Keren gaped. "Tomorrow, Cyrus! I have a mountain of tablets to go through. I couldn't even wash the ink stains from my fingers by then."

Cyrus pinned her with his green gaze. "Are you the one getting married?"

"No."

"Then stop pestering me with your objections. You can attend the ceremony with ink on your fingers. Jemmah?"

Jemmah grinned at the king. "Yes, lord?"

"Is tomorrow too soon?"

Jemmah looked at Jared. When her father nodded, she smiled at Asher. "Tomorrow is perfect, my lord."

"Good. Then let us arrange a wedding. Who does that around here?"

"Your beleaguered senior scribe, Your Majesty," Keren said. "Ah, good. She'd better go about her business then."

*　*　*

Cyrus had assigned Asher and Jemmah a suite of three small rooms within the palace for their wedding night. In his chamber, Asher took off his elaborate wedding garb and donned a green linen robe. From a wrinkled bag, he withdrew a long false beard, somewhat misshapen and patchy, missing a few gold rings. He attached it to his face and grinned as he studied his reflection in a silver mirror.

He knocked upon their sleeping chamber and, hearing Jemmah's soft greeting, entered on silent feet. She stared at him open-mouthed.

The merry laughter died a quick death in his throat at the sight of her. Her wild curls lay loose down her back. The gold-and-turquoise necklace he had given her as a wedding present hung from her neck, the blue jewels dripping against the rise of her chest. She wore a white robe of some fabric so sheer it left little to the imagination.

"Fire and lightning!" he said.

She giggled. "You stole my words."

He forgot about the beard and, pressing a knee next to her on the bed, bent down to kiss her. She shoved a hand between them. "Not so fast, if you please. I did not marry Master Kandalanu."

"We best get rid of him then." Asher stripped off his beard. "Better?"

She studied him and sighed. "I am not sure. I will need to test the merchandise."

He swallowed a burst of laughter. He bent low to kiss her deeply. She made a sound deep in her throat, something like a gulp. He lifted his head. "How was that?"

"I have only one complaint. You stopped too soon, Bijar."

"That will never happen again, Silver Girl."

A NOTE FROM
THE AUTHOR

Speaking to the Judean captives in Babylon, Jeremiah said, "The Lord has stirred up the spirit of the kings of the Medes, because his purpose concerning Babylon is to destroy it" (Jeremiah 51:11).

The kings of the Medes. It was the leaders of Media who would one day destroy Babylon and set the Judean captives free.

Jeremiah most likely wrote this prophecy when Cyrus was a mere boy. Long before he was in any position to win the crown of Media. As I studied the historical accounts of Cyrus's ascension to the throne of the Medes, I realized the fulfillment of this single verse required innumerable miracles. The intricate threads of Cyrus's story fascinated me. He needed countless tiny impossible victories to win that extraordinary conquest.

In another prophecy, Isaiah mentioned Cyrus by name, the only Gentile as far as I know to be called the Lord's anointed:

Thus says the Lord to his anointed, to Cyrus . . .
"I will go before you
    and level the exalted places,
I will break in pieces the doors of bronze
    and cut through the bars of iron."
ISAIAH 45:1-2

God himself promised to make a way for Cyrus. And in doing so, he engineered the freedom of his people from captivity in Babylon.

Cyrus the Persian became king of the Medes. But he did not do so alone. The hand of God was with him. The hands, also, of unknown men and women whose sacrifices fulfilled God's will in these verses. Those were the stories I wanted to capture alongside the famous one, stitching the tale of a few fictional Judeans into the fabric of the historical accounts we have of Cyrus's victory over Media.

Most of us are familiar with Cyrus in the later years of his rule. When he rode down the streets of Babylon and, as its new king, declared freedom to the captives. But before that story could be told, there was this one. There was that tiny fraction of Jeremiah's prophecy that had to be fulfilled. Cyrus had to rise up to become a king of the Medes.

Jemmah, Asher, Zarina, Keren, Jared, and Johanan are fictional, of course. But their journey points to an inconceivable reality. God uses the courage and faith and obedience of nameless people like you and me in order to fulfill his great Kingdom plans.

Not all my characters are denizens of my imagination. Several historical people are running around the pages of this book, including Cyrus, Daniel, Astyages, and Harpagus.

The scythed chariot is a real thing. According to the ancient historian Xenophon, Cyrus made this innovation, which allowed the cavalry to penetrate a closed formation of armed infantry. Using this new technology against the seasoned Lydians, the Persians broke through the deadly hoplite forces and won another unexpected victory.

One of the more well-known features of the Persian Empire

was the legendary guard known as the Immortals. Xenophon credits Cyrus with the creation of this successful military construct. I tried to depict the beginnings of this elite fighting corps at its earliest stages under Cyrus's reign. Incidentally, the Persian king was also fond of his spies. Hence Prexaspes. Cyrus might not have had an actual spy who was a waste remover. But I bet he wished he did.

While it is historically accurate that the Persians lacked a written language, not all scholars agree Cyrus devised the Old Persian alphabet. I found enough evidence to credit him (and Johanan, since I reasoned Cyrus would have needed the help of at least one scholar) with the invention. (See *Discovering Cyrus: The Persian Conqueror Astride the Ancient World* by Reza Zarghamee.) However, written Old Persian never became very popular. If you have been trying to pronounce some of the names in this novel, you know why.

The scenes depicting the events of the last battle against Astyages are based on the reports of ancient historians such as Nicholas of Damascus, Polyaenus, and Justin. The battle seems filled with inexplicable moments where the whole tide of events turns inconceivably in favor of the Persians. Even the role the women of Pasargadae play in encouraging their disheartened army seems the stuff of Hollywood rather than the realm of history. Cyrus had no business winning that victory against such a mighty force. But he did. Miraculous. Told you so.

A word on Zarina's background: The Sakas and their close relatives, the Scythians, were a collection of nomadic tribes spread throughout a vast landmass north of the Persian Empire. Fierce warriors, they spent their days on horseback and welcomed women as soldiers. Recent DNA studies of Saka remains have revealed a blue- or green-eyed, fair-skinned people. However, excavations of burial sites suggest that the ancient Saka lords had a fondness for women with Asian features. Now you know how Zarina came into existence!

If you read *Harvest of Rubies* and *Harvest of Gold*, my other books based in the Achaemenid period of the Persian Empire, you will discover a much more formal world where aristocratic women, though enjoying certain freedoms, live a more constrained life. That is because by the time of Esther and Nehemiah, less than a hundred years after Cyrus, the Persian court had become highly regimented. But in Cyrus's Persia, women still enjoyed a more flexible life. That's why I gave Jemmah the freedom to travel alone with Asher. Although I stretched the bonds of propriety just a smidgen, it felt like a believable choice during the chaos of war.

You can find out more about the story of Keren, Jared, and Cyrus in *The Hidden Prince*.

For updates and to sign up for my monthly newsletter, please visit my website at tessaafshar.com. I love hearing from my readers.

ACKNOWLEDGMENTS

You have read the book and now you are sticking around for the acknowledgments. You are my kind of reader! To be fair, all my readers bless me. Whether you have been with me from the start or just discovered my books, whether you read the novels over and over until your copy starts to fall apart or you read them once and pass them on to (I hope) your favorite friends, you are the reason I write. You keep me going with your grace, encouragement, and commitment to these stories. I have the most amazing fans. Please keep those letters, messages, and prayers coming. Even when I don't have time to answer, I read every word, pray for you in your struggles, and thank God for you.

As for the librarians and booksellers who introduce my books to new readers and keep them supplied with fresh copies, what can I say? Many of you don't have an easy job. Please know I appreciate you so much.

Thanks to my very talented editors, Stephanie Broene and Kathy Olson, who help me write better books. I hope you know I love working with you. I am grateful for the gifted team at Tyndale House Publishers, including Elizabeth Jackson, Karen Watson, Jan Stob, Ron Beers, Madeline Daniels, Andrea Garcia, Cheryl Kerwin, Andrea Martin, and dozens more whose names should be here. I couldn't get these books into readers' hands if it weren't for these incredibly gracious people.

A special mention is due to Jen Phelps and Shane Rebenschied, who created the beautiful covers for both *The Peasant King* and *The Hidden Prince*. Thank you for the unforgettable designs that capture these stories so well.

I am forever thankful for my capable agent, Wendy Lawton, whose continued encouragement and dear friendship have guided me along both level paths and bumpy roads. It's been a challenging year requiring extra time and wisdom, and you have been there through every step. So deeply grateful for you.

So much gratitude to my friend and assistant, Julie Kieras, a joy and a godsend, one of my favorite blessings in my writing life.

My brilliant husband helps me in a thousand ways. He was the one who suggested the storm that saved Jemmah from the well. I am blessed and grateful to have him in my life. This book was written as we rode the wave of a lot of challenges, watching dear friends walk through loss, illness, and more trouble than we could understand. My husband's steady love and strength helped me stay the course and finish this novel. I thank God for you, my love.

This book is about the beginnings of the Persian Empire, where historical accounts intersect with the promises of God. The longer I study the Bible, the more I realize how intricate and miraculous the plans of God truly are. Those thousand-thousand threads have been in play from the start of time. The beginning of Cyrus's empire is one of those threads, which God wove into a remarkable story of salvation. I am filled with gratitude when I think of the tender care of God and the obedience of nameless men and women who allowed for Cyrus's true story to be written in the pages of history.

DISCUSSION QUESTIONS

1. This novel sets a fictional story in the context of the Old Testament and incorporates people we know of from the Bible, such as the prophet Daniel and the prophesied Cyrus. Do you like reading fiction set in biblical times? What are some benefits for contemporary readers? What may be some drawbacks?

2. Did you enjoy the historical information about the lands of Persia, Media, and Babylon and their customs? In what ways does it add to or detract from the story?

3. In chapter 6, Keren tells Jemmah, "It's not Astyages who controls our world. He has his role to play." What do you think she means by this?

4. In chapter 7, Jared has to make a hard decision. How does Jemmah convince him to remain behind? Do you sometimes find yourself fighting God when he asks you to remain behind or stay out of something?

5. Asher and Jemmah are both stuck in certain areas of their lives. Do you have a similar experience in your life?

6. What are the different things that finally help Asher get free of the wounds of his father's abandonment?

7. When Jemmah has to treat her mother's broken arm, she prays using Scripture: "We do not know what to do, but our eyes are on you." Could you relate to this prayer? If yes, in what way?

8. Jemmah has to learn the "little by little" of God in her life. Have you ever had to learn that lesson? How did Jemmah's story encourage you in yours?

9. In chapter 27, Jemmah answers Zarina's practical concerns about the war by reminding her that "our God is the Lord of hosts and the God of armies." In what ways do you see faith and practical realities clash in your own life? How do we live a balanced life between the two?

10. Toward the end of the story, Asher talks about the way God fulfills his promises by weaving a thousand different strands together. "Each one of us was a tiny strand in his hands. Insignificant in ourselves. And yet he used the insignificant in order to bring about his glory." What do you think Asher means by this? Do you see your own life as one of those strands in God's hands? If so, how important does that make you in the eternal schemes of God's plans?

ABOUT THE AUTHOR

Tessa Afshar is an award-winning, ECPA bestselling author of historical and biblical fiction. Her awards include the Christy and the INSPY. Her novel *Land of Silence* was named by *Library Journal* as one of the top five Christian fiction titles of 2016. *Harvest of Rubies* was a finalist for the ECPA Christian Book Award in the fiction category, and *Daughter of Rome* was a Carol Award finalist in the historical romance category. Tessa's first Bible study and DVD, *The Way Home: God's Invitation to New Beginnings*, won the Christian Book Award for best Bible study of 2021.

Tessa was born to a nominally Muslim family in the Middle East and lived there for the first fourteen years of her life before moving to England. She settled permanently in the United States, where she converted to Christianity in her twenties. Tessa holds a master of divinity from Yale University, where she served as cochair of the Evangelical Fellowship at the Divinity School. She worked in women's and prayer ministries for nearly twenty years before becoming a full-time writer. Tessa is a devoted wife, a mediocre gardener, and an admirer of chocolate from afar. Visit her website at tessaafshar.com.

DON'T MISS

"Tessa Afshar combines adventure and romance in a fast-paced novel that kept me turning the pages. I highly recommend *The Hidden Prince*!"

Francine Rivers, *New York Times* bestselling author

CP1909